THE
ENEMY
INSIDE

WILLIAM CHRISTIE is the author of:

The Warriors of God

Mercy Mission

The Blood We Shed

Threat Level

THE ENEMY INSIDE

WILLIAM CHRISTIE

PINNACLE BOOKS
Kensington Publishing Corp.
www.kensingtonbooks.com

PINNACLE BOOKS are published by

Kensington Publishing Corp.
850 Third Avenue
New York, NY 10022

All Kensington titles, imprints, and distributed lines are available at special quantity discounts for bulk purchases for sales promotions, premiums, fund-raising, educational, or institutional use.

Special book excerpts or customized printings can also be created to fit specific needs. For details, write or phone the office of the Kensington special sales manager: Kensington Publishing Corp., 850 Third Avenue, New York, NY 10022, attn: Special Sales Department; phone 1-800-221-2647.

PINNACLE BOOKS and the Pinnacle logo are Reg. U.S. Pat. & TM Off.

ISBN 0-7860-1708-2

First printing: November 2006

10 9 8 7 6 5 4 3 2 1

Printed in the United States of America

For Beth, once again.

ACKNOWLEDGMENTS

Once again, I'd like to publicly thank the members of the military and law enforcement communities who helped me out. And once again, of course, I can't.

Then there are my friends, who put up with me shamefully neglecting them during the writing of this book. Some are still serving or otherwise prone to embarrassment, so first names will have to suffice for all. The Bull and Joan. Jad and Peg. The Zooman. Erich and Vicki. Rick and Melissa. Ské and Guia. Dan and Sonita.

The always fantastic, unintentionally neglected Nelson and Donna.

Jim and Beth, as always, for everything. Anne and Howard, my second set of parents.

Karen, who isn't all that evil. And Kevin.

Jason and Valerie. Philip and Sally, Lee, Kimberly, Neil, and Will.

John and Shirley.

Hope, Anne, Jackie. Hobe and Gwynn. And Mary.

My family, of course.

Gary Goldstein, the editor of this book. Once again both a total pro and a lot of fun to work with.

My agent, Richard Curtis of Richard Curtis Associates, whose evil plan continues. Thanks, Richard.

And my mother, who both made me and made me a writer.

I can be reached at christieauthor@yahoo.com.

"To become the enemy" means you think yourself into the enemy's position. In the world people tend to think of a robber trapped in a house as a fortified enemy. However, if we think of "becoming the enemy," we feel that the whole world is against us and that there is no escape. He who is shut inside is a pheasant. He who enters to arrest is a hawk. You must appreciate this.

—Miyamoto Musashi,
A Book of Five Rings, 1645
(tr. Victor Harris, 1984)

Chapter One

It was early afternoon, and the cigarette smugglers weren't even knocking off for siesta.

The two Americans were leaning over the railing of the Bridge of Friendship over the Paraná river, watching the action. An accident of geography allowed them to stand in Paraguay and view two other countries: Brazil on the other side of the bridge, Argentina just slightly downriver.

It wasn't just one or two smugglers. It was a whole column of them, walking like army ants down the pedestrian walkway across the bridge from Ciudad del Este, Paraguay, toward the Brazilian side. They were all carrying big cardboard cases of cigarettes, wrapped in black plastic. Once they were over dry land, they all lined up at the hole that had been conveniently cut in the ten-foot-high fence lining the bridge and pushed their cases through, letting them drop onto Brazilian soil about 120 feet down.

Brazilian crews appeared from under the bridge, tearing off the plastic wrapping, extricating the cartons of cigarettes, and stuffing them into homemade backpacks.

Master Sergeant Edwin Storey, U.S. Army, had been timing them. Under two minutes from tearing off the plastic to disappearing into the bushes. "Those boys got it down to a science."

"Sure as shit *is* the Friendship Bridge," said Petty Officer

First Class Lee Troy, U.S. Navy. Shredded black plastic lay on the ground as thick as garden mulch. "All those smokes'll be on sale in Brazil tonight, tax free."

Everyone knows Miami and Hong Kong are the first and second largest tax-free commerce zones in the world. Ciudad del Este, population 240,000, was actually number three. This was mainly due to geography and politics. The Paraná let cargo move back and forth among Buenos Aires, Montevideo, and the Atlantic Ocean. The government of Paraguay did not collect income or sales tax, or tariffs in Ciudad del Este because the country's chaotic political history and lack of national tradition for the rule of law led it to believe, correctly, that no would pay them anyway. So why not take advantage of it? Ciudad del Este was responsible for 60 percent of Paraguay's gross domestic product.

Low or no tax areas abutting high tax areas are always boomtowns. Ciudad del Este was a boomtown, a trader's paradise. Low or no tax areas abutting high tax areas are always a smuggler's paradise. Ciudad del Este was no different.

It was estimated by the Paraguayan police that 70 percent of all the vehicles on the road in Paraguay were stolen in neighboring countries. Or the United States. They arrived in trailer trucks and shipping containers, and were traded for Paraguayan marijuana and Colombian and Bolivian cocaine. Firearms made by Taurus and Rossi in Brazil came across the border and went right back into Brazil, and Argentina, and elsewhere, without documentation.

Boomtowns tended to attract entrepreneurs. A large Chinatown had grown up in Ciudad del Este. And, of much more interest to the United States, an Arab community of more than 30,000 had established itself there as well. Investment dollars, clean or not, poured in from the Middle East because there were big profits to be made on merchandise like bootleg movies, music, designer clothing, and software. Consumer electronics, even computer chips, were major commodities. Any hot vehicles in excess of local needs went overseas, many to the Middle East. SUVs stolen off the streets of the United States were the vehicles of choice for suicide bombers in Iraq. The money moved back and forth with few controls and almost no oversight.

The lines of cigarette smugglers continued remorselessly across the bridge. The vehicle traffic was all backed up. It was always backed up. Forty thousand people came over from Brazil every day, to work and shop. And smuggle. "There's never a cop around when you need one," said Troy.

"Five hundred U.S. buys you a cop with a serious vision problem," said Storey. "The law around here don't pull in much salary, but they all drive Mercedes or BMWs."

"I don't know," said Troy. "Seems to me it takes all the fun out of smuggling if it's this easy. High noon? In public? Where's the juice in that?"

"Businessmen run this," said Storey. "Not thrill seekers like you. Take a good look. When the State has power, criminals are a minority. When the State loses power, criminals take over."

"I've seen this everywhere I've been," said Troy.

"That's what I mean," said Storey. "We're looking at the future. If we don't win."

Troy glanced at his watch. "Our boy's running late."

"He's a creature of habit," Storey said reassuringly.

"If these guys ever showed an ounce of tradecraft, we'd never find them. Makes me wonder how many sharp ones are running around we don't know anything about."

"Rule Number One," Storey said in a warning tone.

The first of Ed Storey's operational rules was that, when working covertly, you always operated under the assumption that you were under visual or audio surveillance twenty-four hours a day. So you never broke your cover, and you never, ever, discussed any mission details in any insecure space. And in these days of ultrasensitive parabolic microphones and computer-enhanced audio, even the open air wasn't a secure space.

It always annoyed Troy when Storey mentioned his rules. Especially when Storey was right to mention his rules. And Storey had a tendency to be right all the time, which was even more annoying.

The point was driven home by how they'd located their quarry, an ordinary Arab businessman who regularly ran up $5,000 a month in phone bills calling Saudi Arabia, Pakistan, Egypt, and the United States.

When most people thought of spies, they pictured high-level politicians snapping photos of secret documents with miniature cameras. But the most valuable agents were people like the moonlighting phone company employee who passed you lists of people making interesting calls for a retainer of $1,000 a month.

Of course, the target could have been just an Arab businessman with a lot of contacts. But the National Security Agency, whose mandate it was to intercept communications and break codes, had a worldwide network of listening stations and satellites to allow it to listen in on international phone calls. And after listening carefully to all the Arab's numbers, they discovered he wasn't calling Pakistan about DVD players.

Storey's cell phone rang. One of the first things they did upon arriving in a new town was to buy a bunch of cell phones, all local numbers, that they could use a few times and then discard. He listened carefully. "That's right," he said in almost accentless Spanish. "Twenty minutes." Then to Troy, he added, "We're moving."

A casual observer would have had no idea they were Americans. Clothes are always the tip-off. Move someone from one country to another, and even if they don't say a word everyone knows they're a foreigner.

One of Storey's other rules was to travel with only a small bag—which had the added benefit of allowing him to move like lightning when necessary—and buy clothes wherever he landed. All he had to do was look around a bit, see what the majority of men in his age group was wearing, and go shopping. The goal being anonymity, not cutting-edge style.

So all the casual observer saw was a nondescript white man in his mid-thirties, with brown hair and a closely trimmed beard, wearing an inexpensive suit and no tie. And a similarly dressed black man in his late twenties with a moustache and an Afro that wasn't quite large enough to call attention to itself. Nobody you'd remember. Just part of life's background.

The motorcycles were parked at the end of the bridge, helmeted riders waiting atop. Storey had learned from having them used against him that nothing was better at getting you through the traffic, narrow streets, and alleys of the Third World than the "mototaxi," a motorcycle and driver that operated just like a taxi. Flag one down, hop on the back, and get dropped wherever you wanted. If you had the balls, that is. For local cover, they were perfect.

Everything of importance in Ciudad del Este was concentrated near the bridge, so it was a short drive. The streets were a madhouse. Nothing but horns, shouting, exhaust, and gridlock. Except for motorcycles.

Storey slid off the bike and passed his helmet to the driver. He cast a professional eye down the street. The only thing worse than walking unawares into your own trouble was blundering accidentally into someone else's. After one outrage too many, Brazil had turned its army loose on the Rio drug gangs, and the pressure was causing the leaders to relocate to Ciudad del Este. Drugs and terrorists. Always looking for a friendly home.

To an orderly North American, it would seem like just too much. Too many people literally running back and forth, moving merchandise carrying all the logos of all the world's manufacturers, genuine or not. Door to door shops, and shoppers pouring in and out of them. Even the sidewalk vendors were elbow to elbow hustling trinkets, CDs, perfume, and soccer jerseys. All it took was one slightly interested glance and they'd attach themselves to you like remora fish to a shark. There wasn't even enough space for all the brightly colored signs and billboards, so they were slapped up almost overlapping one another.

It was only April, but even without all the bodies it still would have been too hot, and jungle humid. One of those places where everything felt illegal, and even the most insensitive blockhead could pick up the danger radiating from the streets along with the heat.

Storey gingerly inserted himself into the pedestrian traffic. You didn't go shoving your way through a crowd of overheated, short-tempered Latins unless you were looking for trouble.

The shops were all on street level, offices and apartments on the upper floors. Storey went through a glass door that was nearly opaque from the ever-present brown dust, mixed with rain splatter and hydrocarbon emissions. In the entry alcove he was confronted with a line of apartment buzzers along the wall, and a glistening steel security door. The object that slid out from Storey's sleeve looked like an electric toothbrush, except it was flat, black, and had, instead of bristles on the end, a steel pick. The pick went into the deadbolt lock's keyhole and the unit vibrated just like an electric toothbrush, knocking all the pin tumblers from their cavities. A twist of the tension wrench in Storey's left hand, and the lock snapped open. Five seconds, start to finish. He went up the stairs, the door closing and locking automatically behind him.

The upstairs hallway was dark, smelling of old wood

and musty carpet. Storey fitted the plug into his ear and squeezed and released the transmit bar of the Motorola walkie-talkie five times. He received five clicks back. The lookouts were reading him, and in position. Now, if none of the other residents showed up, life would be perfect.

Storey waited. By now he considered himself the duty expert on waiting. He could do the biofeedback techniques taught to all Delta Force operators without even having to think about it, reducing his heart rate and relaxing his body while keeping his senses sharp and his mind alert. He did not look at his watch.

The radio broke squelch four times. The target was on the street. Three times. Coming in, alone. The acoustics of the empty stairwell made the lock sound like a gunshot.

Storey edged along the wall until he was even with the stairway opening.

Feet on the stairs. Trudging. Storey could tell by the pace of the steps, and the little grunt as he started up, the poor guy was tired. Too bad.

Storey had counted the steps on his way up. Now he was counting them again. Twenty-six, twenty-seven.

Black hair, leaning forward, looking down at his feet. A second later enough of the head. Catching sight of Storey, the look of alarm, but by then it was too late.

Storey's arm swung down, and he delivered an open-handed slap to the back of the skull, just above the ears. Ordinarily the kind of blow that was just an attention-getter, the prelude to more serious action to come. But the guy dropped like a rock, facedown on the stairs. Out.

Storey had tried everything from Taser stun guns to Halothane anesthetic in a handheld vaporizer mask. And they had all let him down at one time or another, sometimes with embarrassing results. Everything except the palm sap: a leather pocket shaped like a small ingot filled with powdered lead, stitched to a leather band that went around the back of the hand, to hold it in place.

You could walk up behind someone and give them a casual slap to the back of the head, and it didn't look like you'd hit them with a club. And in a situation with multiple adversaries, knocking the first guy unconscious with a simple open hand to the side of his head usually made the others reconsider their motivation. The best part was that in your luggage or pocket the palm sap looked like some kind of exercise equipment, not an obvious weapon.

Storey slipped the sap off his hand and keyed the radio, still speaking in Spanish. It wouldn't do to have anyone with a scanner hear English being spoken. "Clear. Move."

Lee Troy emerged from the darkness at the other end of the hallway, where he'd been covering the back steps. He was carrying a Glock pistol, the compact Model 26 9mm. Twelve-round capacity and 6.29 inches long. The Gemtech Aurora sound suppressor can screwed on to the end of the modified barrel added another three inches. "He's alive, I hope."

"He's alive," said Storey, who had just finished checking the carotid pulse. He pulled both hands behind the back, securing them with flexible plastic handcuffs, like the ties used to hold together bunches of electric cables. Another around the ankles, and a strip of duct tape over the mouth and around the head.

Troy went down the stairs and opened the door for a member of their support team dressed as a deliveryman who was rolling a wooden box strapped to a hand truck.

They fitted the unconscious body into the box and latched it shut. The deliveryman rolled it back down the stairs and out to the unmarked van double-parked on the street.

The van didn't wait around. It drove across the Friendship Bridge into Foz do Iguaçu, Brazil. Unlike their Paraguayan counterparts, Brazilian customs actually searched vehicles. But not this one. The driver and passenger carried red U. S. diplomatic passports, granting them and their vehicle diplomatic immunity.

At the Foz do Iguaçu airfield the box was loaded aboard an unmarked Gulfstream V business jet. Once the hatches were shut the passenger was extracted and examined by a medical technician.

Anyone curious enough about the jet's tail numbers to do a little research would discover that it was registered to Aero Contractors, Ltd., of Smithfield, North Carolina. They would not discover that Aero was a CIA front company.

The jet flew directly to Guantánamo Bay, Cuba.

Storey kept two souvenirs from his victim. The nylon briefcase he'd been carrying, and his keys.

He and Troy let themselves into the apartment.

Storey was surprised. They were always as neat as a prison cell. But this guy was a slob.

"You sure you don't want to toss the room?" Troy asked.

"I don't want *anything* out of place," said Storey. "Let's stick to the plan." He unzipped the briefcase and handed Troy the laptop computer.

Troy turned it upside down and paused, the screwdriver poised in his hand. "What if it's wired?"

"I expect you'll be bitching at me for all eternity," Storey replied.

Troy grinned and exposed the guts of the laptop. There were no explosives inside. He removed a plastic box from his pocket, took out a computer chip, and plugged it into the board.

Storey dialed his cell phone. "Stand by for a test."

Troy reassembled the laptop. Even when turned off, computers still drew tiny amounts of power. Enough for their purposes. "Testing, testing, one, two, three," Troy said in a normal voice.

"Got it?" Storey said into his phone. He nodded to Troy. "Location? Good." He snapped the phone shut.

Troy zipped the computer back into the briefcase. "On the bed?"

"Yeah, good spot."

Troy tossed the briefcase onto the unmade bed, the way he would if he'd just come home. "You sure you don't want to give the room a quick toss?"

"We could tear down the walls and pull up the floor, and still not find everything. Let's give this a chance to work."

"You're the boss," Troy replied.

Storey spoke into his radio. "Coming out. Clear?"

They locked the door behind them. The motorcycles were waiting in the street.

The safe house they were using wasn't a house. Or an apartment. Another of Storey's rules. Someone moving into a house or apartment, even if it's purchased furnished, shows up with a big truck full of all their stuff. If you didn't it raised suspicions. If you did it was a lot of time and money to maintain your cover. And the neighbors were always watching you. So Storey believed in hotels for short-term operations, no longer than a week. Anything longer and he'd rent a business office. No one paid any attention to office space, even if it was occupied all night. And it always took time to open for business, so that wasn't a problem. All you had to do was throw some air mattresses on the floor.

Back at one of the two offices they'd rented, Storey peeled off his beard, and Troy his Afro and moustache. Their appearance would be completely different from now on, just in case anyone had noticed them on the street.

Storey and Troy's four-man support team were electronic intercept specialists, mostly former members of Gray Fox, an electronic intelligence unit formed to support Joint Special Operations Command. The team's noncommissioned officer in charge, Army Sergeant First

Class Peter Lund, called Storey over to his table of computers. "Bad news from Washington, Ed."

"What now?" said Storey.

"They turned down your request," said Lund. "No help."

"What?" Storey demanded, bending down to read the message off the screen. He'd asked for either a troop from the Army Combat Applications Group, originally known as Delta Force, or a few boat teams from the Naval Special Warfare Development Group, originally known as SEAL Team Six.

"What's the excuse?" Troy asked, coming up behind them.

"Same as always, Afghanistan and Iraq," Storey replied. Of the three Delta squadrons, one was nearly always in Iraq, another in Afghanistan. The same for two of the three SEAL assault groups. The remainder was on alert or in the process of working up to deploy, which could mean anywhere else in the world.

"So what?" said Troy. "This is what the fucking alert elements are for."

"I was afraid this was going to happen," said Storey. "You can't convince anyone there's a problem down here—it's a backwater theater of operations."

"Backwater," Troy said in disgust. "Khalid Sheikh Mohammad came here in '94. What did they think the guy who planned 9/11 was doing, vacationing in the fucking jungle? The guys who shot up the tourists at the Luxor Temple in Egypt ran here, not to Afghanistan."

"It's all Colombia and drugs and guerrillas," said Storey. "Terrorism's got the backseat."

"I guess I should have known when they told us at the briefing that there wasn't a single CIA case officer in the entire country," said Troy.

Just like the military, the CIA had found itself totally overwhelmed by the demands of Iraq and Afghanistan. Unwilling to pull people out of their old Cold War

playgrounds of Russia and China, they'd instead stripped
Latin America nearly bare. Things were so bad they had
to fly the few remaining case officers from country to
country every month, like circuit riders, to pay off and
debrief the agent networks.

"I'm used to the CIA leaving us in the lurch," said
Troy. "I just didn't think we'd get buddy-fucked by our
own people."

"Everyone's stretched to the breaking point," said
Storey.

"Somebody correct me if I'm wrong here," said Troy.
"But isn't our job to find these motherfuckers, and if
there's more than one or two, call in the shooters to take
them out? Well, that doesn't fucking work if the shooters won't show up to take them out."

"Don't hold back," Storey urged. "It's not healthy to
keep it all pent up inside."

Whenever he did that, Troy usually went back to
keeping it all pent up inside. Which was probably Storey's
intention.

Storey found a chair and sat down in silence. All the
kids knew to keep quiet when the Master Sergeant had
his thinking cap on.

They'd followed their target for two weeks, and only
identified two of his contacts. There had to be more.
Storey's idea was to spike his laptop and leave it in the
apartment, hoping it would lead them to the rest.

Troy had been openly skeptical.

"What would you do if I got snatched?" Storey had
asked. "You'd go to my place to look for clues or anything
incriminating. Then you'd sanitize the area and take away
my computer, phones, files, weapons, and equipment."

Troy had gotten it then. It was Storey at his absolute
sneakiest. "We'd all get together and do a damage
assessment."

"Exactly," Storey had replied. "Have I only run off with

the petty cash? If the enemy has me, what do I know that could hurt the unit? How much do I know about networks, future plans? So do you stand pat? Do you look for me? Do you split up and run?"

"You think these Tangos are going to play it the way we would?" Troy had countered, using the military phonetic designation for both the letter T and terrorist. "Get together and have a meeting?"

"*We* are," Storey had pointed out. And at that all the support team had cracked up laughing. "And what's the alternative?" he'd asked. "By the time they break our guy at Guantánamo and he gives it up, the rest of the network's going to be long gone. I'd rather take a shot at chopping up a whole network that be satisfied with bagging one or two more."

And so it stood. Except how they were going to chop up the whole network now was anyone's guess. Or Storey's.

Who finally emerged from his meditation and said, "We're sticking with the original plan."

"Oh, really?" said Troy. "How are we going to do that?"

"If they do get together, we'll check out the location and the number of players. We may just have to shoot pictures and try to make identifications. But if we can, we'll take them."

"And how are we going to do that with what we're got?" Troy demanded. It was his way, without making too big an issue of it, of mentioning that even though the support guys were trained soldiers, they were techies. Which wasn't entirely fair, but reflected current prejudices. Many members of Gray Fox were actually former Green Berets, but the unit was widely seen as being manned by guys who hadn't made Delta Force.

"We'll have to wait and see," said Storey. "No sense in making up a plan now with so many variables hanging in the air."

Troy had been working with Storey long enough to

know that probably wasn't true, that he had a pretty good idea of what he was going to do. Any reluctance to spring it on them meant that it was probably going to be hairy. Storey was the best operational planner he'd ever seen, always thinking outside the box. But he was so good, and had such big balls, that sometimes he took it right up to the edge. They'd pulled off every mission, so far, but a couple had been damned close.

So they sat tight, and the tech guys watched their screens, waiting for the laptop in the apartment to either move or pick up human voices.

Most tracking devices were based on global positioning system technology. Signals from three satellites, triangulated, told the bug exactly where it was. Then the bug transmitted that information to a base station. But GPS didn't work all that well in jungles and cities, where foliage and buildings blocked out line of sight to the satellites. And most GPS trackers could only relay a position every twelve to twenty-five seconds. A quarry in a car could move a good long way in that amount of time.

The very latest equipment used radio frequency identification, or RFID. The same tiny chips that Wal-Mart used to locate and track every item in a store had other, more martial uses. These sent out a signal every two seconds, and could be mated with microsensors so sensitive they could pick up the sound of a human footstep from thirty feet away. They didn't have the same range as a GPS, but compensated for that by much smaller size, lower power, and longer battery life.

The receiver was a modified laptop linked to an antenna that looked like the ones used for car phones back in the day. The display was a street map of Ciudad del Este with a blinking cursor representing the bugged computer.

While they waited to see if the bait would work, Storey composed some message traffic to their operations center back in Washington. It was actually part message, part shopping list. Despite all the vows of brotherhood and reform, the war on terrorism was as much a turf battle as the Cold War had been. Especially since the Pentagon was trodding heavily on what had been the CIA's exclusive turf. Previously, to keep their message traffic secure from both foreign intelligence services *and* the other branches of the U.S. intelligence community, they had communicated using a modified personal digital assistant. Messages written into it were encrypted, the PDA was then plugged into an Iridium satellite phone, and the message transmitted. Worldwide-secure communications on equipment that could be carried on a belt, and that any legitimate businessman might carry. The military used encryption sleeves that attached to Iridium phones so secure voice calls could be made, but businessmen didn't carry those.

Lately, a little Silicon Valley firm working for the Defense Intelligence Agency under a black program outside all the usual contracting rules had figured out how to stuff the guts of an Iridium phone into a high-end PDA and downsize the bulky antenna. So Storey and Troy carried what looked like regular PDAs, on which they could talk to anyone in the world, write and send encrypted text, take photos, and determine their precise location with a GPS chip and map display. Any customs or police inspection would only reveal the files and address book matching the cover identities they were traveling under. The other stuff could only be accessed by password, and any attempt to break into the unit would wipe the drive clean.

Storey got the usual reply back to his message: *Why do you want this?* It hadn't always been that way, but their unit was getting bigger and the careerists and armchair commandos were starting to filter into the staff positions.

He let Troy read his reply: *If you aren't going to support us, then at least supply us.* Troy loved it.

Another unmarked Gulfstream flew into Foz do Iguaçu the next day, carrying items from a cache maintained in Colombia. Two of the technicians picked the cargo up in the van and drove it over the border without any problems. They didn't even have to use their diplomatic passports. The Brazilians didn't care about anything *leaving* Brazil, only coming in. And Paraguayan customs didn't care at all.

While they waited the technicians fiddled with their gear and read novels. Troy and Storey continued what was shaping up as a possible world record for the longest continuously played game of hearts. They threw the cards down mechanically while Troy listened to the Grateful Dead—exclusively—on his iPod. The military gave you a connoisseur's appreciation for personal eccentricity, and Storey saw nothing at all unusual in being partnered with a twenty-eight-year-old Navy SEAL Deadhead from rural Maine.

After all, it had been his choice. And he'd actually come to regard Troy's idiosyncrasies as an excellent gauge of both his own personal cool and ability to distance himself from his immediate surroundings. Most people, after listening to "Sugar Magnolia" wafting over from some-one's earphones for the thousandth time, would have laid hands on the nearest heavy object and crushed their skull.

It took three more days for the laptop cursor to move. By then the safe house was feeling mighty small.

"Pack everything up; wipe everything down," Storey ordered. "I doubt we'll be coming back."

The cursor stopped on the outskirts of Ciudad del Este. Not quite out on the edge of the jungle.

Storey rode behind one of the technicians on a motor-cycle. Everyone else was in the van.

Time spent in reconnaissance is never wasted, but Storey didn't figure the meeting, if in fact there was one, would be lasting very long. It was an upper-middle-class neighborhood. Though individual homes pressed tightly together, every house was surrounded by a wall. Absolutely common in places where there was no law and order—like Los Angeles, for instance.

Storey knew there would be lookouts. He made one circuit around the block in the van, and only one. No stopping, no pausing to look at house numbers, or pretending to consult a map, or pretending to pull into a drive to turn around, or any of the other obvious tip-offs.

They parked a full six blocks away. "What have we got in there?" Storey asked Lund, who was listening to the bug while it was being digitally recorded.

"Seven distinct voices," Lund replied. "All male, and all speaking Arabic."

"They're our boys, all right," said Troy, who was also listening in and also spoke conversational Arabic. "You got your props, Ed. They're having the damage-assessment meeting about our boy."

Storey's face failed to reveal how he felt about that. He sketched the house on a piece of paper. "There's probably a couple more than seven. I saw one in an upstairs window, watching the street with binoculars. Thought if he turned the lights out he couldn't be seen. Okay, we're got a two-story stucco house, around eight rooms or so. Wall is concrete or adobe, maybe a foot, foot and a half thick. Driveway gate and pedestrian gate in front. An alley between the backyard and the property directly behind, so there has to be a door or a gate. They picked the right house. Good lines of sight, hard to approach. Neighbors probably have dogs in the backyards. We're talking a platoon-size assault force to take it, along with a couple of nice loud charges to breach the wall."

"I can't wait to hear how we're going to take them down all by our lonesomes," said Troy.

"You know I hate to disappoint you," said Storey. "So here goes."

And he told them. And it wasn't at all what Troy had been expecting. That was Storey for you. What you got when the Army paid for a shrewd old country boy to get himself a masters in psychology. Even more scary, the gear Storey had ordered turned out to be exactly what they needed.

Troy still wasn't totally confident. Ordinarily something like this would take a full day or two, minimum, to plan, brief, and rehearse. Anyone who'd ever done any kind of military operation, not to mention a special operation, knew there were always a million things that could go wrong. And they were pulling this one out of their ass.

Lund didn't like one aspect of the plan. "At least let one of us go with you, to back you up," he said to Storey.

"Nothing against you boys," said Storey. "But two attracts a hell of a lot more attention than one."

They talked it through a little more, until everyone felt reasonably comfortable.

"You going to roll out of the van while we're moving?" Troy asked.

Storey shook his head. "You SEALs love sneaking around like ninjas. If someone notices you sneaking around, you're compromised. If you're just walking around like everyone else, you're part of the scenery."

Troy made no reply, probably because there was a large amount of truth to it.

They dropped Storey off on a side street near the entrance to the alley running behind the back of the house. He loudly thanked them for the ride and wished them a good evening in Spanish.

Storey walked right down the alley, carrying a suitcase. Dogs were barking. He liked that. Because where there were dogs who barked all night long, there were people who paid no attention to barking dogs. TVs and stereos were blaring. People were arguing. It made its own kind of camouflage.

He was wearing blue jeans, a dark gray long-sleeved T-shirt, running shoes, and tight-fitting leather driving gloves, so if he happened to be stopped by the cops he didn't look like the local cat burglar dressed all in black.

The alley was lined with garbage cans, and rats scurried back and forth in the moonlight. He was carrying an Israeli ORTEK night vision scope, small enough to be concealed in his cupped palm. No U.S. equipment in case he had to leave anything behind. The Israelis sold a lot of equipment in Latin America. He'd flick his hand up to his eye, then down, looking for security cameras. He didn't see any. Or infrared beams or trip wires on the top of the wall he was approaching. Storey slid in between a cluster of garbage cans. It smelled worse than putrid, but he was out of sight. He pulled on a hood made from Spandoflage, a stretchable camouflage mesh. A lot cooler than a black balaclava, and easier to put on and take off than camouflage face paint.

He checked the wall one more time with the scope. It looked clear. There was no gate in the wall, just a solid metal door. A gate would have let anyone see the backyard and house from the alley.

He'd taped a small metal folding stepladder to his suitcase, on the side concealed by his body. He cut the tape with his folding knife and set the ladder up against the wall. Something brushed by the leg of his jeans. Probably a rat. Storey didn't move a muscle. Then he began to unzip the suitcase. Very quietly, an inch at a time. He stopped when he heard something on the other side of the wall. It sounded like a door closing.

Storey strained to hear, but there was too much background noise in the neighborhood to make it out.

Then, clearly, a key going into a lock. The door in the wall came open with a creaking of hinges. A man stepped out cautiously, a plastic bag in his left hand and his right inside a jacket, despite the heat.

Storey could accept only two possibilities. Either there was a surveillance camera, and it had picked him up. Or this was a lookout doing a routine check of the alley in the guise of taking out the trash. Since it was only one man, it had to be the second option.

Storey's silencer-equipped mini Glock pistol was in the shoulder holster under his shirt. A hell of a place for it, because right now he couldn't get it out without attention-attracting movement.

The man took a few steps toward Storey's hiding place. An Arab, not Latin or Indian. Now Storey didn't even dare lift one eye above the garbage cans.

No garbage in the bag, Storey thought, as if to will it to be so. The bag is just camouflage. Go back through the door.

No. Feet moving closer. Storey could feel the adrenaline surge, his heart beginning to race. He held his breath, afraid it would be heard. Crouched behind the garbage can, Storey knew that as long as he couldn't see the Arab he couldn't be seen himself.

The footsteps were right there. A shadow fell from a security light farther down the alley. Then the top of a head.

Storey drove himself up off the ground, and the web of his open outstretched hand into the Arab's throat. That shut off every noise but a strangling sound. The blow caused the Arab to instinctively throw his hands up to his throat, giving Storey enough time to dart around the trash can. A fast kick to the groin bent the Arab over and brought the hands down from the throat.

Storey stepped forward, swinging his arm around the Arab's neck and tucking the head into his armpit. He put all his weight down on the back of the head, driving his opponent's chin down onto his chest. Except under the chin was Storey's forearm, as a fulcrum, grasped by the other hand, violently lifting up. There was a loud snap, like a piece of green wood broken in two, and an electric shiver ran through the Arab's body. The broken neck flopped nauseatingly in Storey's arms, and he eased the body down onto the dirty alley. The dirty alley and the unclean feeling after fighting hand to hand.

He swept out the pistol and trained it on the open doorway. There was no time to lose now, he had to initiate the attack before they missed the garbage man. Heedless of the noise now, he ripped the suitcase open and keyed his radio four times.

At the sound of the fourth click, Troy turned to the driver and said, "Go!" He jammed the other earplug into his ear—it was going to be really loud.

They were only at the end of the street, just out of sight of the house. The driver, a young sergeant all fired up to be on his first real combat operation, floored it. Troy almost yelled at him to slow down but held his tongue, afraid the sergeant would stop instead.

Troy did keep a close eye on their location. When people got excited strange things happened, like stopping in front of the wrong house.

The sergeant in fact didn't slow down in front of the house. He stood on the brakes, sending everyone in the back flying. Troy almost went out the open side door.

Giving vent to a "Goddammit!" he picked himself up off the floor and picked up the RPG-7 rocket launcher. Nothing more than a 37.43-inch-long piece of steel pipe sheathed in brown wood, with two handgrips, a bell-shaped flare at the end, and an 85mm antitank rocket sticking out of the front.

Troy scrambled up on the roof of the van so he could see, and shoot, over the top of the wall. He balanced the launcher on his shoulder, aiming for the second-floor window where Storey had noticed the lookout. A spin of the thumb to cock the hammer on the back of the hand-grip, an intake of breath to steady the aim, and a squeeze of the trigger.

A thunderclap of a roar; a brief tongue of flame and longer belch of rolling dark smoke from the rear. But for Troy no sensation of recoil, just a flare of light out in front when the rocket sustainer motor fired downrange. The rocket hit the window and detonated with a bright flash and an even louder roar.

But by that time Troy had been handed another rocket from inside the van. He slid the slim tail down into the launcher tube, careful to line up the prominent screw on the rocket with the indent on the launcher.

There was a downstairs room with lights on behind the curtains, and another next to it that was dark. Troy fired his second rocket into the darkened room, per Storey's instructions.

The other technicians were covering both ends of the street with AK-47s, careful to stay out of the RPG back-blast area.

Troy put his third rocket through the lighted window. That ought to do it, he thought.

After his radio call Storey had rushed to finish assembling the Minimi Para light machine gun. The same gun was used by the United States as the squad automatic weapon, but this one had Belgian markings. With the chopped barrel and collapsing tubular stock, it was only thirty inches long. Storey snapped on the Gemtech Halo sound suppressor, one of the few that could be used on a machine gun without melting into a puddle of molten metal. The plastic box holding the 200-round belt clipped under the receiver. The last step was to cock the bolt and position the first round on the feed tray.

The now open door to the backyard meant he didn't have to use the stepladder to aim the machine gun over the wall.

When the first rocket hit, pulling everyone's attention to the other side of the house, Storey slipped through the doorway, pulling it closed behind him and throwing himself down onto the grass. He extended the machine gun's bipod legs to give himself a stable firing platform.

When the second rocket hit a few seconds later Storey pushed the button safety to "fire."

A few seconds later the back door to the house exploded open, sending a column of light onto the lawn. The stampede had begun. He wasn't worried about being seen—they were coming from a lighted house into darkness.

They were running hard, panicked, heading for the door into the alley. Storey counted them out. Four, five, six.

The first one was getting close, but Storey waited patiently for more to leave the house. He could hear the panting; the lead man was almost on top of him. Storey held the trigger down.

The metal clacking of the bolt cycling back and forth was louder than the hissing of the suppressor. One round in every five was a tracer, and the stabbing red lines cut across the lawn.

The lead man dropped right in front of Storey, blocking his view, so Storey had to rise up on one knee to get a clear field of fire. He fired five-round bursts, finger bouncing on and off the trigger, just like the well-disciplined Ranger private he'd been seventeen years before, sweeping the gun back and forth across the width of the backyard. When the bullets hit the wall or ground and ricocheted, the normally orderly tracer lines skipped off wildly, some flying up into the night sky.

The sheer focus on the technical shooting problem demanded that Storey shut his ears to the cries. He watched the bodies pile up in front of him and then quickly shifted his fire. They didn't have a chance, which is the precise goal of any ambush. They couldn't make it back to the house, and the walled backyard—intended to keep out enemies—instead trapped them in a killing ground. The ones in back charged him when they saw the front-runners go down. They had as much chance against a single man with a machine gun as the Ndebele tribesmen who'd been the first to try and charge a Maxim gun in 1893.

When they were all down Storey rose up into a crouch and moved forward. Each body received a short burst as insurance against anyone playing possum.

Then he paused and made a quick radio call, mainly so Troy wouldn't come looking for him. "Clear."

Storey cautiously peered through the open doorway into the house, but did not go in. Anyone who wanted to stay alive didn't go trying to clear houses by themselves.

Someone had been carrying papers—they were scattered across the lawn. Anticipating this, Storey had a nylon mesh shopping bag tied to his belt and stuffed into his hip pocket. As fast as he could, he shoveled the papers inside. He stopped at each body and frisked it, using his own quick field expedient technique of pressing the fingertips of one hand into a middle page of a passport to preserve the prints for later recovery.

Two of them had computers in their arms. Storey appreciated them not leaving the machines behind. They were added to his bag.

Another radio call. "Make the move." And almost immediately the sound of a motorcycle roaring up the alley. Storey went to pull open the door to the alley. It had locked automatically. And at least one key was out in the alley. Now that was embarrassing. Darting back to get a running start, he leaped for the top of the wall. Weighed down by computers, papers, and machine gun, he only got it with his fingertips. Storey swung his hips, using the momentum to bring his legs up. He managed to hook one heel over the top of the wall, and kicked hard with the other leg to lever his body up on top. He rolled over the wall and dropped to the other side, angry with himself for wasting so much time.

Covering the alley with the machine gun, Storey hopped onto the back of the waiting motorcycle.

No sirens, no neighbors in sight other than curious faces in the windows. In the tropics people stayed up late to do as much living as possible in the cool of the evening. But everyone was staying out of this one. Sensible.

They came out the other side of the alley, and the van was waiting for them two blocks away. Storey passed the Minimi and the shopping bag through the open door, and they all got moving again.

The next stop was two miles down the road. Everyone removed their personal baggage from the van, and then hoisted the motorcycle inside. It would remain there, along with the Minimi, the RPG-7, and the AK-47s. Before they locked the van, Troy gave a twist to the egg timers taped to the two plastic jugs full of gasoline and detergent, each topped with an electric blasting cap. It was always a good idea to light two of everything—one might turn out to be a dud. As the SEALs say: one is none, two is one. In about ten minutes all the incriminating evidence, along with any fingerprints and DNA they might have left behind, would be burned up along with the van.

A short walk to another van—different make, different color—and once again they were off. Now to the Freedom Bridge, and Brazil. A one-way trip this time, because the town was about to get kind of hot.

Their fake passports were tucked away, and they went back to being U.S. diplomats with diplomatic immunity. Even though the names on those documents weren't genuine.

Storey busied himself during the drive by emptying out the shopping bag, making neat piles of passports and identity cards, some of them badly bloodstained.

"How many?" Troy asked.

"Seven," Storey replied. "Good shooting on the RPG."

"Made a real mess."

"If you'd just sniped through the windows with a rifle, they would have hit the floor, thought it over, and decided to stay and fight. But rockets hitting the house turned it into a stampede."

"Think we got 'em all?"

"Don't rightly know. If any stayed in the house, good luck to them. We'll get intel later, check the police reports."

"Speaking of the cops, they weren't in any hurry to show up, were they?"

"You're a city cop, and a call comes in someone's shooting RPGs into a house. Would you want to be the first responder?"

"Nope, don't think so."

They all flew commercial to Rio de Janeiro, then split up, taking different airlines and different connections back to Washington so they'd be harder to trace.

Chapter Two

Once you get off the main drags in Studio City, California, you find quiet neighborhoods of neat, single-story homes. The grounds mostly immaculate and the house numbers, according to the local custom, painted on the curbs.

A pickup truck equipped with commercial toolboxes and a ladder on the back cruised slowly down the street. The cable companies had all moved to independent contractors to do their service and repair work, to cut costs, so nowadays you saw more and more generic trucks and vans with vinyl magnetic signs slapped onto the doors.

The pickup stopped in front of a house near the end of the street, and two workers got out instead of the usual one. A man and a woman, wearing jeans and cable company polo shirts, laminated clip-on ID badges, and tool belts.

The man crossed the street. The woman knocked on the door of the house. She had fine auburn hair, tied in the back. There was no answer.

She passed by the next house, knocking at the one on the other side.

This time, an old lady's voice said from behind the door, "What do you want?"

The redhead smiled into the peephole and said,

"Adelphia Cable, ma'am. Are you having any trouble with your TV?"

"No."

"Well, we've had some power fluctuations in the neighborhood, so we're checking all the homes."

The door opened and revealed a silver-haired lady in her seventies, wearing a turquoise nylon jogging suit. "I don't believe it! You're from the cable company?"

"Yes, ma'am."

"The last time I had a problem with my Internet service, I called you up. And the recording said the customer service number changed, and to call another number. But by the time I got a pencil and paper, the recording was over and I had to call all over again. When I called that number do you know who I talked to? A man in Colorado. Colorado! You have to call Colorado for a service call in Los Angeles. I made an appointment, and you never showed up. Then I was out shopping, and a man called my cell phone saying he was waiting at my front door. On a day I didn't even make an appointment! After that nonsense I went back to dial-up, and I don't even want to tell you how long it took to get them to stop sending me bills for the service I cancelled. I'm thinking about satellite TV now . . ."

"I know just how you feel, ma'am," the redhead replied, for a cable company employee strangely unperturbed about the amount of time she'd been standing there. In fact, she was all sympathy and warmth. "They mess up all our appointments, then send us out to try and put everything right. But you're not having any trouble with your TV reception?"

"No, honey. I was just watching Judge Judy. And aren't you a sweet thing. Are you single?"

"No, ma'am. I'm married."

"You're not wearing a ring. Are you separated?"

The redhead smiled. Her faint freckles nicely accompanied wide cheekbones and merry brown eyes. "No, ma'am. I just don't wear my ring while I'm working. I don't want to get it caught in anything."

"That's too bad. I've got a wonderful nephew. But he can't seem to meet any nice girls."

"Don't worry, ma'am. I'm sure he will. I'm so sorry to have bothered you. Have a very nice afternoon."

As she turned down the walk, the homeowner called out, "Honey!"

The redhead turned. "Yes, ma'am?"

"I used to have a rear end like yours. Enjoy it while you've got it."

The redhead laughed heartily. "Thanks, I will."

She was already down to the sidewalk and out of range of any reply. Stopping in front of the house she'd originally passed by, she waited for her partner to return from knocking on all the doors in view on the other side of the street.

"Nobody at home," he said. "You?"

"One little old lady next door."

"Should we have gotten her all interested?"

"She'd be watching us out her windows anyway. Now she's satisfied, she knows what we're doing."

"Okay."

"Let's go around back."

They still didn't knock on the door, but went around to the backyard through a gate in the wooden fence.

"Nice," the man said. "The fence *does* cover the windows."

"You never know," she said. "Don't take any chances. Sell the thing all the way."

"All right, all right."

They both paused to put on gloves. But not work gloves. Latex gloves.

They appeared to trace the cable down the side of the house, stopping at the electric meter. The redhead produced a pair of cutters from her tool belt and clipped the wire seal on the meter and stuck it into her pocket. Grasping the glass barrel with both hands, she pulled the meter out of the socket, gave it a twirl so the plug wasn't lined up, and left it resting there in the box. To all appearances still connected.

While tracing the cable wire around the nearest window, the redhead took a thin-bladed palette knife from her belt and slid it in the crack between the upper and lower window frames. She yanked the knife sharply toward her, and the window lock popped open.

After sliding the window open she paused for a moment. There wasn't supposed to be any dog, but if there was it would show up shortly. No dog. And no power in the house meant no burglar alarm. The vast majority of alarm buyers failed to shell out that extra money for the backup unit that sent a radio signal if the power and phone were cut. The phone had already been cut.

The redhead leaned through the window, as if looking for something. Then she was inside. Having learned from experience that she might need it, she checked again to make sure her walkie-talkie was on.

She walked through the living room, checking the layout, making her decisions.

Cops like to say that every burglar has a pattern. The redhead went directly to the light switches. Why? Because she wasn't stealing anything. She had in her pocket a court order issued by a U.S. magistrate judge, authorizing Special Agents of the Federal Bureau of Investigation to physically enter the target location in order to deploy, maintain, utilize, and remove the means to effect video and audio surveillance upon the interior of the target location. The document ordered further that Special Agents of the FBI were authorized to enter the target location surreptitiously, covertly, and by breaking and entering, if necessary, in order to deploy those means.

Special Agent Elizabeth Royale went right to the light

switches because they were the best place to install cameras in a house that didn't have drop ceilings or overhead light fixtures. And she preferred not to do any drilling, spackling, or painting—even when she had the time. People in their own homes reacted like deer on forest trails. They immediately sensed if anything was out of place.

Audio bugs didn't require a lot of power. A unit the size of the waist button on a pair of pants could go for days on a power source the size of a hearing-aid battery.

Video needed a lot more juice. A wireless camera half the size of a Zippo lighter would only run for a day on a battery pack as big as a paperback book. So they had to be wired into a power source. Which was why Beth Royale loved using light switches.

She picked the one that gave an unobstructed view of the whole living room. The screws and plate came off, and she was pleased to see that the switch box was plastic. Metal played hell with wireless transmissions.

The first thing she did was see if the box was firmly attached. Al-Qaeda operatives loved to hide documents and guns in wall cavities behind and below switch boxes. It wouldn't do to install her equipment in the same place they were using as a cache.

To be sure, Beth used the endoscope on her tool belt. Holding the scope up to her eye, she ran the lighted fiber optic cable all the way around and below.

No, nothing there. The tiny plastic box that contained both camera and transmitter, only one and a quarter inches square and three eighths of an inch thick, could be wedged in the space behind the light switch because the pinhole lens was mounted on the end of a fine fiber optic cable. Like a miniature version of the endoscope. The cable threaded right through the screw hole in the switch to reach the outside world. Beth had a plastic container filled with every kind of screw for every color switch and plug plate made. But they were dummy screws, with the centers drilled out to receive the fiber optic cable and a small lens hole masked by the darker screwdriver slot.

In addition to the lens cable, the camera box had two other wires trailing from it. One thin wire antenna to transmit the picture out. And a thicker one branching out into two leads with alligator clips that Beth attached to the light switch power lines.

The plate went back on, and the lower screw secured it to the wall. The lens had a sixty-degree field of view, enough to cover the whole living room. Beth knew from experience exactly what the camera would see.

The audio bugs went in the same way, but closer to the furniture to pick up the sound better. Electric plugs were best for those. The microphones were shielded so the current didn't bother them.

Beth had practiced her technique to the point that she could install a camera in under a minute, and a bug in under thirty seconds. Limiting their exposure inside the house was critical. Ironically, when working in a residential neighborhood broad daylight was better than night. People were at work during the day, and those who weren't didn't pay attention to things out of the ordinary they way they did at night.

She was soon in the kitchen putting a camera and microphone in the combination light fixture/ceiling fan that hung right over the table. Her partner was out on the back deck bugging the lawn furniture. Very alert to her surroundings, Beth heard a muffled thumping sound. She stopped work to listen, but didn't hear it again.

But some feeling kept her from shrugging it off. She climbed down from the kitchen chair she was standing on. As soon as her feet touched the linoleum, a small shape dashed through the doorway.

Beth nearly had a heart attack. It was a little girl, a

toddler. Just walking. A baggy diaper, a cute top, and two big brown eyes.

Beth froze, for longer than she would ever admit later. No, no, the parents *couldn't* be right behind her. Not without her having heard about it over the radio. This was more of a prayer than a statement of belief.

The little girl let out a happy baby cry that snapped Beth out of her trance. She gave the child a big smile and an exaggerated wave, and was rewarded by the kid holding out her arms to be picked up and hugged.

Beth did just that, while hurrying to the doorway to check out the living room. No one there. She'd seen everything on the job, but in this case the target's wife was a super-protective mother—not the type to leave a baby home alone.

Still carrying the little girl, and rubbing noses to keep her quiet, Beth checked out the rest of the house—the house that was supposed to be empty. They'd gone in through one bedroom. The doors to the bathroom and the adjacent bedroom were open. The third bedroom door, closed, gave Beth a sinking feeling in the pit of her stomach. Someone was in there, and if they came out all the smooth talking in the world wasn't going to explain why the power was out and a couple of cable installers were inside the house.

Beth immediately turned off her radio. Right then nobody needed the sound of an incoming call.

Her partner picked that very moment to come in from outside. At the sight of the little girl in Beth's arms his mouth opened, very wide, forming the word "what." He very excitedly aimed a thumb at the back door, but Beth shook her head. This family was always at home— no shit—and they might never be able to get back in.

The little girl was getting antsy in her arms, starting to squirm. She was going to start howling any minute.

Beth flew through the kitchen cabinets, almost settling

on an eggbeater as a toy before coming across a box of Cap'n Crunch. She dumped a pile of cereal on the floor, set the kid down, gave her the box for her very own, and let her have at it.

Whispering in her partner's ear, Beth said, "You watch that bedroom door. It opens, you go out the back door here and get to the truck."

He shook his head vehemently, pointing toward the door again.

Beth shook her head just as vehemently, ending the discussion by walking out of the kitchen, through the living room, and into the parents' bedroom. It had the crib in one corner. She put two microphones in electric plugs, not wanting to risk one going down in such an important space. No video, though. No time. She'd do this room, then finish up next door, the room she came in, and then exit through the window.

Beth was just screwing the plate back on when the other bedroom door opened. She looked out through the open doorway, weighing the odds. The window in this room was closed and locked. Opening it was going to make noise. No way was she getting under the bed.

She went for the closet. No squeaks from the door, thank God, and she released the knob a millimeter at a time so the latch wouldn't click.

A crackling floorboard let her know someone was in the bedroom. A mature female voice with a strong accent said, "Nadimah?" Then louder, sharper, and more concerned. "Nadimah!"

Beautiful, Beth, she told herself standing there in the darkness. Always pushing it. Couldn't get out of the house when you had the chance, could you? Now what are you going to say when she opens up the closet door looking for the kid? You let yourself in to fix the cable, didn't want to disturb anyone, and then decided to try on some shoes. Just a little fetish she was trying to come to grips with.

Beth thought about hiding behind the clothes, but didn't want to make the slightest kid-like sounds that might provoke an investigation.

She waited for the sound of the hand on the closet doorknob, her heart thumping in her chest. Then a "Nadimah!" that was outside the bedroom.

Beth opened the door a crack, so she could hear. The woman was in the next bedroom. Super, the one with the open window. Well, maybe that was okay—go look for the kid outside.

Beth was thrown into a moment of uncharacteristic indecision. Move or wait? Anything might happen if she waited. With her luck everyone else would come home.

Gingerly opening the closet door, she went across the carpet on the balls of her feet, crouching down to peek through the doorway.

The woman was over by the front door. Another Pakistani, family or friend obviously, about fifty. The calls to Nadimah were getting more frantic. She was moving again. Shit! She was heading back to the bedroom. Beth knew she was too far away from the closet. And to get behind the door she'd have to cross the open doorway.

Beth could hear the footsteps and then the woman's breath as she approached the doorway. A feeling of resignation—the case was blown. Then from the kitchen the sound of a cereal box falling on the floor. Beth could feel the woman stopping short. She'd heard it. Beth heard the footsteps turn away, and peeked around the corner. The woman was heading to the kitchen. Not even waiting for her to get there, Beth bolted through the doorway and into the adjacent bedroom.

As Beth popped the buckle on her tool belt she heard a relieved but stern "Nadimah!" from the kitchen. She threw the tool belt out the window and dove through right behind it, sailing over the shrubs along the side of the hose and hitting the grass with both outstretched hands.

Beth rolled and was up, grabbing the tool belt and sprinting for the electric meter. She jammed it back into the box and both felt and heard the surging hum of electricity. Digging into the tool belt at her feet, she snapped a new seal onto the meter collar. Fortunately, there were no windows in view.

Trying to casually clip her tool belt back on while still shaking from the adrenaline surge, Beth left the back-yard through the fence gate. Inside of passing in front of the house, she crossed through two backyards to reach the pickup. Her partner in crime, Special Agent Russell Behan, was sitting behind the wheel, looking singularly distressed.

"Jesus Christ!" he exclaimed in relief.

"Yeah, I know," said Beth, dropping into the passenger's seat. "You were trying to figure out how to tell the bosses you left me inside." One glance over at Behan confirmed the accuracy of her thesis and got her laughing. "Hey, I told you to get out."

"Like they'd believe that," Behan grumbled. "Are we going to leave the power off?"

"I reconnected it," said Beth. "Didn't close the window behind me, though. Oh, well. Auntie'll think she left it open."

"That was way too close."

"Lesson learned: check out the entire house, every room, before you start work." Beth let out a big breath. "I think I'm going to give up black bag jobs for a while," she mused. "The last few have gotten really weird."

"I think I'm going on suspension," said Behan.

"You did fine," Beth said reassuringly. "As long as the video and audio come through all right, this was a perfect entry. Hairy, but perfect."

"That's not what I'm going on suspension for," said

Behan. "I'm going on suspension for kicking the shit out of those two assholes from the LA office who told us the house was empty."

"No you're not."

"Oh yes I am."

"No, you're not," Beth replied firmly. "You've got a family, you can't afford to lose a couple weeks' pay. Not to mention your job." She gave Behan a smile that he found very unsettling. "I'll take care of them."

Chapter Three

The six-lane, Korean-built superhighway was a marvel to everyone accustomed to Pakistani roads. There were actually police enforcing the traffic regulations and the 120-kilometer-per-hour speed limit. The trucks actually used signals and stayed in their designated lane. Unbelievable.

The Japanese Hiro bus was comfortable and air conditioned, but crowded. Everyone's shopping had overflowed the overhead baggage racks and migrated into the middle of the aisle. Abdallah Karim Nimri felt as though he'd spent a week on the wretched vehicle.

Nimri had previously based himself in Karachi, but that city had become unfriendly to him. He had lately been spending most of his time in Belgium. It was more congenial there.

However, he'd received a summons to return to Pakistan. He had flown into Lahore and boarded the bus from there.

The traffic was stopped up ahead, and the bus squealed to a stop inches from the bumper of the truck in front. It had to be another checkpoint. They took forever.

Every ten minutes the bus crawled forward another few meters. Then finally they reached it. The soldiers finished swarming over the truck in front, and waved the bus up.

The driver rushed out to open the baggage compartment. Four soldiers stepped aboard. Two covered each row of seats with their rifles. The other pair made their way down the aisle, everyone scrambling to pull their bags out of the way.

A *sepoy*—private—and a *naik*—corporal—wearing khaki shirts under greenish-brown sweaters and matching trousers, combat boots and khaki web belts. Carrying Chinese AK-47s. Nimri recognized the insignia. The Baluch Regiment. A jeep was parked at the checkpoint, an alert soldier behind the Chinese Type 54 12.7mm heavy machine gun mounted on it. What the Russians called Dashika, or little darling. Nimri knew it well from Afghanistan. If the soldiers on the bus ran into any trouble the gunner wouldn't care—he would cut loose. And those huge .51-caliber bullets would reduce the bus and everyone aboard into much smaller pieces.

The *sepoy* and *naik* checked the overhead and under the seats, and frisked all the men. Anticipating this, Nimri was uncharacteristically unarmed. Years before he had spent more than a year in prison in his native Egypt, and nothing on earth would ever send him back. To ensure this, he almost always kept a hand grenade taped to his stomach. Today this was not possible, so he had to rely on the cyanide pill inside his shirt collar.

Nimri watched them closely as they made their way toward him. When it was his turn he handed over his Pakistani identity card—forged, of course—then stood up and stretched out his arms to accept the frisk. He watched their eyes. If they were looking for someone in particular, if they had a face in mind—and it was his—he would know from their eyes.

His own dropped to the *naik*'s AK-47 with professional interest. It was obviously old but spotlessly clean, and the selector bar was one stop down from safe to fully automatic. What to do if they tried to take him? Grab a rifle or go directly to the tablet? Better to be sure and go for the tablet. If he didn't get the rifle, or was only wounded, it would go very badly for him. Very badly.

The frisk revealed nothing, of course. He was carrying no bags. Everything was in his head.

His identity card was handed back without a word, and they continued down the aisle. Nimri had gone through many checkpoints before, but it had been a long time since he had traveled this far north. He had never seen them search so thoroughly.

Nimri left the bus in Rawalpindi, before it continued on the short ten-kilometer hop to Islamabad, the national capital.

Rawalpindi was the older of the two, standing atop the ruins of an ancient city destroyed by the Mongols. A garrison town during the British Raj, it was still the headquarters of Pakistan's army. An irony Nimri appreciated. But with a population of nearly a million and a half, easy to be anonymous in.

The bus had arrived on time, as guaranteed. An unheard-of thing in Pakistan. It meant Nimri did not have to hurry. He hailed a motor rickshaw and ordered the driver to take him to Murree Road.

He immediately regretted choosing the rickshaw over a taxi. The sun was setting, though a drop in temperature was only a dream. The pollution was thick as a fog, and he was sitting right out in the middle of it. It seemed his fate to put himself into situations where he was bound to be aggravated.

Rawalpindi, and Pakistan, looked ragged and beaten down. The backed-up sewers overflowed into the streets, and there were piles of garbage everywhere. Nimri realized he was only noticing it because of Belgium. That had been their mistake, seeing this and feeling that Pakistan was ripe for an explosion. Pakistan was always on the verge of exploding, but never did. The Pakistani masses accepted everything, because they could never imagine a government doing anything for them.

The stadium was all lighted up. Nimri already had a ticket, sent to him in Lahore. The cricket grounds held 15,000, and the stands were nearly full even though it was only a match between club teams. Pakistanis were absolutely mad for cricket, while to an Egyptian the game was inexplicable.

But he wasn't there to watch. Wearing a beige *shalwar kameez*, the indigenous garment—loose knee-length tunic and matching trousers—he looked like almost every one of the 10,000 men there.

Always alert for a trap, before he sat down he checked for extra police or plainclothesmen in his section. He couldn't see any surveillance. Which meant Nimri did not have to worry about the authorities. Or their American masters. He only had to worry about *them*. And that was worry enough.

His seat was on an aisle—the only adjacent seat was to his left. And it was occupied by a young man in his early twenties. No beard, just a moustache. Also wearing a *shalwar kameez*. Inexperienced, because he had made a point of not looking over when Nimri sat down. And everyone looks at the person who sits down next to them.

Nimri nudged him and said in Urdu, "Am I in the right seat?" and handed over his ticket stub.

The young man looked at the ticket carefully, turning it over to note the faint handwritten markings on the back. "Yes, this is the right seat." He kept the ticket stub. Nimri knew the boy would have to produce it later.

"Do you want to finish the inning?" the young man asked.

"No," Nimri answered emphatically.

The young man seemed disappointed. He stood up and motioned for Nimri to move.

Nimri waited on the steps for the guide to lead the way. He didn't like strangers behind him.

They hailed a cab outside the stadium. If Nimri thought he could determine his reception from his guide's manner, he was disappointed. Other than giving directions to the driver, the young man never said a word.

The taxi stopped near the Saddar Bazaar, and they walked the streets to throw off any followers. The young man led them into a tiny cupboard of a tailor shop. A nod to the proprietor and they went into the back. The young man pointed toward a changing room. "Strip naked and hand all your clothing out to me."

Nimri did as he was told, placing his billfold and identity documents into his shoes and wrapping the *shalwar kameez* around them. "There is money in the belt," he said as he handed the bundle through the curtain. He remained standing to wait, none too impressed by the cleanliness of the bench.

The young man came through the curtain, brandishing an old Pakistani army Walther P38 pistol.

"If you had not noticed," Nimri said, "I am not armed."

These young ones, unfortunately, had been taught that a sense of humor was not Islamic. He moved sideways to make room for a stockier fellow in a skullcap and full beard who, Nimri immediately noticed, had not bathed in quite some time. He was holding what looked like a handheld radio.

The scanner was passed over Nimri's body. They were being *very* careful. Which was good for all concerned.

Nimri was left alone again. He knew that if the scanner had detected any radio emissions coming from his body he would have been shot instantly. And now his clothes and papers were being checked.

No, he was handed an entirely new outfit, complete with shoes that were too tight. But it was not the proper circumstance for complaints. He just hoped he would not have to walk too far. Even his money and documents were in a brand-new billfold.

He left the tailor shop with the young man again. They walked through the bazaar, the young man checking their backs for surveillance. Not willing to trust his fate to anyone else's competence, Nimri was doing the same.

Outside the bazaar a parked car suddenly opened its doors in front of them. Nimri flinched, ready to run, but the young man grabbed his arm and pushed him into the backseat. There was a driver and passenger in the front.

Nimri was blindfolded and pushed to the floor, a blanket thrown over him. He could have done without the hot, scratchy blanket, not to mention the young man's foot on his back to hold him down, but he still approved. Not just the precautions, but the fact that they wouldn't be taking such precautions if they intended to kill him out of hand.

With little else to do, he tried to keep track of their route. But there were too many turns, and he didn't know Rawalpindi well enough. Then, from the echoing sound, they were passing through a tunnel. But they stopped, so it wasn't a tunnel. That was it—an underground garage.

Nimri was removed from the car and pulled to his feet, still blindfolded. Told to walk, he ended up in an elevator. He couldn't imagine what kind of apartment building it might be, where a blindfolded man could be led about with no one taking any notice. That was right—an office! An office building at night had no workers, only watchmen who could be persuaded to look the other way.

Nimri was led down halls and through doorways. Then roughly pushed down into a chair. At least it was padded. The treatment had Nimri's temper, never too long to begin with, at the boiling point.

The blindfold was taken away. He was in an office sitting at an oval conference table. The room was warm. Nimri imagined that the air-conditioning was turned down at night, to save electricity. With limited circulation, the room smelled of new carpet and stale cigarettes.

Blinking at the bright light, Nimri almost failed to recognize the man sitting across from him. When he had last seen Abu Faraj al-Libbi in Afghanistan in 2001, the man had a closely trimmed beard. Now he was several kilos lighter and the beard was untrimmed, the wisps of black hair growing almost up under his eyes, making him look as if he had a skin disease. Together with the hatchet face and the beady eyes, he looked even more like a thug than before. But then Nimri had never cared for the man. Egyptians always regarded Libyans as desert bumpkins.

Nimri's mood wasn't improved by the realization that al-Libbi must be the new al-Qaeda head of operations. He actually did not know for sure who the head of operations was, except that it was not him. That the Americans kept capturing them made it hard to keep track. Under such pressure, the organization had splintered even further into self-contained cells, and few of the old communications links were still active. It had taken weeks for him to receive this summons, and even more time to arrange the travel details. And still he did not have complete knowledge of all the paths the messages had taken.

"I speak for Abu Abdullah," al-Libbi announced.

Nimri was not impressed. It was one thing to use Osama Bin Laden's code name and claim you spoke for him. It was another thing for it to be true. And the insult! No greeting between brothers at war. No "peace be upon you." No blessing. Intolerable. But just like a Libyan. No manners whatsoever.

Nimri merely looked over his shoulder at the two musclemen who had brought him up from the car, as if to ask why they were speaking in front of so many ears.

Al-Libbi made a curt gesture, and the two left the room.

Nimri's own anger had subsided, and it pleased him to see al-Libbi's rise.

"I have told you I speak for Abu Abdullah," al-Libbi repeated.

"And I continue to hear you say so," Nimri replied.

"Abu Abdullah is angry at your failure."

Nimri doubted it. Bin Laden knew how many operations failed for every one that succeeded. He would not let the Libyan goad him. "Failure? I penetrated the heart of America, into Washington, D.C., itself, and was within thirty seconds of destroying the Jew Donald Rumsfeld."

"And failed," al-Libbi pointed out.

"I noticed from the newspapers this morning that Musharraf is still alive," Nimri countered. And from the way the Libyan reacted he knew the reports had been true, that it had been al-Libbi's operation. The previous December, right there in Rawalpindi, two attempts had been made on the life of General Pervez Musharraf, the president of Pakistan. In the first, a huge explosive charge was detonated while the president's vehicle convoy was passing over a bridge. Even the most heavily armored limousine was not proof against a charge of 225 kilos. But it was thwarted by the same thing that had earlier saved Donald Rumsfeld from the explosive-rigged gasoline tanker truck Nimri had placed in his path: a radio frequency jammer that blocked the detonation signal from being sent.

"A fine idea for an attack, though," Nimri continued. "How ever did you think of it?"

Al-Libbi was so furious his mouth was moving though no sound was coming out.

"The second was well conceived," said Nimri, almost in the form of a compliment. "You adapted very quickly."

Twelve days after the first attempt was defeated, al-Libbi sent a *shaheed*, a martyr, in a car bomb to ram the convoy. But could not get past the security vehicles to reach Musharraf's limousine.

The hollow compliment fell on deaf ears because, of course, the second attempt had also been a failure. "Now

you will tell me you counseled against killing the apos-
tate Musharraf," said al-Libbi.

"I will not deny it," said Nimri. "My position was clear."
In response to demands for Musharraf's head after the
al-Qaeda operations chief Khalid Sheikh Mohammed had
been captured by the Pakistanis and turned over to the
Americans, Nimri had counseled restraint. Under intense
pressure from the Americans, Musharraf had moved
against only the highest al-Qaeda leaders hiding in
Pakistan after the fall of Afghanistan, and rather listlessly
at that. After all, Pakistan had helped to create the Taliban
in Afghanistan, and used al-Qaeda–trained militants to
fight the Indians in Kashmir. When the Americans had
attacked al-Qaeda Afghan camps with cruise missiles after
their embassies were bombed in Africa, more Pakistani
Inter-Services Intelligence officers had been killed than
al-Qaeda fighters.

Nimri had predicted that if they tried to kill Musharraf, and failed, he would purge his army and intelligence
services of all those sympathetic to al-Qaeda. And there
were many who were sympathetic. Al-Libbi had had no
trouble obtaining Musharraf's top-secret travel itinerary
and constantly varying routes. With his personal survival
at stake, Musharraf would come after them, no holds
barred. And so it had come to pass. After the failed attempts, thousands of brothers had been thrown into jail,
including hitherto untouchable army officers. Al-Libbi
had a reward of twenty million rupees on his head—
$340,000 American. A fortune in Pakistan.

Nimri was a little surprised that al-Libbi was still in
Rawalpindi, though of course policemen were the same
the world over. They were hunting him in every corner of
Pakistan, because of course he would never be fool
enough to remain at the scene of his crimes. So of course
that was where he was. Though he actually had no
idea, Nimri would not have been surprised to hear that

bin Laden was comfortably ensconced in a penthouse apartment around the corner from the presidential palace in Islamabad, rather than the tribal village on the Afghan border the Americans imagined.

"What became of Kasim al-Hariq?" al-Libbi demanded.

Nimri had been rather enjoying how al-Libbi had begun full of authority and accusations, and been thrown onto the defensive. Now the sweat began trickling down his own spine. And it was not just the heat of the office. Kasim al-Hariq was a Saudi, one of the old men in bin Laden's inner circle. "He was captured by the Americans."

"It is known he was captured by the Americans. He was captured by the Americans after he traveled to Karachi to meet with you. He was captured by the Americans in the safe house where he met with you, shortly after he met with you."

"He was betrayed by Imram Hasan, as you must know." Formerly Nimri's assistant. "If I had not left to begin the American operation, I would have been taken too, by God."

"Which begs another question. Your operation. You were to have assassinated George Bush during his visit to the Philippines. How then did you come to attack Donald Rumsfeld in Washington?"

This was why Nimri had come to the meeting believing his life was in jeopardy. "I persuaded Kasim al-Hariq that an attack on Bush was not feasible, given the level of security on his tour of Asia. I offered the alternate plan of attacking Rumsfeld in Washington while the attention of the American intelligence services was focused on Asia. Al-Hariq approved the plan, and released the funding to carry it out. He was captured before he could return and inform the leadership of the change."

"He approved the plan?" said al-Libbi.

"He did. How else would I have received the funding?" This was not true. Al-Hariq had come to him with orders to shoot down Bush's helicopter in Manila with surface-to air-missiles. It would have been a fiasco, but the stubborn old Saudi bastard would not listen to reason. Why should he? He did not have to be the one to execute a hopeless attack. But God had intervened. Only days before, Nimri had learned from a contact in Pakistani Inter-Services Intelligence that his assistant had become an informer for the rival Federal Investigative Agency, which was more closely aligned with the Americans. So he agreed to execute the foolhardy plan, took the money, and intentionally left the Saudi in the care of the traitor Hasan.

But God did not grant him the successful attack that would have made him al-Qaeda operations chief. But God also did not save Kasim al-Hariq from the Americans. So Nimri's secret was known to no one. Al-Libbi and even bin Laden could suspect all they wished.

"He approved your change in plan?" al-Libbi repeated.

At that Nimri knew they had nothing against him. "He approved it. Is it any wonder my operation failed, with him in the hands of the Americans? By God, I was hunted every moment, yet still nearly succeeded."

"At the cost of a network in the Philippines, one in Thailand, and an important cell in the United States," said al-Libbi. "The coordinators for the Philippines, Thailand, and Southeast Asia. All dead or captured."

"And all my friends," Nimri shot back.

"And you alone escape."

"God is merciful," said Nimri. "God is great."

"All praise to God," al-Libbi replied automatically.

There was a pause then, which led Nimri to believe that al-Libbi had fired all his ammunition yet hit nothing. He decided to remain on the attack. "I have a plan for another operation."

"Where?"

"America."

Al-Libbi shook his head. "Iraq is the decisive battle-ground. Almost all our resources have shifted to Iraq. Even the European networks have put aside their other work to move young brothers and money into Iraq."

Nimri had no trouble reading between the lines of that statement. "I have been in Europe, as you know. The networks have little direction, so they are focusing on Iraq."

Al-Libbi's eyes flashed at the insult. "Iraq is the decisive battleground. Iraq will prepare the next generation to fight the way combat against the Russians in Afghanistan prepared us."

"Iraq is the path of least resistance," said Nimri.

"This is not true," al-Libbi said heatedly. "Iraq will be our salvation. The Americans have brought the battle to us, and we will defeat them there."

"In ten years."

"It took Vietnam ten years to defeat them. Their defeat will be in God's time."

"God's time, yes," said Nimri. "But do we, as an organization, have that much time? In ten years we will be nothing."

"God will choose the time, and the place, and the form of victory. And the caliph who brings the world of believers together."

It was useless, Nimri thought. They could not see past their own noses. Only bin Laden could look into the future and make plans that were not dreams. And bin Laden was now isolated, by necessity out of touch with the organization he had so painstakingly built. "What if the Americans are able to hold their election in Iraq this fall, and their Iraqi puppets take over?

"We will stop this election, God willing."

"As we stopped the election in Afghanistan?"

Al-Libbi glowered. "Iraq will be different. We will drive out the Americans, and hang their Iraqi puppets from the corner of every street."

"If we do, the Kurds and Shia will combine to destroy the true believers, the Sunni. Or the Iraqis will fight their civil war, and whoever wins, even the Sunni, will turn on us. You know the Iraqis."

"Our brothers will not turn on us!" al-Libbi shouted.

"Our Afghan brothers did."

Al-Libbi was keeping control of himself, but with difficulty. "You speak nothing but defeatism. What is *your* plan for victory?"

Just what Nimri had been waiting for. "The Americans were forced out of Vietnam. What difference did it make to them? Nothing. They were forced out of Lebanon. Did that prevent them from sustaining the Jews and oppressing the true believers? No. Somalia? The same. They are immune to every humiliation. If they are forced from Iraq, will they abandon the house of Saud and their puppets Musharraf in Pakistan and Mubarak in Egypt and Abdullah in Jordan? I think not. This is why we must not succumb to the easy path. We must strike them directly, make them change their minds about keeping their thumb on our world. Their government will never do so, but, hurt badly enough, their people will force their government."

Al-Libbi actually put his hands together and applauded Nimri, slowly and with supreme irony. "A beautiful speech. So inspiring. And how do you propose to accomplish this?"

Nimri did not let al-Libbi see it on his face, but he vowed one day to revenge himself. "Disrupting the Iraq election may, in the end, mean nothing. Why not, instead, disrupt the American election this November?"

"What did you say?"

And then Abdallah Karim Nimri told him exactly how to do it.

Chapter Four

His head swimming with Arabic, Nasser Saleh decided he needed a break. As he passed by his neighbor's cubicle he held up his empty coffee mug, making the gesture into a question. Farah was on her cell phone, as usual, instead of translating Pashto. She'd figured it out. There were only ten Pashto translators in the entire FBI, so Farah did as she pleased. The supervisors rode everyone else, but they pleaded with her.

She handed him her mug without a pause in her conversation.

While he was pouring coffee Barry, the supervisor, stuck his head into the break room. "Nasser, how close are you finishing that audio file?"

"Pretty close, Barry." He'd learned it was no joke when they said that the "B" in FBI stood for bureaucracy. If you told them you'd be done in an hour, as soon as the minute hand ticked over there'd be three more jobs on your computer.

He'd been in his senior year at the University of Maryland, considering his options. With a degree in political science, a contradiction in terms if there ever was one, he was looking at some $20,000 a year entry-level gofer job in Washington, that first rung in fighting his way up the political food chain. Or maybe the State Department

Foreign Service exam. Every political science major in the country took that.

Then 9/11 happened, and in the spring he saw the ad.

He was first generation, his parents had come over from Egypt. His father started as a janitor cleaning offices, and now ran his own small janitorial company.

Immigrant parents always insisted on the first generation learning the native tongue. They usually felt more comfortable speaking it at home, and they wanted the kids to stay in touch with their roots.

Learning Arabic from two native speakers wasn't enough. Nasser's parents sent him to classes. Which had been like piano lessons when you wanted to go out and play ball. But unlike all his American friends, there was no arguing with *his* parents. In college it had been an easy language elective, then a dual major that might improve his job prospects. It was actually easier for him than taking English.

When the FBI advertised it was looking for translators, it had sounded exciting. He took the language tests and they instantly offered him a job, contingent upon receiving a Top Secret security clearance. He wouldn't be a permanent FBI employee, just a contract worker. Nasser found out later that was because Congress tightly controlled both the FBI budget and the number of employees. The FBI did have linguists as permanent employees, called Language Specialists. But the more Language Specialists, the fewer Special Agents. So all the new hires went on contract.

He'd had to fill out the SF-86 questionnaire, the background investigation form. Basically, everything he'd done and everyone he'd known his entire life to date.

Then he was polygraphed. Mostly questions about whether he knew any terrorists or had been a member of any groups. No problem there. Then more questions about his relatives in Egypt. He barely knew them. His father brought his grandparents over to visit every other year or so, but no one else. His parents never went back, not even for visits. And he'd only been to Cancún on spring break.

So he passed, even though the blood-pressure cuff and all the wires and contacts had scared the crap out of him. They told him later that was the whole point, since the machine measured your physiological response to the questions, not your truthfulness.

Then came the personal security interview, which after the drama of the polygraph was a major letdown. Probably because the agent who conducted it did five or six of them a day. Nasser got the impression that you passed if you didn't go out of your way to make him dislike you.

The whole process took more than a year. Even though he'd applied at the start of his last semester in college, he still had to take another job after he graduated. Yes, the $20,000 congressional staff errand-boy position, which he'd happily quit when the FBI finally called.

Most of the contract linguists were farmed out to all the FBI field offices. But because of Nasser's Arabic proficiency, and the fact that he was an American citizen, he was assigned to the Language Services Translation Center at FBI headquarters in Washington. It was the command and control center for translator assignments, and also had twenty FBI and thirty contract translators who handled urgent taskings from the field offices and legal attaché offices in the embassies abroad.

After all the excitement of recruitment, and the first day walking into the J. Edgar Hoover building wearing his own ID badge, the reality of an office crammed full of cubicles was another letdown.

He started off as a Contract Monitor, only allowed to provide summary translation and analysis for internal dissemination. It had taken him a while to get the hang of it. It wasn't the Arabic—that was easy. You didn't need to translate everything in an audio session, and it took time to recognize what was important and what wasn't. And the military terms and euphemisms terrorists used were like a whole other language.

But pretty soon he moved up to Contract Linguist, which meant he could perform the same job as a permanent-employee Language Specialist. He could act as an interpreter in FBI interviews, though that had never happened. His material could go out for external dissemination or be used in court, and he could testify as an expert witness. That hadn't happened either. He just translated conversations. Lots of conversations.

Which usually ended up with Barry saying exactly what he was saying in the coffee room now: "I'm going to need you to send that off to the New York office before the end of the day."

"Okay, Barry."

The pressure was always on, because the bottom line was that FBI couldn't translate all the foreign language material they collected. They were at the point where 98 percent of the audio material was being translated, since that was the priority. Like most government statistics, it sounded really impressive. As long as no one mentioned that the 2 percent was nearly 8,000 hours of recorded audio. And no one really knew if there was anything important in those 8,000 hours. The supervisors spent so much time preparing reports for the FBI leadership on how much was getting translated—not what wasn't—that they didn't have any time to monitor the priorities of most cases. The Counterterrorism Division rarely set priorities, and the field offices gave almost everything the highest priority to keep it from getting stuck in the backlog.

And all the emphasis on audio meant that only 2 percent of the text material was getting translated. Nasser hadn't worked on a document in a month.

Farah was finally off the phone. Passing her coffee, Nasser said, "If you're not careful, when you get your one-year work review they're going to fire you."

"Who cares?" she said.

It had gotten to the point where everyone felt that way, even those like Farah who did half the work everyone else did.

Nasser mostly translated counterterrorism Foreign Intelligence Surveillance Act audio sessions. This was electronic surveillance of conversations obtained by warrants from the FISA court in Washington.

The policy was to review FISA audio within twenty-four hours of interception. And al-Qaeda FISA audio within twelve hours. When the field offices couldn't meet the deadline, they passed it on to the Language Services Center.

It wasn't easy, and the FBI's computer systems made it even harder. Nasser had been amazed to discover that the University of Maryland's computer system was like Star Wars compared to the FBI's.

Everything was sent back and forth from the field offices over a secure communications network called Arachnet. But the system had trouble forwarding material. Then the office that sent it didn't know it hadn't been received, and the receiving office had no idea anything had been sent.

And the computer systems had unbelievably limited storage capacity, particularly for audio files. So sometimes the automatic system deleted files on your computer to make room for new audio sessions. Without warning and without review. The traffic was so heavy that sometimes a file disappeared after only three days. A few times Nasser had come back from a break to find that audio files he was just about to start work on were gone. When it deleted them, the system didn't distinguish between completed work and unreviewed files. There were no system controls at all.

The deleted files didn't disappear, they were archived. But the archived audio sessions didn't include status information. Not even "reviewed" or "unreviewed." So when you did drag something back up from the archives, you had to go through it all over again.

One of Nasser's jobs was to review the work of the Contract Monitors. Some of them might work on the same audio session. And the computer kept track of only the last person to work on a particular task. So that was overwritten if someone else worked on it later. A lot of the Contract Monitors were really sloppy. Nasser had seen some stuff that made him wonder if they really understood Arabic. But sometimes you couldn't even tell who had screwed up. So the sloppy translators kept doing sloppy work.

Nasser sat down at his desk and put the earphones on. The first time he'd seen a document with a black "Top Secret" stamp across the top had been a rush. As was translating a recorded conversation between two Arab diplomats.

But for every bit of excitement like that, there were days of listening to Arab men slurp tea and lament the state of their bowels. Hours and hours of constipation. It was probably all the tea.

That and the pressure and fighting the computers was wearing him down. It was probably time to see what that Top Secret clearance could do for him. Congressional staff, maybe. Or a think tank or contractor. Something better than this.

His phone rang. He picked it up. It was his mother. "Hey, Mom. Well, I'm really busy right now. What? I don't know. I don't know, I'll see. Yes, *Umma.* Yes, I'll come for dinner this weekend. No, not Saturday night. Sunday. Yes,

I promise. I have to get back to work now. Love you, *Umma*. 'Bye."

Nasser sighed. His mother could teach the FBI a thing or two. Every time he came to dinner there was some chunky Egyptian girl with hair on her upper lip. And his mother calling him every day for the next week asking how he'd liked her. Not only that, but she wanted him at mosque for Mawlid al-Nahi, the Prophet Mohammad's birthday. It wasn't one of the main Muslim holidays, and some parts of the Arab world considered it undignified and refused to celebrate it. But in America there was music and dancing. Kind of like St. Patrick's Day for the Irish. The exiles celebrated it with a lot more enthusiasm than the natives. Dancing around the mosque with a bunch of old farts instead of hitting the clubs at Georgetown. Wouldn't that be great?

But if he blew off his mother then the old man would be on the phone, without a doubt. Except he'd call only after work. And then Nasser would get the faith, heritage, and tradition lecture. Not forgetting your roots. The old man might as well put that on a CD—it never changed.

He was going to have to think of something good to get out of it.

Chapter Five

Ed Storey was damned if he was going to stand at attention in front of a desk and get his ass chewed like a private. So after reporting as ordered he'd snapped into parade rest without asking for or receiving permission. Such damned foolishness. They were all in civilian clothes, and there was no one in the unit under the rank of staff sergeant. They weren't even on a military base—they were in an office park in Northern Virginia for crissakes.

The unit didn't even have a name. It had a Joint Task Force number that, for security, changed as often as the seasons. So often that no one who worked in it, other than the admin clerks, even bothered to keep track. "What are we this week?" was the running joke. Everyone called it "the office." Which, for purposes of operational security, was ideal anyway.

On the front door was the seal of the Defense Security and Cooperation Agency (DSCA), the arm of the Pentagon that handled selling weapons and organizing military training around the world. The unit was inside the DSCA budget, though it was a certainty that no one in DSCA knew anything about them.

It had its origins as a cell within the headquarters of Joint Special Operations Command at Fort Bragg, North Carolina. JSOC was the umbrella command responsible for the nation's Tier-1 counterterrorist units: Combat Applications Group/Delta Force, Naval Special Operations Development Group/SEAL Team Six, and the Army's 160th Special Operations Aviation Regiment, along with some smaller spooky units and Air Force aviation assets.

The JSOC headquarters cell had been known as Advance Force Operations (AFO). Not manned as a regular unit, it drew very senior personnel from Delta or SEAL Team Six for specific missions. These could be four operators living in a hole dug into a hillside overlooking an Afghan village for two weeks, collecting every scrap of information that would be needed for a raid by a Delta squadron. Or two men in civilian clothes photographing a terrorist safe house in the heart of urban Samarkand, Uzbekistan, that would be hit later by a combined Uzbek Spetsnaz and SEAL Team Six assault group. Hence the name Advance Force.

After 9/11 the secretary of defense had run into a few problems taking the fight to terrorists around the world. Basically, he couldn't get anyone to do what he wanted.

The CIA had vivid memories of doing exactly what the president wanted, and then being screwed over by Congress and the press for the Bay of Pigs, the Phoenix Program in Vietnam, and Iran-Contra. Even their greatest success, the covert war against the Soviets in Afghanistan, was now regarded as the breeding ground of modern Islamic terrorism. So they would play in Afghanistan and Iraq with their Special Activities paramilitary people, but they always felt the covert action mission was something they could do without. As a perfect illustration of this, the paramilitaries were almost all contract employees instead of regular CIA officers. Most of them retired military special operators.

In the Pentagon, the generals and admirals who ran the U.S. military were very careful, orderly men who had gotten where they were by making few waves and no mistakes. Special Operations wasn't their cup of tea, but they recognized the necessity of it in wartime. But sending military teams to snatch or—even worse—gun down terrorists on the streets of countries they weren't officially at war with was something else entirely. If anything went wrong careers and reputations could be ruined. But they were willing to sign off, as long as the lawyers reviewed every mission and the decision was unanimous so everyone's ass was covered. Unfortunately, this process took days or weeks, and most missions had to be pulled off in hours or not at all. Worse, if the generals didn't want to do something they didn't salute and carry out their orders. They'd blow the operation by leaking the details to the press.

Then there was the State Department. Who ensured that the military had to get prior permission from the ambassador of every country involved. And ambassadors either didn't want gunfire or kidnappings disrupting their friendly relations with the host government, whether the host government was friendly or not, or they wanted to play armchair general and direct the operations themselves.

In frustration over this state of affairs, the secretary of defense had formed his own unit. He snatched the AFO cell away from JSOC and took sixteen men, one troop and four boat crews, from Delta and SEAL Team Six respectively. All senior men with AFO experience. He made it into a Special Access Program, as deep black as stealth aircraft, which reduced the people who knew about it to such a small number that they wouldn't dare leak. And he received permission from the president for a command system of only two people: himself and the national security advisor. If they gave the okay a mission could be launched instantly with the transmission of a code word from the Pentagon Command Center to the team in the field. No military involvement at all.

Small teams, usually two men, would be sent around

the world to hunt terrorists and act on breaking intelligence. They would operate undercover in unfriendly countries, or liaise with the intelligence and special operations units of friendly countries. If the target was small enough, they'd take it out themselves. Otherwise they were supposed to prepare the ground and then call in anything from a Delta troop or SEAL platoon all the way up to a 600-man Army Ranger battalion.

The office building headquarters in Rosslyn, Virginia, kept them away from the clutches of the uniformed military. Including, surprisingly enough, U.S. Special Operations Command, which was transforming from an administrative to an operational war-fighting command, and didn't want to give up any units or control over them.

At first it was totally ad hoc, commanded by the kind of snake-eating special operations officers who didn't care about risking their careers in a new deep black unit and expected to retire at the colonel level as a badge of honor. The total strength was around fifty, broken down with uncharacteristic bluntness into the subsets of the classic raid mission: assault, security, and support.

Support was the technical surveillance specialists, like the boys Storey had with him in Paraguay.

Security was the assault team backups: medical specialists, snipers, and operators being groomed for assignment to the assault teams.

Assault was the elite two-man teams.

The problem, Storey reflected as he stood in front of the desk, had been their success. When, out of gratitude, Rumsfeld made a general out of the first commanding officer, an animal of an Army full colonel who hadn't even been considered refined enough to command Delta, the floodgates had opened. The unit had gotten bigger, as special ops units always did. Of course, there weren't many who wanted to put on civilian clothes, travel on a false passport with no diplomatic immunity, and live by their wits on the streets of Khartoum. But there were a hell of a lot more who wanted to be staff officers and have the duty on their resume. And so the generals began trying to slip their little butt-boys into the organization.

It seemed like every unit Storey had ever been in, the executive officer (XO), or second in command, was always a weasel-dick with high-ranking friends trying to give him a career leg up. And now, with the commanding officer traveling in the Middle East, the XO was in charge of the unit.

And he obviously didn't like the fact that Storey was standing at parade rest in front of his desk. But was just smart enough not to try and call a Master Sergeant to attention.

He was doing the old "read through the papers on my desk and make you stand there and sweat" routine. Storey always wished they'd come up with something original.

Finally he glanced up, as if he was surprised to see Storey there. "Master Sergeant, this unit's mission statement is low visibility operations."

"I'm aware of that, sir," Storey replied in a neutral tone of voice.

"You think what you did in Paraguay was low visibility?"

"Yes, sir. I do."

"Oh, you do? You think firing rockets into a building in a residential neighborhood is low visibility?"

"High noise, sir, but low visibility."

"Don't try to be funny, Master Sergeant. Do you know what a diplomatic incident is?"

He was the type of officer who couldn't speak to the troops without either sneering or talking down to them. "As a matter of fact, sir," Storey replied, "I do know what a diplomatic incident is. And it's only a diplomatic incident if the host country knows who created the incident. In this case they have no idea."

That set the XO back for a moment. "The point,

Master Sergeant, is that you fired rockets in the middle of a neighborhood full of civilians."

"Yes, sir. If you'll check the after-action report, you'll see that no property other than the terrorist safe house in question was damaged. And no one got hurt except the ones who were supposed to get hurt. And it was done in such a way that the local authorities believe that either drug gangs or terrorists did it."

"That's my point. You acted like terrorists."

"Yes, sir, that's how we fight them. That's why we're successful."

"Master Sergeant, you're going to start briefing us before you pull off these little ops of yours."

Storey's warning systems went off. "Excuse me, sir, but the protocol is that we inform the Pentagon Command Center of a prospective operation. And when we receive the go word, we execute. There is no other chain of command."

"I know how you work, Master Sergeant. You wait until the last minute, give up as few details as possible, and get your permission that way."

"I accept total responsibility for every operation I execute, sir."

"These out-of-control ops are going to change that, Master Sergeant. People like you *need* a chain of command, and you're going to keep us informed of everything you do."

"Since that contravenes what I understand to be my previous orders, sir, I would have to speak with the CO *and* see those new orders in writing."

"Get out of my office, Master Sergeant."

Storey came to attention for about a nanosecond before he faced about. He said, "Good morning, sir," but only because it was required.

He found Troy down in the basement equipment cages, cleaning his weapons. Each operator had his own cage, as a big as a single-car garage, holding everything from parachutes to high altitude mountaineering equipment, and a range of personal weapons from the mini Glock pistol to the new SEAL Mk-48 7.62mm machine gun.

"XO chew your ass?" Troy asked idly.

"What makes you say that?"

"Because that's all that pussy ever does around here. Sneak around and chew people's asses. He did, didn't he?"

"He tried."

"SEAL officers might be stupid," said Troy. "And they might be assholes. But at least they're never pussies like these Army guys."

Storey wasn't really in the mood to spring to the defense of Army officers. "He's the kind of guy who does one tour in Special Forces as a captain, and his A-Team hates his guts. Then he burrows into the special operations staff like a tick. Next time you see him he's a lieutenant colonel who didn't get command. Some general pulls some strings for him, and he gets stuck into a unit like this to get himself a good fitness report."

"It must have been a real fine ass chewing. He doesn't usually get under *your* saddle."

"I'm more concerned than pissed off." He told Troy about the conversation.

Troy shrugged. "The usual shit."

"No, it's not," said Storey. "That's why you have to listen. He's talking about changes in the chain of command. Because he's stupid he's talking about them to someone like me. Lieutenant Colonel XOs don't talk about changing the chain of command in units run by the Secretary of Defense. But generals send people like him to be XOs of units they're trying to get back under their control."

"You think they might?"

"Secretary's a busy man. He may think we're running well enough to take his hands off the wheel."

Troy shrugged again. "That's officer shit. First thing I leaned from my first platoon chief—officer politics is for officers. Enlisted get involved in officer politics, they get burned every time."

Storey grinned. "Is that Troy's rule?"

"Bet your ass it is."

"It's a good one. If I ever forget it, make sure you remind me." It was too bad, Storey thought. They'd had a lot of success running missions their own way, without ten-page messages filled with detailed guidance from all the staff officers back home. Pretty soon, there'd be officers as team leaders. Well, he'd be in the zone for Sergeant Major pretty soon. With any luck he'd be able to get back to Delta. Maybe it was time to start thinking about making a few phone calls.

Chapter Six

The scene was a dingy warehouse. Cars pulled up to the loading dock. Trunks were opened, and cans of baby formula were handed up. Money changed hands. Then trucks appeared and the formula, now repackaged in cardboard cases, was loaded inside. Back and forth. Back and forth.

"I'm bored now," announced Supervisory Special Agent Benjamin Timmins of the FBI.

"Hold your water," said Special Agent Beth Royale.

A Pakistani man showed up. Late fifties, carrying more than his share of comfortable, easy-living weight. Obviously dyed jet-black hair all combed back and gelled up. Dressed like someone who had never played a round of golf in his life but was a member of a country club. Like Rodney Dangerfield in *Caddyshack*. The lime green slacks were the highlight. He flipped through a clipboard full of papers, stuck his head in the trucks, shook hands all around, and left.

Timmins picked up the remote and turned off the TV. "I've seen about a hundred hours of this surveillance video already. Or maybe it just seemed like a hundred. It's like watching paint dry. At least you had fun putting in the cameras and listening devices."

"Yeah, it was just heaps of fun," said Beth Royale.

They were in a borrowed office in the Federal Building on Wilshire Boulevard in Los Angeles. Timmins was in charge of a Fly Away Team, or Fly Squad as it was called in FBI slang. Formed after 9/11, these were specialized teams within the Counterterrorism Division, based out of Washington, that flew out to the local field offices or elsewhere when needed in major cases. The teams were composed of the most experienced counterterrorism agents, language specialists, technical people, and intelligence analysts.

"You've got to give him credit, though," said Timmins.

"For what?" Beth demanded.

"For a vertically integrated company. He hires South American shoplifting gangs to boost cans of baby formula. He pays them five bucks a can. He sells them in his markets for fifteen a can. That's a damn fine profit compared to the pennies per can the honest merchants are making. If they steal too much he unloads the excess on eBay. If they can't find baby formula they boost cold remedies, which he sells by the gross to all the home methamphetamine cookers without reporting it. How many markets does he own now?"

"Five," said Beth.

"I thought only Hezbollah and the Palestinians were into the baby formula scam."

"Everyone follows the money," Beth replied. "Why wouldn't al-Qaeda get into it?" This case had begun, the way they usually did, when an alert local cop made a traffic stop of a truck full of stolen baby food with an Arab driver.

"So we have receiving stolen goods, transporting stolen goods, tax evasion, and money laundering. But no terrorism case. And I can't justify tying up a Fly Squad without a terrorism case."

"Just because we don't have a case we could take to the grand jury doesn't mean we don't have a terrorism case," said Beth. "Shakir's careful. He only has serious discussions in places that don't have walls."

"So maybe he's just a crook, and we should go home."

Beth knew Timmins was just yanking her chain, but she clucked her tongue and gave him a loud "tsk" anyway. She'd tried to make herself stop doing that, but it was no use. It was habit. "Ben, nobody has that many serious discussions in backyards and park benches. How many times do *your* friends, the ones you aren't even doing crime with, show up at your kid's soccer games, just to shoot the shit? And how many hundreds of thousands of dollars do *you* wire to Pakistan every year? Dollars that disappear as soon as they get there."

"So it's a terrorism case," Timmins said defensively. "Which means there's never enough to take to court. So Shakir does his fifteen years or so, and we deport his family and friends. And that's one more network out of our hair. Feel free to complain about me not pushing to make a bigger case."

Beth tsked again. "I'm not complaining about that. He'll be lucky if he gets only fifteen years."

"Well, then, you're here to complain about the aunt and the kid being inside the house in Studio City?"

"We're just lucky the aunt was taking a nap," said Beth, "and the baby was a crib climber and let us know we had company in there. I should have checked the whole house before I started work. I'll never make that mistake again."

"I thought you'd be ballistic."

"Hey, Ben. That team from the L.A. office was doing the surveillance and they told us the house was empty. So they're either incompetent or they wanted the Counterterrorism Division to get embarrassed. Either way, that reflects on *you*. It's none of my business."

Beth knew her statement, delivered matter-of-factly, would have more impact on Timmins than all the yelling in the world would have. The Fly Squads had to deal with a lot of jealousy and resentment from the local field offices. Those L.A. boys were toast now. Even though yelling at Timmins would have been a lot more fun.

Timmins let a tone of amazement creep into his voice. "Then you're not here to complain about that?"

"Don't be silly, Ben."

The tone changed to suspicion. "Then what are you here to complain about?"

"Ben, Ben, Ben. I'm not here to complain about *anything*."

"Imagine my surprise."

"You know, Ben, if people could hear you talking like that, they wouldn't call *me* a bitch."

Yes, they would, Timmins thought. But what he said was, "My profound apologies, Beth. Then why, may I ask, did you want to see me about the baby food guy?"

"I think we've got a substantial network here. I want to put an informant inside."

"And just how the hell do you propose to do that?" Timmins's bureaucratic antennae sprung up. "Are you working something I don't know about?"

Beth tsked again. "Ben, Ben, Ben. Have I ever screwed you, in either the personal or professional sense?"

"No. Now . . ."

"Have you ever taken a hit for anything I've ever done?"

"We've come pretty damn close, Beth . . ."

"On the contrary, you've received a considerable number of pats on the back for the cases I've worked, haven't you?"

Timmins opened his mouth to say something, then abruptly halted. "Wait a minute. Why am I even thinking about apologizing to you before I hear about whatever game you're trying to run on me?"

Beth smiled sweetly. The auburn hair tended to fall across her face when she was too focused to attend to it.

"You know, Ben, stress can be a real killer. And you're starting to move into that high-risk age . . ."

"Okay, Beth."

"I want to put an informant inside."

"And just how do you propose to do that?"

"Shakir's brother-in-law, Roshan."

"Are you working him?" Timmins asked suspiciously.

"Not yet. I'm just looking him over."

"We don't have anything on the brother-in-law."

"I know. That's why he's my guy. Quiet. Family man. Runs all the markets single-handed. He probably knows where the baby formula and cold medicine come from, but not enough to make a case on. He works his ass off, lives in a little house in Studio City, and sends his money to his actual extended family in Pakistan. Shakir the big-ass brother-in-law doesn't do shit except count his money, live in Bel Air, and wire his tithe to al-Qaeda. There's got to be some major family dynamic going on here. Big-time resentments. Roshan knows all the players and probably hears more than he lets on. He's perfect."

"And you'll do this, how?"

"When we arrest Shakir, we bring Roshan in and charge him, too. He's not the type who'll enjoy being in custody. He's a put-the-kids-to-bed-every-night kind of guy. And unless I miss my guess, he does *not* want to go to prison. More important, he definitely does not want to go back to Pakistan, tell the relatives there's no more money coming in, and start all over again."

She did this to him all the time, and Timmins always looked at her the same way. "So you threaten him with deportation?"

"I *save* him from deportation. He becomes our confidential informant. His brother-in-law Shakir goes to jail. The U.S. Attorney refuses to file on Roshan—lack of evidence. His time in the slammer radicalized him, made him want to get into the game as a player, and he becomes the link between Shakir in prison and his network. If we're lucky, maybe Roshan takes over the network. If not, at least he's inside it."

Timmins leaned back in his chair and began tapping his fingertips together.

Beth knew he was going over all the angles. She'd worked for him for nearly two years now, and knew what made him tick. White male, white shirt, dark suit. Supercompetent, no waves. But in his early forties, just *that* close to getting the boost up to Special Agent in Charge. And like so many who were close enough to taste it, he fretted every day about blowing it. The Counterterrorism Division was high visibility in the Bureau. Being in charge of a Fly Squad was even more so. You could launch yourself with a single case. But you could also cast yourself into perpetual darkness.

She waited just long enough, then put in the shot. "It's time we stopped playing the terrorism game like cops. Otherwise we'll just be deporting people without making cases. And Congress and the press are going to say: it's been three years since 9/11 and you haven't made any terrorism cases. But if we start thinking like counterintelligence professionals we'll start turning terrorists and playing them back into their own networks. Now that's something we could really hang our hat on."

Timmins's face exposed him as imagining the possibilities. "How will we know he's not agreeing to everything, and then playing *us*?"

Beth just pointed to the TV screen.

Then the moment of realization. "Jesus," Timmins exclaimed. "This is why you insisted on making the warrants on the warehouse and markets criminal ones from the local magistrate judge, and the ones on the homes from the Foreign Intelligence Surveillance Act judge in Washington: so we could keep them separate."

"If we don't use any of the home surveillance at Shakir's

trial, Roshan will never know we're watching him. Roshan's not the outdoor type—he won't be having meetings on park benches."

"This could be the perfect way to confirm an informant's reliability," Timmins exclaimed. "You debrief him, then you go watch what he's actually doing and saying." And then another pause, as another realization took hold. "Is this why you pushed so hard for video as well as audio on them?"

Beth only smiled sweetly, once again.

"You were making the moves to put this together from the get-go."

"It just doesn't work if we try and throw something together *after* we make arrests," said Beth. Then added, "The way we usually do." And then immediately reproached herself for it. Always having to hammer the point into the ground. Shut up, Beth.

"And I was the one who bitched about the expense of doing video as well as audio," said Timmins. "Okay, Beth, if you're going to play me like that, I give you permission to keep playing me. Not that you won't anyway. Be ready to do a full-bore brief on your plan for Roshan. Power-Point and all. We'll definitely have to take this up to the Deputy Assistant Director for Operational Support. Then probably the Division Assistant Director. We may even have to brief the Director himself."

"I'm all ready to go right now."

"Why am I not surprised? This is great work, Beth."

"Thanks, Ben."

Chapter Seven

Whenever he used the train station in the old city of central Antwerp, Abdallah Karim Nimri made a point of walking along the Pelikaanstraat to pass through the Jootsewijk. He loved how they would cross the street before reaching him, do anything not to have to look at his face. One of them could never walk alone in the Arab ghetto unharmed, and here he walked and they were afraid. Nimri loved to see the Jews afraid. It was good for them to fear an Arab.

They had been in Antwerp for 400 years, and there were 20,000 of them. There they were in their black coats and fur hats, their diamonds and riches. But now there were 30,000 Muslims. And every day more. One day, Nimri promised himself. One day the Jews would all die.

When he had sufficiently pleased himself he turned east toward Borgerhout. And in the Arab district the faces became comfortingly familiar to him again, and the music of Arabic found his ears.

Nimri was watched by young men as hard as the old stone buildings they were slouching against. The sight of them always made him happy. Belgium was perfect. In the Arab world the masses were seething but crushed. America was a disaster. In America Muslims did nothing but work. They made money, bought things, made more money, bought more things, and were gradually turned into creatures of luxury that were no longer Muslim.

Europe was their only hope. Only there were the conditions ideal. A culture of plenty, but not for Muslim immigrants. The professions were closed, so there was nothing but day labor—cheap labor—the only reason the Turks and Moroccans had been admitted in the first place. No one would rent them apartments or sell them homes, so they crowded into the poor districts like Borgerhout, whose overwhelming Moroccan population caused the Belgians to call it Borgerokko. It kept the people together.

The young men born there were neither Arab nor Belgian. Molded into ferocity by the teeming government housing blocks, street fights with the skinheads, drugs, petty crime, and the contempt the Europeans had for them.

All good, because eventually the suitable were drawn into the mosques seeking a path out of the emptiness. And unlike America, where they built rich mosques to their heart's content, the Europeans would never issue building permits, so the Faithful were forced to worship in garages and warehouses, the better to build their righteous anger. So the angry began to work for the cause, with the necessary skills they had already learned on the streets. The unemployment benefits and proceeds from crime allowed them to work for the cause full-time, also relieving the organization of the burden of supporting them.

And while the Belgians might not speak to Arabs, the Belgian government was so tolerant and open-minded that the assured way of getting it to abandon any policy was to accuse it of intolerance. For fear of giving offense, the government left them alone to do their work. But if that changed, it would still be fine. As a matter of fact, Nimri felt it would be perfect if the right-wing Vlaams

Belang, or Flemish Interest Party, took control and instituted anti-Islamic policies.

Belgium was perfect.

Nimri turned off the Milisstraat and wove through side streets. He felt the eyes on him, and he approved. Strangers could not enter the neighborhoods without the neighborhoods knowing. The police rarely left their automobiles. If they did they were followed by young men with video cameras to record the activities of the racist police. Rather than be drawn into incidents that would cause the government to wring its hands and fire them, they stayed away.

Nimri stopped at a run-down brick house. He had never been to this one before. The neighborhood was mainly Moroccan, but this house was Chechen. In striking contrast to the rest of the façade, the front door was new and solid steel.

Nimri did not bother to knock. They knew he was standing there. He braced himself, as he always did before dealing with the Chechens. They were serious men. Ferocious fighters and implacable foes for whom every insult had to be avenged. They lived by blood feud, which, once entered into, could last for centuries with each new generation swearing to prosecute it. What a Chechen swore a Chechen did.

The door opened, Nimri nodding to the Chechen with the pistol stuck in his belt. He did not miss the Kalashnikov rifle propped up in the corner behind the door.

Once past the guard, Nimri found himself embraced by another young Chechen.

"Abdallah," the Chechen exclaimed. "*Assalam alaikum.*"

"*Walaikum assalam,*" Nimri replied. Peace be upon you also. "How are you, Lecha?"

"Well, very well. And you?"

"Well also. How is your uncle?"

"He waits to receive you."

"He is too kind."

The house was swarming with Chechens. Nimri had grown up in such a house in Cairo, but unlike most Arabs he was a natural loner and had never liked it.

Weaving their way through the throng, they passed a room that caught Nimri's eye. At first he just glanced, but the sight made him stop. A long table with bags of yellowish white powder on one end. Chechens wearing surgical masks were emptying them into large bowls and mixing in other white powders. At the end of the table others were weighing smaller amounts on scales and loading it into smaller bags.

Nimri was privately appalled. Not by the heroin, of course. The river of drugs began in Afghanistan, flowed through Central Asia, and into Russia. The Chechens handled a great deal of the business in Russia, and transshipment into Europe. Belgium was a favorite entry point.

No, it was not the drugs. Anything that weakened the infidels was permissible, as long as the Faithful did not indulge. It was that, instead of a safe house, the Chechens had brought him to this place where they did this business. It was incredibly insecure. But then they were always reckless. The only saving grace was that Chechens kept such business within their own clan groups. So betrayal was uncommon, and penetration next to impossible. No matter his misgivings, of course he could say nothing. He was a guest, and it would be an insult.

Lecha of course noticed his interest. "Business is good."

Nimri only grunted and kept walking.

He was ushered into a large room, with fine carpets and many chairs. A room for meeting, receiving guests, and doing business. A man waited at the head chair. A small man, but packed with lean muscle. Bald at the top of his head, the hair at the side cropped close the scalp like a prisoner. A hawk's beak of a nose, and burning black eyes.

Arbi Temiraev had come to Antwerp after breaking

with the Riyad us-Saliheyn Martyrs' Brigade, the largest of the Chechen resistance groups fighting the Russians. He maintained that it was because they were not Islamic enough. Nimri suspected tensions between the domestic Chechen fighters and those, like Temiraev, who had trained with al-Qaeda in Afghanistan. When the Russians had invaded Chechnya the world had offered sympathy. But only al-Qaeda had offered money, weapons, training, and brother fighters to battle the Russians. To the Chechens it became a blood debt. But later there was tension. Most of them were only interested in killing Russians, while al-Qaeda fought jihad, holy war, against all infidels everywhere.

Then again, Temiraev might have come to Belgium in the aftermath of a clan dispute. The only thing that could cool the heat of a Chechen clan feud was a temporary truce to kill Russians.

Temiraev rose and embraced Nimri warmly. "Peace be upon you, my brother."

"And upon you also, my brother."

"Sit, rest. My house is yours."

They spoke in Arabic. Nimri had no Russian, and Temiraev's French was poor.

Nimri followed the forms. Chechens were strict about courteous and formal public behavior. "I am grateful for your hospitality."

Properly hooded and gowned women brought a silver tea samovar, glasses, and plates of cookies. Neither Nimri nor Temiraev spoke a word to them, though Temiraev watched intently to make sure the serving was done properly. When it was, the women and Lecha were dismissed and the door closed.

"God be praised, you look well and strong," said Nimri.

"You look tired," Temiraev observed. "We have not seen you."

Nimri of course would never have mentioned it, except

he needed to make the point that the proposal he had brought was not from him alone. "I have been abroad."

"Oh?" The disinterest was feigned but not unexpected.

"To Pakistan."

"If I am not mistaken," said Temiraev, "it has been some time since you visited there. A pleasant trip?"

"Very. I saw the family."

Temiraev knew that Nimri's family, what was left of it, was in Egypt. So he also knew which family Nimri was speaking of. "Really? And how is the family?"

"God be praised, still strong."

"God is great, my brother. This news is welcome. Because there has been much talk that the family is no longer strong, I am sorry to say."

"I can report with pleasure this is not the case."

"I am relieved to hear it," Temiraev replied, without a great deal of conviction.

"We spoke of upcoming business."

"We?" Temiraev repeated politely.

"The Libyan."

"The *Libyan*?" Temiraev said in disbelief. "It is the Libyan?"

"It is."

Temiraev made a sound of disgust. "It should be you."

"That is a matter of no importance. I received approval for my business."

"From the *Libyan*?"

Nimri smiled. "I understand your surprise. No, he desires me far from Pakistan and his own position. And if God calls me during this business, the Libyan will shed no tears."

"Do not sell yourself short, my friend. God grant you old age, but upon hearing the news, the Libyan may well commission a celebration."

"Not if he has to pay the bill for it," Nimri replied.

Temiraev laughed appreciatively, slapping the arms

of his chair. "Good, very good. Now tell me about this business of yours, which is why you have come."

"Oh, I have come only to see my old friend and taste his well-known hospitality after too long a time," Nimri said quickly. "My business will not interest you."

A sudden change in mood, eyes flashing. "Why not?"

Nimri knew he was on dangerous ground, even *seeming* to impugn a Chechen's courage. "Oh, you have your business here, my friend," he said lightly. "It appears you are successful. My business is abroad. I will most likely not return."

"Martyrdom? You?"

"If I am martyred, then I pray God receive me to Paradise. It is not my intention to become a martyr, but the business is very hazardous."

"You think that frightens us?"

Nimri chose every word with exquisite care, having seen for himself what lay beneath the veneer of Chechen ritual courtesy. "Of course not, my friend. Your courage is known to me. It is known to all."

"You think that because we handle the *Tozhu*, the Horse, that we have lost our *yajtza*?"

Nimri did not know the Russian prison slang word for testicles, but Temiraev's meaning was perfectly clear nonetheless.

Temiraev sprang up from his chair. "Come with me."

Nimri felt sudden alarm. One never knew when one had pushed a Chechen too far, except when it was too late. But of course he could do nothing but follow. There was no other way out of that house.

Temiraev led him to the back, to another steel door with a massive padlock that he unlocked. Then down creaking wooden stairs into a basement. It was cold and damp, and smelled strongly of mildew. Antwerp stood beside the North Sea, and all its old basements were damp.

Instead of the open space Nimri had been expecting,

the cellar was blocked off by fresh brickwork. A narrow hallway, obviously new brick walls, and a line of metal doors. Dim light from low-wattage bulbs dangling from the ceiling.

Something unknown, something just barely touching his senses, made Nimri feel incredibly uneasy.

Temiraev unlocked another padlock on one of the doors, threw the bolt, and pulled it open. He flicked on a light switch.

Nimri leaned into the open doorway, blinking as his eyes adjusted to the brighter light. Then he jumped back in alarm.

It wasn't just the overwhelming stench of urine, feces, and vomit. It was the naked body hanging upside down from the ceiling, the rope around its feet tied to a hook.

Odd the details that caught one's eye at such a moment. The legs were a different color than the body. Nimri held his breath against the smell and looked closer. By God, all the skin from the feet to the thighs had been cut away. What he was seeing were red muscles. He took another step backward before remembering he had to control himself before Temiraev.

Just in time, hands on both shoulders moved him out of the doorway. Temiraev passed by and into the room. Looking for something else to look at, Nimri noticed that the walls and ceiling were covered with thick dark padding, like life preserver material.

Temiraev gave the body a kick. What Nimri had thought was a dead body moaned. By God, it was still alive.

Temiraev threw a few more kicks, as if he were practicing on a boxing bag. The moans turned to screams, and the noise backed Nimri out into the hallway.

Finally noticing this, Temiraev bent over and whispered something in Russian into the dangling man's ear. Then he joined Nimri in the hallway, bolting and locking the door.

"Russian," Temiraev said with a pleased smile. "Federal Security Bureau. We found out the agent he was running, and persuaded him to call for their next meeting at a bar owned by some friends of ours. We watched, hidden, as his security checked it out before the meeting and left. Then he arrived." Temiraev grabbed Nimri's upper arm. "You should have seen the pig's face when we all walked in a few moments later. The pair covering him were still out in the street. We left them there like the fools they were, wondering what had happened."

Hearing the rest of the story, Nimri did not ask why they did not simply cut the Russian's throat then and there, instead of wrapping him in a carpet so they could take him out the back and remove his skin at their leisure. He knew how Chechens felt about Russians.

There was also a lesson in it. Belgium was so hospitable because its security service, the Sûreté de l'Etat, was spectacularly ineffective. They had no right to even tap telephones. Unfortunately that ineffectiveness allowed other, more aggressive services, like the Russians and the Americans, to operate freely.

As they made their way back up the stairs Nimri glanced at the other doors in the cellar, wondering what was behind each of them.

Returning to the audience room, Temiraev shouted something in Chechen. Just what soon became clear. As they were settling back down another woman brought a bottle of vodka in an ice bucket, a loaf of black bread, and pickled cucumber.

Temiraev gestured toward a glass as the vodka was poured. Of course Nimri shook his head but said his thanks. Alcohol was *haram*, forbidden.

The Chechens were not good Muslims. This was known. It was said that they had originally embraced Islam out of characteristic defiance, because it was associated with resistance to Russian conquest. And Russian conquest in the Caucasus was not just something of the past two centuries.

Temiraev toasted Nimri's health in Russian and threw down a shot.

Nimri drained his now cool glass of tea. Anything to put some moisture back into his mouth.

"Now you see that I have not become soft," Temiraev stated.

"I never doubted it, my friend. Not for a moment. But my business is not with the Russians."

"Americans?"

Nimri nodded.

"Did we not fight them together in Afghanistan? Did they not shed the blood of my clan with their bombs, the cowards, instead of fighting like men? Is there not a debt that must be paid?"

"All these things I know, my brother," Nimri replied. "But it was not for me to speak them. I desired to hear you speak them to me."

"Am I not under obligation to you? When the American bomb hit the bunker, was it not you who dug me out and returned me to life, all praise to God in His mercy? And did we not both bury my sister's son Islamov in that place, with our own hands?"

Nimri remembered the day. The idiot Taliban digging their trenches and bunkers in Kandahar, as if fighting World War I. The American planes so high up they were only tiny streaks of white contrail across the sky. And then the earth erupting without warning, the bombs with eyes dropping on each bunker in succession, leaving the positions looking as if they had been turned over by a giant's spade. God had been with him that day. He had been inside the bunker but awoke outside, deaf but still living.

"I remember all these things, my brother," Nimri told him. "But understand that you are under no obligation this day. None. I do not invoke it."

"You are a true Arab, my brother," said Temiraev. "You will not come to the point unless I take *your* skin. And perhaps not even then. Now tell me this business of yours with the Americans."

Temiraev was right, the time had come. Nimri laid out his plans. In detail.

Temiraev heard him out impassively. "And your role in this?"

Nimri had been waiting for that. The al-Qaeda chiefs sent others off to execute their plans. But he had a different reputation. "Beside my fighters, as always. As before. As in Afghanistan. I would not have come here otherwise."

Temiraev closed his eyes and thought for a very long time.

Nimri poured himself some more tea and waited patiently.

"There will be fame in this," Temiraev said finally. "Great fame."

Nimri only nodded. They were all God's instruments. Every one of them fought for a different reason—it was only important that they fought. Temiraev loved to fight. And to see himself, and have others see him, as a great battle leader meant that he needed constant battle. Trapping a Russian agent in a comfortable European city was a poor substitute. The young brothers fought to be part of something big and important. And of course there was the thrill of living a clandestine life as a servant of God while others were condemned to normality. One traveled the world, lived undercover, planned attacks, built bombs. Much more exciting than selling shoes. Again, how they came into it was not important. It was that they embraced jihad. God was great.

Temiraev closed his eyes again and thought some more. "We will need forty men. At least."

"We may need forty men, my brother, but we will take fewer than twenty."

"Not enough."

"Every extra man is a risk. They cannot all travel together. Even two of our brothers on the same airplane, even if they are not sitting together, will cause if not a panic then at least suspicion."

"I see. So therefore none of them can know anything until the attack."

Nimri was glad he did not have to make an issue of that and risk another insult. "None but you and I, my brother."

"I see the necessity, but it will make things difficult. Each man will have to travel in foreign lands by himself. There are good fighters, and there are men who can do this. Fewer who can do both. How will we travel?"

"Several brothers, who knew nothing and still know nothing about the mission, have done detailed work in preparation and reconnaissance. Each a piece, in isolation. Only I know how they all come together. Over the course of a month, we will take flights to Brazil."

"Brazil?"

"Yes. Our mistake before was to use countries friendly to the Americans to launch operations. The Philippines. Thailand. Pakistan. It made it easy for our enemies. The new leftist government of Brazil is not inclined to work with the Americans. They were infuriated when the Americans insisted on fingerprinting and photographing Brazilian citizens who traveled to America. I doubt they will allow the Americans to conduct operations against us. This means only a few American secret agents. They worry me not. The odds will be even. We will treat them like your Russian."

"Yes, I see it now."

"Each brother will be met at the airport and taken to a safe house," said Nimri. "New documents and flights to Mexico. All I require are passport photographs for each of our fighters. I will make all preparations here. All the documents, tickets, and flights. Then I will fly to South America and prepare the way there. On my signal, the movement will begin."

"Direct flights? That will make it easier for the less experienced."

"No, my friend. There must be as many connections as possible. To make tracing our routes all the more difficult."

"Very well. How will we enter the United States?"

"I will not even tell you that, my brother. But we will enter, and we will strike them to the marrow of their bones."

"How will the operation be financed?"

It was ever the same, Nimri thought. The Chechens were fighters, but they were also businessmen. They were willing to die fighting, but not to open their purses. "The operation is fully financed, my brother."

"The Libyan?"

Again the tone of surprise. "From him a small part of what is required."

"It must be the smallest part."

"It is," said Nimri. "But the old way of centralized financing and disbursement is no longer safe or secure. Neither are the charities by which our brothers around the world supported us. Now our wealthy brothers in the Gulf no longer send their contributions to the center. Each of us who continue in an operational role have made contact with a few of these rich brothers, and they have become our personal patrons. They give us access to personal accounts of theirs, relying on us to use the money well."

Tamiraev was visibly impressed. "This is a much better system. No bank, no government will interfere with the private money of an Arab millionaire. And since they go everywhere and do business everywhere, money wired everywhere raises no alarms. Brilliant." And then a wolfish grin directed at Nimri. "But a considerable temptation."

A Chechen was a Chechen, Nimri thought. They would happily throw themselves on a hand grenade with the name of God on their lips. But if you were not under their protection they would steal the last gold tooth from your mouth, whether you slept with it open or not. "We are all responsible to The Base, for everything we do," he said pointedly. This was the literal translation of al-Qaeda. The Base. "All of us. With our lives."

"Of course, my brother," said Tamiraev, still grinning wolfishly. "Of course."

"Then we are in agreement, my brother?"

"Unlike some of these idiots, like the Libyan, you know how to plan an operation, my brother. Where you go, I will go with you. Where you fight, I will fight beside you. Until the end. This I swear."

Chapter Eight

Nasser Saleh had his earphones on and was really hitting his computer keyboard. Two Palestinians in Charlotte had gotten in touch with a military surplus dealer who evidently had some crooked Marine combat engineers at Camp Lejeune working for him. The Palestinians were negotiating to buy C-4 plastic explosive to ship to Gaza.

A hand touched Nasser's shoulder, and he almost jumped out of his skin. It was Barry, his supervisor.

"Sorry, Nasser. I need to talk to you for a second."

"What is it, Barry?"

"Why don't you come to my office?"

Something was wrong.

Nasser followed him in. Barry shut the door. "Sit down, sit down."

Nasser did, and Barry put the desk between them. "We need to talk about your evaluation of the New Orleans audio."

"What about it?"

"The case agent complained."

"About the translation?"

"No, about your evaluation. They're putting a lot of effort into that case, and they didn't appreciate you telling them it was nothing."

"That's not what I wrote."

"Now, don't get excited. You certainly implied it."

"Barry, they asked for an evaluation. And I gave it to them."

"And they didn't think it was either fair or correct."

"Barry, I listen to these conversations all the time. These guys are Salafist fundamentalists. They like to pretend they're radicals. They go to mosque, listen to some violent sermons, get themselves all fired up, and go home and drink tea and talk."

"And they're talking terrorism."

"They talk about jihad and loving death and martyrdom. But it's all talk. Barry, Arabs talk. They talk big. And nobody talks bigger than an Arab."

Trying to cool him down, Barry said, "Hey, if I said that, there'd be a grievance filed."

The attempt at levity didn't go over. "It's like most things, Barry. If it's about what I am I can say it—you can't."

"Okay, whatever. But you've got to understand that talk turns into action, Nasser."

"I've done a lot of listening, Barry. There's the ones who talk about what they're going to do. And then there's the ones who just talk. These guys in New Orleans are just talk."

"I'm not going to keep arguing the point with you. You aren't trying to cut down on your workload, are you?"

Typical. The Arabs were always trying to get over. "Barry, the less unimportant stuff I have to wade through, the more time I have to translate something important."

"Listen, Nasser, you're a young guy."

And it always got said in that condescending tone. Nasser really hated that.

"This happens all the time with translation," Barry went on. "You've been doing it just long enough to *think* you're an expert now. But you've got to understand you've got a lot to learn. Right?"

"I may have a lot to learn, Barry, but I'm right on this one."

"Hey, hey, calm down here. This just makes my point. With a little more experience under your belt, you'll realize that we support the field agents, we don't direct them. I'm going to expect you to keep that in mind in the future. Evaluate the conversation you're translating, and leave the analysis to the professionals. Okay?"

"Whatever you say, Barry."

"Good. I don't have time to deal with complaints from the agents in the field. I hope you took this the right way. I'm just looking out for you here."

"Sure, Barry."

"Better get back to work."

Back at his cubicle, Nasser felt like putting his fist through the monitor screen. His stomach hurt, because he didn't stand up for himself. "Come suck my cock, you bastard son of a whore!" He whispered it in Egyptian Arabic, and Udi in the next cubicle started giggling. Nasser stopped, now furious *and* embarrassed.

He'd practically been accused of disloyalty. That was the tone. Looking out for the Arab homeboys. So now Barry was going to be looking over his shoulder. He didn't need this shit. He could walk out the door and triple his salary working for the Rand Corporation or one of the military contractors. He'd checked. That's what he got for working his ass off and being conscientious. People who didn't do squat in the office didn't have to take half the shit he did.

And the field agents didn't appreciate it. How about that? They were recording conversations they didn't even understand. It could just as well have been cows mooing for all they knew. But they didn't want to listen to someone who actually spoke the language telling them they didn't have anything. Then they might have to get off their ass and investigate a real case.

That was it, he was quitting. No, he'd put out his resume and get a new job lined up. *Then* tell them to go fuck themselves.

At that moment the computer blinked. More incoming files. Well screw them, he was on a work slowdown.

But after a couple of minutes curiosity overcame him, and he clicked to see what they were.

Overload from Guantánamo. He didn't see many of those, because there wasn't a big FBI presence there. But there was the National Virtual Translation Center, which definitely wasn't virtual but did tap into FBI, CIA, and Defense Intelligence Agency translators whenever someone had more requirements than capacity. And that was like all the time.

The military translators at Guantánamo were pitiful. Guantánamo was another circus. The Taliban commanders claimed they were only Afghan farmers, and they got released to go back to fighting. So then the translators thought the real Afghan farmers were Taliban commanders, and kept them locked up.

Nasser clicked on one of the audio files. Another interrogation. Forget it. He'd get around to that when he felt like it.

In between the new Guantánamo arrivals was a text file. He never got text. Wait a minute, it didn't have his address on it. Another computer screwup. Nasser started to send it to Barry. Let him deal with it, he's so busy. But then he stopped. Screw them. They couldn't even send files to the right place, let them figure it out for themselves.

Curiosity gnawing at him again, he clicked on the text file. Classified Secret. A memorandum to the Deputy Assistant Director of the Counterterrorism Division.

Nasser looked over his shoulder to make sure no one could see his screen.

It was from the Inspection Division. About interrogation of detainees. Looked interesting. Nasser read on.

. . . members of the Behavioral Analysis Units were deployed to GTMO [that was Guantánamo] to observe interviews of detainees and provide interview strategies and other behavioral assistance as needed . . .

There were many comments made by investigators during my tenure at GTMO that every time the FBI established a rapport with a detainee, the military would step in and the detainee would stop being cooperative . . . The next time detainee was interviewed, his level of cooperation was diminished. There were also accusations made by different investigators that Military Interrogators would present themselves as FBI agents to detainees. See attachment . . .

Nasser clicked on the attachment. It was a bunch of e-mails, all classified Secret. He clicked on the one the memorandum had referred to.

I am forwarding the Electronic Communication up the Counterterrorism Division chain of command. MLDU requested this information be documented to protect the FBI. MLDU has had a long standing and documented position against some of DOD's [Department of Defense] interrogation practices, however, we were not aware of these latest techniques until recently.

Of concern, DOD interrogators have impersonated Supervisory Special Agents of the FBI during interrogation where extreme physical pressure has been employed . . . These tactics have produced no intelligence of a threat neutralization nature to date and CITF believes that techniques have destroyed any chance of prosecuting this detainee . . .

If this detainee is ever released or his story made public in any way, DOD interrogators will not be held accountable because these torture techniques were done by the "FBI" interrogators. The FBI will be left holding the bag before the public.

Torture techniques? Nasser clicked on another e-mail.

Following a detainee interview exact date unknown, while leaving the interview building at Camp Delta I heard and observed from the hallway loud music and flashes of light. I walked from the hallway into the open door of a monitoring room to see what was going on. From the monitoring room I looked inside the adjacent interviewing room. At that time I saw another detainee sitting on the floor of the interview room with an Israeli flag draped around him, loud music being played, and a strobe light flashing. I left the monitoring room immediately after seeing this activity.

Nasser clicked on another e-mail.

Special Agent was present in an observation room at GTMO and observed a DOD female, name unknown, conducting an interrogation of an unknown detainee. Special Agent was present to observe an interrogation occurring in a different interrogation room. DOD female entered the observation room and complained that curtain movement at the observation window was distracting the detainee, though no movement of the curtain had occurred. She directed a Marine to duct-tape a curtain over the two-way mirror between the interrogation room and the observation room. Special Agent characterized this action as an attempt to prohibit those in the observation room from witnessing her interrogation with the detainee. Through the surveillance camera monitor, Special Agent then observed DOD female position herself between the detainee and the surveillance camera. The detainee was shackled and his hands were cuffed to his waist. Special Agent observed DOD female apparently whispering in the detainee's ear, and caressing and applying lotion to his arms (this was during Ramadan when physical contact with a woman would have been particularly offensive to a Muslim male). On more than one occasion the detainee appeared to be grimacing in pain, and DOD female's hands appeared to be making some contact with the detainee. Although Special Agent could not see her hands at all times, he saw them moving toward the detainee's lap . . . Subsequently the Marine who had previously taped the curtain and had been in the interrogation room with DOD female during the interrogation reentered the observation room. Special Agent asked what had happened to cause detainee to grimace in pain. The Marine said DOD female had grabbed the detainee's thumbs and bent them backward and indicated that she had also grabbed his genitals. The Marine also implied that her treatment of detainee was less harsh than her treatment of others by indicating that he had seen her treatment of the other detainees result in detainees curling into a fetal position on the floor and crying in pain.

FBI agents observed detainee after he had been subjected to intense isolation from over three months. During that time period detainee was totally isolated (with the exception of occasional interviews) in a cell that was always flooded with light. By late November, the detainee was evidencing behavior consistent with extreme psychological trauma (talking to nonexistent people, reporting hearing noises, crouching in a corner of the cell covered with a sheet for hours on end). It is unknown to the FBI whether such isolation was approved by appropriate DOD authorities . . .

Transfixed, Nasser clicked to another attachment.

On a couple of occasions, I entered interview rooms to find a detainee chained hand and foot in a fetal position to the floor, with no chair, food, or water. Most times they had urinated or defecated on themselves, and had been there for 18, 24 hours or more. On one occasion, the air-conditioning had been turned up and the temperature was so low in the room that the barefoot detainee was shaking with cold. When I asked the MPs what was going on, I was told that interrogators from the day prior had ordered this treatment, and the detainee was not to be moved. On another occasion, the A/C had been turned off, making the temperature in the unventilated room probably well over 100 degrees. The detainee was almost unconscious on the floor, with a pile of hair next to him. He had apparently been literally pulling his own hair out throughout the night. On another occasion, not only was the temperature unbearably hot, but extremely loud rap music was being played, and had been since the day before, with the detainee chained hand and foot in the fetal position on the tile floor.

Nasser felt sick to his stomach all over again. It was unbelievable. Of course the stories had come out about Guantánamo. But from the people and groups you'd expect to want terrorists set free. But this . . .

No one expected terrorists to be treated with kid

gloves. But how could you get information from them by driving them insane? Or having a woman grab a man's balls during Ramadan? Even the FBI was saying that no one could be prosecuted after using these techniques. How could you justify it?

Nasser heard a noise behind him. He grabbed the mouse and closed the file.

An old girlfriend who worked in sales for a computer company had given him his key ring with the portable storage drive on it. He'd never used the flash memory stick—he just thought it looked cool.

Without really thinking about it, Nasser fished the key ring out of his pocket and popped the drive stick out of its holder. He inserted it into his computer's USB port. And saved the file to it. Then he sent the file to the archives.

When he snapped the drive stick back onto the key ring, his hands were shaking.

Chapter Nine

The operations workroom was nothing more than an interior office. A table for everyone to sit around, big whiteboards and cork bulletin boards on the walls. And in the corner a computer loaded with all the special operations software planning tools.

It wasn't a SCIF, or Sensitive Compartmented Information Facility, a special location supposedly shielded against electronic eavesdropping where matters of the highest security classification were supposed to be conducted. Terms like "code word clearance" or "above top secret" were bandied around by the ignorant. It was SCI, Sensitive Compartmented Information.

Ed Storey thought it said something that the unit's founders had decided not to piss away a few million dollars building themselves a SCIF on one of the nearby military bases. Instead they chose for a headquarters one of the literally hundreds of nondescript office parks in Rosslyn, Virginia.

It was the same security philosophy adopted by the CIA in embassies behind the Iron Curtain during the Cold War. They assumed, as a matter of course, that the Russians had everything in the embassy bugged: walls, typewriters, copy machines, toilets. So they held all their meetings and debriefed walk-in agents in the janitor's broom closet among the mops and jugs of floor wax. Because who bothered to bug a broom closet? And what enemy intelligence service wastes their resources conducting surveillance on suburban office parks instead of the Pentagon?

The unit operations officer was Lieutenant Commander Moneymaker, formerly an assault group commander at SEAL Team Six. About as far a cry from the XO as you could get. He, Storey, and Troy were the only ones in the room.

Moneymaker passed around folders. "Your guy in Paraguay made ten trips to Brazil, Rio to be exact, in the last three months."

There was a long pause after that. Troy looked over at Storey, who was wetting his fingers and flipping through his folder. When Troy couldn't take it anymore, he said, "Do we know why, sir?"

"No idea," Moneymaker replied.

Troy knew what was going to happen as soon as he looked over at Storey. But he did it anyway. And, yes, Storey was giving him that *you dick* look.

The silence continued apace and then, still unable to help himself, Troy repeated, "No idea at all, sir?"

"He hasn't mentioned it to the interrogators yet," said Moneymaker. "DIA checked his various passports against flight records. His credit cards show rental cars and meals but no hotels. So he stayed with someone. Whoever that someone is, that's the next link in the chain."

Storey was thinking about the incredible waste of time and resources having the Defense Intelligence Agency do the work the CIA should have been doing. All because of the continuing intelligence turf war between the Pentagon and the CIA. It was going to get someone killed someday, Storey thought. Probably him.

"That's it, sir?" said Troy.

"That's it," said Moneymaker.

At that point Storey looked up from his reading and spoke his first words. "We're going to need someone who speaks Portuguese, sir. As fluent as possible, and has some experience with low-visibility operations."

"You got it," said Moneymaker. "Anything else?"

"Not right off the top of my head, sir."

"Well, if you think of anything, let me know. When you've got a plan put together, I'll hear the brief-back."

"Yes, sir."

Moneymaker gathered up his papers and left, shutting the door behind him.

"Okay," said Troy. "I can tell just by looking at you. Let me have it."

Storey hadn't looked angry, just a little exasperated. "I've told you time and time again," he said. "Never put officers in a position where they're tempted to tell you how to do something. *Especially* when they don't have a clue themselves. Because not having a clue never stops them."

"That's all well and fucking good," Troy replied. "But the bottom line, as usual, is we're getting sent somewhere to try and find someone. With nothing to go on. Zip. Not that it bothers anyone but me."

"People are creatures of habit," said Storey.

"Ed, what the fuck are you talking about?" said Troy. Storey always did that. Always laying some statement into the conversation that had nothing to do with anything that had come before.

"People are creatures of habit," Storey repeated. "Just like they always ask the same questions, even when they know they're not going to get a good answer, they fall into routines and patterns and stick to them. It's natural behavior. Look how hard we have to train ourselves to analyze everything we do and always vary our times, routes, and procedures. It's like tactics. You have to spend a hell of a lot of time teaching troops to attack. Running away don't take any training at all."

Troy was a sniper by trade. On operations he could lie in the weeds for days at a time, moving nothing but his eyelids. But outside the operational environment he was like a different person. Like someone with attention deficit disorder. Storey found that dichotomy fascinating, though he was always trying to change it.

"Okay," said Troy. "What did I miss?"

"Check the credit card receipts. Is there a restaurant in Rio de Janeiro listed more than once?"

Troy flipped through the folder, knowing of course something was going to get stuck up his ass. "Yeah, there is."

"You have a good time, a nice meal," said Storey. "You go back."

"But he ain't going back there anymore."

"You ever work in a restaurant?" Storey asked.

"Nope."

"Restaurant owner doesn't survive on people coming in one time for dinner. You live and die by your regular customers. Someone comes in regular, you take care of them. More important, you remember them. Restaurant owner'd forget the names of his kids before he forgot a regular customer."

"Pretty damn thin," said Troy, trying to salvage a little pride.

"Big things come from small things," said Storey. "Especially in intelligence. We had nothing—now we have a little something. We've had less before and made something happen."

They flew into Rio on three separate flights. Following Storey's rules, they registered at three separate hotels. That way if one of the hotels was compromised, the other two became ready-made safe houses for all of them.

They outfitted themselves in Brazilian clothing and the

usual large number of cell phones. All prepaid, because those were the hardest to trace.

Neither Storey nor Troy had ever operated in or even visited Brazil before. So they were dependent on Sergeant First Class Gary Poett, an Army counterintelligence specialist who was used to traveling around the world and operating undercover in small teams.

Poett was black, about 6'3", and built like he sprinkled steroids on his Wheaties every morning. And like a lot of guys with the early male-pattern baldness thing going on, he shaved his head.

All in all, not the visually inconspicuous look Storey usually preferred, but he had a few ideas about using Poett's appearance to his advantage. Besides, he liked him. And when you had to live in close quarters with someone for indefinite stretches of time, that had a way of becoming a prime consideration.

The first thing Poett had said, at their first meeting, was, "Okay, let's get all the shit about my name over with right now."

Storey had only lifted his eyebrows quizzically.

"What do you mean?" Troy asked innocently.

"Motherfuckers," said Poett.

And a couple of beats later they'd all had a good laugh.

Storey had insisted on spending a week training with Poett before they went operational. And Storey's training days, as Troy had warned Poett, usually lasted around eighteen hours.

At the end of one of them, Poett had grabbed Troy and said, "Goddamn. He works you like a mule, don't he?"

"That he does," said Troy, hoping he wasn't going to have to hear any whining. He hated whining. Complaining was a military necessity. But only pussies whined.

But that wasn't what he heard. Poett said, "I learned more in the last week that I did in ten years doing counterintelligence."

"That's Storey," said Troy. "He was learning how *you* move, too. This is how he works. Once everyone's singing off the same sheet of music, he can do his planning on the fly and not worry about you. And Storey improvises like Miles Davis."

"He's that good?" said Poett. "I heard a lot about him, but he's really that good?"

"He's that good," Troy confirmed. "Started out in the Rangers when he was eighteen. Then Special Forces. Then Delta Force. Assault troop, then reconnaissance and surveillance troop. There's only one in each Delta squadron, and they're the best operators. Then the operational support troop, the ones trained to infiltrate cities and do recon undercover. Advanced Force Operations. When it comes to low visibility, he's the best. Three Purple Hearts, and even I don't know how he got them."

"He's kind of . . . remote."

"If you need a lot of maintenance, he's not your guy," said Troy.

"Okay, I can handle that. If half the stories about him are true . . ."

"Half of them are," said Troy. "The ballsiest half. Problem with Storey is, he'll throw your shit out in the breeze. He's so good he'll take chances nobody else would. Someone else'd look at the mission, say forget it. He'll figure out a way, then pull it off."

"Well, you been working with him for a while." Which was a way of saying he couldn't be that reckless.

"He's so good, after he throws your shit out in the breeze he'll bring your ass back home, too."

"Couldn't ask for more than that, I guess," said Poett.

"No," said Troy. "You couldn't."

The restaurant was in the Centro, or central zone of Rio. Near the Avenida Rio Branco. One of Rio's prime walking and shopping areas. Narrow streets, two-story shops, and small squares. Storey had looked it up in the guidebook. A neighborhood place. Brazilian home cooking. Good food, very popular, but not fussy or expensive enough for more than two stars.

In the rental car nearby, Storey asked everyone, "Are we all clear? No matter what happens, I'm not saying a word. He might think I'm an American, but I'm not going to confirm it for him."

Poett glanced at his watch. "We're early for a Rio restaurant."

"That's what I want," said Storey. "I want the kitchen busy doing prep, and the owner's complete attention. Now, we've got to lay out the cover story exactly."

Troy let out a barely audible groan. Storey had put it together like the headshrinker he was, fussing over every word and detail, making Poett rehearse it until both the brothers were ready to start screaming.

"*I'm* ready to go," said Poett.

Storey gave no indication that he'd heard Troy's groan. Troy dropped them off down the street, and they walked up, ignoring the valet.

Storey was wearing eyeglasses and a mustache. He was willing to let Poett start out with the bare scalp, but had brought along a collection of wigs for later.

It was just after 6:00 P.M., by Brazilian standards too early for even the senior citizen's early bird dinner.

At the door the maitre d' tried to tell them the restaurant wasn't open, but Storey hit him with $20 in Brazilian reals and Poett said they wanted to discuss a business matter with the owner.

The maitre d' eyed them both, but especially Poett, with more than a little alarm. "Do you gentlemen have a card?"

"Yes," said Poett, without making any move to hand him one.

After a prolonged silence that made the maitre d'

begin to fidget, he managed to get out, "How shall I announce you?"

"As the impatient men who wish to speak with the owner. Now."

The maitre d' dashed off. Storey gave Poett a little approving nod. He had no idea what had been said, but he liked the tone.

No more than a couple of minutes later, the maitre d' reappeared and ushered them to an office in the back. It was the kind of place Storey liked. Nothing too loud, from the décor to the music. Comfortable.

The owner was a small, fat man. The kind of small, fat man who just couldn't get his suits to fit right, not matter how much money he spent on them. He was sweating, and seemed afraid to offer to shake hands, so he gave them both awkward little bows.

Where the restaurant's décor was just right, his office paneling was too bright and plastic looking, the desk too big for the room.

"Gentlemen, I am Luis Franzini, the owner of this establishment. How may I assist you?"

Storey immediately realized the guy thought he was about to get strong-armed. Asked to pay protection or something. Which wasn't a bad thing. Without waiting to be asked, he moved a chair up to the desk and sat down.

Poett followed his lead.

Flustered to find himself the only one standing, Senhor Franzini dashed around his desk and sat down. His chair squeaked badly.

Storey noticed the adjoining door open a crack. As Poett began, "Senhor Franzini," Storey shot from his chair and yanked the door open. He came back into the room dragging a man in a tuxedo by the hair and holding the revolver he'd taken away from him. Storey guided the man over his outstretched leg and onto the floor, placing a shoe on his throat to cut down on the noise.

Poett improvised beautifully. He actually started laughing, a deep bass laugh that startled Storey momentarily, and the owner for much longer. "Senhor Franzini, you are in no danger. We have a business proposal, one that could be very advantageous to you. An opportunity for you to realize a considerable sum of money. But we do wish to discuss it with you privately." He nodded, and Storey removed his foot from what he assumed was the restaurant manager's throat.

Being a restaurant owner, Senhor Franzini did mad very well. "A thousand apologies, gentlemen. You," he shouted at the manager on the floor, "what are you doing eavesdropping on me? Get out! Get out this instant!"

The manager looked up at Storey for permission. Storey casually gestured toward the door. With the pistol. The manger sprang up and left rapidly. Storey made sure the door was closed and regained his seat, smoothing his trousers. He placed the pistol in his lap.

"My younger brother," said Senhor Franzini, as if that explained everything.

Now that things had quieted down, Poett began anew. "We are representing a party in a legal matter. And we are looking for a man whose testimony could be very important to the case. All we know about this man is that he is a regular customer of yours, and he has dined here several times with *this* man."

Following another nod, Storey passed a photo they'd taken of the Arab in Paraguay across the desk. And from the eyes it was clear the owner knew exactly who they were talking about.

Storey knew the cover story sounded thin, bordering on fake. This was intentional. He wanted the owner to start thinking about Arabs and come to the conclusion that he was in the middle of something serious. So serious that he'd be too scared to notify either the police or the target.

He nodded to Poett.

Poett said, "You know who we are talking about." He did not put it in the form of a question.

Senhor Franzini thought it over, sweated some more, and eventually nodded.

"Do you know his name?" Poett asked pleasantly.

"Ijaz Wazir," Senhor Franzini muttered.

Pakistani, Storey thought. For a moment there he was frozen by indecision, unsure of his next move. There couldn't be many Ijaz Wazirs in Rio. So this might be a good time to walk right out the door, put the intelligence community on to the name, and let them track the guy down. But if was just another nom de guerre, and he didn't have a credit card, car, or apartment in that name, they were screwed. And if they didn't take care of Franzini, of course he'd either tell Wazir or, more probably, sell him the information that people were looking for him. No, better to stick with the original plan, no matter how risky.

"Do you know his address?" Poett asked.

Senhor Franzini shook his head.

"How often does he eat here?" said Poett.

Senhor Franzini really did not want to say anything. But he most certainly did not want to say nothing at all. "Once a week, sometimes twice."

"Describe him."

"How do you mean?"

"I mean describe him," Poett said curtly. "Height, weight, hair color."

"Perhaps a meter and three quarters, seventy-two kilos, dark brown hair, brown eyes."

Poett realized that wasn't getting them anywhere. "How old is he?"

"Perhaps thirty years."

"Is he a native Brazilian with an Arab name, or is he an Arab?"

"An Arab. Definitely."

"Does he pay his bill by credit card?"

"No, cash always."

"What we require, then," said Poett, "is that the next time this gentleman comes in, you notify us. We will return and you will point him out. Nothing more. This will not be done in public, of course, but perhaps from the kitchen. We will not speak to him in your establishment, or disturb your business in any way. And for your time and trouble in this matter we are prepared to pay you twelve thousand reals." A whisker over five thousand dollars, U.S.

At another glance, Storey removed an envelope from his suit jacket and fanned out the cash before replacing the money in the envelope and the envelope in his jacket. The sum had been arrived at after much debate. Too small and he'd blow off the job. Too big and he'd think they wouldn't deliver. It had to be just enough to tickle his greed.

Senhor Franzini gave the matter some more thought, then, looking directly at Storey, said, "Twenty-four thousand."

Storey, having absolutely no idea what was being discussed, stared back stonily.

This caused Senhor Franzini to panic. "My apologies, gentlemen. I misspoke. Twelve thousand is more than generous for such a small service."

"Then you accept?" said Poett.

"I accept." And then the timid request. "Half in advance?"

"All upon completion," Poett said firmly.

"Of course, of course."

Using Senhor Franzini's desk pen and pad, Poett wrote down two of their cell phone numbers. "Do not misplace these."

"Never! Never!"

"You may now write down your mobile phone number, for us."

Franzini scribbled it on the back of one of his business cards.

"We will await your call," said Poett. He rose from his chair, and Storey followed suit.

As Senhor Franzini ushered them out, Storey turned suddenly and clapped a hand on his shoulder, gathering up a bundle of muscle and skin and giving the man his best platoon sergeant stare, one that had terrified more than its share of Army privates.

Which was Poett's cue to say, "Upon reflection, you may feel the urge to tell us that Senhor Wazir has ceased to frequent your establishment. Or become tempted to act as an intermediary and notify Senhor Wazir that we wish to speak to him. Or tell anyone else about our arrangement, other than your maitre d' that you wish to be notified when Senhor Wazir arrives, for confidential reasons of your own. Giving in to any of these impulses would break our agreement. And since it might affect our case, we would look very unfavorably on it. Do you understand?"

"Yes, yes of course. We are in agreement, gentlemen. You may rely on me."

Poett signaled Storey to release him. "We certainly hope so," he said. "We will pay in cash, at the moment you identify Senhor Wazir to us. And then we will not trouble you again."

"Of course, gentlemen, of course. Are you sure you would not wish to stay and dine? As my guests, of course."

"Thank you, no," said Poett, almost laughing again at the insincerity of the invitation.

"Then a drink, perhaps, before you go."

"We regret having to decline your generosity. We have further business this evening."

Before they left the office, Storey flicked open the revolver cylinder and emptied the cartridges into his palm. He tossed the empty pistol onto a chair.

As soon as Senhor Franzini ushered his two guests out

the door, he went right to the bar for a large whiskey that he did not linger over.

The manager rushed up. "What was all that about?"

"Nothing," Franzini snapped. "Get back to work!"

The manger fled yet again.

Franzini impatiently gestured to the bartender to refill his glass. For half an instant he thought about calling the police, who he of course paid off every week. Then he called himself a fool. The police? If those two strangers, who he was certain were Israeli secret agents, were arrested, their associates would toss a bomb through his window one night and blow his restaurant into matchsticks. Probably after tying him to a chair inside. Wazir was a dead man, no matter what. If they got what they wanted, and his prayers to the Virgin were answered, no one would know he had helped them and he would be left in peace. With the money. That cheered him for a moment, then thinking about what might go wrong had him loudly calling for another drink.

Poett waited until they were back in the car to break out laughing.

As he was rolling around in the backseat, Troy turned to Storey and said, "What happened that was so funny?"

"You got me," said Storey.

"Ah," said Troy. "Then *you* must have done something to crack his ass up."

"Offhand, I can't recall any humorous moments," said Storey. "But I'm sure he's going to tell us as soon as he gets his shit together."

"You're damn right I'm going to," said Poett, wiping his eyes. He gave them the play-by-play of everything that had been said.

"You took a revolver away from him?" Troy broke in to ask Storey.

"He barely knew which end to hold," said Storey.

"Didn't mean he couldn't manage to shoot your ass with it," said Troy.

"O-kay," Poett said firmly, to direct their attention back to his account. "We offer five grand. He thinks for a while, then says how about ten? And he looks at Ed, real hopeful like a little puppy. Ed has no idea what the guy just said, but he's not even blinking, just staring at the guy like he was a cockroach running across the floor that he really wanted to step on. And you can just *hear* the shit hitting his skivvies, and he goes: five grand will be just fine, thank you very much." Poett started laughing again.

"Just your little contribution to holding down information price inflation," Troy said to Storey.

"Is that what he was asking for?" said Storey. "I was just thinking I ought to act pissed off at everything he said."

"Oh, man," Poett exclaimed in relief after he finally stopped laughing. "You did. You surely did that."

"You handled yourself real well in there," Storey told him.

"Thanks."

"It wasn't just great work," Storey went on. "It was sheer poetry."

The smile got wiped off Poett's face. "Man, that was bad."

Troy cracked up.

They drive around for a while, making sure their back was clear of any surveillance.

While they waited for Franzini's call, Storey sent the name Ijaz Wazir to Washington. His instinct had been correct. Incredibly, there were six Ijaz Wazirs living in Rio and the surrounding area. But all were either older men or younger boys, none within the age range of their target. This was confirmed through their own local research of phone directories and property records. As Storey had feared, they were stuck with Senhor Franzini.

Troy wanted to stake out the restaurant. Storey vetoed

that. Any kind of close-in surveillance was too risky. If it got made the target was gone and the game was over.

But he understood Troy's feelings. Their position was one no operators wanted to find themselves in. Not only dependent on one informant of unknown, but probably shaky reliability, but committed to show up at a location known to that informant, at a time to be determined by the informant. Totally contrary to every last rule of intelligence tradecraft.

So they made sure their escape routes out of the country were updated on a daily basis. Their luggage could be abandoned at the hotels. Their operational equipment was staged in a rental car parked not at any of the hotels, but in a well-secured car park.

Three days later one of the cell phones rang. It was just a few minutes after 9:30 P.M.

Poett picked it up. "Yes? Yes, it is I. What? Very good. Remain calm—I will call you back." He snapped the phone shut. "We're on."

Storey knew there were three possibilities. The first was that everything was going to happen as planned. No one was counting on that. The second was that they'd walk into the arms of Brazilian security. The third was that al-Qaeda would be waiting to greet them.

To deal with the second possibility they were all carrying diplomatic passports in addition to the ones they were actually traveling under. Neither in their real names, of course. Diplomatic immunity would at least keep them from a long stretch in a Brazilian prison. But it would also mean a very embarrassing, high-profile diplomatic incident. One that, Storey knew, would make certain they'd never get promoted again and would be reassigned to await retirement or end of enlistment in the shittiest possible jobs at the most asshole bases imaginable.

To cover the third possibility they'd visited the cache that the DIA maintained for the unit everywhere they had safe houses, which was most of the major cities in the world. So they didn't need to have weapons flown in, as in the case of Paraguay.

Storey and Troy were wearing MP5K 9mm submachine guns slung under their armpits. Only thirteen inches long, with no stock. A short-range, 900-rounds-per-minute, get-your-ass-out-of-trouble insurance policy. Short fifteen-round magazines in the weapons for concealment, and thirty-rounders in their belts. Along with a few Austrian Arges HG86 mini–fragmentation hand grenades, just a shade larger than a golf ball. There was even a collapsing bullet-trap target in the cache, so they could test-fire the weapons, with sound suppressors of course, in the safe house basement. None of the weapons were traceable to the United States.

Fortunately it always rained in Rio in the summer, so their raincoats wouldn't attract any attention.

When they reached the restaurant they circled around the block, looking for people sitting in cars and pedestrians hanging around instead of doing something.

In the movies there's always a parking space available, but it's never like that in real life.

Storey thought it over. "Let the restaurant valet park it," he told Troy.

"What?"

"It'll actually be better that way." He explained his thinking to Troy, who began to grin.

"It *is* better that way."

Storey and Poett got out of the car about fifty yards from the restaurant. They could just barely see the sign.

Troy drove up, gave the car to the valet, and went inside.

"Make the call," Storey said to Poett.

"Hello again, Senhor Franzini," said Poett. "No, we will not be coming in at this moment. You will call me when Senhor Wazir has paid his check and is preparing to depart. Yes, that is correct. You understand? Do not fail us." He broke the connection. "He's panicking," he told Storey. "A million questions, first being when does he get the money."

"Ought to keep him on his toes," said Storey. "If he don't melt down first. You relax here and keep an eye on the front. I'm going to take a little walk."

That hadn't been in the plan. "What if he calls before you get back?"

"I doubt that'll happen. But if it goes, you call Troy and tell him Wazir's on his way out. That's all you need to do. And just sit tight." Then, as if an afterthought. "Of course, if I don't show up in, say, an hour, don't sit tight. Get the hell out of the country."

"Fantastic," said Poett.

Inside the restaurant, Troy declined to check his raincoat and took a seat at the bar. Before the bartender could ask him something in Portuguese, Troy caught his eye and said, "Caipirinha."

If anything could be called a national drink, caipirinha was it. The bartender tossed some lime slices in a wide glass, then poured in a few spoonfuls of sugar. Using a special wooden tool, the fetish aspect of these things always being important, he crushed the lime in the glass and mixed the juice with the sugar. Then he poured in a big slug of cachaça. The Russians have vodka, the Caribbean has rum, and the Brazilians have cachaça, distilled from sugar cane. The bartender added ice and slid it over.

"*Obrigado*," said Troy, passing over a ten-real note. He took a sip. Jesus. A few of these and you'd step off the barstool and find out the hard way that your legs didn't work anymore. The bartender returned with his change, and Troy hit him with a good though not memorable tip. The first time he'd gone overseas undercover he'd tipped big. It was fun when it wasn't your money. And he'd had bartenders and waiters stuck to him like barnacles all

night long. He'd become memorable instead of anonymous. Luckily, that had happened before he met Storey.

The bar was crowded enough that he didn't have to
worry about being bothered by the bartender. Unfortunately, that wasn't the case with the clientele. The Brazilian on the stool next to him was totally shitfaced. And
started talking to him in Portuguese.

Troy tried to ignore the drunk, but the guy kept talking
to him and patting him on the arm to get his attention.

Deciding that English wasn't the way to go, he spoke
to the idiot in Spanish. "I'm sorry, friend, but I don't
speak Portuguese."

It didn't do any good. The attention only encouraged
the asshole, and the Portuguese kept pouring out of him
at the rapid rate.

Troy didn't know what the hell to do. He finally
caught the bartender's eye and appealed for a little help.

The bartender leaned over and spoke to the drunk, slowly
and loudly. "HE DOES NOT SPEAK PORTUGUESE."

The drunk paid him no mind. Didn't even look at
him. Just kept up the conversation with Troy. Then he
draped an arm over Troy's shoulder.

Oh, Christ, they were best friends now. Troy picked out
a spot on the side of the guy's forehead and dreamed
of planting an elbow there. But a scene was out of the
question.

Troy had scanned the dining room on the way in, and
was sure he'd made his man. There weren't many thirty-
year-old Arab/Pakistanis in the restaurant, not to mention eating alone and not drinking alcohol. Seemed to
be pretty far along in his meal.

Out in the street, Poett was beginning to get a little
antsy until he saw Storey heading toward him. There
were quite a few people out. Hitting the bars, window-
shopping, going to dinner.

"Everything okay?" Storey asked him.

"So far. No call yet."

Storey only nodded, apparently unconcerned. Poett had heard how cool Storey was, but the people who'd told him had no idea. No idea at all.

"Neighborhood looks clear," said Storey, just mentioning it. "If we don't get the call in a couple of minutes, we'll start walking. No sense attracting attention standing here."

Poett's phone rang.

"Ever notice how often that happens?" said Storey, taking out his own phone.

"Yes?" Poett said into his. "Very good." He put his hand over the phone and said to Storey, "Our guy's on his way."

"Tell him to stay on the line," said Storey, dialing a number.

Troy's phone rang. *"Hola?"* he said into it, keeping up the Spanish cover. The drunk was still talking. Troy held up one finger to call a time-out, but the bastard just wouldn't shut up. Troy knew if he did anything it would only get the guy agitated. And louder.

It was Storey. "Our boy's heading out. You got him?"

"Absolutely," Troy said in Spanish, one finger in his ear in a feeble attempt to block out the noise. The guy paying his check was the one he'd already picked out.

"You need anything from us?" Storey asked.

"No, gracias," said Troy, putting his phone away. The drunk was still draped all over him. Troy had never wanted to kill anyone so badly in his life. He slipped under the arm and off the barstool. Now the son of a bitch was off *his* stool and following him, still running his mouth. Troy decided there was nothing to do but wait until they were outside, then lay the guy out and hope it didn't screw things up too badly.

* * *

Storey pocketed his phone and said to Poett, "Tell Franzini his money's taped under the lid of the trash can outside his kitchen door."

Poett grinned and passed on the news. "He forgot to say thank you," he told Storey. "Actually, he didn't even say good-bye."

"Too busy running for that money," said Storey. Even if there were Brazilian security inside, neither Franzini nor anyone in the restaurant had ever laid eyes on Troy. Not a bad way out of a rotten tactical situation.

Troy was concentrating on his target going out the door, which wasn't easy with the stream of maddening, unintelligible talk buzzing in his ears like a fucking mosquito. But just as they were leaving the bar area, there was a commotion behind him. Troy shot a quick glance over his shoulder, and saw the bartender and a bouncer grabbing the drunk by both arms. The drunk was howling now, probably that he wanted to go with his new best friend. From what Troy could decipher, the drunk hadn't paid his tab. Thank you, God. With no idea how long the respite would last until the drunk found his wallet, he hurried for the door.

The Pakistani was standing on the curb. One of the valets was gone, probably getting the car. Troy handed his ticket to the other. He could feel the Pakistani watching him, but when he turned he was being ignored.

Troy patted his pockets as if looking for his keys.

The first valet drove up in the Pakistani's car, a blue four-door BMW sedan. How about that, Troy thought, impressed.

As the Pakistani was getting in, Troy dropped his keys and a handful of change onto the sidewalk, cursing his clumsiness. The Pakistani turned and Troy waved a hand—no help needed—and bent down to start picking it up. The Pakistani continued into his car anyway. Rude prick, Troy thought. The valet crouched down to help him.

When the door slammed Troy duckwalked forward to pick up a coin, placing his left hand on the BMW bumper. His fingers crept underneath, and he attached the radio frequency tracker, mounted on a magnet, to the frame. And not a second too soon, because the car shifted into gear and roared off, giving him a face full of exhaust.

Troy retrieved the last of his change and straightened up. The valet poured the coins he'd recovered into his hand. Troy tipped him more than their value for his trouble.

Now his car drove up. He tipped the second valet and was off.

Troy stopped at the end of the street and popped the trunk. Poett got in the back. Storey retrieved a briefcase from the trunk before sliding in next to Troy on the passenger side.

"Give him a minute to put some distance between us," said Storey. "We don't want to bump into him if he hits some traffic." He opened the briefcase and fired up the laptop computer inside, extending the small antenna. The computer took its own sweet time booting up. "Did you put both chips on the car?"

"All I had time for was one," said Troy. "And almost got dragged down the street at that."

Storey wasn't pleased by the news, but he didn't say anything. If that one tracking chip wasn't working, or went down before the Pakistani got home, it was back to square one.

The computer finally booted up, and couple of taps on the keyboard brought up a street map of Rio. Another tap and a cursor began blinking on the screen. Storey could feel himself calm down. "We got him."

They stayed close enough to remain within range of the tracker. It was obvious that the Pakistani was dirty. He did the same thing they'd done after their last visit to the restaurant. Driving around, doubling back, speeding up, slowing down. Looking for the pair of headlights that stayed with you.

The Pakistani made sure he got onto the Avenida Presidente Vargas, which was always a traffic-choked wasteland. It didn't matter. The Americans watched his every move. He could drive the wrong way down all the one-way streets he wanted. They just laughed at him.

Then all the bobbing and weaving was over, and they headed south, toward Copacabana.

"You don't think he's a beach boy, do you?" said Troy.

"I've seen stranger," said Storey.

But before the Pakistani reached the beach he turned left.

"Pull over the first chance you get," said Poett. "He lives in Urca."

"Urca?" said Troy.

"It's a little neighborhood out on the peninsula," said Poett, leaning over the seat and pointing it out on the map. "It's nestled around the front of the Pão de Açúcar, Sugarloaf Peak. Part residential; the rest is the naval training college. The peninsula makes it isolated, and the only reason for anyone but the people who live there to visit is to take the cable car up to Sugarloaf for the view, then come down and leave. Otherwise it's not a tourist destination."

"That's good," said Storey.

"Well, not good for keeping an eye on him," said Poett.

"That's not what he means," said Troy. "He always likes it better when the other guy's a pro."

"Why wouldn't you want him to be a jerk?" Poett asked.

"Amateurs are unpredictable," Storey replied.

The cursor finally stopped, just as Poett had predicted, in the Urca neighborhood.

"Let's give him a chance to get in and get settled down for the night," said Storey.

They circled Botafogo Bay on the Avenida Pasteur, then took the Avenida Portugal onto the little peninsula.

It was very un–Rio-like. "Damn, it *is* quiet around here," Storey said. He checked the map. "Only about five main avenues on the whole peninsula."

"Mostly military lives here," said Poett. "The naval college. Fishermen. It's one of the safest locales in Rio."

"One way in, one way out," said Troy.

The BMW was parked at a modern, six-story concrete-and-glass apartment building.

"You want to see what apartment he's in?" said Troy. "Our only hope for surveillance is renting one in the same building."

"No, keep driving," said Storey. "All we'd need is some neighbor asking our boy if the men inquiring about him found him. He'd be gone. We've got his car. We've got his registration. We've got his neighborhood. We'll send it off to Washington, see what they give us."

"You going to ask for a support team to take over surveillance?" said Troy.

"Not yet," said Storey. "I want to see what this guy does first. He may not even live here full-time. If he doesn't we'd be moving surveillance all over town, and that can get messy."

Sitting in the car Storey wrote out a short report on his PDA, encrypted the text, and sent it off via satellite phone.

Washington's reply a day later proved the power of both databases and easily bribed public officials. The BMW was registered to one Jan Mohammad, as was apartment 505. He'd been in Rio for four years. Pakistani passport, which said he was from Hyderabad. Not that any of that was necessarily true. Work permit had him as the owner of a carpet import company.

"Jan Mohammad what?" was the first thing Troy said. "In Pakistan it's always Jan Mohammad something."

"That's it," said Storey, reading the screen. "I guess he was fresh out of ideas for this pseudonym."

They trailed Jan Mohammad for a week, recording his patterns. They rented three cars at a time, used a different one every day, then turned them in and rented three more. He didn't spend any time at all at his carpet business. Or any other job that might have paid for that BMW.

He went food shopping every day, and then drove up to the Glória neighborhood, on the opposite side of Botafogo Bay. Glória was an old neighborhood. Once tony, then gone to seed, now rediscovered and turned trendy again by urban yuppie pioneers. Big old nineteenth-century houses, one of which Jan Mohammad lugged his groceries into every day.

"That's a lot of damn chow," said Troy. "Who's he feeding?"

"More than a couple of people, that's for sure," said Storey.

One the third day of surveillance there was a change of routine. Jan Mohammad visited the house in Glória, then made the twelve-mile drive north to Antonio Carlos Jobim International Airport on Governor's Island. With a passenger in the car. As usual the traffic was crazy, and no Brazilian worth his salt stopped for red lights.

Instead of parking in front of one of the two terminals, Jan Mohammad drove to the short-term lot.

Poett was driving the surveillance car, with Troy in the backseat and Storey, as usual, watching the map display.

"Okay, great opportunity," he said. "He's not dropping the guy off, he's going in with him. Lee, he's seen you already. You stick with the car. I'll get off at Terminal 1. Gary, you take Terminal 2. Whichever one they go to, we'll already be inside waiting. We'll leave our pieces here, we might have to go through security."

Storey and Poett ducked out of sight, opened up their shirts, and removed the Null USH shoulder holsters they'd been wearing next to their skin. They stashed them and the silenced Glock pistols under the seat.

The two terminals were almost side by side. Storey went though the doors and quickly oriented himself before buying a newspaper and finding a seat with a good view.

A few minutes later Jan Mohammad entered the terminal with his companion, who was definitely not an Arab or East Asian. Only the companion was carrying a suitcase. They turned down the concourse and disappeared around a curve.

Storey gave them a little time, then got up and followed. They were checking in at the TAM-Meridional counter. Storey continued on and passed through security. He kept walking until he found the TAM gates, picking the first one with people in it and taking a seat where he could see the aisle.

Jan Mohammad and his companion soon appeared. And turned right into that particular gate. It was a local flight to São Paulo. Had to be a connection to somewhere else.

Storey was plotting how to get a look at the boarding pass when the two of them sat down in the only two remaining adjacent seats. Right next to him.

Which might have sounded like the ideal situation, but really wasn't. Because it was like having his fly unzipped in public, magnified to the tenth power. Storey couldn't pay too much attention to them. But ignoring them would be equally suspicious. Every single move he made had to be carefully contemplated and calibrated.

So of course his nose itched. His ass itched. He wanted to fidget. For a second there he even thought his eyelid was beginning to twitch. A million insecurities blew up from nowhere. Should he cough a couple of times, or would it sound unnatural? Blow his nose? He couldn't get up and walk away. He had to sit there and sweat.

Storey read his newspaper page by page, and even that was a nightmare since it was in Portuguese and he couldn't understand a word. He was praying they wouldn't make conversation or ask him about a headline.

He needn't have worried. They didn't even say a word to each other.

This torture lasted for thirty minutes until the plane began to board. When the third economy row was called, Jan Mohammad and his companion stood up and embraced, Jan Mohammad saying in Arabic, "God be with you, my brother. A safe journey and all success. Our prayers follow you."

"God be with you also," the other replied, also in Arabic. "A thousand thanks for all your labors."

While they were saying their good-byes, Storey got a good look at the boarding pass in the companion's hand. He committed the rows and seat numbers to memory.

Storey couldn't hang around and be the only one left at the gate with Jan Mohammad. He waited until they both began moving down the line, then slipped away. Three gates down he found a pillar to both lounge against and conceal himself.

Jan Mohammad watched until the aircraft pulled away, then headed back into the terminal.

Since he was now a familiar face, Storey gave him a lot of room. Jan Mohammad got onto the travelator that connected Terminal 1 to Terminal 2.

Storey stayed put, not wanting to get caught short if Jan Mohammad doubled back. He dialed Poett on his cell phone. "Our friend's about to join you. Alone, so don't worry about anyone but him. I'm staying here."

"Okay," Poett replied. "Here he comes. I've got him."

"Call me if he leaves." He'd just been sitting at an airline gate for a half hour, but Storey felt drained by his ordeal. He bought a couple of Cokes to ram some caffeine into his system. And he didn't stop fretting, because now he was fretting about how Poett would handle himself. Poett may have been an experienced counterintelligence man making a tail in an airport terminal, but the only things Ed Storey *didn't* worry about were the ones he did himself. His armpits were soaked.

As he drank his Coke he thought he ought to call Troy, who was probably having his own little battle with impatience.

The conversation was conducted in Spanish, and as soon as the connection was made Troy said, "What's going on?"

"Number two got on a flight," said Storey. "Number one is now in Terminal 1. You're not double-parked anywhere, are you?

"No, I'm on the top of one of the car parks. Got a nice view of the entrances of both terminals."

"Good, stay there. I'm staying here at 1. Nobody moves until we hear from our friend."

"Oh, it's one of those," said Troy. "Okay, staying put."

While he waited, Storey made a call with his satellite phone. Back in Washington they manned a twenty-four-hour toll-free number that was like your own personal concierge. They booked flights, hotels, and rental cars anywhere in the world. And instantly answered all of the different kinds of information requests that popped up in foreign countries. Storey gave the operator his work name and ID number. When she confirmed his identity he said, "AeroMexico flight 17 from São Paulo to Mexico City. What's the plane's next stop?"

A pause and clicking of computer keys. "No next stop. The plane overnights in Mexico City. Do you want its schedule for tomorrow?"

"No thanks," said Storey. "That's all I need."

Mexico City. Unless there was another flight from

there on another airline. But he wouldn't ask them to trace the seat number and name on a voice call, in the clear. It would have to be sent as encrypted text later.

An hour passed. Storey wanted to call Poett, make sure his phone hadn't gone down. But he didn't. He didn't believe in bothering people while they were working.

Three very long hours later Poett finally called. "Flight just came in, and he's waiting at Customs."

"Okay," said Storey. "You get eyes on the arrival. After they leave the terminal, call again and we'll pick you up."

"Understood."

Storey broke the connection and dialed Troy. "Pick me up at Terminal 1. Don't go to Terminal 2."

They drove around until Poett called back. When he got in the car he was beaming with the excitement. "He met TAP Portugal flight 177 from Lisbon. One man."

"Let me have the phone you used," said Storey.

Poett passed his over. Storey had already collected Troy's. He made sure they were turned off, since a cell phone that was on sent out a continuous signal, which made its location easy to trace to the nearest tower. The phones had been purchased with fake ID. But if the police or Brazilian security ever picked them up with the phones in their possession, or if the numbers were some-how compromised, then every call they made and their exact whereabouts could be traced. He wiped the phones down for fingerprints and put them in a paper bag. Then he stomped on the bag. The debris would go in the nearest trash can, and their next calls would be made from a new set of phones, which was why they always bought so many.

"I didn't get eyes on the new arrival," Troy said to Poett. "What did he look like?"

"Enough like the guy he took to the airport to be his brother. Caucasian."

"Caucasian is right," said Storey.

"What are you talking about now?" said Troy.

"I mean Caucasian, like from the Caucasus," said Storey. "The one who flew out was a Chechen."

"And just how the hell do you know that?" said Poett.

"Heard him speak," said Storey. "I heard that Arabic accent in Afghanistan. Only the Chechens speak it that way."

"Shit," said Troy. "You were close enough to hear him talk?"

"Not on purpose," said Storey.

"Where did he go?" said Troy.

"São Paulo to Mexico City."

"One goes out and one comes in," said Poett. "Regular little conveyor belt they've got going. No wonder all the groceries in that safe house in Glória."

"They're running a rat line," said Storey. "They're moving people, and this is a way station."

"Europe to Mexico?" said Troy. "That's not good. One person from Europe to Mexico is an agent. A bunch of people from Europe to Mexico is an attack."

"Washington better pay attention to this one," said Storey. "We're going to need a full-strength support team, maybe two, to do that surveillance. And then I reckon we're going to have to hit that house."

"I don't know about Washington," said Poett. "But I think I know how the Brazilians are going to feel about that."

"That's what worries me," said Storey. "It's not so much that I'm worried about the Brazilians as I'm worried about Washington being worried about the Brazilians."

"Translated," Troy said to Poett, "we're going to get fucked again."

Chapter Ten

"If you're going to do the interrogation and try to play him back into the network, you definitely shouldn't be arresting him," said Supervisory Special Agent Benjamin Timmins.

With just a bare desk and a computer, his voice echoed around that borrowed L.A. office. Of course L.A. wasn't going to give the Washington interlopers anything good. Beth Royale knew they were lucky they weren't working out of the bathrooms. "Ordinarily, Ben, I'd agree with you. But you know what's going to happen if someone else brings him in."

"No, Beth, I'm pretty sure I don't. Other than placing him under arrest, cuffing him, Mirandizing him, and driving him down here. Besides that, I'm not following you."

"They're going to kick down his front door and arrest him in front of his wife and kids. Or they'll go to the market and arrest him in front of his employees. Either way, he'll be so humiliated that he'd rather go to jail than do anything for us."

Timmins just looked at her and sighed. Beth loved hearing that sound. She always knew she was right when he sighed.

"You know," said Timmins, "I could always order them not to do that."

"Oh, Ben, do you really want me to say what I'm thinking right now?"

"Not particularly. Go pick him up yourself." Then Timmins gave her the kind of smile that let Beth know something unpleasant was on the way. "But before you make the collar," he continued, "I want you to meet your new partner."

"A partner? We team up with whoever's available."

"Yes, we do. But we have an agent that's new to counterterrorism, and I want her to learn the ropes from you."

"Her? Ben, I thought you'd evolved beyond that old 'team the chicks up together so they don't bother the guys' technique."

"Ordinarily, I have—and nice try, by the way. But in this case I want her to learn the ropes from you. Did I mention that before?"

"Where is she?"

Timmins slowly rose from his chair, opened his door, and pointed out into the office.

He was pointing at a pert blonde in a very stylish cream-colored suit, sitting with her legs crossed and delicately holding a coffee cup, smiling, surrounded by four equally smiling male Special Agents.

He had to be kidding. "You mean Miss Legally Blonde is my new partner?"

"Yes, Beth, she is. Paul Moody's taking medical retirement after you got him all shot up. So you need a new partner."

"I did *not* get Paul all shot up."

"The fact remains that he did get shot up. He's not coming back, and that is your new partner."

"She looks like she lettered in baton twirling."

"I really don't know. You'll have to ask her. Let's get the introductions done, and then you can coordinate with the other teams rolling on the arrests."

"You know I'll get you for this, Ben. I don't forget, and I don't care how long it takes."

"That particular threat has been communicated before. Come along now."

They walked up to the little group, Timmins saying, "Excuse me, guys."

That only turned off the conversation. Then Timmins stared at them until they left. "Beth Royale—Sondra Dewberry."

Beth almost said: cut the crap and tell me her real name. Except her hand was being shaken, and she was hearing, "Oh, I've heard *so* much about you."

Wonderful, she had blue eyes, too. "I'll bet you have."

"I'll leave you two to get acquainted," said Timmins. Then he scampered off like the little weasel he was.

"Richmond?" said Beth. That deep molasses and honeysuckle accent was unmistakable.

"Why yes. And you picked it up right off."

"UVA?"

"No, Virginia Tech. And yourself?"

"Colombia."

The nose wrinkled up. "Oh, New York. I was almost assigned there out of the Academy."

That just happened to have been Beth's first posting. "What happened?"

"Oh, I managed to get it changed."

I'll bet you did, Beth thought.

"Everyone has been telling me that counterterrorism is just like working the streets."

"That's what nearly everyone in the Bureau thinks," said Beth. "And everyone who thinks that is full of shit."

"Oh."

"That's my entire orientation speech, in case you were wondering," said Beth. "Where are you coming from?"

"Atlanta."

"What did you work?"

"White-collar squad."

Ah, yes, the mean streets of white-collar crime. Beth wasn't

sure she really wanted to know how her new partner had
gotten on a Fly-Away Team with that kind of background.
"Well, we're going to make some arrests today. Ostensibly for
receiving and selling stolen goods and money laundering."

"What goods?"

"Baby formula, mostly."

"That's getting popular on the East Coast, too."

She almost sounded professional there, Beth thought.
"The ringleader also runs a network of sleepers, in our
opinion. But we can't make a case. And if you can't make
a case, then make the news. So while the bosses are in
front of the cameras, we are going to very quietly pick up
the ringleader's brother-in-law. No perp walk on TV for
him. And I'm going to see if I can convince him to be a
C.I., and run him back into the network."

"Is he dirty?"

"Probably peripherally. He knows what's going on, but
we couldn't charge him with anything major anyway. But
that's beside the point. Deportation is what he's going to
be worried about." Beth looked at her watch. "Arrest
briefing's in ten minutes."

"I have to visit the powder room first."

"The powder room?"

"Yes."

As Sondra Dewberry crossed the office, to the accom-
paniment of all the agents leaning over their desks to
check her out as soon as she'd passed, Beth just thought
to herself: the fucking powder room.

"Hey, Beth. New partner?"

It was Karen the Spook, the CIA analyst assigned to
their Fly Squad. And, being CIA among FBI, an outsider.
And maybe because of that one of Beth's best friends.

It came out of Beth's mouth like a warning. "Karen . . ."

Karen was a short, trim, busty, really funny brunette who
walked with a slight limp. She'd been a case officer, one of
the real spies. But some kind of overseas accident—she

claimed it was a car crash, though Beth doubted it—forced her to leave the field and switch to analysis. It had also gotten her stuck with the FBI, which she didn't particularly enjoy either. She'd confided to Beth that she'd never seen so many tight asses in one place before. It was like an insurance company with guns and police powers.

Other than that, Karen liked to say that her only real regret about her accident was not being able to wear high-heeled boots anymore. She'd had an impressive collection, and sensible shoes just didn't make it for her. "So tell me," she said breathlessly. "What's Scarlett O'Hara really like?"

Beth had known this was going to happen. "Karen . . ."

"And what state did she represent in the Miss America pageant?"

"Karen, don't even fucking start . . ."

"Was joining the FBI her way of working for world peace?"

"You know, Karen, we should be ashamed of ourselves. Here we are, women working in a predominantly male environment. And we've got a new sister joining us, whom we should be embracing in the spirit of feminine solidarity. And instead we're acting like a couple of evil bitches."

"You're right," said Karen, staring down at the floor and nodding solemnly. "We should be totally ashamed of ourselves."

"Definitely," said Beth.

Then they both burst into laughter.

"You know what would be fun?" said Karen. "Trying to guess which model Barbie she looks like."

"Yes, it would," said Beth. "God help us."

They were parked at the back of the market.

"Okay, we're not going in," said Sondra Dewberry. "Are we waiting for him to come out?"

"Ordinarily, I'd say yes," Beth replied. "But we've got two carloads full of impatient testosterone waiting to execute the search warrant and rip his office apart. So, rather than argue with them . . ."

She took out her phone and consulted her notebook for a number. "May I speak to Roshan Malik, please? Mr. Malik? Sir, this is Providence St. Joseph Medical Center calling. Yes, sir. Your son Umar has had an accident. He just sprained his ankle, sir, no other injuries. He's being treated as we speak. Yes, he's fine. Your wife is here but she's quite upset and asked us to call you. Yes, sir, in Burbank. I'll tell her."

Beth tucked her phone away. "He'll be out in a minute."

"That's against policy," said Dewberry.

"So is getting yourself or the suspect hurt while making an arrest," said Beth. "Or at least it ought to be." She started the car and moved it across the lot, parking right next to his.

Four minutes later Roshan Malik came rushing out the back door. He was quite tall and his body seemed too thin for his head and hands, which seemed too large for his neck and wrists. He was clean shaven and dressed in a suit. But a cheap haircut and a department store suit. The car was a Honda Accord. Four-cylinder. He didn't spend money on himself, but the kids were in private school.

Dewberry exited out the passenger door right in front of him. "Are you Roshan Malik?"

She'd startled him. "Yes . . . I'm sorry, I don't have time right now." His English had a faint British accent to it.

Sondra flashed her credentials at him. "Sir, I'm Special Agent Dewberry, FBI. You're under arrest."

Anxiety turned to agitation turned to panic. "What? What is this about?"

Dewberry swept her jacket back and placed her hand on her holstered pistol. "Put your hands behind your back."

Everyone has instincts. All different, but they all tell a story. He obeyed her.

Beth had come around the back of the car, behind him. She grabbed his wrist and snapped one handcuff on. Then the other. She frisked him quickly, then turned him around to face her.

"My son," Malik said.

"Your son's all right," said Beth. "He's at school, not the hospital. We just didn't want to arrest you in your place of business." Grasping the handcuff chain, she herded him to their sedan and opened the back door. "Watch your head." She pushed him into the backseat, locked the door, then went around to the other side. She plucked the walkie-talkie from her belt and spoke into it. "We've got him; go ahead."

The other agents moved into the market to execute the search warrant.

"Roshan Malik," said Beth. "You're under arrest for violation of Title 18, Section 2315 of the U.S. Code: sale or receipt of stolen goods. You have the right to remain silent." She read him the rest of the Miranda warning, finishing with, "Do you understand these rights as I've explained them to you?"

"Arrest . . . stolen goods?"

Beth hit it a little more sharply. "Do you understand your rights?"

"Yes, I understand." And then more vehemently, "I have received no stolen goods!"

"Really?" said Beth. "Well, look at it this way. If *we* didn't think so, we wouldn't have arrested you."

They didn't discuss the matter further until they reached the Federal Building. And not even then. Beth had Malik kept in a holding cell for two hours. Then had two male agents bring him to an interrogation room and handcuff him to the bar on the table.

In the room was a television set ready for video playback.

And a video camera on a tripod. The FBI had an unwritten rule that it did not record interrogations in any way other than agents taking notes. The belief was that an agent's word in court was more than good enough. But Beth had seen that raise a few doubts in juries' minds, so she made a point of recording all of hers. She'd never had a confession thrown out or lost a case on appeal, so Timmins let her get away with it. You'd think defense lawyers would love it, but they didn't. Juries loved it, because they loved cop shows and didn't mind seeing a defendant get tricked. And video left no reasonable doubts.

Beth, Dewberry, and Timmins were watching through the one-way mirror next door.

"Okay, he's been simmering nicely," said Beth. "Now it's time to start cooking."

Dewberry started to follow her out the door, but Beth raised a hand. "This needs to be one-on-one."

"You're joking."

"No. You can watch from here."

She left the room, and Dewberry was furious. "Ben, I should be in there with my partner."

"Did Beth want you in there?" Timmins asked. But he didn't wait for an answer. "Then stay here and watch. I've never seen anyone better than her in the room."

"I know how to handle myself in an interrogation room."

"I don't doubt it. And as soon as Beth doesn't, you'll be in the room. When you see how she works, you'll understand." Timmins knew Beth was showing some attitude. But he also knew that one piece of wrong body language, without a word spoken, could blow an entire interrogation. Especially up on the high wire where Beth worked.

Beth walked into the interrogation room and turned on the video camera, checking to make sure the viewfinder was covering everything. Then she unlocked Malik's handcuffs.

This was the time when the real al-Qaeda would start

screaming about being tortured, especially with a camera present. Malik just rubbed his wrists and glowered at her.

"My name is Special Agent Elizabeth Royale of the Federal Bureau of Investigation. You are Roshan Malik, is that correct?"

"Yes."

She was matter-of-fact, but not official or hostile. He was wounded and resentful, the innocent man hounded by the State.

"You have been advised of your constitutional rights and understand them fully, is that correct?"

"Yes. I am innocent . . ."

Beth could sense when someone was about to lawyer up, so she decided to try a new move she'd been thinking about. "You know what you should do? You should remain silent. I'm not going to ask you any questions. You just listen carefully, and I'll tell you what's going on.

"What's going on is, your brother-in-law Shakir is in the room next door, telling my colleagues that you were the one receiving the stolen goods and reselling them in the markets. I was just in there listening. He gave his brother-in-law Roshan a job out of the goodness of his heart. You ran the business for him, you were in charge of all the inventory. He didn't know anything about it."

When a person is angry their face turns red. When they're under great stress the body calls all that blood back to the core to protect itself. Roshan's face was chalk white.

"From our point of view," said Beth, "we really can't argue with that. After all, you *do* run the stores. But don't worry, we don't think Shakir is innocent."

She turned on the TV and showed Malik the warehouse tape. "So you see, no one's denials are going to work."

It burst out of him. "I know nothing of this!"

"Ssshhh. Just listen. Because you know what? *I* believe you. And that isn't some kind of trick. I've been watching you for quite some time. I've been watching your family. Your wife is a fine woman, and you have beautiful children. I think you're a good guy. You care about your family, and you take good care of them. And I think Shakir's the criminal here."

It came sputtering out. "Then . . ."

"But it doesn't matter what I think," Beth said regretfully. "Because all my superiors, and the U.S. Attorney, they all think you're in it with Shakir. They won't listen to me, and you're not going to convince them. And the sad part is, you're not going to convince a jury either. They're going to look at all those videotapes, and believe me we have a lot more. And they're going to ask why, if you're innocent, why didn't all that baby food get delivered by your regular distributors? And it didn't. It got delivered by your brother-in-law's cronies in a rental truck. And you didn't notice? So of course you had to have been involved."

Roshan opened his mouth to speak.

"You don't have to say anything. I think Shakir duped you, told you he'd gotten some special deal somewhere. Something like that. But you know what? You can't prove it, and no one else is going to believe it without proof. It's going to seem like a weak attempt at an alibi instead of the truth. And you're going to prison. And the government's not only going to seize the markets, but also your home in Studio City. And your family is going back to Pakistan."

Beth spread some photos out on the desk. Shakir speaking furtively with various Middle Easterners in various settings. "And why is your family going back to Pakistan? Because of Shakir's associates here. He ran with a very suspicious crowd, people we've had our eye on. Because of all the money he sent back to Pakistan. He sent back a lot of money, and it didn't end up with your family. Like I said, I think you're a good guy, but your brother-in-law wrecked your life."

Roshan Malik covered his face with his hands and began to cry.

Beth got up and left the room.

"He's going to smash the TV and video camera," Dewberry said to Timmins.

"No, he won't," said Timmins.

Beth came in.

"You peeled him like an onion, Beth," Timmins said. "What's next?"

"I'll let him have a good cry and visualize the end of his life as he's known it. Then I'll go back in and save him. Anyone want a soda?"

"Ah, no thanks," said Timmins.

"No, thank you," said Dewberry.

"Okay." Beth left them staring through the window.

She returned to the interrogation room a half hour later with a Diet Coke and a box of tissues. Roshan was haggard, in the depths of personal depression. Beth was all maternal sympathy. She urged the soda and tissues on him. Had him take a drink and blow his nose, just like a little boy. Then he was ready.

"I've been talking to my bosses," Beth told him. "It was tough. They say they've got enough to put you behind bars, so why should they bother?"

"Look at that," Timmins said in the other room. "Now she's the coconspirator with him, against us."

"But look," Beth went on. "You know they're interested in the radical community. They don't care about Shakir anymore, he's as good as in jail right now. But if you agreed to give them information on Shakir's friends, that would interest them. If you did that, I think I can keep you out of prison, and your family in their home."

If you stare into the pit long enough and someone drops you a ladder, you don't stop and read the warranty on the ladder. You start climbing out of sheer relief.

"You have to decide," said Beth. "They won't wait long— they'll put you into the system." She slid a printed form and a pen across the table. "If you waive your right to a lawyer, and your right to silence, I think I can get them to make a deal."

Malik looked at the form, and hesitated.

"No, no," Timmins whispered urgently, as if he were watching a ball game. "Sign it, you asshole."

"But listen to me," Beth said confidingly. "Don't tell them anything until they agree to the deal."

Roshan signed the form.

"Got him!" Timmins exclaimed from behind the mirror.

Beth picked up the form. "Try and relax, and drink your soda. I'm going to go put this together."

"Thank you," said Roshan Malik.

Beth gave him a brilliant smile.

When she came into the room, Timmins said, "I told you once that your session with the Michigan al-Qaeda ought to be a training tape at the Academy. Well, this one tops that. You not only got him to waive before you asked a single question, you put him on the payroll as a human source before you asked him a single question. Any defense lawyer who saw that tape would go outside and blow his brains out."

"Except no one's seeing the tape," said Beth.

"It's now classified Top Secret and going in the safe," Timmins assured her. "Beth, you've done some great work in the room before, but this is the very best."

"Thanks, Ben. Like my dad always said: if you have what people want, the only question is the price. Now I need you to come in and be the hard-ass."

"What do you want me to say?"

"Just come in with the attitude that it's all bullshit. You say: I understand you want to help us. But like you think it's bullshit. Dig your heels in any chance you get. I'll play with my earring if I think we're going down the wrong track. That happens, you say you want to see me outside. And we'll regroup."

"Okay."

An anxious-looking Beth held the door open, and a scowling Timmins entered the interrogation room.

Beth told Roshan, "This is my boss, Supervisory Special Agent Timmins."

"I understand you're prepared to offer us some information?" Timmins snapped.

Roshan looked at Beth, and she nodded encouragingly.

"Yes, sir," said Roshan. "My brother-in-law Shakir . . ."

"I don't care about his brother-in-law," said Timmins, ignoring Malik and speaking directly to Beth. "This man doesn't know anything. He's just trying to stay out of jail."

The naked hope on Roshan's face was now crumbling into despair.

"Excuse me, Mr. Timmins," said Beth. "I think if you'd just give this man a chance, he could provide some important information on his brother-in-law's radical Islamic associates."

"Well?" Timmins demanded.

Beth nodded to Roshan again, with a pleading look, as if imploring him to make it good.

"My brother-in-law Shakir is friendly with a group of men who belong to a mosque in Lodi," Roshan said haltingly. "They are very hard line. Four of them have had military training in Pakistan."

"What, you mean they were in the Pakistani army?" said Timmins. "There are a lot of ex-soldiers running around. I'm one myself."

"No, sir," said Roshan. "They did not receive training from the Pakistani army. They received training at a terrorist camp in Pakistan."

"You mean Afghanistan, don't you?" Timmins said sharply. "A lot of people passed through the Afghan camps before 9/11."

"No, sir," said Roshan. "In this camp they learned weapons. They learned to make bombs. They learned to be terrorists. They went to Pakistan for this. From

Rawalpindi to a camp in Mansehra. Last year." He looked to Beth for approval, and she nodded encouragingly.

"We might be interested in that," said Timmins, still ignoring Roshan and speaking directly to Beth. "We could probably get some time taken off his sentence."

"Mr. Timmins, *please*," said Beth. "This sounds like first-class information. And I'm sure he has more." She looked over at Roshan and he nodded enthusiastically. "Couldn't we find some way to get him immunity?"

"Drop the charges?" said Timmins. "You must be joking. We've got him dead to rights."

Roshan's face fell again.

"Mr. Timmins," Beth implored. "Think about this. He's Shakir's brother-in-law, after all. What if he got in touch with those people? Joined their circle, so to speak. And then let us know what they're doing." She looked over at Roshan again, and he nodded eagerly. "Maybe he could even be the intermediary between them and Shakir?"

"You think he can do it?" Timmins asked skeptically.

"I'm sure he can," said Beth. She looked over, and the hope had returned to Roshan's face.

"I don't know," said Timmins. "If we do this, I'm making it your responsibility."

"That would be fine, sir," said Beth. "I know he won't let us down." She tugged on her earring.

"Let me speak to you outside," said Timmins.

When he turned to leave, Beth gave Roshan an "everything's fine" hand signal.

On the other side of the door, she said, "That was great, Ben. Everything we needed.

Timmins had actually been afraid she was going to jump on his ass about something. He kind of knew how Roshan felt. "He's hooked like a mackerel. What's next?"

"I work fast with him, because I'm sure Shakir's lawyer is going to show up pretty soon. Then I'll talk to the Assistant

U.S. Attorney. When he's arraigned, we'll accept minimal bail. If he doesn't have the cash to make it, we'll put it up."

"I don't think I'd like to have that getting around," said Timmins. "Bailing out our own arrest."

"Bailing out our own informant," Beth replied. "And before they come up for arraignment we'll have to arrange for both him and Shakir to be put in isolation. I don't care about Shakir, but I don't want Roshan to get shanked. Or gangbanged. It might affect his enthusiasm for working for us."

"I don't see any problem with that. Let me know if you run into any. By the way, Beth, since I had to clear this all the way up to the Director, the Director will probably want to see that tape."

Beth shrugged. "What the Director wants, the Director gets."

"It'll be a feather in your cap."

"With all the feathers sticking out of my head, how about a new partner?"

"No."

"Okay, then I'll just be happy with the Director's approval. The last time that happened I got that big-ass thousand-dollar bonus. I paid off a credit card and bought five pairs of shoes."

"Are you questioning the Bureau's generosity, Special Agent Royale?"

"No, sir. Serving my country is reward enough for me. Just don't tell me how much your bonus was."

"Don't worry about that. By the way, Beth, I really enjoyed you calling me 'Mr. Timmins' and 'sir.'"

"Gee, that's great, Ben. I hope you won't be crushed when it never happens again."

Chapter Eleven

Abdallah Karim Nimri carefully watched every move the men in black made.

The leaders checked the four black Ford Expeditions. They checked the cargo. Then they checked each man, his equipment, and his weapons.

They were all wearing black military-style fatigues. Nimri stood out among them in his jeans and T-shirt. The last thing they did before moving out was check all their radios. Nimri noticed that they had top-of-the-line equipment. Each SUV carried two walkie-talkies, a citizens band radio, and a scanner.

It was as professional a mission preparation as any Nimri had seen. These Mexicans reminded him of Chechens.

Nimri got into the backseat of one of the Expeditions. No interior lights came on when the doors were opened. All the vehicles wore Texas license plates. Sitting beside him was a grinning teenager with a loaded 7.62mm FN MAG machine gun resting on his lap.

The driver and the leader slammed the doors behind them. The leader was named Rafael, a handsome man in his late thirties with distinguished streaks of gray in his hair, a dark tan, and straight, brilliantly white teeth.

He leaned over the front seat. "You understand," he

said to Nimri. "You're here only to observe. So you sit and observe. You don't do anything unless I tell you. We run into trouble, stay in the car unless I tell you." He knocked on the window. "Bulletproof."

"Against rifles?" said Nimri.

"That's all we need," said Rafael. He wedged a folding stock AKM rifle between the windshield and the dashboard. The lighter, modernized version of the AK-47. Almost identical visually, seven versus nine and a half pounds. Only poor countries like Pakistan used the old AK-47 anymore.

"You like the Kalashnikov?" Nimri asked. He hadn't been expecting to see any in Mexico.

"It penetrates cars," Rafael said. "The M-16 doesn't."

"Hard to come by?" said Nimri.

"Not for us. They come up from Nicaragua and Colombia."

"If there's trouble," said Nimri, "I know how to use one."

Rafael nodded. "Only if I tell you."

"I understand."

"Your English is good," said Rafael.

"Thank you, so is yours." They had discovered it was their only common language.

"Where did you learn it?" Rafael asked.

"University."

"Where?"

Nimri ignored the question.

Rafael smiled. "Okay. I learned mine at Fort Benning."

"Fort Benning?"

"Georgia. School of the Americas."

Nimri of course knew that the founding members of this gang, Los Zetas, had originally been soldiers in the GAFES, which translated as the Special Air Mobile Force Group. Or more accurately, the Mexican Army Airborne Special Forces Group. Before they'd deserted in 1991 and become the enforcers for the Gulf Cartel.

"The Mexican Army trained us," said Rafael. "Then the gringo Special Forces trained us. Then we trained our sons and nephews. Los Zetitas." He flicked a stern, parental glance in the direction of the machine gun–toting teenager sitting beside Nimri.

The U.S. Army Special Forces had trained GAFES to intercept drugs. Such skills were readily transferable, and Nimri imagined that the other side paid much better. Los Zetas took their name from their unit radio code. There had been sixty-eight founding members, now known as The Black Commandos, and the gang currently numbered more than 700, including former Mexican military and federal police officers. Nimri had been told that they operated training camps in Tamaulipas and Michoacán, where they taught a six-week course in weapons, tactics, and intelligence gathering. "Very professional," he said.

But Rafael was listening intently to a stream of Spanish coming over the radio.

He spoke a command, the garage doors opened, and the vehicles pulled out into the Mexican night. A patrol car of the Nuevo Laredo police department appeared in front of them. As an escort. This was how it used to be in Afghanistan, Nimri thought wistfully. So much easier when you controlled a country. A pity it would be many years before Mexico found Islam.

The SUVs were moving on column, with great dispersion between them. Mexicans were all watching the streets carefully. Nimri said nothing, not wanting to distract them. Los Zetas and the Gulf Cartel had been fighting a bloody gang war with the rival Sinaloa Cartel for control of the border region. Los Zetas took 10 percent from each drug or human smuggling shipment, the ones that they didn't run themselves. Previously these people had paid protection money to local, state, and federal Mexican officials. It was measure of their power, and violence, that now all that money went to Los Zetas. Those who didn't want to pay ended up dead.

Once they were outside Nuevo Laredo everyone relaxed and the column of SUVs tightened up. They drove northwest on Highway 2. The terrain was relatively flat, with a few slight rolling hills. Dry land, arid desert scrub. The farther they drove, the fewer lights from dwellings could be seen off in the distance.

They drove for a half hour at considerable speed. Then pulled off the highway onto a dirt road. All five vehicles stopped.

From his window Nimri watched them take two motorcycles from the back of one of the Expeditions. Dirt bikes. The drivers donned helmets with something attached to the front. Nimri was puzzled until he realized it was night vision goggles. This was confirmed when the dirt bikes sped off into the darkness, showing no lights at all.

"Reconnaissance?" he asked Rafael.

"Reconnaissance."

They waited for another half hour. To let the bikes get out ahead and make sure the route was clear, Nimri thought.

"We'll cross soon," said Rafael. "If anything happens on the other side, stay in the car. If anything happens to the car, stay with me. If anything happens to me, go with them." He gestured toward the driver and machine gunner. "If all else fails, run to one of the other cars. If you lose everyone, then get clear. Follow the North Star. Don't bother to hide. Give yourself up to the Border Patrol."

"You must be joking," said Nimri. Give himself up to the American Border Patrol. What an idea.

"I do not joke. Your documents are clean, yes?"

"Belgian."

"No problem, then. Do not let them know you speak English. They will take you to their station and check to see if the name in your passport is in their computers.

If it is not, they will issue you a summons to appear in immigration court and let you go."

"Now you are joking."

"No, this is the way the gringos do it."

"Even for an Arab?"

"We have brought Arabs across the border before. As long as your name and fingerprints are not in the computer, they will let you go. The gringos catch a million a year coming across the border. They do not have a million jail cells. The Border Patrol calls it 'catch and release.'"

"Catch and release?"

"You know fishing, eh?"

"No."

"Okay, you catch your fish, you have your sport, you put it back into the water. Catch and release."

Incredible. "You are not joking with me?"

"On my life, no."

Nimri cursed himself for not thinking of this years before.

A call came over the radio, and all the Mexicans donned night vision goggles. Rafael handed a pair to Nimri. "So you can keep watch for us out your side."

Nimri had never worn them before. The young machine gunner showed him how to don them, turn them on, adjust and focus them.

It was incredible. Nimri kept lifting them up and down, to go from inky black night to able to see everything. No wonder the Americans had been unstoppable in the Afghan darkness.

The world revealed itself in different shades of green, clear but with a fine snow like a television set with imperfect reception. Like looking through a tunnel, the image seeming to float as he turned his head.

He soon forgot how far the goggles extended from his face, and the end hit the window with a clank. All the Mexicans laughed. Nimri burned with embarrassment.

"A quarter moon is not perfect for the goggles," said Rafael. "They intensify what light there is: stars, moon, whatever. But never forget the gringos use them also. Along with thermal imagers that see the heat."

So the image could be better than this? Amazing.

The police car remained behind. The four Expeditions were moving along the dirt road without any headlights.

The brush became higher and thicker; the dirt road bumpier and narrower. The branches scraped against the side of the SUV.

Soon they stopped, and the Expedition in front disappeared from sight. Although he wanted to say something, Nimri knew he was not the only one who had seen it go. He had no wish to be laughed at again.

The road before them abruptly stopped in a wall of low brush. But they didn't stop, slowly bulling right through it. An upward slope, ending atop a bank. There was water below.

"The Rio Grande," said Rafael.

Nimri had thought the Rio Grande would be the great river of its name. But in the heat of late summer it was nothing more than a stream. The Expedition that had been in the lead was slowly crossing without any trouble.

"A few trucks full of rock, an underwater bridge," said Rafael.

When the first vehicle had crossed they slowly drove down the bank, Rafael passing sharp orders to the driver. There was no grading or ramp for the SUVs. The bank had a relatively gentle slope, and they descended in the ruts made by the tires of the first Expedition.

The driver inched across the river, bouncing and sliding on the wet rock. They had to be large rocks—the tires would have sunk into gravel. Nimri looked down, alarmed because the water was almost to the top of the tires. If water entered the engine they were finished. Something about the bouncing and the goggles were making him feel a little sick to his stomach. He lifted them up to give his eyes a rest.

The feeling went away before they crossed the river, and he pushed the goggles back down. Off to the left he noticed something. It looked like a tall pole with an object on top of it. "Do you see that?" he said, leaning forward and pointing over the seat to Rafael.

"ISIS," said Rafael.

"ISIS?" Nimri repeated, confused. The ancient Egyptian heathen god?

"Integrated Surveillance Intelligence System," said Rafael. "There is a day and night camera on top of the pole. Have no fear. A disaster for the gringos. The few that do not break on their own, we break them."

Up on the bank above them there was something tied to the brush that showed up bright in his goggles. Nimri wanted to ask, but Rafael was now talking on the radio. The driver went up the bank slowly, the engine grinding away, aiming the Expedition right in between the two markings. They went up and over, and once again right through the brush.

"Welcome to the United States," said Rafael.

Nimri felt a thrill. The last time had been in a small boat across Lake Superior, and he had nearly frozen to death. It was much better in an air-conditioned four-wheel-drive vehicle, surrounded by armed men.

"What were those markings on the brush?" he asked.

"Glitter tape," said Rafael. "Shows up in the goggles. No need to cut the brush to make a road for the gringos to see."

"Then this is a regular route?"

"There is no regular route," said Rafael. "If the gringos find this one, they can wait here for us to return for a month if they wish. Only when they get tired and go somewhere else will we return this way."

"Then being random is your technique?" Nimri asked.

"One of them," said Rafael. "The last in our line drags a truck tire on a chain to wipe out our tracks. The gringos plant ground sensors all along the border. They think Mexicans are children. We hire a Mexican electrical engineer to find the frequencies these sensors transmit to the Border Patrol cars. He builds us a transmitter with more power than the sensors, so as we drive through the signal is drowned out. We have people with cell phones all along the gringo side. We know where their patrols are, all the time. Someone fires a few shots in the air a hundred kilometers away, and all the Border Patrol rush there while we get through here. We use all these things together."

"I see," said Nimri. They did know their business. And it certainly seemed to be a business.

Once again the streamside brush turned into a narrow trail. The foliage was much taller and thicker on the American side. Vines draped over the windshield as they drove.

"The Border Patrol doesn't like coming in here," said Rafael. "You never know who you might bump into."

The lead vehicle had halted up ahead. They stopped also, waiting for the other pair behind them to cross.

A quick radio message, and they were off again. The trail widened, and they were able to drive much faster.

Nimri knew they had nearly reached their destination when Rafael took down the AKM and, as all good fighters did, checked that there was a bullet in the chamber—even though he had put it there. He propped the rifle between his knees, barrel pointed at the roof.

Nimri looked up. The trees were even thicker now, and the foliage overhead much more lush. Such a route had to be intentional, to hide them from aircraft with thermal cameras.

The vehicle up ahead slowed. Nimri realized what he had been missing all this time. The brake lights had all been disabled. Not that it was a surprise. If you were going to drive without headlights to remain unseen, brake lights were also unnecessary.

Nimri hated not knowing what was happening almost as much as he hated not being in control. The Mexicans were tensed up and holding their weapons ready. The driver peered through the windshield, looking like an insect in his night goggles.

They let the lead Expedition get a considerable distance out in front. Nimri knew that in an ambush you wanted as few vehicles in the killing zone as possible, and the ones outside free to maneuver against the enemy.

A flash of light up ahead on the road. Nimri lifted his goggles and saw nothing but darkness. The light must be infrared.

They were moving faster now. The lead Expedition was stopped on the road, but with the front end facing them. There was a truck behind it, a small delivery truck with lettering on the side. Nimri couldn't make out the lettering through the goggles.

The driver spun the Expedition around so it was also facing back the way they had come.

The youth with the machine gun got out quickly and disappeared into the brush on the side of the road. Nimri watched men from the other vehicles do the same, forming a cigar-shaped security perimeter around them.

The driver popped the rear hatch. "You can get out and help us if you wish," said Rafael.

Nimri eagerly opened his door.

"Leave the goggles on your seat and stay with me," Rafael ordered. "Do not wander off."

He need have no fear of that. Abdallah Karim Nimri was not about to go wandering off into the Southwest Texas wilderness with no weapon and no real idea where he was.

They all formed a line and passed duffel bags from the Expeditions into the back of the delivery truck. It took only a few minutes. Nimri estimated 20 bags at approximately 45 kilos—100 pounds—each. A ton of drugs. He did not know if it was cocaine or heroin, and had no plans to ask.

In a way it worried him. They obviously moved such quantities on a regular basis. That was an enormous amount of money. To do the job he wanted with equal professionalism, he would have to offer a sum large enough to hold their interest. The Gulf Cartel leader, Osiel Cardenas, was in prison, though he continued to direct his organization. Perhaps they required every possible dollar to prosecute their battle with the Sinaloa Cartel? He would have to think hard on the best approach to make.

Only because it was light colored was Nimri able to see that the delivery truck had the name of a restaurant supply company on the side.

Rafael grabbed him by the arm. "Back to the car. Quickly."

There had been no lights and no sound. The security men collapsed their perimeter at the sound of the engines starting.

The delivery truck drove off first. Only a few moments later, after a series of quick radio calls that Nimri guessed were to confirm that everyone was accounted for, the convoy pulled out.

At the next road junction they turned away from their original route in. Never take the same route coming and going, Nimri thought. Though he neither saw nor heard them, he imagined the dirt bikes were out ahead.

By now the bouncing of the SUV and his lack of familiarity with the goggles had left him seriously sick to his stomach. Nimri knew he could not vomit in front of these men—they would take it as evidence of fear and he would be ruined. He removed the goggles and leaned back in his seat, keeping his eyes closed. Breathing through his nose seemed to help.

As did turning his thoughts to the problem at hand. Los Zetas had to be a part of his plan. To do it himself would be reckless, too much risk of failure. These men knew the terrain; they had their routes prepared; they knew the American border security arrangements. They had intelligence and reconnaissance resources he could not hope to match. And they took no chances.

The Rio Grande was recrossed by a different ford. They were third in line now, the former point vehicle bringing up the rear. The radio came alive as they prepared to go down the bank. Nimri could tell by the tone of the voices that something was wrong.

Rafael snapped out orders to the driver, and he went down the bank much faster than before.

The Expedition in front of them was stalled out in the middle of the water.

"Put your goggles back on and watch the sky," Rafael ordered Nimri.

Nimri obeyed, beseeching God to keep the American helicopters away while they were so exposed.

The driver went into the river and came up behind the stalled Expedition. As the front and rear bumpers of the two SUVs came into contact, he gave it more gas.

They moved forward about a foot, then stopped. Nimri hoped the driver of the vehicle they were pushing had the intelligence to shift it into neutral.

Possibly Rafael had the same thought, because he was issuing orders into the radio.

The driver gave the Expedition more gas. They still didn't move forward, though Nimri could feel their rear wheels digging into the streambed. If they became stuck also . . .

Rafael was shouting at the driver, who eased up on the

gas. He applied it again, much more lightly this time, and they moved forward a few inches.

Now Rafael's tone was more encouraging. They made more progress, agonizingly slowly.

Nimri scanned the sky in between quick glances at their situation. The American helicopters would probably be flying without lights, as they did in Afghanistan.

Finally the front tires of the stalled vehicle went up onto dry land. But when it tilted up, the front end of *their* SUV dropped and slid under the stalled one's rear bumper.

Wedged under the bumper they could no longer push, and in that nose-down position the water was dangerously close to their engine.

The driver shifted into reverse and tried to back away, but that made their front end dig deeper down into the water. And the stalled Expedition began sliding back, threatening to push them even deeper.

Rafael shouted at the driver, who quickly shifted back to drive and reestablished forward pressure.

But now they were both stuck. Nimri decided that if the Americans appeared he would leave the vehicle, no matter what he had been told, and seek cover on the Mexican side. He took another quick look away from the sky. The lead Expedition, which had already crossed, was backing down the bank. Two men got out and hooked a tow strap to the front of the stalled vehicle.

They tried to pull it out. If both vehicles in the river were locked together, Nimri doubted the towing vehicle had enough power, especially on an uphill grade. At least, God be praised, their own engine had not stalled out yet.

The towing vehicle was rocking back and forth, trying to free them. Nimri could hear the sound of grinding metal.

Then the metal screamed at a higher pitch, and the stalled Expedition popped free. The tow vehicle threw up a fountain of sand from its rear tires as it went up the bank.

Rafael shouted at the driver, and he gave it more gas. The engine died. Now *they* were stalled. Rafael was still shouting. Nimri watched the driver cross himself quickly and turn the key again. The engine came to life. More shouting, more gas, and they lurched out of the river.

With all that gas going into the engine they shot up the bank and sailed over the top. Touching ground again, and they were racing right for the back of the stalled Expedition. Rafael was screaming now. The driver jammed on the brakes, and they came to a stop inches from the other Expedition.

The driver crossed himself again. Rafael let his breath out in a loud rush of relief. As did Nimri. The boy beside him with the machine gun had neither moved a muscle or said a word the whole time. He'd kept scanning the sky, exactly as he'd been told.

Nimri gave thanks to God for delivering his servant once again. Now safely back in Mexico, the escorting police car reappeared and everyone turned on their headlights. Rafael collected the night vision goggles, and the Mexicans in the other vehicles crowded around the stalled Expedition, trying to get it started again.

Nimri heard it before he saw it. A helicopter coming down the river. It stayed about five hundred meters inside the American border, just above the trees. Nimri was surprised that all the navigation lights were on.

The helicopter paused and hovered opposite them. Nimri's first impulse was to run, but none of the Mexicans did. Laughing and shouting insults, they extended their middle fingers toward the helicopter. Two unzipped their trousers and waved their penises at it, making the others laugh even louder.

Nimri didn't join in the fun. He pulled his shirt over his head to conceal his face from the cameras he was certain were taping them. He moved closer, so Rafael could hear him say, "The auto license . . ."

Rafael was laughing even louder at Nimri's head covering. "The plates will all be different next time," he shouted.

The helicopter stayed in position for a few minutes more, as if to show it would not be intimidated. Then it continued down the river.

The Mexicans soon gave up trying to get the stalled Expedition running again. Led by the faithful police car, they towed it back to Nuevo Laredo.

It pleased Nimri that their destination was a different garage than the one they'd set out from.

He thanked Rafael for the trip, and left the garage on another blindfolded car ride. He was used to those by now. All that he could make out was that dawn was breaking. That, and he hated Mexican pop music.

It was a long drive—he'd have to check his watch when the blindfold came off. The car finally parked, and he was taken out, stood up, and thoroughly searched. They led him across pavement, then dirt, and what felt and sounded like stone. Inside a building a television was playing loudly, and it smelled of Mexican cooking and marijuana.

Nimri was sat down, and the blindfold taken off. Experienced now, he held his hand over his eyes before he exposed them to the light.

He almost laughed. Almost. Because Persian Gulf sheiks, Las Vegas hotels, and now Mexican drug lords all seemed to have the same taste in interior design. Ornate marble floors, pillars and arches, large carved wooden furniture, and bright, bright colors.

There were the usual bodyguards hovering about. And Nimri's companion Acmed, the al-Qaeda coordinator for Mexico, who had arranged his evening test ride.

And who, from the look on his face, had spent a very anxious time waiting for its end.

In the largest chair sat one of the leaders of the Gulf Cartel, whom they called El Traca. Something about him reminded Nimri of his Chechen friend, though El Traca was much stouter than Temiraev. It wasn't the face. El Traca actually bore a certain resemblance to Manuel Noriega, the former dictator of Panama, though with better skin. No, it was the flat black eyes. Pitiless eyes. El Traca was wearing a silk shirt, slacks, and no socks with his shoes.

He was one of the most wanted men in Mexico, and was free because he paid the police more than the government did. The Americans had a reward on his head. Reason enough to recommend him to Nimri. And, along with the nature of his business competitors, reason enough for all the security precautions.

"Welcome to my home," he said to Nimri.

Nimri was relieved that El Traca's English was good enough to not require translation. In such negotiations small misunderstandings of language often had serious consequences. "Thank you for your hospitality."

"May I offer you something to eat, drink?"

"Just water, if you please." Nimri had learned that Mexicans always gave foreigners bottled water. But if you specifically asked for it they became insulted, as if you were implying that they were trying to make you sick.

It was brought on a silver tray and poured into a crystal glass. Nimri raised it to El Traca. "Thank you."

"I like a man who insists on seeing with his own eyes before he does important business," said El Traca. "My men took care of you?"

Nimri had seen this pose before. El Traca affected the languid air of a supremely powerful man who hadn't a care in the world. But those eyes betrayed him. There was no relaxed indifference there. They bore in on the object of his attention as if prepared for a challenge. "Very well," Nimri replied.

"You have a good time? See everything you need to see?"

"It was very interesting."

"You see how good my men are."

Nimri hadn't grown up in Cairo without learning how to get a price down. "They were good. But we were lucky."

El Traca's air of royalty suddenly abandoned him. "Luck! What do you mean, luck?"

"We were lucky the Border Patrol did not arrive while we were stuck in the middle of the Rio Grande," Nimri replied calmly.

With a stab of one finger, El Traca summoned a lieutenant over to his ear. As the whispered conversation went on, Nimri looked over at Acmed, who was giving him an imploring look in return. Nimri returned nothing but scorn. Every negotiation was a bargain, in one way or another. And this was not the first dangerous, or even crazy, man he had bargained with.

Hearing the story, and having lost some face in the presence of strangers, El Traca was angry.

What he said next, Nimri thought, would guide him on how to proceed.

El Traca didn't put his anger on display with the volume of his voice. He turned cold, staring Nimri down with those snake eyes. "You doubt our skills, why are you here? You don't want to make a deal, go. Leave now if you like."

"I'm sorry you feel that way," Nimri replied pleasantly. "I was looking for a man who hated Americans to help me."

Since Nimri hadn't given him anything to bounce his anger off, El Traca replied sullenly, "Of course I hate the gringos. Who doesn't? You complain about my men, why do you want me help you?"

"I did not complain about your men. I only mentioned what happened. They were very skillful to move the vehicle out of the river before the American helicopter arrived."

Those eyes kept evaluating. "You Arabs are very strange. First you complain, then you compliment. Then you ask if I hate the gringos, and you ask for my help. All right. I hate the gringos. But I don't hate them enough to work for nothing."

Nimri turned to Acmed with an expression of almost theatrical disapproval, and made sure El Traca saw him doing it. "If any of my people was disrespectful enough to suggest you work for nothing, I will shoot them myself." He knew how these gangsters talked. Like Saudis, actually.

El Traca laughed at that. He was on top of his world, controlling millions of dollars. And just waiting for someone to either shoot him or betray him. No wonder even his laughter was mirthless and cold. It was a reminder to Nimri of what was in store if he ever became al-Qaeda operations chief.

"Spoken like a man after my own heart," El Traca said. "Now, what do you want from me?"

"Twenty men, moved across the border, without any problems."

"Twenty of *your* men?"

"I am not prepared to pay for twenty strangers."

El Traca laughed again. "I know who you are, my friend. And I am surprised you still wish to cross the border."

Now Nimri was puzzled. "Why not?"

El Traca motioned again, and one of his men passed Nimri a newspaper. There was something about Russia; a picture of soldiers. "I'm sorry, but I don't read Spanish."

El Traca said something fast and harsh, in Spanish, and his men started rushing about. One returned in a few moments with another newspaper, *The Dallas Morning News*.

Nimri scanned the front page with a sinking feeling of

despair. Chechens holding hostages at a Russian school. How could this be? He set the paper down, trying to think. Al-Libbi. That son of a whore. Faithless, worthless, bastard son of Libyan whore.

Always plotting against him, always attempting to betray him.

Nimri's first impulse was to call the operation off. But all attention would be on Russia. There would be heightened security alerts, of course. But they would already be in place for the election, in any case. Two months . . . enough time for the Americans to relax a bit. "This means nothing to me. We were speaking of twenty men, to cross the border."

El Traca registered first surprise, then respect. "Very well. But this is not like taking twenty farmers from Puebla across the border. Not now. One hundred thousand dollars. Per man."

Nimri made no reaction, other than to please himself by imagining if al-Libbi had been there when the sum was mentioned. "That is very kind of you. But it will not be necessary to transport my men across the border in limousines with champagne, caviar, and women. Therefore, six hundred thousand dollars for all twenty should be sufficient."

While he was talking El Traca had continued to stare him down. But at the end he laughed again. "I like you, my friend. But what you ask will not even pay my expenses. I am not a charity. If you want charity, go to the Church. If you want to pay six hundred thousand, go to Mara Salvatrucha. They are crazy, and not reliable. But they are cheap."

Mara Salvatrucha, or MS-13, was a Salvadoran street gang that operated in many American cities in addition to Mexico. Nimri had actually considered them. And then decided against it, for precisely the reasons El Traca had mentioned. He knew the going rate across the border was

$30,000–$50,000 per man. But that was an argument he did not intend to become involved in. "Some men fly first-class," he said regretfully. "And some must fly economy, and save their money for more important things."

El Traca considered him carefully. "Four million dollars. You want the job done right, that is what you pay."

Nimri folded his hands together and played his card. "I understand the leader of your organization is in prison. Senor Cardenas?"

"You know this," El Traca stated, moving him onward.

"My organization has some expertise, as you know. We would be prepared to offer our assistance in creating and executing a plan to free him."

"*And* execution?" said El Traca, putting all his emphasis on the first word.

"That is correct," said Nimri. "And for a sum of eight hundred thousand dollars, I will require transport for my men from the airport in Monterrey to Nuevo Laredo, accommodation in a safe house, your protection the entire time, then transport across the border on a date that I choose. All twenty at one time." It was nearly three times what the entire Operation of the Blessed Tuesday, 9/11, had cost al-Qaeda. But this was 2004, not 2001, and there would be difficulties enough without stumbling blindly on foot across the desert at night.

Instead of flying into the expected rage, El Traca said, "Documents?"

"They will have their own documents when they arrive."

Now El Traca's stare was much less aggressive, and much more knowing. "You make a deal with me, the deal is final. You make a promise, you deliver. You understand?"

"I understand," said Nimri.

"Then the deal is done. Only if you promise me that I will see your work on television."

"I would not be at all surprised," Abdallah Karim Nimri replied.

Chapter Twelve

For some strange reason Nasser Saleh felt like a little kid waiting to see the principal.

He ought to feel comfortable back at College Park. After twelve years in public schools with the name Nasser Saleh, the University of Maryland was the place he'd felt most at home.

That was really why he was there. He had to talk to someone. It never even occurred to him not to. The only question was who.

His parents would be no help. They'd tell him to do his job and stay out of trouble. His friends the same, but in a different way. He doubted whether any of them could even spell Guantánamo, let alone find it on a map. And secretly he wasn't sure, if push came to shove, how many of them cared about *anything* that was being done to Arabs. The mosque? No way.

He needed someone who would understand, so he drove up to see his old professor of Arabic and faculty advisor, Dr. Jafar al-Hakan.

It wasn't the professor's regular office hours, but Nasser knew he always came back to his office right after lunch. That was when they'd used to talk before, and being invited to do it outside office hours felt like a privilege. It was a good memory. Now the different circumstances made him feel the way he did, sitting on the floor beside that locked door.

The hallway was abandoned during the lunch hour, so he was able to feel the footsteps through the floor first. Catching sight of the professor, he stood up.

Seeing just another student in front of his door, the professor said with more than a little annoyance, "I'm sorry, but my office hours are . . . Nasser?"

Nasser felt almost pathetically glad to be recognized. "Yes, Professor."

As always, Professor al-Hakan was an endearingly roly-poly figure in his always rumpled suit, salt-and-pepper stubble of a beard, and double chin spilling down over his collar. "Nasser, I don't believe it."

"I'm sorry I haven't kept in touch, Professor."

Professor al-Hakan was pumping his hand. "Nasser, no one your age keeps in touch with anyone who isn't a pretty girl. So I'm flattered. Do you need another letter of recommendation?"

Nasser flushed. "Actually, Professor, I need to talk with you. If you have time."

Now he was looking at Nasser a little more closely, while unlocking his office door. "Of course. Come in, come in."

The office was exactly as Nasser remembered it. Still a cluttered mess. Still with that weird smell of Turkish tobacco that wasn't nearly as unpleasant as American cigarettes. The framed Arabic calligraphy on the walls. And the professor still had those same two photos on his desk. One of him shaking hands with Bill Clinton. The other doing the same with Yasser Arafat.

"Sit down, sit down. You look like you have a problem."

Nasser moved the only chair without papers on it close to the desk. "I do have a problem, Professor." He said it in Arabic.

The change in language caused the professor's eyes

to narrow. And to reply, also in Arabic, "Then tell me, if you wish."

Without saying much about his job, Nasser told him about seeing the e-mail from Guantánamo.

"These things have been in the news. But you saw the reports with your own eyes?"

Nasser nodded.

"What is the FBI doing about this?"

"The agents there complain about it. But in Washington they seem to be concerned only with not being blamed."

"I'm sorry, Nasser, but this is difficult to believe."

Nasser handed over the sheaf of papers he'd printed out at home from the jump drive.

The professor spread them out on his desk and read carefully. The more he read, the angrier Nasser watched him become. Nasser felt pleased that they'd both had the same reaction.

The professor got up suddenly and started pacing around his office, the papers in his hand. "Nasser, this is a crime. If you have knowledge of a crime and do not report it, you are culpable."

"Report it to who, Professor? The FBI already knows about it. Those papers are classified. I have already broken the law by letting you see them."

Professor al-Hakan abruptly stopped moving and said, "Wait here."

He left the office and shut the door behind him. It took Nasser a moment to realize that his absentminded professor was walking around with a sheaf of e-mails stamped Secret still in his hand. Feeling sick to his stomach, he charged out the door into the hallway. Standing there, bouncing back and forth looking in both directions like a bobble-head doll, he couldn't see the professor at all.

Nasser's impulse was to run after him, but just as quickly he stopped himself. Run where? And if the professor came back another way, and found his office empty? He might very well go on to his next class. And leave the papers God knew where. Nasser forced himself back into the office, and forced himself to sit down. He felt like he was going to throw up. Or cry. He begged God to help him. And then felt guilty about doing that.

A few minutes later the professor came back through the door, still preoccupied. Nasser shot up out of his chair.

"I am sorry, Nasser. I needed to walk and think in private. I forgot I still had these." He handed the papers back.

Rather than make Nasser feel better, the relief made his stomach roll over in just a different direction. He fought through the urge to flip through the e-mails to make sure they were all there.

"This is very delicate," the Professor said, emphasizing that last word—which had multiple meanings in Arabic. "With your permission, I will consult with a friend in the law school. I will not use your name, but he can advise us of the legal ramifications. If you went to the press, or Congress, the administration would surely try to destroy you. Perhaps send you to jail. You have a good heart, Nasser, not to be silent about this injustice. A brave heart."

Nasser was so relieved to get the papers back that he barely heard the oration. But that didn't last long before the frantic feeling returned. A law professor? This could get out of control. "Please remember not to mention my name or my job to anyone, Professor."

"Have no fear." He shoved a pen and pad across the table. "Here, write your address and phone number. Your cell and e-mail also. I will let you know what I find."

Nasser was even more relived that he didn't have to make any more decisions for the time being. "Thank you, Professor."

Professor al-Hakan shook his hand again. "I am honored you came to me, Nasser. I will not fail you."

Outside the office, beyond the closed door, Nasser checked the e-mails. They were all there.

Chapter Thirteen

Copacabana Beach in Rio is only about three miles long. But most days that strip of bright white sand has a population density to rival Calcutta's. Not as rich, not as chic, and not as safe as Ipanema, it was just packed with virtually naked humanity sizzling in the summer sun. And drinking and eating and making sand castles, and playing volleyball, and surfing and strutting and dancing and flirting. The tourists came to watch the Brazilians and the Brazilians came to watch the tourists. The poor watched those with money, and everyone else stayed the hell away from the poor.

Copacabana was one of the few places where Ed Storey let everyone gather to talk business. Following his rule of always assuming you were under surveillance, why not all show up at the beach separately and throw the towels down in the same general area? Better than meeting in a hotel room with a paper-thin cover story. The roaring throng of sun worshippers made electronic eavesdropping out of the question, and when they were done they could split up and disappear into the crowds.

"I can't believe the SEAL isn't going into the water," said Gary Poett.

Lee Troy tapped his baggy shorts. "I get these babies

wet, everyone's going to be saying: is that a Glock nine millimeter in your pocket, or are you just glad to see me?"

"Yeah, the Glock is a lot bulkier," said Poett.

"A little respect. My mighty equipment puts this Glock to shame."

"With suppressor, or without?" said Poett.

"Suppressor, flashlight, you name it."

"Too bad, then," said Poett. "If you'd worn your thong, you would've fit right in."

"If these Brazilian chicks saw me in a thong," said Troy, "this meeting would be over."

"Speaking of the meeting," Peter Lund interrupted them. "Are we going to get on with it so I can get a beer? I spend all my time in a goddamned van, and I don't get many days off." The surveillance team had paired off and was running twelve-hour shifts. Which for the man in charge meant twenty-four hours some days.

"Okay," said Troy. "Pete needs some liberty. So let's break down what we've got. One Pakistani in charge. Always four Chechens in the house in Glória at one time. They stay for a little less than a week—individually, not together. One goes to Mexico—one arrives from Europe and joins the house party. They never make any phone calls from the house, either hard line or cell. Jan Mohammad makes no calls from his apartment in Urca. But he's got to be talking to someone to be handling all these travel arrangements."

Just as in Paraguay, Sergeant First Class Peter Lund and his support team had been doing the surveillance. "He's supercareful about his physical security. Which is why you guys spiked his car in the first place, so we didn't have to follow him too close. Three times a week he goes to an Internet café. Once we got in there right behind him and took a look at the computer he used. No joy there. He loaded Window Washer onto the computer, and when he was done he wiped out everything. Run history, registry streams, find/search history, documents, Internet Explorer cache, address bar, cookies, and temporary files. The café staff is clueless anyway. Without getting ahold of the computer and physically yanking out the hard drive, we're out of luck."

"Starting to look like we killed all the *stupid* terrorists," said Troy.

"The next time he went to the café, Tommy put on his backpacker clothes and went in right behind him," Lund went on. "Couldn't get too close, but saw he was using Hotmail. Probably an e-mail dead drop."

"Okay, hold up," said Poett. "I know e-mail. I know dead drops. But what the hell is an e-mail dead drop?"

"Latest al-Qaeda wrinkle," said Troy. "Same principle as a physical dead drop: communicate without face-to-face meetings, beat surveillance. Leave your message in a hollow rock or something, put up a signal, your contact picks it up."

"I think I mentioned I know what a dead drop is," Poett said impatiently.

"Try and stay with me," Troy urged. "You set up an e-mail account with Hotmail or some other free service that doesn't require ID. You write your message. But you don't send it, because you know the National Security Agency is always trying to intercept interesting-looking international e-mails. Instead, you save your message as a draft. Your contact knows your e-mail address and password. He logs into your account, reads the draft, and then deletes it so you know he read it. An e-mail dead drop."

"That's fucking brilliant," said Poett.

"It's fucking hard to break into," said Lund. "If we do they just set up a new account and pass the address and password over some message board. Or they'll send their e-mails to look like spam. Penis enlargement shit. And it's not just plain text—they encrypt everything. Strong encryption, too."

"Dead end there," said Troy. "What about the phone?"

"He uses satellite, not cellular," said Lund. "Globalstar. And he does what we're doing right now. Makes all his calls from the middle of a park, where we can't get close enough to him to snag the signal. He goes to different parks, and makes his calls at different times of the day."

"Natural selection," said Troy. "We thin out the herd; only the fittest survive."

"Cellular is easy to intercept," said Lund. "Satellite goes straight up. The way he's doing it, the only way to grab his signal is off the satellite itself. And only the NSA can do that."

"And without a time window and a damn good reason, NSA's not going to allocate the assets," said Troy. "We're too small potatoes."

"Chechens moving into Mexico is too small?" said Poett.

"Washington probably asked the Brazilians for help and got a hell no," said Troy. "Either that or they were too scared to ask the Brazilians for help."

"Nobody wants to get involved," said Lund.

"It's a fucked-up situation," said Troy. "You got a country important enough you don't want to risk pissing them off by running an op on their soil without them knowing about it, and unfriendly enough not to let you run that op on their soil even if al-Qaeda's involved."

"Brazilians probably think they've got enough trouble without getting on al-Qaeda's list, too," said Poett.

"Bottom line," said Lund, "we don't have a lot of credibility these days."

"Bottom line is we get no help," said Troy. "And that's getting to be the plan of the day from Washington. It's up to us if we want to take them down. If it works, it works. If it doesn't, it's our ass."

"Beautiful," said Poett.

"It's always been like that," Troy told him. "Only difference is, we used to get help. Everyone's going batshit about Russia, and South America's still off the radar."

"Makes me nostalgic for the good old days in Ciudad del Este," said Lund.

"It was okay to pull that shit in Paraguay," said Troy. "Fucking place was like Deadwood. We can't go around shooting off RPGs in Rio. No way."

"RPGs?" said Poett.

Everyone suddenly remembered that Poett not only didn't know about Paraguay, he had no need to know.

"Different op," said Troy, and left it at that.

"If we can't drive them out into the open," said Lund, "we have to go in. Hit 'em at zero dark thirty in the morning, when they're all asleep."

"That's a big damn house to clear with seven people," said Poett.

"If all seven go in, no one's covering the outside," said Troy. "So that's a nonstarter."

"The Chechens don't leave the house," said Lund. "Except one trip in from the airport, and one to fly out."

"Ed, feel free to jump in here anytime you feel like it," said Troy.

Ed Storey was lying on his back, pale redneck body glistening with sunscreen. With his shades on he might as well have been asleep while everyone was talking. Except everyone knew Storey would never sleep while they were talking shop. "Y'all are thinking like counter-terrorists," he said.

"Don't anyone say 'what the fuck,'" Troy told them. "He'll make his point sooner or later."

Storey raised himself up on one elbow and gave them all a look at themselves in his sunglasses. "Washington's right. This time, at least. Without bringing the Brazilians on board it wouldn't make any difference if we had a couple of Delta troops to hit that house. As soon as we kicked the door all the local cops and half the Brazilian army would be all over us. Even if we snuck in and used suppressed weapons, *someone's* bound to make some noise. A counterterrorist assault is out. We have to be terrorists instead. And how do terrorists plan operations?"

"Christ, someone besides me please answer him," Troy pleaded. "I've been doing this Socratic dialogue shit for over a year now."

"Okay, they look for vulnerabilities," said Lund.

"Which we haven't found yet," Poett added.

Troy knew how Storey thought, and he couldn't stand waiting any longer. "The Chechens don't leave the house. Jan Mohammad drives everyone to the airport, brings the chow, runs whatever the fuck they do in the week they stay here. Take out Jan Mohammad while he's away from the house, and those Chechens are up shit's creek."

"It would be really interesting to see what they do," said Storey. "They'd probably start using the phones. Emergency numbers lead to people who make decisions. People we want to know about."

Poett was seriously impressed. Storey was one scary motherfucker.

Storey lifted up his sunglasses and closely examined his reddening torso. "I think I'm done. Let's get back to work. Except Pete. Pete can have a beer and see how friendly these Brazilian girls are."

Jan Mohammad was pushing a cartload of groceries out of the Extra supermarket in the Botafogo neighborhood, near the safe house in Glória. The parking lot was scorching hot, and one of the wheels on his cart kept wobbling. He kept shaking it, but it kept bearing to the left.

"Your pardon, senhor?" a voice said in Portuguese.

Jan Mohammad looked up from the cart to the enormous black man in front of him. "Yes?"

"Can you tell me the best turn to reach the Biblioteca National?"

As Jan Mohammad turned to point, Ed Storey appeared behind him and in one fast motion seemed to brush the back of his head.

Jan Mohammad hit the ground in a heap.

Storey and Poett bent over him, Storey slipping the palm sap back into his pocket.

"My God, what happened to him?" said a middle-aged matron from behind her cart.

"He passed out right before my eyes," Poett told her. He and Storey gently turned Jan Mohammad over onto his back. His eyes rolled up into his head.

"Is he dead?" the woman asked.

"No," Poett told her. "Unconscious."

A crowd was gathering.

"The heat?" said one.

"A heart attack?" another offered.

"Call an ambulance," said someone else.

"He'll be dead before *they* arrive," came from the back.

"Help me put him into my car," Poett said to Storey, as if he was talking to a stranger who spoke Portuguese. "I'll take him to the hospital." He rushed to open the back door of his car, which was conveniently parked nearby.

Two other men helped Storey, and they slid Jan Mohammad into the back seat.

"Bless you, son," the matron told Poett behind the wheel.

He smiled bravely at her.

As he drove away, no one really noticed that Storey had gotten into the backseat.

"What a good man," the matron told everyone.

"A true Christian," added one of the helpers.

"God reward him," the matron said.

Feeling good about themselves, the crowd disbursed into the parking lot and went about their business.

Once they were clear Storey dumped Jan Mohammad

onto the floor, taping over his eyes and mouth and cuffing his hands behind his back and his ankles together.

"*Is* he alive?" Poett asked.

"Oh, yeah," said Storey. He spread a blanket over the prostate form.

"You know, these Chechens don't rattle easy," Troy was saying. "If the guy running *my* safe house didn't show for two whole days, I think I'd be shitting the bed right about now."

"But you're a well-known spaz," said Storey.

Troy just swung off onto a different riff. "Maybe. All I know is, I hate vans. Pete, how can you stand being cooped up in vans all the time?"

"Better than freezing my ass off on top of some Afghan mountain," Lund replied, bent over his screens.

"I'll take the mountain anytime," Troy grumbled.

"Here we go," Lund announced. "Just turned their phone on. Eighteen hundred megahertz, GSM cellphone."

Whenever a cellular phone is turned on it emits a control signal, called a handshake, that identifies itself to the nearest network base station. The network determines if the signal is coming from a legitimate registered user by comparing it to its subscriber list. When that's done, the network emits a control signal through the base station that allows the subscriber to place calls at will. All these signals were visible on Lund's screen, and recorded onto his computer drive.

"They're dialing out," he said.

Cellular providers like to tell their customers that, unlike the old days of analog phones that anyone with a scanner could listen to, their modern digital encrypted phones could not be monitored. Which was not true. Radio Shack scanners didn't work anymore, but Pete Lund's million dollars' worth of portable electronics did.

The antenna, receiver, and laptop computer fit neatly inside a briefcase.

A ring tone went off in the van, startling everyone.

"Shit," said Troy.

Storey glanced at Jan Mohammad's cell phone before showing the number to Lund.

"That's it," Lund said. "They're calling Jan Mohammad."

"Jan Mohammad ain't going to be answering," said Story.

"I love this," said Troy.

Everyone turned to look at him.

"Fuck you, I do," Troy retorted. "I love seeing the terrorists get terrorized for a change."

"Well, when you put it like that," said Storey.

Jan Mohammad's cell phone stopped ringing.

Storey checked the screen. No voice mail. "Okay," he commanded the Chechens inside the house. "Now yell at each other a while, then call your emergency number."

"You want to hear?" Lund asked. "They left their phone on."

Troy answered for everyone. "Shit, yes."

Now that he had the International Mobile Subscriber Identity, the fifteen-digit number that was the country, network, and station identification number; and the International Mobile Equipment Identity, which was that phone's unique identification code, Lund sent the unit inside the house a maintenance command on its control channel. This placed the phone in diagnostic mode. Which effectively turned it into a microphone, transmitting all nearby sounds over the voice channel.

All cell phones were capable of this, and there was no way for anyone to tell that their phone was in diagnostic mode until they tried to place a call.

Lund tapped a key, and over the laptop speakers they could hear the Chechens talking.

"I guess they're speaking Chechen," said Troy. "What the hell is that language called anyway?"

"Chechen," said Storey.

"You fucking with me now?" Troy demanded.

"You?" said Storey. "Never."

"You know," said Poett, "even not speaking the language, it does sound like they're hashing something out."

"Oh yeah," Troy said wearily. "They're trying to decide whether to call the emergency number. Don't bet against Ed on that."

Lund recorded it all for future translation. Then the conversation tapered off. "I think they're getting ready to call," he said, remotely cycling the phone in the house off and then back on again, taking it out of diagnostic mode.

The graph on his screen began to register again. "Another call going out."

Storey nodded. Lund never got caught short. It wasn't just the technical side—he was an artist at this.

"Let's see what the phone number is," said Lund. "International access code, they're calling out of the country. Country code fifty-two. Mexico. City code eighty-one. What's that?" He tapped on another laptop keyboard to answer his own question. "Monterrey."

"Damn close to the border," Troy muttered.

"Not picking up," said Lund. "They're leaving a message on the voice mail."

"Smart," said Storey. "The controller keeps his phone turned off, so he can't be tracked. That's probably why they waited until now to call. Controller checks his voice mail a few times a day. This must be one of them."

"It's in French," said Lund. He played the message back.

"Please tell me someone in this van speaks French so I don't have to wait on Washington for a translation," said Troy.

After a pause, Sergeant Sarver said hesitantly, "Just high school."

He left that hanging too long, and Troy blurted out, "Well, do you fucking understand it or not?"

Sergeant Sarver was an electronics technician, not a special operator, and by now nicely rattled by the attention. "Something about his mother being sick."

"Word code," said Storey.

"He says their brother hasn't . . . I guess hasn't been seen for two days. And he wants to know what to do," said Sergeant Sarver. "I think."

"That's fine," Storey said to Sarver, before Troy could get on Sarver's ass again.

"Damn, Ed," Poett exclaimed. "That *was* the emergency call."

"It's one of his little party tricks," Troy explained. "He's always predicting what people are going to do or say."

"You mean guessing," said Poett.

"No, I mean predicting," said Troy.

Storey had his PDA out and was writing something. Then he extended the antenna and held the PDA out the van window, since satellite phones needed line-of-sight to work. And the camouflaged antenna on his PDA wasn't as powerful as the bulky cigar-shaped one on an Iridium phone. After transmitting his message to Washington, he said, "Now Lee's going to ask me what I'm doing."

"Wow, that's fucking amazing," Poett said dryly.

"Let's hope I get my callback before they get theirs," said Storey. "Pete, can you send them a text message and identify it as coming from the number they just called?"

"Sure," said Lund. "I just duplicate their ID codes."

Storey's PDA began to vibrate. Answering the call, his reply came up on the PDA screen. He showed it to Lund. "Send them this as a text message from the Mexican number. Then send the one below as text *to* the Mexican number, from them. As soon as you're done, jam the house so they can't get any more incoming calls."

"Let me have that," said Lund, grabbing the PDA and propping it against his laptop screen. "I want to make sure I send it exactly."

Everyone except Storey looked over his shoulder. The text was in French.

Troy knew Storey had called Washington to get the translation made. "What does it say?"

"For security, move your phone one kilometer and call again," Storey replied. "To Mexico, it's: phone problem—stand by."

Poett was skeptical. "You really think they're going to go for text instead of voice?"

"Yeah, and they used word code to confirm their identities and show they weren't under duress with the voice call," said Troy. "Why wouldn't there be a code for text, too?"

"I'm sure there is," said Storey. "But if you were sitting there and the shit was hitting the fan, and a couple of minutes after you made the emergency call a credible text message came in from the right number, you'd think they were just rushed and rattled and forgot about the code, wouldn't you?"

"Okay, I see what you mean about him," Poett said to Troy.

"You better believe it," Troy replied. "And after Mexico gets that text message, he's going to try calling and not be able to connect. Because we'll be jamming. So he'll buy that, too."

Among his bag of toys Lund had a transmitter that mimicked a cell phone base station and was equipped with a horn antenna to concentrate the signal from a ten-milliwatt power source in a single direction. The signal would trick any phone in the house into thinking it was within range of a new network base station and block it from any genuine stations in the vicinity, allowing Lund exclusive access to send any message he wanted, disconnect a phone, or keep it from receiving any incoming calls.

"Let's be ready to improvise," said Storey. "Whoever steps out to make the call, I want to take him as soon as he's out of sight of the house."

"How do you want to do it this time?" Poett asked.

"He's not going to be a Portuguese speaker," said Storey. "So I think it'll be me and Lee. We'll do a front and back," he said to Troy.

"Okay," Troy replied. "Each end of the street? Who's front and who's back depending on which way he goes?"

"That's it," said Storey. "But don't make him nervous until we're a ways away. I don't want him running back to the house."

"No prob," said Troy.

Fifteen minutes later one of the Chechens left the house. He turned to the right, which put Storey in front of him at one end of the block, and Troy behind.

The Chechen wasn't unschooled, because when he reached the end of the street he checked his back. The traffic was still buzzing by, but there weren't many people on the sidewalks in the heat of the afternoon. So the Chechen saw two couples going the other way, and Lee Troy behind him. Instead of continuing straight he turned left and went down the next block, slowing his pace.

The Chechen stopped halfway down to look in a store window. Out of the corner of his eye he saw Troy appear, look both ways, and turn toward him.

Concerned now, the Chechen started walking faster. So did Troy. The Chechen ducked into a storefront entrance and waited a few moments. When he reappeared Troy was closer. Troy saw him, stopped, and clumsily turned to look into a store window.

Now the Chechen had no doubt he was being followed.

Which happened to be exactly what Troy wanted. Once you know someone's behind you, that's where your attention is fixed. The Chechen was looking back over his shoulder at Troy, and Troy was driving him right into Storey.

The Chechen was moving again. Quickly, almost skipping down the sidewalk.

Troy was pleased. He could practically smell the panic.

The Chechen bolted. But he didn't go in the expected direction. He sprinted across the street. Two cars jamming on their brakes had a nice little fender bender. Horns blew in rebuke.

Shit. Troy took off after him. He didn't see Storey. And if Storey hadn't seen this they were in trouble.

The Chechen had stopped the traffic, and Troy made it across the street before it got going again.

The Chechen was in a flat-out sprint. With the lead he had Troy didn't think he could take him over the next couple of hundred yards. But if he kept it near the aerobic threshold the Chechen was bound to run out of gas first. Troy didn't think Chechens were used to running ten miles at a shot the way SEALs were.

Troy thought they'd be attracting a lot of attention, but that wasn't happening. Mugging was the national sport, after soccer, and men running after each other in the streets wasn't all that uncommon. Pedestrians saw them coming and got out of the way, but that was it.

Troy had now closed the gap to less than twenty yards, and the Chechen could feel as well as hear him behind.

Troy knew he'd have him before the next intersection. The Chechen knew it too, and made a hard turn into an alley.

Troy yelled, *"Halto! Polizia!"* but the Chechen wasn't having any of it.

There was a gate across the alley. The Chechen went over it. Shit, this wasn't the right situation to go flying over gates. Troy pulled up short and quickly ducked his head over. No Chechen in sight. The alley was over a hundred yards long—no way he could have made it to the end. Troy looked up—no one going up the fire escapes. He reached inside his shirt, got ahold of the Glock, and gave the pistol a sharp twist to release it from the shoulder holster. He was all ears now, listening for the sound of a door along the alley. Those steel doors were going to make noise if opened. Or knocked on to be opened. It was Rio—alley doors weren't left unlocked.

This wasn't a one-man job, unless you were suicidal. Keeping one eye over the gate, Troy dialed Storey on his cell phone.

"What?" Storey's voice told Troy he was running.

"Did you see which way I went?" Troy whispered.

Storey had stopped. "I'm paralleling you on the next street over."

"Two intersections up," Troy whispered. "There's an alley before you get to the third intersection. We're both inside—he's playing possum. I'm behind the gate. You need to close off the other end."

Storey was running again. "I think I'm past it. Hang on."

With the tall buildings and afternoon sun in descent it was almost as if the alley was in twilight. Troy realized that Storey might not be able to see an arm waved over the gate. But he could easily see the bright alley exit onto the street.

A half minute later a head cautiously poked around the corner. "You're there," Troy whispered.

"Okay," Storey whispered back. "You sure he's still around?"

The fuck. "No, I'm not. I'm going over the gate, and off the net."

"Okay."

Troy tucked his phone away. He breathed to settle himself. Go over left or right? The alley was an ambusher's paradise. Some of the doorways had columns holding up metal rain roofs. Some had stairs going down to basement doorways. And there were trash cans and bigger metal Dumpsters lined up all along both walls. If the Chechen was right-handed like the majority of the population, he'd probably stopped along the right wall so he could shoot with his body behind cover. A crossing shot would be easier for him, so Troy decided to stick to the right side, too.

He took a few steps back for a running start and then went over, one hand atop the gate and the other holding the pistol. As soon as he touched ground he ducked behind the nearest Dumpster.

No shots fired. That wasn't good. If the Chechen was still in the alley, it meant he'd kept his cool and was waiting for a sure hit.

Troy couldn't just dash from cover to cover. He had to come up on the opposite side of the alley from the nearest obstacle, carefully, trying to see what might be behind it before he committed himself.

The low light and shadows didn't make it any easier.

Troy halted all his inner decision-making dialogue and shifted every last bit of concentration toward his senses. This was hunting, except between two predators who could both be prey. Whoever heard the sound or saw the movement first was going to live.

Troy made sure his footfalls were silent. The first Dumpster loomed up. Was he waiting behind it? Troy had his pistol out in front, locked in his hands, front sight following his eyes. He inched forward, and bit by bit the far side of the Dumpster was revealed. Nothing. He grabbed the side door and threw it open. No other sound. He bobbed his head into the opening. Nothing but trash.

Shit, this was going to take forever. Or if he moved faster he was going to get killed. Or after he went by, the Chechen was going to come popping up out of one of the Dumpsters and shoot him in the back. Or if he kept sticking his head inside them he was going to get it blown off. Shit.

A row of small metal trash cans next. From the cover of the Dumpster, Troy fired a round into each one. The sound of bullet hitting metal was louder than the hissing *pfft* of the suppressor and the snap of the slide cycling back and forth.

Maybe he could flush the game. Moving now, Troy snatched the lid off the last can and hurled it like a Frisbee at the next Dumpster. It sounded like a gong being struck. The sound echoed away to nothing. No sound from inside the Dumpster. Troy took a step forward and was engulfed in a wall of black, deafening sound and a gale-force wind.

It threw him to the ground. But the adrenaline was pumping, and he drove himself back up to his feet. Whoa, there was smoke everywhere and the alley was wobbling around. A hand grabbed his arm.

Storey knew you never asked someone if they were all right. They always said they were even if they were missing an arm. Instead he looked for blood. Finding none, he guided a woozy Troy back to the alley gate he'd jumped over. "Okay, up and over," he said.

All Troy needed was a little guidance, and instinct took over. He pulled himself over and dropped to the other side. His head was clearing, and he looked back over the gate. The smoke was wafting away. The top of the Dumpster was gone; the metal sides were bulged out and split down along the seams like a peeled banana.

Storey grabbed Troy's pistol, stuck it back into his holster, and led him out of the alley. People were running up to see what had happened, and Storey picked up the pace to get them clear.

Four blocks away Troy's wits had returned, and Storey sat him down at a bus stop bench.

"A grenade?" Troy asked. His hearing was still a little tinny. He opened and closed his jaw to see if that would improve things.

"In this particular case impatience served you well," said Storey. "He must have jumped into that Dumpster. And if you didn't pass him by he was waiting to take you with him. I reckon that trash can lid sounded like you opening the door, and he let go of the spoon."

So he *had* flushed the game. But like most things in this

business, the final result didn't much resemble the plan. Troy looked himself over. Other than his clothes being messed up, and stinking of burned explosives, he was okay. "Dumpster must have absorbed most of the shot."

"That wasn't exactly the outcome I was hoping for," Storey observed. "But no blood, no foul."

"You mean none of our blood."

"That's always my aim."

"I'd rather have taken him alive."

"My fault," said Storey. "Every time I go light on the planning something like this happens."

"Couldn't be helped." Troy knew Storey was genuinely annoyed with himself, though as far as he was concerned *he'd* been the one who screwed up the snatch. "We had to get them to do something before Mexico called back."

"We can't risk anything like this for those last three," said Storey. "You sure you're all right?"

"Yeah, I'm fine."

"Okay. I don't want to retrace the route of our little chase. I see a bus coming. Let's take it and clear the area. Then I'll call Poett to come get us." He bent over to check Troy's ears and nose. No blood, so hopefully no concussion. "How many fingers am I holding up?"

"One," Troy groaned. It was the *middle* finger. "And fuck you, too."

"You seem normal to me," said Storey.

There was a crash of nearby thunder, and dark clouds were building up overhead.

"I needed to cool off anyway," said Troy.

"I expect I do, too," said Storey.

There was a pool on how long it would take before the three remaining Chechens picked up the phone and called Mexico again.

Troy had chosen the soonest time. One hour. And

was seriously ticked off when that passed. "Don't these assholes watch the news?"

Storey said, "If you don't speak the language, what's an explosion in an alley going to tell you?" He'd guessed three hours, and was proved wrong.

Poett took three and a half. No dice.

The technicians chose increments between four and five, and were disappointed.

Lund had picked seven hours and forty-five minutes. And at seven hours and fifty-five minutes after the Chechen left the house to make his phone call, he announced, "Cell phone just came on."

"Son of a bitch," said Troy, looking at his watch.

"If they try to dial out, let it go through," said Storey.

"Why don't we send them some more text?" Troy suggested. "Tell them to do exactly what we want instead of sitting around with our thumb up our ass?"

"I thought about that," said Storey. "But they're going to be mighty paranoid right about now, and I don't think they'd go for it. Instead of us telling them what to do, we should step back and let the guy in Mexico try and manage the situation."

"We could harvest some good intelligence off that," said Lund.

"Suppose the guy in Mexico tells them to split up and run?" said Troy. "We'll either have to cowboy up or risk losing one or two of them."

"I'll take that chance," said Storey. "The way this thing has been set up, these guys are not experienced operators. If they run, they'll run together. Either that or Mexico's going to send someone to get them out. I'd like that. The more the merrier. We'll let them do the work."

"They'll probably do exactly what we don't want," said Troy.

"Maybe," said Storey. "But I'm thinking if we get Mexico

all riled up, it might knock them off their timetable. Maybe even make them call off their operation."

"That I didn't think of," Troy conceded.

"Dialing Mexico," said Lund. "Same number."

This time they didn't need Sergeant Sarver and his high school French. Lund had managed to hijack a wireless Internet connection from the van. So everything his equipment was picking up was being sent online, encrypted of course, to a French-language DIA translator at Fort Belvoir, Virginia. Who would be listening and translating in real time, just like TV closed captioning.

The Chechens left another voice mail.

The DIA translated it immediately: Uncle George is still very sick. Please call as soon as you can.

"I guess Mom got better," said Poett.

"After this long a wait, Mexico's going to be stone suspicious and definitely not wanting to make this call," Storey predicted. "But if the code's right he's going to have to."

At three minutes past eight a call came through to the house, and was answered on the first ring. The operators crowded around Lund's laptop screen to read the conversation.

Mexico: Hello?

Brazil: I send you greetings from your Uncle Thomas.

Mexico: Is my Aunt Catherine well also?

Brazil: She is well.

"Okay, that's the identification," said Storey. "Probably a duress code too, in case someone's talking with a gun to their head."

Mexico: Why have you not called?

Brazil: There was no call?

Mexico: No. What happened?

Brazil: He who left to make the call has not returned.

Mexico: Not returned? From this afternoon?

Brazil: Yes.

Mexico: How many have not returned now?

Brazil: Two.

Mexico: Two have not returned? Two have left the house and not returned? Is that correct?

Brazil: Correct. What shall we do?

Mexico: Do you see anything?

Brazil: We see nothing. But what else can we think?

"No shit," said Troy. "I'd be thinking my ass was pretty much surrounded right about now, too."

Mexico: You see nothing?

Brazil: Nothing.

Mexico: Hold the line.

"He's thinking it over," said Storey. "Can't you feel the paranoia? Watch him wrap this call up double quick."

"Rescue or write-off," said Troy. "If he's smart he'll write them off. I can't wait to see how he's going to do it. Wish we had some popcorn."

Mexico: Are you still there?

Brazil: Yes.

Mexico: Pack quickly. Discard any mementos. Go to the airport and wait. I will fly in to get you.

"Bullshit," said Troy.

Brazil: How should we get to the airport?

Mexico: Take a taxi, you fool. And take precautions on your journey there. Leave immediately. Wait at the airport. Do not call again—I will be flying to you. Or I will call. Do you understand?

Brazil: We understand.

Mexico: Until we meet again.

The connection clicked off.

"You know, it would be poetic justice to leave those assholes sitting at the airport for the next year," said Troy. "Because sure as shit no one's going to be flying in from Mexico to get them."

"If they were a little less desperate, they'd be thinking the same thing," said Storey. "But what are they going to do, stay in the house and sooner or later starve to death?

They'll go to the airport. Either to wait, or, if they got enough money or a credit card, to catch the next flight leaving to anywhere else."

Lund was racing away at his computer. "Okay, I've got the Mexico network base station ID from the incoming call. Good old Telcel." He scrolled down, searching all his databases, then said triumphantly, "The cell phone number is Monterrey. But this call was made from Nuevo Laredo. Don't ask me to narrow that down any more, but the base station it came through was definitely in Nuevo Laredo."

"Motherfucker," said Troy. "That's *right* on the border."

Storey rubbed his eyes. "We got to get this done quick."

"You want to borrow a cab?" said Troy. "Have Gary give them a ride?"

Poett didn't think that was such a smoking red-hot idea. But before he could say anything Storey came to his rescue.

"These boys are going to be ready to blow themselves up as soon as they step out the door," he said. "Let's see if we can all keep from getting taken along on *that* ride."

"Hey, I would've written you up for a medal," Troy said to Poett.

"Thanks," Poett replied.

"Drive by?" Troy said to Storey.

"I reckon that's best way," said Storey.

Troy sat down at one of the laptops. "You start scheming, I'll get this intel off to Washington."

Lund was counting the thirty dollars he'd won in the pool.

Watching him, Storey said, "Pete, what made you go with them waiting that long to call?"

"I figured the controller checked his voice mail on either a four- or eight-hour window," said Lund. "And that the Tangos inside the house were afraid of getting in trouble if they called Mexico and a minute later their boy walked back through the door because Mexico sent him off to do something."

"Good thinking," said Storey. "Stay on top of them, Pete. I'll need to know fast if they make another call, like for a cab."

"I'm always on top of it," Lund said testily.

Storey was feeling the effects of cramped quarters and twenty-hour days, too. He grabbed Lund's shoulder and gave it a hard squeeze. "I know you are, Pete."

An hour later the SOPHIE thermal imager showed three human figures glowing bright white against the cooler sidewalk and parked cars. "They got their bags," said Troy. He, Storey, and Poett had vacated the surveillance van for one of the pair of emergency getaway rental cars they'd stashed nearby. Except in special circumstances, like Paraguay, a van wasn't the preferred vehicle for high-speed escapes.

Troy was in the passenger seat and pointing the imager, like a large bulbous pair of binoculars, through the windshield. The light rain that was falling didn't affect the thermal image the way it would a night vision scope.

"They must've taken that no calls order literally," said Storey, in the backseat. "I guess they're planning on hailing a cab on the street."

"After all this, *I'd* think if I called one, the cops would be driving it," said Troy. "Shit, the way they're moving, we're pointed in the wrong direction."

"I don't want to drive past them and have to turn around and come back," Storey told Poett, who was behind the wheel. "Get us around the block before a cab shows up for them."

Driving like a Rio native, Poett popped a U-turn in the middle of the street. He stepped on the gas to get up to the next intersection, made a hard left against traffic, sped down the cross street, then another hard left. Now they were racing parallel to their original street. Another left and they had almost completed the square. Except this was a main street, and much busier. Poett stood on his brakes as he almost got broadsided by oncoming traffic. Someone was yelling out his window, but Poett bulled his way into the line of cars.

Storey gave the thirty-round magazine of the MP-5K submachine gun a slap to make sure it was seated properly, and drew the bolt back a half inch so he could see the gleaming brass 9mm round in the chamber. Finally a little twist to make sure the sound suppressor tube was attached tight to the barrel.

Poett was getting frantic, because they were stuck trying to make a left back onto that first street. Traffic wasn't stopping, and there were no gaps in it for him to make the turn. Goddammit, it wouldn't be long before the three of them made it out to the intersection or a cab came along.

Poett was pouring sweat; the back of his shirt was stuck to the car seat. He was not going to be the reason the Chechens got away.

"C'mon, go for it," Troy said between gritted teeth. His MP-5K was resting on his lap.

Spying the slightest of gaps between cars, Poett gave it the gas and leaned on the horn. He made the turn, hearing skidding tires and horns behind him but no sounds of a crash.

Now they were driving on the same side of the street the three Chechens were walking on. The wipers were beating against the windshield. Poett nearly had his nose against the glass so he could see. There they were. Seemed to be in their twenties. No beards.

As Poett came up on them, Troy said, "Normal speed, not too slow." A metal click as he flicked off the submachine gun's safety.

The Chechens' hands were in their jackets. Their

faces were grim, as if they were waiting to be halted by lights and bullhorns.

Troy shifted slightly in his seat, left foot braced on the floorboard for the stop. "Now!"

Poett drove his foot onto the brake. Troy and Storey leaned out their respective windows.

Storey's field of fire was blocked by the roof of a parked car. He grabbed for the door handle.

Troy picked up the nearest one on his front sight and slapped the trigger down. With the suppressor on it was just the metal clacking of the action cycling back and forth. Three-round burst, shift to the next target, three-round burst.

The Chechens had turned sharply at the squeal of tires on wet pavement, but by then it was too late. Two spun and went down, obviously hit. The third? The third had also disappeared from sight.

Storey was out on the street, cutting between two of the cars parked in a tight row along the curb. Trying to stay at least fifteen yards away, the effective casualty radius of the average hand grenade.

He ducked his head underneath the nearest parked car, looking for the telltale sight of legs to point their location out to him. Dammit, the raised curb didn't let him see anything.

Storey crouch-walked around the back of the car. A flash of movement off to his right. Someone was running for the nearest house. Away from the streetlight it was too dark for Storey to see his sights; he swung his body and the weapon at his shoulder came along like an extension of himself. When his eyes and the barrel caught up with the running figure he fired two fast bursts. The figure stumbled, went down on the grass. Storey fired again. Then he swung back down along the line of the sidewalk. Looked like two of them huddled up behind the car. Storey fired a longer burst into both of them.

Then he heard something metal hit the concrete sidewalk right beside him.

Storey pushed himself up, lunged into the gap between the two parked cars, and dove over the hood of one out into the road, twisting his body in midair to land lengthwise behind the front tire.

The *whap* and shock wave of a grenade explosion. Dark smoke bloomed up; the blast rocked the car back and forth on its tires.

Storey loved using grenades because they knocked the other guy out of his game plan. He hated being on the receiving end for the same reason. Angry, he jumped back to his feet. He cut back between the two parked cars, changing magazines. Leaning out, he fired another long burst into the two bodies down on the sidewalk, then finished off the magazine on the figure lying on the lawn. Houselights were popping on all along the street. That settled it—no searching bodies and taking fingerprints tonight. Storey jogged back to the car. "Let's get out of here."

Poett burned rubber obeying him.

As soon as Storey made his move Troy had automatically stayed in the car to cover the street. Of course he'd noticed that his partner hadn't given the Chechens the usual final two in the head. "What if someone's still alive?"

"They can explain everything to the cops," Storey replied tersely.

Troy leaned over the front seat. "I can't believe you saw that frag coming in in the dark."

"I didn't," Storey replied. "I heard it. I was just lucky it landed on the sidewalk instead of the dirt."

"I wish people would stop selling grenades to terrorists."

"This whole day has been a little less professional than I would have liked," Storey commented mildly.

Troy just smiled, knowing his partner would keep

playing it out in his head until he'd identified every wrong move.

Lund and the other surveillance pair that had been watching the back of the house were already checking out of their hotel rooms. They'd head right to the airport, turn in their rented vehicles, and fly out under diplomatic passports.

Storey, Troy, and Poett dumped the car a mile away, leaving it unlocked and the keys in the ignition to ensure it would be stolen. They transferred to the very last rental car.

"Where to?" Poett asked.

"Just head north," said Storey. "We've got to get rid of some stuff."

While Poett drove north Storey and Troy broke down the submachine guns. Whenever they saw a sidewalk trash receptacle Troy got out and threw some parts in—a bolt here, a trigger group or magazine there. Since they were a ballistic match with the bullets in the Chechens the MP-5Ks had to go, but Storey didn't want to make anyone a gift of any intact automatic weapons.

Passing the Praça XV square, Poett turned left onto a side street near the Ordem Terceirao do Carmo church and Troy got rid of the last of the parts.

Poett had been ready for it. He'd been watching it. But it had still jarred the shit out of him. He was glad to be driving, because his hands had been shaking ever since leaving the van. He'd been in the Army for fifteen years and had never seen a weapon fired outside a range or someone killed in front of him. Storey had been out of the car before he'd even processed what was going on.

And he and Troy had already calmed down like nothing had happened. Storey was checking the car floor with a flashlight for anything they might have missed. They didn't leave anything to chance, and didn't trust anyone with the crucial details except each other. It pissed Poett off, but it also made him yearn for their respect. Of course, Storey's compliments were always perfunctory, like he was just making them for the sake of your morale.

The rain had stopped, and clouds had begun to break. As Poett turned the wipers off he chanced to glance up. Christ the Redeemer was looking down on him from atop Hunchback Mountain, the statue lit up like ivory in the night sky.

Troy got back in the car. "That's it."

"Good work," Storey told Poett.

Poett had to chuckle. Yeah, it did sound perfunctory.

"What?" Troy asked him.

That made Poett chuckle even harder. Storey never would have asked that question. If you didn't want to tell him why you were laughing, and he couldn't figure it out, then it was none of his business. "Nothing," he told Troy.

Troy shook his head, and said to Storey, "I'm still tempted to check out that house."

"And get caught in there when the cops start swarming all over the neighborhood? No thank you. The CIA can go over the house to their heart's content. If they want to."

"Ah, the CIA," said Troy. "What comes next is Ed's favorite part of every op. Right, Ed?"

"I was thinking of having you do it this time," said Storey.

"No way," Troy said happily. "Senior man's job. Gotta be the senior man."

Troy's unconcealed joy had Poett smiling, even though he was in the dark. "What's he talking about?"

"Happens every time we have to send back a prisoner or some shit in the diplomatic bag," said Troy. "Didn't happen in . . . our last job, but that was a special case. Happens everywhere else. And it's going to happen this morning."

"*What?*" Poett demanded.

"Ed gets his ass reamed by the CIA Chief of Station," said Troy. "If you could bet it in Vegas, we'd all be retired now."

"The Chief of Station's at the main embassy in Brasília," Storey lectured. "This one's just a lower-ranking guy who runs their shop at the consulate here."

"Is that better, or worse?" Poett asked.

"Worse," said Storey. "The Chief of Station pisses on your leg just to get it out of his system. Lower level pisses on your leg thinking you're actually going to do what they say."

"And since you ain't going to do what he tells you," Troy added, "you might as well wear your wet-suit bottoms."

"Can I come along?" Poett asked. It sounded like something to see.

"He's already met me," said Storey. "I don't want him getting a look at anyone else."

Troy said, "If he had a shit fit when you dropped Jan Mohammad in his lap, this is going to be a thousand times worse."

"He weren't too pleased then," Storey confirmed. "And he won't be now."

The head case officer in the Rio Consulate was posing as one of the commercial attachés. The name on his office door was Crozier. In such circumstances that was usually the truth.

Storey got to the embassy at 8:00 A.M. The CIA guy rolled in around 9:30. And kept Storey cooling his heels until 10:30.

Crozier was in his mid-thirties. Mustache. Soft. The kind that looked like he smoked a pipe, whether he did or not. Just the sight of Storey back at the consulate was enough to get him going. Because his Chief of Station had been, to put it mildly, very upset to hear that the military had dropped off his al-Qaeda counterpart in a basket on his doorstep, with everything except a note pinned to it saying he needed a good home. That had not been a happy call over the secure phone.

Then he had to tell his Chief of Station that this Army Sergeant, who seemed to be making a career out of embarrassing Chiefs of Station all around the world, had lost his CIA surveillance ten minutes after leaving the consulate by the simple expedient of turning in his rental car with the CIA-installed tracker and disappearing into the streets. That was an even worse phone call.

When Storey handed over the keys to the apartment in Urca and the safe house in Glória, the fireworks began.

"You just forgot about these when you dropped off the Arab, is that it?" said Crozier.

"He's a Pakistani, sir," said Storey. Who was standing, though of course not at attention.

That didn't touch the match to the fuse, but it did light the match. "And I don't suppose you know anything about someone getting blown up by a hand grenade about a mile from this house in Glória, do you?"

"News to me, sir," Storey said.

"Or what about the three guys who got machine gunned just down the street? Not to mention another grenade going off."

"I'm in the dark, sir. What happened?"

"I want a complete briefing on everything you've been doing in Rio. Not on paper later. Right now."

"No, sir," Storey replied politely.

"What the hell do you mean, no sir?"

Storey looked him directly in the eye, and answered in the same polite tone. "I mean that just because I call you sir doesn't mean I work for you. I answer to my chain of command. If you want a briefing, you need to take it up with them. Sir."

Crozier came up out of his chair. "Who the fuck do you think you're talking to, *Sergeant*? Don't think I haven't heard about you."

"I haven't had the same pleasure, sir," Storey replied cordially.

"So you think you can just drop an Arab in my lap, and some house keys on my desk, and I'll clean up your mess for you?"

"My orders were to deliver my prisoner and the information on his residences to you, sir. What you do with him and his apartment and safe house is up to you and *your* chain of command."

Storey was of course implying that his report was going up the chain, and it might be a good idea for Crozier if it bumped into his somewhere along the way.

Storey added, "Since I've executed these orders, sir, is there anything else before I leave?"

Crozier sat back in his chair, defeated. "Just get out. Not just my office. Get the hell out of Rio, and the hell out of Brazil."

If Crozier had been looking carefully, which he wasn't, he might have seen a little crinkling of amusement around Storey's eyes. "Then good morning, sir."

He met Poett back at the only hotel room they hadn't checked out of yet. Troy hadn't returned from turning in the last rental car. Storey never liked to do it at the airport.

"How did it go?" Poett asked.

"Just like Troy said," Storey replied. "Same song and dance. Not even worth remembering." Which was not strictly true. He actually used the digital recorder in his PDA to record every conversation he ever had with every CIA officer. And with military officers giving him verbal orders. He knew he'd burn, and burn good, if he ever got caught doing it. But after nearly twenty years in the Army and seeing quite a few good men burn, Storey had learned that honor and integrity were personal characteristics, not institutional ones. He kept the recordings in a very safe place, and never told anyone about them.

"And this happens all the time?

"Just like handling officers," said Storey. "The last one to get mad wins. They rant and rave—you just talk to them like you're the most reasonable fellow in the world."

"I never mastered that. I always get pissed."

"You just got to keep it all business. If you're right, you make the case. If you're wrong, you admit it. He talks bad about your momma, well, he don't know your momma. You care about what he's saying, but not what he's saying about *you*."

"That's hard," said Poett.

Storey nodded solemnly. "But it's how you win."

Poett didn't quite know what to say to that.

"Before Troy comes back," said Storey, "I want you to know that you really did an outstanding job on this trip. The whole way through. I'd work with you again in a heartbeat."

"Thanks," was all Poett said. Mainly because he felt like crying. And wasn't quite sure why. Maybe because it had that kind of impact when someone didn't give it up that easily.

Storey went in the bathroom to clean up. Poett knew he'd come out with his appearance totally changed for the flight home.

The shower was on when Troy returned.

Poett told him what Storey had said to him. "Did he really mean that, or was he just playing me?"

"If Storey gave you props he meant it," said Troy. "But as far as answering your question: you figure that out—you win the lottery."

"You two work together pretty good," said Poett.

"I think you noticed—we are definitely the odd couple. But man, we *operate* together. And we do get along. I love giving him shit. And he loves ignoring me while I do it. Then he'll give it back to me, in that desert-dry Storey way. You won't even know he tagged you until you feel yourself bleeding."

"I saw a little of that. Not much."

"When he's working Storey's like an all-star goalie—nothing gets past him into the net. And if something does, he doesn't get over it easy. Off duty he takes things a little easier. A little. But whenever you think you've got him figured out he always surprises you."

"He's scary good."

"He's the best I've ever seen." At that Troy smiled wryly. "And I do *not* make a habit of talking about the Army that way. Thing is, he's not only getting it done—you start thinking about shit, and you realize he's been training you to take over your own team all along."

"You know, that cracker accent kind of messed me up at first."

Now Troy started laughing. "Same."

"Every other white master sergeant I ever worked for, he'd get all paranoid thinking the two brothers were going to get together and start plotting against him. But Storey's not that way at all."

"Old Storey wouldn't even give it a thought," said Troy. "But if he ever did decide we really *were* getting together on him, two things would happen. He'd make sure he was right, and then you wouldn't want to be us."

"No," Poett said thoughtfully. "There's a Pakistani and four Chechens who'd give you their testimony on that."

Chapter Fourteen

It was late enough in the morning that the 110 Freeway through Los Angeles wasn't the nightmare it had been during rush hour. They were driving south, toward San Pedro Bay.

Beth Royale had been sneaking glances from behind her sunglasses. Her partner was fidgeting in her seat. Beth had been dreading this kind of private time. The questions were bound to come sooner or later, and she'd been hoping for later.

"So," Sondra Dewberry began. "Are you seeing anyone?"

Beth had been expecting the indirect lesbian query. A Kewpie doll like Dewberry wouldn't consider her nearly girly enough. "I'm seeing someone." She wanted, oh so very badly, to say that her significant other was a powerlifter named Denise. But she'd been getting the feeling Dewberry wasn't overly receptive to irony, and that little joke would probably end up all over the office, in various versions, by suppertime.

"Someone in the office?"

"No." God, no. She'd done a lot of stupid things in her time, but never a nightmare like that.

"What does he do?"

Jesus. "He's in the Army. Special operations."

"Oh, that's nice. Did you meet him on a case?"

"We worked together a couple of times."

"What is he?" Dewberry asked. "A major? A colonel? My daddy was a colonel when he retired from the Army."

Daddy. Daddy was a colonel. This was going to be fun then. "He's a Master Sergeant."

"Oh."

Beth had to admit it. Her partner could put more different spins on that one favorite word than she ever would have thought possible. Sensing an opening for even more fun, she said, "But the nice thing about dating a special ops soldier is the gifts. They give great gifts."

Dewberry brightened up at the mention of presents. "Really?"

"Oh, yeah." Beth lifted her left leg, and the bottom of her suit pants, exposing a pistol in an ankle holster. "He gave me my backup gun."

"He gave you a gun?"

"He sure did. It was so *sweet.*"

"As a present?"

"Uh-huh. We'd been involved in this shooting, and he noticed I was using a revolver as a backup piece. He pointed out that if I had to fire all six rounds I was in trouble. So he bought me a Glock 27, the mini .40 caliber. So in a pinch I could reload it with the spare magazines from my full-size model 22. It was so thoughtful."

"That's . . . nice. You were in a shooting?"

"Uh-huh."

"I've never had to use my weapon."

"Well, don't worry. One of these days."

"How long have you been going out?"

Questions, questions, questions. Maybe she wasn't girly enough after all, because Beth only asked people questions on the job. "I guess about eight months."

"Oh."

A much sunnier oh this time, Beth thought.

Then came the follow-up question, though this time it was more of a statement. "Then it's serious."

"I don't know about that," Beth said. "We've had four dates."

"Four dates in eight months?"

A good octave higher on that one, Beth thought. Not quite enough to crack a wineglass, but still impressive. "He isn't in the country all that often. The war on terrorism? You know. And when he is we're on different coasts. Like now."

"Four dates."

If Beth had only known Dewberry could get dejected so easily, she'd have opened up long ago. The uncomfortable silence was luxurious.

Then her cell phone rang.

Beth held it up so she could see the screen. A disapproving look in the peripheral vision. No doubt there was some Bureau policy about cellphone use while driving. "Uh-oh. My mom. I'd better get this." She brought the phone up to her ear. "Hi Mom. Okay, what's wrong? You're calling me in the middle of the day—I don't have to be in the FBI to figure out something's wrong. Is it Dad? No reason, just a wild guess. You called, Mom, you might as well go ahead and tell me. Is he all right? He what? He *what?*" Beth let out a loud chuckle. "Yeah, Mom, I didn't think that was the way you wore them. Yes, I am laughing. I'm sure you don't think it's funny—we're just going to have to agree to disagree on that. Did you try? Uh-huh. Uh-huh. You know I can't do that, Mom. Because he'd kill himself if his little girl tried to talk to him about something like that. Did you? What did he say."

Finding it hard to drive while shaking with laughter, Beth pulled into the breakdown lane. "Yes, Mom, I'm still laughing. I realize that, but I can't seem to stop. No, I don't think so. Not any crazier than usual, at least. Yes, I know I shouldn't talk about my father that way, even if he is nuts. Mom, if talking to him didn't work, it might just be easier to let it go. If anyone else sees it? Mom, if anyone sees it you've got a lot worse problem on your hands. Yeah. Yeah. Okay, Mom. I've got to go now. Right. Call you when I can. Love you. 'Bye."

Beth put her phone away and cleaned up her running

mascara before pulling out again. She didn't say a word. Just waited for it, knowing Dewberry was being eaten alive by curiosity.

Then it came. "Everything all right?"

"My dad. He just had surgery for prostate cancer."

"Oh, I'm so sorry."

"Everything came out all right, but now he has to wear those adult diapers. You know what I mean?"

"I understand it's pretty common after that procedure."

Grinning wickedly, Beth said, "Yeah, got himself a leaky garden hose now."

Not the kind of thing well-bred Southern belles expect to hear. "Oh, you don't have to tell me anything so personal."

"No, really, it's okay," said Beth. "We *are* partners, after all. My parents were getting ready to go out. And my mom walks in the bedroom." Beth had to pause to deal with another attack of the giggles. "My mom walks in the bedroom, and there's my dad, standing there. And he's wearing the diaper *over* his boxer shorts." The laughter came snorting out of her—she almost had to pull over again.

Dewberry was only puzzled. "Why was he doing that?"

Beth was trying to hold the steering wheel straight, but the car kept shaking. She had to struggle to get the words out. "He said they were more comfortable that way." Another roar of laughter. The road was getting hazy through her tears.

"But you're supposed to wear them next to the skin," said Dewberry, dead serious.

Beth was afraid she was going to go off the highway. Fortunately their exit was coming up. She took the Harbor Boulevard off-ramp, and entered the Port of Los Angeles.

They skirted the long lines of trucks waiting to pick up a trailer and have a shipping container deposited onto it. Of course all the trucks were running while they waited, and there was a fog of burned diesel in the air. There were a lot of trucks. The ports of L.A. and Long

Beach next door handled 40 percent of the entire nation's seaborne imports.

With Dewberry calling off the directions, Beth headed toward the shipping basins. They flashed their credentials at the L.A. Port Police checkpoint and continued toward the berthing slips.

It was like driving through another city, but one made out of a giant child's blocks, stack after symmetrical stack of red, blue, and white shipping containers. The spaces between them arranged into avenues and streets, stretching out over acres. Toward the water the individual berths could be picked out because over every one towered cranes and gantries like giant Erector sets.

"Fries Avenue," said Beth, making the turn. "What was the berth again?"

"Berth 176," said Dewberry.

The berths weren't the piers Beth had been imagining. It was more like a giant parking lot that ran right down to the edge of the channel, with the container ships parked in a row, one after the other, just like cars.

As they got closer they could see the line of Port Police and Customs vehicles, lights flashing of course.

"What the hell?" Beth exclaimed. She could feel her face flushing, as it always did when her dander was up.

She brought the car to a quick stop and charged out her door, flashing credentials at the uniformed cops and ducking under the crime scene tape.

The center of attention was an open container and a forklift pulling out pallets of large metal ingots. Except the ingots weren't solid. A few were sitting on the asphalt cut open, revealing folding stock AKM rifles sitting on the plastic and cloth they'd been wrapped in, each with four magazines, magazine bag, sling, cleaning kit, and plastic oil can. Farther down were the dull green metal cans of ammunition, the Russian kind that opened with a key like a can of Spam.

It was all lying out there in the open, as if for display.

Immigration and Customs Enforcement (ICE) had a bench set up, and an agent in a blue jumpsuit wearing a plastic face shield was cutting open ingots with a metal saw.

Supervisory Special Agent Benjamin Timmins was holding a paper cup of coffee amid a huddle of other suits watching the action.

Beth was sorely tempted to embarrass him in front of the others. Perhaps fearing exactly that, when Timmins caught sight of her he broke away from the group and put himself on a course to intercept her.

"Now, Beth . . ."

"Jesus Christ, Ben. Why didn't you get the USC marching band to make the spectacle complete? Did the TV crews get stuck in traffic or something?"

"Beth . . ."

"Why the hell isn't this being done under wraps in a warehouse? Didn't we talk about putting transponders in these weapons and sending them on to see where they ended up?"

"As you've no doubt guessed, Beth, it's been decided not to let these weapons get out on the street. We're making the seizure right now."

"For the love of Christ, why?"

"It was decided—*above my pay grade, Beth*—not to take the risk of letting them get loose."

"But why? We could spike every single piece of ordnance and scoop up every single one of the perps literally on the way to do whatever it is they had planned."

"No one wanted to take the chance of the transponders being discovered."

The realization of bitter defeat seemed to mark a change in Beth's aggressive body language. She slumped a bit, and began talking slower. "No, of course they wouldn't. And this is going to be publicized, isn't it? So the Bureau and Customs can let the nation know we're on the ball."

"Probably."

"And what about my C.I.? How do we keep Roshan from getting killed? Those Russian arms dealers are going to wonder who tipped off their shipment. They're going to wonder about the Arabs they were going to sell their guns to. And the Arabs are going to wonder about each other. Incidentally, has anyone thought about how we're going to make our case?"

"The U.S. Attorney says the wiretaps will be more than enough."

Beth pointed to the ingots. "I assume that's lead, or something like it. So out of all the thousands of containers that got unloaded today, how did we find this one? Not by x-ray."

"The cover story's all ready to go. An experienced inspector noticed that the container was too light for that amount of metal." Timmons waved his head in the direction of a large Customs truck. "So they used one of their new gamma ray scanners on it."

It wasn't bad. At least they weren't complete idiots. But Beth was still bitterly disappointed. "And you think that's going to fly?"

"The Russians weren't going to have that container delivered to their homes. They've got cutouts between it and them. They're going to look at the seizure as just part of the price of doing business."

"Yeah? Well, let me ask you something else then, Ben. Now that we've got this shipment of arms, are those Russians going to get suspicious and throw off all the surveillance we have on them right now? Or discover the surveillance and decide to leave the country? This can't have been their only shipment. What if they fill the order from guns they've already got stored someplace else? Did everyone above your pay grade think about that?"

"Whether they did or they didn't," said Timmins, "it's out of yours and my hands right now."

Just then Karen the Spook walked up and said, "Excuse me, Ben, but I need to speak with Beth for a minute."

"No problem, Karen," said Timmins. "I was just finished."

Seeing Karen's move, Dewberry took the opportunity to join them, saying, "What's going on?"

"Excuse us for a minute, Sondra," Karen said pleasantly, taking Beth by the arm.

"What's up?" Dewberry asked Timmins.

"Nothing," Timmins replied. "But I recommend you don't go over to those two until they finish talking."

"You and your fucking bat ears," Beth said once they were out of earshot. "Or are you doing this electronically?"

"Just part of my continuing effort to keep you out of trouble," said Karen.

"Good luck," said Beth.

"I often feel that way," said Karen.

Beth gestured angrily at the scene. "It's like *Groundhog Day*, it just keeps happening over and over again. Can't anyone in this organization make a right decision, except by accident?"

"Nobody's really a bad guy here," Karen observed. "They all think they're making the right call. They're just making it according to a different set of criteria than you."

"Yeah, as idiots."

"Not necessarily. No one's a dummy. Well, most of them anyway."

"Assholes?"

"That's not quite . . ."

"Idiot assholes?"

"No," said Karen. "Good street agents like to work the streets—not become supervisors. So management is always going to be a breed apart. You can't be surprised when bureaucratic politicians make decisions according to the rules of bureaucratic politics."

"They're screwing up by the numbers."

"Not with that particular goal in mind. They're

organization men, and women, who made their rank by acting like the organization men who selected them. They're thinking about the Beslan school siege in Russia, and they don't care about anything except making sure something like that doesn't happen on *their* watch."

"Well, that makes all the difference in the world. By the way, are you still working on your thesis?"

"No. Why?"

"It just sounded like it," said Beth. "I try not to care about what they do, but I can't help it. And now they're putting my C.I. in danger."

"So what?" said Karen.

Beth was taken aback by that. "What do you mean?"

"I mean: *so what.* He's not your friend, he's your Joe."

"I love it when you use those CIA spy terms."

Karen was totally serious. "Your C.I. is a scumbag. If he was a decent, law-abiding American he wouldn't be your confidential informant. Feeling sympathy for the guy helps you run him well, but don't get carried away. You run an agent to gather good intelligence, not so you can dance at their retirement party. You run them like a professional, but you always have to use them and every now and then you have to risk them. And whatever happens, happens."

"Sometimes I forget you haven't always been an analyst."

"Just remember what happened to those FBI agents in Boston who forgot they were supposed to be running criminals as informants and got run by them instead. Keep your perspective."

"Okay, I will. Now tell me what kind of intelligence we're getting off this seizure?"

"I don't want to extrapolate too much. This could be one piece of a bigger, multipart shipment. Or the Russians might be selling off parts of this to more than one buyer."

"Jesus, Karen, now you're starting to sound like the bosses, always equivocating. What do you *think?*"

"Okay. I think this looks like a complete assault package for twenty men. Sixteen AKs. Two Dragunov SVD sniper rifles with the whole kit: telescopic sight, night scope, and the special Russian 7.62mm sniper ammo. Two PKM machine guns. Two RPG-7 rocket launchers. Ammo and accessories for all the weapons, including RGD-5 hand grenades. And two SA-14 surface-to-air missile launchers, shoulder-fired heat seekers."

"I thought the next thing they'd try would be suicide bombers," said Beth.

"Twenty men can do a lot of damage with all that ordnance."

"Can the weapons mix tell us anything about the mission?"

"No," said Karen. "You could use that package for anything from ambushing a limousine to raiding a nuclear power plant to shooting down a helicopter or a plane."

"Super."

"All the weapons and ammo are Russian manufacture. Probably from the Ukraine, but could just as easily be Belarus or Russia proper. You pay off the right colonel, all you have to do is drive onto the base, stop off at the armory and ammo magazines, and pick out what you want. It's going to take a while to trace this container back to point of origin and get a picture of their smuggling technique. If we can, that is. Russians haven't been too helpful lately. What does your guy say?"

"He's not all the way into the group yet, but he is hosting the meetings and parties. They're still a little skittish about talking in front of him, but they do talk. The video and microphones caught two of them sitting off by themselves talking about meeting with some Russians, so we followed them to the meeting and found the Russians. Russian mafia, of course. We couldn't hear what the meeting was about, but it was enough to get a warrant. And those Russians like to talk in their cars. We got lucky and heard about this shipment. The Russians run a bunch of small businesses to launder money, including a trucking company and a metal broker, which is where these ingots were heading to. It'll be closed and empty by tonight."

"That electronic surveillance was a nice touch. Is your C.I. still giving you straight reporting?"

"So far."

"Still, it's good intelligence work. You FBI gumshoes are learning. It never comes in on a platter. You have to pick out the thread and tease it out bit by bit."

"We live for the CIA's approval," said Beth. "But it just raises a bunch of new questions. Are the twenty guys already in the country and ready to go? Are they from outside, or are they part of this California group that went to Pakistan for training? And do these Russian mobsters have enough guns already salted away somewhere so they can fill this order anyway?"

"All great questions," said Karen. "And all ones I can't answer. At least now."

"Hope we have time."

"We're already past the 9/11 anniversary."

"And I don't think Halloween is a significant event," said Beth. "But we all know what happens the first Tuesday in November."

"Election Day. God forgive me, but let's hope it's the Inauguration, if only to give us more time."

"Seems like only the worst-case scenario ever comes to pass."

The events of the day had Beth seriously dejected, and Karen hated to see her that way. "Speaking of worst case. We're getting into the playoffs and you haven't put your World Series bet down yet. What's it going to be?"

Karen loved making her bet on sporting events. Not money, just something evil and humiliating for the loser. When Karen's Redskins beat Beth's Patriots in a regular season game the past year, Beth had to dress up in a red cowboy hat and boots and ride the mechanical bull at a cowboy bar. And almost lost her handgun when she got bucked off.

But revenge had been sweet when the Patriots won the Super Bowl. A Redskins season ticket holder, Karen was going to have to attend this year's home game against the Cowboys wearing a white leather cowgirl skirt, vest, boots, and gloves, all trimmed in blue fringe. And a white cowboy hat. And a large blue star painted on each cheek. And give up her husband's ticket so Beth could watch.

"I think it's the Cardinals this year," said Beth.

"The Bostonian isn't betting on the Red Sox?"

"That you would ask such a question only reveals the depth of your ignorance. We might live and die with the Sox. We might bleed Red Sox red. But no New Englander is going to *bet* on them to win the World Series. You just can't do that. Killing the Yankees was miracle enough. So I have to pick the Cards."

"In that case I have to pick the Red Sox."

"You're picking the Red Sox to *win* the *World Series*?"

"Why not?"

"Okay," Beth said quickly. "It's a bet."

"What exactly is the bet?"

"Let's say next season we go to New York for a weekend when there's a Yankees-Sox series. You have to buy the tickets. Bleacher tickets will be fine. And you have to sit in the bleachers wearing a Red Sox hat and jersey."

"That can't be any worse than dressing up as a Cowboy fan in Washington."

"Of course it can't," said Beth, fighting to be convincing. "And your bet?"

"I'll let you know. I've got to think about it."

"Bitch. The CIA picked you for that evil mind, didn't they?"

"You better believe it. And if the FBI had known about yours, they *wouldn't* have picked you. Bitch."

Chapter Fifteen

After the call from Rio, Abdallah Karim Nimri sat on the wooden bench twirling the cell phone between his fingers.

God, all praise to Him, never ceased testing His servants. It was maddening. Everything was an irritant. A disaster in the making in Brazil. Another in America. Sitting in this park, under almost leafless palms, surrounded by huge fiberglass sculptures of pagan Mexican gods that seemed to be poking their heads up from the grass between the brick walkways. Idolatry and graven images, as if God felt he needed to be reminded of being surrounded by evil in these infidel lands. He almost felt as if the Los Zetas driver had brought him here intentionally. Even the furnace heat, which did not irritate him but instead made him homesick for Egypt, a feeling he had not had for a long time.

And the United States was just over the international bridge, one street away, almost close enough to touch.

Nimri stared at his phone, thinking. Then he dialed a number in Monterrey. Acmed, the Mexico coordinator, picked up after one ring.

"There is a compromise in Brazil," said Nimri. "I will not discuss how I know, but it has happened. Is there anything there that can link to here? No? I told the brother in Brazil nothing but his mission—if he somehow learned more tell me now. You are sure? Good."

Then something occurred to him. "Was there any connection between Brazil and the brother in Paraguay?" Listening, Nimri's anger flared up. "Why was I not told of this? Enough excuses. Notify the last four in Europe and tell them they will not be needed. No. And cut all links to Brazil—no contact at all. What? Do you wish to go there? I did not think so. In any case, no one who has any knowledge of this task is to travel to Brazil, even to change planes. What? Call them if you wish, they will not answer. If they do? Then send tickets for the soonest flight back to Europe. Then change your location and never use that phone again. Yes, not where you are now, and not Mexico City. Yes, the next number. I will call you if I need you. You are ordered not to call me again. Yes, computer only. Go to a place of safety and take precautions. Very good. God be with you, brother."

Nimri turned off the phone and smashed it down on top of the bench, startling a little old lady who had been shuffling by. The fool. Not to tell him about the connection between the coordinators of Brazil and Paraguay. If he had known, then after the incident in Paraguay he would have brought all new people into Brazil to run the operation. Especially after what had happened in Thailand the previous year.

He had first thought that Paraguay had been the work of the Iranians. Or that the brothers there had somehow run afoul of one of the criminal or narcotics gangs while doing business.

But it was now clear that it had been the Americans all along. They had been clever in their methods to buy themselves more time to track him down. After his last operation he had sworn off the use of satellite telephones. And now they had used the brothers in Rio to trick him into revealing himself again. Devils.

And now the seizure of the weapons in Los Angeles. Another compromise? He had never been happy with relying on American brothers. That had always been the weak link in the plan. Perhaps they were communicating to him under American control? He could not take the chance. Fortunately, they knew nothing of the objective.

His choices were also clear: cancel the operation or alter his plan.

To be so close and cancel? Unthinkable. Every day, every setback was a sign of God testing the worthiness of His believers. All praise to God. To show fear, to show doubt, was to tempt His judgment.

Then the plan must be changed. They no longer had the luxury of time. Or of complication. Fortunately, he had learned from the past and built that flexibility into his plan.

Nimri sat on the bench and planned it all out. He wrote nothing down. He never wrote anything down. The Americans had captured too many brothers with their diaries and their computers.

As the day's heat rose shimmering into the air the park and surrounding streets emptied of people. It was time for *Zuhr*, the noon prayer, but Nimri knew he could not pray in public. God would forgive whoever marched to war in the earth in His name for neglecting his prayers. God was ever merciful.

Hovering nearby were Nimri's driver and bodyguard, both young Los Zetas. Hungry for their lunch, longing for siesta, anxious with responsibility for their charge. They had been told what would happen to them if anything happened to the Arab.

Finally Nimri rose and walked to the car. The driver and bodyguard fell in with him front and back. "*La casa*," Nimri said.

Returning to the safe house, he sought out Temiraev. He found him in front of the television surrounded by his men and the Los Zetas guards. Every day they had to watch a Mexican soap opera that, Temiraev had explained to him, was also incredibly popular in Russia. Bizarre. Through enormous effort the Chechens had surmounted the language barrier in order to get updates on the current condition of their favorite characters from the Mexicans.

Nimri could care less, as long as it kept them occupied. But now he could do with a little less devotion. He caught Temiraev's eye and motioned him out of the room. Temiraev pointed to the screen. Nimri signaled the urgency.

Temiraev shook his head and snapped out an order to the Chechen sitting beside him. Probably to keep him updated on the plot.

Picking his way through the bodies, Temiraev met Nimri at the doorway. "Is this important, my brother?" he said crossly in Arabic.

Nimri motioned for him to follow. They went upstairs to one of the bedrooms, which was currently unoccupied for the duration of the soap opera but carpeted with inflatable mattresses and piles of clothing. Nimri made a mental note to get them to clean up the room.

They sat cross-legged side by side on an air mattress. Literally mouth to ear, since Nimri did not want to be overheard. "A problem in Brazil," he whispered.

"What has happened?" Temiraev asked calmly.

Nimri had to think of the future before giving his answer, weighing what words might come back to haunt him. "The coordinator has not returned to the house for two days. The brothers called the emergency number."

"Defected, captured, or run away?" Temiraev asked.

"Only God knows," Nimri replied.

"What will you do?"

"I have given the order for the four brothers still in Europe not to come."

"And the four in Brazil now?"

Nimri had given careful thought to what to tell him. "They have been ordered to the airport. Tickets have been purchased for them to return to Europe."

Now Temiraev surprised him. "If they have been discovered, they will lead the Americans back to my family in Antwerp. And then perhaps Russia also. All could be lost."

"I could not give that order on my own, my brother. If you desire it, I will do so now."

Temiraev might as well have been discussing the characters on the soap opera. "We have no choice."

"Very well."

"What of our operation?"

Nimri was on firmer ground now. "We will still go. But I will step up the timetable and make a few changes."

"What changes, my brother?"

It was less of a question than a statement, and Nimri recognized the unspoken threat in his voice. Handling Chechens was like making your own nitroglycerine. "Speaking to you frankly, I desire to cut the American operatives completely out of the operation. All except the one in Texas."

"Can you do that?"

"It depends on the Mexicans. If they agree, and give me the answers I hope for, we will leave here very soon. We may even be able to do a rehearsal or two before."

"Good." Temiraev grabbed Nimri's arm in that iron grip. "Very good. Is there anything else?"

"Not now."

The words had barely left his mouth when Temiraev rushed off to return to his program. Nimri shook his head. All was on his shoulders alone, as it ever had been.

The Los Zeta responsible for the safe house was Rafael, who had taken Nimri across the border previously. Nimri found him sitting in the shade of the back portico, sipping from a brown bottle of beer that was sweating much more than he.

"Have you eaten?" he asked Nimri. Los Zetas had imported several women to do the cooking and cleaning for the house. The women told him they had never seen anything like these Muslims, who did much praying but no flirting.

Nimri shook his head.

"You should have something," said Rafael. "I thought these men of yours would find our food strange, but they each have the appetite of four."

"They have been hungry enough times to appreciate any food," said Nimri.

"The mark of a soldier," said Rafael. "A pity I cannot speak the language of the leader among them. He seems a man of much experience and many stories. I think I would enjoy sharing a bottle with him. Except you Muslims do not drink, of course."

"You might have more success with him than you imagine," said Nimri. "But I have something else I wish to discuss with you."

Rafael raised his beer. "This house is yours."

"I would like to purchase arms from you before we cross the border."

Rafael eyed him carefully. "This was not your plan originally?"

Now Nimri realized that Rafael was smelling a last-minute renegotiation after all the hard bargaining on the price for the crossing. "No, it was not. My plans have changed, and I was hoping you could accommodate me. I realize it is short notice."

Rafael looked a little less suspicious. But only a little less. "This can most likely be arranged. What arms do you wish to buy?"

Nimri knew he would have to be almost as careful with this one as Temiraev. "Thirteen pistols, 9 millimeter. Glock, SiG, Heckler and Koch, it does not matter. But they must be new, and they must have the large magazines.

Holsters, like you wear under your shirt. Two magazines each. Magazine pouches. Ammunition enough for two magazines, and to refill them again."

"That is no problem. Anything else?"

"Ten Kalashnikovs. Six magazines each, magazine pouches, slings, cleaning kit. Six hundred rounds per rifle."

"Easy."

"Two machine guns. Three thousand rounds per gun. Cleaning equipment."

"What kind?"

"What do you have available?" Nimri asked.

"The Spanish Ameli in 5.56 millimeter. The MAG in 7.62 millimeter. Mexican army issue. Anything else will take time."

"The MAG will be fine. Armor-piercing ammunition if possible."

"Perhaps. Spare barrels? Tripods?"

"Not necessary. One sniper rifle, with telescope. Not bolt action, if possible."

"Then it must be the German G-3 sniper rifle, the G-3 SG/1."

Nimri guessed that was Mexican army issue also. "Very well, with two hundred rounds. Magazines, pouches, cleaning kit, sling. Also, four pairs of binoculars. Thirteen handheld radios—good ones. And thirteen pairs of the night glasses." After using them on the last trip across the border, he had to have them now.

Rafael had to think about that for a moment. "We can do thirteen."

"What about an RPG?"

"The Russian?" said Rafael.

"Yes, the RPG-7."

"It would have to come up from Nicaragua. Can you wait at least two weeks?"

"No. Do you have anything like it?"

"The American LAAW. Very light. Shoot the rocket and throw away the fiberglass tube."

"Are they difficult to learn?" Nimri asked.

"Very easy."

"Range?"

"Two hundred meters."

Much less than the RPG. "I will want twenty-five."

"That many?"

"I will want to practice with them. As a matter of fact, I will want to practice and test fire everything before we leave. Is that a problem?"

Rafael aimed his thumb. "The desert is out there. No problem."

"Hand grenades. Fifty."

"American okay?"

A grenade was a grenade, as long as it worked. "Fine."

"We have smoke and gas too, if you like."

Nimri's ears perked up. "Gas?"

"Tear gas."

Now that was an interesting idea. "Fifteen of each. And thirteen gas masks."

By now Rafael was writing the whole shopping list down. "Anything else?"

"Antiaircraft missiles?"

"Madonna, my friend, you are ambitious."

"Do you have them?"

"Not for you, I regret. It would have to be Nicaragua again. And I warn you, they will be very expensive."

"The same two weeks?"

"If not more."

"Never mind then," said Nimri. "What about explosives?"

"What do you want?"

"I prefer plastic."

"Plastic is available, but expensive."

Nimri did not want to fool with civilian dynamite or

gelatin if he could help it. Too sensitive. One stray bullet strike at the wrong time meant disaster. "I want plastic."

"It is your money. How much?"

"Ten kilos. Bags to carry it. Two dozen time detonators, two dozen electric. A roll of time fuse, two dozen igniters, two crimping pliers. A roll of wire and two blasting machines—small ones. I think that will be all. How quickly can you have everything?"

"How quickly do you want everything?"

"Two days."

Rafael chuckled grimly. "Two days can perhaps be done, my friend. But for two days there will be no bargaining."

The quick reply told Nimri that Los Zetas would be taking the weapons and explosives out of their own stores. With a hefty commission for Rafael, no doubt. "You tell me the price, and I will tell you if I will bargain or not."

"The price I will perhaps have for you this evening."

"And delivery in two days," said Nimri.

"And delivery in two days."

"Then we will test fire and practice with the weapons on the third day, and cross the border on the fourth."

"That soon?" said Rafael.

"And I wish to make a small change to the crossing arrangement."

"You are filled with changes. Tell me and I will give you my answer."

"A small change. Instead of dropping us off in America, add two vehicles to your convoy. With Texas licenses, as before. Your men will drive them across the border. Then you leave, and leave the vehicles with us—we will continue on our way."

"I wondered why you did not ask for that at first," said Rafael. "Bulletproof vehicles?"

Nimri thought about the cost. "Not necessary. Can it be done?"

Rafael closed his little leather notebook. "It can be done. But you must share some information with me."

"I will not discuss what I will do after I cross the border," Nimri warned.

"This I have no desire to learn. But you are now twelve men plus yourself. You buy weapons for twelve men plus yourself. I was told to expect at least another eight men."

Nimri had been right. He would have to be careful. "My plans have changed. No more will arrive."

"Very well. Your plans have changed. Now, when it seemed you had plenty of time, you wish to buy weapons and leave in four days. Your plans have changed, and this is your business. But something seems to be pushing you across the border. You have hired Los Zetas to do this thing, so it concerns Los Zetas. Los Zetas have guaranteed your safety, which is my responsibility. But the safety of Los Zetas is also my responsibility. So I ask you to share this information with me. And I beg you, for your own sake, to tell me only the truth."

Nimri knew it would be madness to underestimate this man. Or his organization. He also knew that the entire operation was resting on his answer. "It is possible that our travel route has been compromised by the Americans. I do not know this for certain, but I cannot take the chance. I intended to move across the border without arms, but now I feel that is another chance I cannot take. The faster I move, the less risk for me. And for you."

Now Rafael's expression was frightening in its intensity. "How much do your travelers know about us?"

"They did not even know they were going to Mexico until they stepped on the plane to Mexico City. They did not know they were going to Monterrey until they stepped on that plane. And they did not know about Nuevo Laredo until you drove them here from Monterrey."

Rafael had watched Nimri's face with that same unnatural focus the entire time. "I believe you. Not because I think you cannot lie, but because I have watched you and think you are a professional. You will not discuss who was to have met you in the United States. Fine. But we will use a different route and I will leave you in a different place than we discussed before. This we will not negotiate."

"It is acceptable to me," said Nimri. He knew it would be useless to try and convince Rafael that his American operatives had not been told of the crossing location.

"For everything else, I will have to speak with my leaders before you have my answer on the arms and the border."

Nimri knew that if the answer was no they would all be killed. Only half the agreed-upon money had been paid. He had to gamble that Los Zetas would want the other half. Without torturing him for the bank wire codes, he reminded himself. Yet another trap to plan a way out of. "I understand. I have not led the Americans here."

"Perhaps. But you still think they may appear, looking for you."

"They may," Nimri admitted.

"This is our city," said Rafael. "It would be their misfortune."

Chapter Sixteen

When Nasser Saleh heard the message inviting him to lunch, at first he thought it was something his parents had gotten him into. The North American Islamic Friendship Society sounded just right for them. And how else would the guy have gotten his number? So he'd ignored the message on his machine. But the guy kept calling.

Which gave Nasser the idea that maybe his resume had found its way around town, and he was calling about a job. So he returned the call. The guy was pretty vague, but he did invite him to lunch. Nasser could always blow him off—after the free lunch.

Nasser didn't know the place, but a deli on K Street north of the White House was going to be packed at lunchtime. The things you did for a free meal.

At lunchtime FBI Headquarters spilled out onto Pennsylvania Avenue, and Nasser joined the throng heading north.

The deli was mobbed. One look inside and he almost turned around and walked out, except a waving arm attracted his attention. A guy in a booth by himself, who was the only other Arab in the place. With any luck no one would call the police. That had happened to Nasser before. He made his way over.

"Nasser?" He was a few years older, closer to thirty,

taller and with a thick shock of straight black hair that fell down onto his forehead.

"I'm Nasser."

"Samir Bakri. Call me Sam. Thanks for meeting me."

He wasn't a native-born American. Nasser had gotten pretty good with accents, and this sounded Algerian. The fast-talking lobbyist type. The free lunch might not be worth it. Nasser grabbed a menu and started looking for something expensive.

"You know, I did the same thing you do now," said Bakri.

A harried waitress, who had obviously been waiting for someone to arrive to justify the booth, arrived to take their order. Nasser had hot pastrami on a roll, and a Diet Coke. Bakri kind of creeped him out by ordering the exact same thing.

After she left, Bakri repeated, "Yes, I did the exact same thing you do. Translation."

"Really?" said Nasser, just to make conversation. "For who?"

"I applied to the FBI, but you know how long that takes. I got a better offer."

Nasser was getting all kinds of strange vibes. "I don't want to be rude or anything, but if you don't mind, what did you want to see me about?"

"Dr. al-Hakam suggested I talk to you."

Nasser's stomach began to clench up. "Are you a lawyer?"

"No. The North American Islamic Friendship Society is investigating what's going on at Guantánamo."

The fear hit Nasser like a cold chill all the way through his body. He wanted to get up and run, but his legs were frozen and it was like he was bolted to the bench. "I can't help you."

"Dr. al-Hakam thought you could."

"He was wrong."

"Don't you want to help your people?"

"I have to go. You're going to have to excuse me. I have to go."

As he rose up, Bakri laid some papers down on the table. "Are these yours?"

Halfway up, Nasser looked down and saw his FBI Guantanamo e-mails. He felt like he was going to throw up. The professor hadn't been walking around thinking. He'd been at the copy machine.

"Why don't you sit back down and hear me out?" Bakri suggested.

As if he'd been rocked by a blow to the head, Nasser obeyed.

"The problem is, Nasser, that in order to receive your security clearance you signed a Classified Information Nondisclosure Agreement. You agreed not to improperly divulge classified information. The agreement also described the penalties, if you remember. They're very harsh. I'm sure you know that when you took those e-mails out of your office you violated that agreement."

Nasser couldn't remember many times when he had absolutely no idea what to say.

"I think you've got me all wrong," Bakri said smoothly. "No one wants to get you in trouble. Especially with the FBI."

"Who are you?"

"I told you, the NAIFS investigates the mistreatment of our people by the government. Any violations of their civil rights. That is why the last thing we want is to see *you* mistreated by the government. If you didn't feel the same way, you wouldn't have shown those e-mails to your professor."

Everything stopped as the waitress set two plates down in front of them. "Thank you," Bakri said to her. Then when she was gone, "We would really like you to help us out. Nothing formal like a consulting agreement, of course, that would make the FBI angry. But we would pay your expenses."

The smell of the hot pastrami rising up from the plate, which Nasser ordinarily would have loved, was making him sick. "I have to go to the bathroom."

"Sure," said Bakri. He handed Nasser a thick business envelope. "Take a look at this while you're in there. And please don't run off. No matter how much you'd like to."

Nasser hurried into the men's room, took a stall, and ripped open the envelope. Inside was $5,000 in cash. He twisted around and violently threw up. Then again, losing all his Diet Coke.

He flushed the toilet and wiped his mouth. He was bathed in sweat. His cell phone rang. Even in the midst of all that was happening he was a child of his age, and could no more not answer his phone than stop breathing. Someone was sending him a photo. At least that was something not terrible for his mind to grab onto. He watched hypnotically until it blinked onto the screen. It was him taking the envelope from Bakri, snapped by someone in the restaurant.

Nasser spun around and vomited again. His stomach was empty, but he was wracked by dry heaves.

Even after they ended, the last thing he wanted to do was go back out into the deli. But he was trapped.

He put the envelope back onto the table. "I don't want this. Take it for yourself. Take the e-mails. But leave me alone. Please."

Bakri put down his sandwich. He'd almost finished it. "Nasser, that's quite impossible. Without our help the FBI would surely start a security investigation on you. You would be indicted. Your parents would be bankrupted by the legal expenses. You'd go to prison. We can't let that happen."

Nasser realized that all the pleading in the world wasn't going to save him. He felt like he wasn't getting enough air. And something was happening to his head. He couldn't hear any of the clatter in the deli. All he heard was Bakri's voice.

"You applied to the Bureau, didn't you?" Nasser said. "You didn't pass the polygraph."

Bakri wiped his hands on his napkin, folded up the e-mails, and tucked them under the envelope. He pushed all of it back across the table. "Keep the e-mails. We have copies."

Nasser just sat there.

"You really shouldn't leave that out on the table," Bakri said. "Put it in your jacket."

When Nasser did his recruitment was complete. Another photograph had been taken of him doing it.

"Did you print out the e-mails?" Bakri asked.

"Flash drive," Nasser said tonelessly.

"From *your* computer?"

"Yes."

"That was reckless. FBI security is a joke, but we cannot risk you coming to any harm. I promised you we would protect you, and we will. You'll need to have a new computer. Listen carefully."

Bakri began telling him what he needed to do. Nasser folded his napkin and took out a pen.

"What are you doing?" Bakri demanded.

"Writing it down."

"Write nothing down. Memorize this."

"All of it?"

"Yes, all of it." When he finished he made Nasser repeat it back, correcting him until he got it right.

"Next," Bakri said. "We're very interested in this case in California that's been in the newspapers."

"Not Guantánamo?" said Nasser, perhaps finally realizing what was happening.

"Guantánamo of course. But we feel these people in California have been falsely accused. It's quite possible that their civil rights have been violated. The more information we have, the better."

"I'm not translating that case," Nasser said desperately.

"No matter. I'm sure you'll be able to discover who is, and borrow their computer when they're not using it. In any case, you must always use someone else's computer when you retrieve this information."

"I don't know if I can do that."

"Of course you can, if you apply yourself. And time is of the essence. We can't hope to defend these brothers if we don't have information about the government's case against them. You have to work quickly. But do the other thing first. I'll contact you the day after tomorrow."

"The day after tomorrow?"

"Yes. Please have the California information by then." Nasser looked down at his plate.

"You don't look well at all," said Bakri. "You should eat something."

The next day Nasser arrived at work early, but not too early. He unplugged his computer. He'd bought a fireplace lighter, breaking it apart, discarding the butane tank, keeping only the piezoelectric igniter. Pressure on the piezoelectric crystal is what produced the spark to ignite the butane and produce a flame. A spark hot enough to ignite flammable material is more than 2,000 volts. It only takes 200 volts to destroy a computer chip.

He'd unplugged the computer to remove its ground with the earth. Fumbling with a small screwdriver, Nasser removed a few screws so he could open the back plate a crack. He was sweating and the screws were small. He lost one and it bounced across the carpet.

Nasser knew all the screws would have to be back on the computer when he was done. He crawled under his desk, looking for it on the carpet. People were starting to come into the office. He couldn't see under there, so he felt around with his hands, growing more frantic. His finger hit the screw and pushed it away. He stretched out his arm to the limit, almost under the next cubicle. He felt the screw with his fingertips, and teased it back toward him. A little more. He had it.

Just then his neighbor Udi came into that next cubicle and sat down.

Nasser pulled himself back up into a crouch, and opened the back plate on his computer. He poked the igniter inside and zapped everything he could see.

"Hey, Nasser?"

"Hi, Udi," Nasser said quickly, trying to keep his voice normal.

"What's that strange sound?"

"I don't know," Nasser replied. "I heard it, too."

"Weird."

Nasser pushed the plate back flush and reattached the screws, trying not to scrape the metal with the screwdriver.

He plugged everything back in, and backed his chair away to the length of his arm. He turned his head away and pushed the on button.

There was a loud pop, then a couple of smaller ones. The monitor blinked, then went dark. There was a distinct smell of electrical equipment.

Udi's head appeared over the top of the cubicle. "What just happened?"

Nasser stood up fast, tapping his back pocket to make sure the igniter was all the way in there. "My computer blew up."

"Was that the sound I heard before?"

"I don't think so, I just turned it on."

"Better tell Barry."

"I'm doing that right now."

Nasser found his supervisor out in the hall. "Barry, I've got a problem."

"What's up, Nasser?"

"I just turned my computer on, and it blew on me."

"It blew?"

"There was like this big pop, and it went dead."

"You're shaking."

"Well, I don't have computers blow up on me every day."

"Let me take a look at it."

Barry, of course, was an expert in computers, too. They walked over to Nasser's cubicle, and Barry waved his hand in front of his face. "Jeez, I can smell it. What did you do?"

"I didn't do anything, Barry. I turned it on, and it blew."

"I heard it, too," Udi chimed in from behind his cubicle.

"Okay, take it easy." Barry tried turning it on, but the computer was quite dead. "What a pain in the ass. How much work was on it?"

"I send everything off to the case agents before I leave for the day, Barry. You know that."

"Yeah, you're right. I wish everyone else did that. Okay, I'll get on the phone and have someone take a look at it." He surveyed the office. "Until they get you a new one, work from Jim's desk. He's on maternity leave. Okay?"

"Okay, Barry."

"You just turned it on, right?"

"I just turned it on, Barry. And it blew."

"Okay, don't worry about it."

Nasser felt drained, his arms like rubber bands. But the relief was enormous. He began moving his stuff over to Jim's cubicle. He'd already made up his mind. He'd get them what they wanted, then get out. Quitting wouldn't do any good—they'd just make him join some other government agency.

But he'd get himself fired. If he got fired from the FBI, he wouldn't be able to work anywhere that required a security clearance. They couldn't do anything to him then. He never wanted to see anything secret ever again.

Chapter Seventeen

When they were in the United States, Storey and Troy wore pagers so they could be called when they were off duty. Pagers were more reliable than American cell phone networks.

Storey was watching Saturday night college football with Sergeant Major (retired) Dave Tallchief, an old buddy from Delta Force. Delta always had a significant presence of hardcore Native American warriors.

The Sergeant Major was doing contract work at the Pentagon, making more than three times his last Army salary. Iraq's demands on an overstretched military, and Republican philosophy in general, had caused the government to shovel money at private military contractors to pick up the slack. And in a textbook lesson in the law of unintended consequences, not to mention basic economic theory, the contractors used all that taxpayer money to bid against the U.S. military for the services of its best soldiers. The most senior and by definition most experienced enlisted men in Special Operations found they could make six figures doing the exact same job with less military bullshit. So they were either retiring right at the twenty-year mark or just not reenlisting and leaving the services in droves. A massive brain drain that Special Operations could ill afford with two wars going on.

The game was on the big screen, Storey had his feet up on the La-Z-Boy, and his stomach was full of steak and potatoes.

"You sure you don't want a beer?" Tallchief asked.

"No thanks," Storey replied.

"You need to come over here sometime when you're not on alert."

"Truth is," Storey admitted, "I gave up drinking after divorce number two."

"Did you?" said Tallchief. It wasn't just that struggles with the bottle were a dime a dozen in the military. Senior staff NCOs, who had damn near seen it all, tended to be a lot more understated than civilians would ever imagine.

"Didn't need any more problems," said Storey.

"You gotta do what works for you," said Tallchief. "Whatever happened to Jocelyn, anyway? Pretty little gal—mean as a wolverine."

"Moved to San Diego and married a dentist."

"Did she?"

"Worked out for everyone," said Storey. "She don't hate me anymore, and I'm not as poor as I used to be."

"Remember her from Bragg, Di?" Tallchief asked his wife.

"I remember," said Diane Tallchief. She and her husband were just touching forty. Delta operators were such expert soldiers that they tended to make rank very quickly. "Everyone told her what the life was going to be like. And she was fine, the deployments weren't going to be any problem. Being independent and solving problems yourself wasn't going to be any problem. Then after about a month she was sick of it. Sorry for dragging it up, Ed."

"No problem, Di," said Storey. "Like I told you, everything worked out."

"For everyone but the dentist," said Tallchief.

He and Storey chuckled.

"Don't laugh too soon," said Diane Tallchief. "I'm thinking about what it would be like with a house full of dentists instead of a house full of soldiers."

"Boring, honey," said Tallchief. "Very boring. Just like all those civilians we hang around with now."

"Do dentists sit around talking about the old days when they turn into old farts?" Diane asked. "Ed?"

"Probably," said Storey. "And they talk about fillings and braces."

"You're so sweet, Ed, trying to make me feel better about it."

"And they don't talk about it while the game is on," Tallchief said pointedly.

"Put on the closed captioning," said Diane. "Except you can't read that fast."

"I hate movies with subtitles, too," said Tallchief.

. Lee Troy was in a bar in Old Town Alexandria, checking out the talent. And the talent was there, except the women were all running in posses. It was no trouble meeting them away from the posse, but then you always got dragged back to the table. He'd just as soon avoid that, if at all possible.

Wait up a minute. Killer bod up at the bar. He began circling her, doing the recon. Man, those jeans were so tight—good tight, not bad tight—that it looked like it had taken a working party to get her into them. Outstanding profile in that tight top. And the face? Nice— but that body was 4.0, as they said in the Navy. She looked about thirty-five. That was okay, he liked older women. And no posse in sight.

She got her drink and was waiting for her change. Troy made his move and came up behind her.

She left a tip, picked up her drink, and turned away from the bar.

Troy bumped into her. "Excuse me."

She'd spilled part of her drink on her arm. "So there's no one in the world other than you, is that it?"

Troy was contrite. "I'm really sorry. I'm just a little preoccupied tonight. I'll get you another drink."

The apology took her edge off, and made her take a closer look at him. "What's wrong?"

"Oh, nothing," said Troy. "I'm just shipping out tomorrow. Are you sure I can't get you a replacement drink?"

"Shipping out?"

"To Iraq."

"Really?"

Troy nodded solemnly.

"Why don't you come over and sit down with me?"

"Thanks," said Troy. "I could use someone to talk to."

Storey's pager went off.

"That's a sound I don't miss," said Tallchief.

"Me either," said his wife.

"Excuse me," said Storey. He went outside to call the office.

"Ed looks as tired as you did on your last hitch," said Diane.

"Did I look that tired?" said Tallchief.

His wife nodded.

Storey came back in. "Got to go, folks." He hugged Diane. "Thank you for supper, darlin'."

"Be careful, Ed," she said.

He and Tallchief shook hands. "The next meal's on me when I get back," said Storey.

"Make sure you bring Beth along," said Diane.

"Diane can't wait to look her over," said Tallchief.

"Would you please shut up," she said.

"I promise I will if she's in town," said Storey.

"I was going to say it served you soldiers right to meet

someone with a job like yours," said Diane Tallchief. "But no one really deserves that."

They were making out in the elevator, then did the locked-together tipsy walk down the hall to her apartment. Getting the door open was a team effort.

Troy looked around. "You have great taste, Jane." Actually, he wouldn't know great taste in decorating if it bit him in the ass, but women always liked to hear that.

"Thanks, Lee. How about a drink?"

"That would be great."

"What would you like?"

"Whatever's handy. Don't go to any trouble."

"Be right back."

She disappeared into the kitchen.

Troy took a little turn around the living room, looking for any kind of weird lifestyle indicators he might have to deal with later. Nope, everything seemed normal.

"Here you go." Jane was standing in the kitchen doorway, naked, holding two drinks. She turned and walked into the bedroom.

Troy loved older women. He shucked off his clothes on the way to the bedroom, then leaped onto the bed, making them both laugh.

He was kneeling upright on the bed, and she knee-walked over and put her arms around his neck.

Troy always loved that first full body-to-body contact.

They kissed, and she said, "I want to show you something."

"Okay." What *else* was he going to say?

She opened the drawer to the night table, and Troy was really hoping nothing scary was going to come out.

It was a roll of LifeSavers. She popped one into her mouth. And then she popped him into her mouth.

"Whoa," Troy exclaimed. Wintergreen. The LifeSaver

was being moved around by her tongue, very slowly. "Holy shit."

There was a noise out in the living room. Concerned enough to stop everything, Troy gently held her head and started to move off the bed.

She grabbed his arm. "My husband."

"Your husband?" There hadn't been any wedding ring, and a husband hadn't come up in conversation. Troy was pretty sure he would have remembered.

She put on a robe and opened the window. "Wait out on the balcony."

Well, at least she was thinking fast. And better the balcony than being discovered in the bedroom.

When Storey pulled into the lot the whole office park was dark except for their building with the one lit-up floor. The operations offices.

Lieutenant Commander Moneymaker was waiting for him. "Where's Troy?"

If Storey felt any concern he didn't show it. "He didn't answer his page, sir?"

"No."

Officers tended to lock on to the one thing that was bothering them and forget the matter at hand. "No need to wait, sir. I'll brief him."

"All right."

"What's going on, sir?"

"Everyone's going ballistic over your intel. The CIA put their first team on the Pakistani you grabbed in Rio. He's talking about twenty Chechens heading into Mexico."

"Just curious, sir. Any word on what they were doing the week they spent in Rio?"

"The Pakistani was making them Brazilian passports. Evidently he'd managed to buy real blanks. Had the camera, seals, everything."

"What are these Chechens going to do, sir?"

"Nothing on that yet, but with your intel on Nuevo Laredo they're sure as shit coming across the border. Combine that with Customs seizing a shipping container in Los Angeles with a weapons load for twenty men."

"What kind of weapons, sir?"

Moneymaker passed him a sheet of paper.

Storey looked it over. This wasn't a pistols and home-made explosives operation. No wonder they were going ballistic over at the Pentagon.

"NSA's got all their ears focused on Nuevo Laredo," said Moneymaker. "Nothing so far."

"Nice to know they're on the job, sir. Now."

"Yeah, I know Ed. We need to get you down to Nuevo Laredo as soon as possible."

"Anything on the cell phone that was used, sir?"

"The CIA probably has someone inside Telcel, the Mexican provider. Most likely they'll have the records in a day or two."

Storey almost asked if he was going to bump into the CIA in Nuevo Laredo. That had happened before. If only they fought al-Qaeda as hard as they fought each other. Personally, Storey had no problem either way. But he did not want anyone, not even Moneymaker, knowing exactly where he was and what he was doing until he decided to let them know. People just weren't as careful about operational security when it wasn't *their* ass out on the line.

"What do you need from me?" Moneymaker asked.

Now that was the kind of question Storey liked to hear from an officer, rather than trying to tell him what to do. "I'll let you know once I do my research on Nuevo Laredo, sir." He never went into a city cold if he could help it. It wasn't just looking at maps and satellite photos. He liked to get a bit of the history and what had been going on recently. It nearly always paid off.

"I know you like to be thorough, Ed. But we need to

move fast, here. Not just because we need to move fast, but there's a lot of pressure to move fast."

"I understand, sir." And Storey did. It was why disaster always clung to U.S. Special Operations like a bad smell. Everyone did everything by the numbers in training, then when it was real things fell apart because the officers rushed and half-assed everything.

"Something else I've got to tell you," said Moneymaker. "Lund's support team is already on their way to Nuevo Laredo."

Only someone who knew Storey quite well, and Moneymaker did not, would have realized how angry that made him. "Sir, an assault team always goes in first to check out the ground. And *then* brings in support. That's SOP."

"I know, Ed. I didn't hear about it until they'd already been launched."

Storey didn't bother with a lot of whys. It had already happened, so that would be for the after-action report. This was bad. Lund and his team were good, but the smaller the city, the more care that had to be taken. And four men made a much bigger footprint than two. Now he was really going to have to rush. "Do you have anything else for me, sir?"

"No. I'll stand by in case you need anything before you launch."

Storey knew his preparations would take the rest of the night. "That's really not necessary, sir."

"I'll be here."

As soon as he could get away from Moneymaker, Storey called Troy's cell. This was the wrong time to be missing a page. He got Troy's voice mail. "Wherever you are, get your ass down to the office ASAP."

Troy was standing naked on the balcony. In the darkness of one corner. There was the window to the bedroom. And there was the sliding glass door to the living room. He looked down over the railing. Seven floors down. Not only were his clothes in the living room, but his wallet, phone, and pager. And it was fucking cold out here.

So did he go over the rail and abandon ship? Did he wait until the husband stuck his head out the sliding door and then lay him out? Or did he go inside, lay him out, and hope to clear the building before the cops arrived?

Troy heard Storey's voice in his head. There were some decisions you needed to make fast. And then there were some decisions you didn't want to make *too* fast. Because if he made the wrong move he wasn't just going to be in trouble. He was going to lose his SEAL quals and end up in the black shoe Navy. Anything but that.

The cold made up his mind. He leaned over the railing and planned his moves. Then the bedroom window slid open. It was Jane. She stuck her arm out and handed him his phone, wallet, pager, and keys. She mouthed the word "wait" and shut the window.

Troy took that as a sign. He flipped open his phone and dialed a number.

Storey went down to his equipment cage and put on his blue suit, white shirt, dress shoes, and conservative tie. They always traveled as businessmen, at least to get into a country. Businessmen might get searched at Customs but they didn't get the real treatment the way someone with a ponytail would.

The mini Glock was in the shoulder holster under the dress shirt, which although it displayed buttons was fastened with Velcro. Their Bureau of Alcohol, Tobacco, and Firearms credentials would get them on a plane in the United States. And from then on, no matter the number of connections, it was rare to pass through another metal detector. Even if they did, there were ways around airport metal detectors. That Glock pistols could pass through them unnoticed was an urban legend. The receiver was made from polymer, but the barrel and slide were both steel.

Storey's cell phone rang. He checked the incoming number. Troy. "Where the hell are you?"

Troy was speaking into his phone in a barely audible whisper. "You're going to have to come get me."

Storey didn't ask why Troy was whispering. His partner was obviously in some kind of situation. "So where you at?"

Troy whispered out an address in Alexandria.

"And what exactly is that?" Storey asked, just to be clear.

"Apartment building," Troy whispered back. "Park on the west side. I'll see your truck."

"You don't want me to blink my headlights three times?" Storey asked. "Carry a copy of *Popular Mechanics* under my arm?"

"Just hurry the fuck up," Troy whispered louder.

Storey pocketed his phone. He had a feeling this was going to be good.

The apartment building was on Duke Street in Alexandria. Storey knew it; it was one of the places he checked out when he got orders to Washington.

He parked on the west side of the building as instructed. No one was in the parking lot except one guy on the far side. He was driving a car with D.C. plates and a Support Our Troops bumper sticker and the Christian fish symbol on the back, unloading his trash into the apartment building Dumpster so he wouldn't have to pay the city for the extra bags.

No one was around any of the exits. Storey thought about going into the building, but the entrance was on the other side and there had to be a reason Troy told him to park here.

Deer never look up, because none of their natural predators is in the habit of dropping down on them from above. Which is why deer hunters use tree stands. Humans have the same bad habit, which is why whenever there was an up in the vicinity, Storey made a habit of checking it out.

As always, movement tends to catch the eye first. Someone was climbing down the side of the building, using the balconies. Storey had a pretty good idea who that might be.

He dialed Troy's cell phone number. And was rewarded when the human fly stopped climbing and disappeared into the darkness of a balcony.

"What?" Toy whispered into the phone.

"I'm here," Storey announced cheerfully. "Where you at?"

"I'll be there in a minute," Troy whispered. "Just hold on to your ass."

"Where do I go to pick you up?" Storey inquired.

"Just . . . fucking . . . wait," Troy snapped.

"You were in a such a big hurry," said Storey. "I'll go pull over by the entrance."

"Just . . . fucking . . . wait . . . right . . . there," Troy hissed into the phone.

"Quit fooling around," said Storey, grinning as he looked up. "Where are you?"

"I'm . . . coming . . . down . . . the side of the. . . fucking . . . building. Now shut up . . . and . . . wait."

"Oh," said Storey. "So *you're* the naked black guy climbing down the side of the building. Okay." He broke the connection, still wearing that smile.

The apartments seemed to start on the second floor, which left Troy a very high jump down to the parking lot. Storey was about to show mercy on him and drive over when Troy swung out onto a drainpipe and shinnied down. Not bad barefooted, Storey thought.

Back on terra firma, Troy anxiously waved Storey over before backing away into the darkness.

Storey leisurely started his engine and turned his headlights on.

Troy appeared again to wave him over a little more urgently.

Storey gave a couple of friendly taps on the horn.

When it became clear his partner wasn't moving, Troy sprinted across the parking lot. He obviously tripped on something, because the sprint turned into a very fast hop. He grabbed the passenger door handle. "Hey, Ed, you want to unlock the door?"

There was a bright flash as Storey snapped a photo with the disposable camera he kept, as recommended by his insurance company, in the glove compartment in case of an accident. "One more," he said. "Smile." The flash popped again.

Then the lock clicked and Troy slid into the passenger seat, naked as the day he was born.

Storey paused to snap one more picture.

"Can we leave now?" said Troy.

"Someone isn't coming down with your threads?" Storey asked.

"No," Troy replied. "You wouldn't happen to have a blanket in the redneckmobile here, would you?"

"Sorry," said Storey.

"Don't worry about it," Troy assured him. "Camera but no blanket. I understand completely."

"Don't forget your seat belt," said Storey, putting the truck in gear. "Safety first."

"Yeah, we wouldn't want to get pulled over, would we?"

"Do we need to get your car?"

"No," said Troy. "I was planning on drinking, so I took the Metro and was going to catch a cab home."

"Very responsible of you," said Storey.

"Didn't make any difference. My ass got sobered up real fast."

"It's kind of a cool night. Want me to turn the heater on?"

"Only if it's not too much trouble."

"No trouble at all." Storey turned the heater on the first setting. "So. How did you find yourself in this unfortunate condition?"

"I don't want to bore you," said Troy.

Storey rolled his window down. "Does it feel stuffy in here to you?"

Troy watched his skin forming goose bumps, everywhere, and sighed. "Okay, I was at a bar in Old Town and met this lady."

"Were you shipping out again?" Storey asked, rolling the window back up.

"Well, I *am* shipping out, aren't I?" Troy demanded.

"As a matter of fact, you're shipping out this morning."

"See," said Troy. "I'm always shipping out. I'm not a dog if I really am always shipping out."

"Of course not," Storey said reassuringly. "You crawled down the side of a building naked, but you're not a dog."

"I'm glad *someone* realizes it."

"I'll try not to distract you any more while you're telling me what happened."

Troy took him through it, being careful to emphasize, "And nobody mentioned anything to me about being married. So there I am, out on the balcony, with my wallet, phone, keys, pager, but no clothes. Why no clothes? I don't know, maybe she had to stuff them under the couch or something. But since I don't have my clothes, I'm trying to get that out of my head while I try to decide what to do next. Then I'm trying stay focused and not get hung up on going why me? But all I can think about is my mom. She always used to say that you never ask God, 'Why are You fucking with me like this?' Because

He's just going to do you like Job and say, 'Who made the world, motherfucker?'"

"I'm giving your mom a pass on the motherfucker," said Storey.

"But then I figure, I've got the wallet and keys and shit. So I'm like, okay God, I hear You now. I'm gone. I'm over the balcony."

"Now I'm reading you," said Storey. "But I've got just one question. You were climbing with both hands, I assume. So how did you manage the phone, wallet, keys, and pager?"

"Stuffed the keys in the wallet, clipped the phone and pager to the wallet, and carried the whole thing in my mouth like a fucking squirrel carrying nuts."

It was too easy. Storey let it go. "You're lucky someone didn't shoot you off their balcony."

"Don't think I don't know it. I'm not Alexandria's favorite color at the best of times, even with clothes on. But the Lord was with me, brother."

"I'll say amen to that," said Storey. "So you experienced a religious awakening and you're saved now, is that it?"

"Maybe. But I think I'd better take it slow. Start off by not fucking married women."

"That's probably best. You don't want to rush into anything."

"You're not speeding, are you?" Troy asked, checking the dashboard.

"No, I'd just as soon not have to explain all this to a cop. Even though the Lord is with you."

"No lecture, Dad?"

"Somehow I think you've absorbed all the lessons learned from this little experience, Son."

"Good. Because I learned my lesson about getting laid on an operation last year in Thailand. I was really hoping I wouldn't have to give up getting laid back here."

"That's up to you."

Troy felt strangely satisfied. Anyone else, the first question they would have asked was: Was she black or white? But not old Storey. "By the way, where are we shipping out to?"

"Nuevo Laredo."

"I figured. Are we flying to San Antonio and driving across, or flying to Monterrey and driving?"

"Monterrey. I want to be driving in a car with Mexican registration. And I don't want to pick it up in Nuevo Laredo. We got to hurry. Lund's team already got sent in."

"How the fuck did that happen?"

"Usual big Army stuff. Somebody thinks he's Patton, directing operations from behind a desk."

"That's fucked up."

"That it is. You think we could figure out that al-Qaeda's done best when they decentralized their decision making down to the lowest levels. And we've done best against them operating the same way."

"A few A-Teams taking Afghanistan without one-hundred-page op orders was too good to last," said Troy.

"Hey, I just thought of another question," said Storey.

"Shoot."

"Any money in your wallet?"

Caught off guard, Troy flipped it open and peered inside. It was empty. "Son of a bitch."

Chapter Eighteen

"Something is wrong," said Roshan Malik. "They suspect me."

Beth Royale knew that every informant got paranoid. Some felt those accusing eyes on themselves twenty-four hours a day. Some only got twitchy every now and then. It was their handler's job to get them through it.

"What makes you think so?" she asked. You never wanted to tell them they were imagining things. Mainly because you wanted them alert to danger, within reason. As the saying went, sometimes paranoids really did have people out to get them.

"They were always cautious speaking around me," said Roshan. "Now they do not speak at all. Only small talk, and they act as if they are making sure of every word. Before they came to my home, now they have excuses. I can tell they suspect me by how they look at me. You must please get me out of this, Beth. Put me and my family into the Witness Protection Program. I will testify. I promise."

"Take it easy," said Beth. "First of all, we're with you all the time. You're safe. Second, this type of behavior from them is perfectly normal. They're suspicious of everyone. Don't skulk around and confirm their suspicions. Come right out and ask them why they're acting strangely. If

they accuse you of anything, ask them how that can be if
they haven't told you anything yet? If they want to suspect
someone, suspect someone who knows something."

Her calmness seemed to restore Roshan's confidence.
"Yes, yes, that is very good."

"Then say that if they're looking for someone who's
been talking too much, they should use you since you
haven't been involved. Don't push it, though. Just throw
out the suggestion and then drop it. Leave it to them."

"Yes, Beth, very good. Throw their suspicions back
into their face."

"But don't push it too hard. You and your brother-in-
law are under indictment, after all. *You'd* like to know
who's talking. But take it easy on that."

"Yes, good."

"Is there anything else that made you suspicious?"

"No, no, Beth. I was being nervous. I see it now."

"Don't worry. You're doing great. Everyone's very
happy with you."

"Even this Mr. Timmins who never liked me?"

"Even he's coming around," said Beth. "Now how's
your little girl? I've been worried about her."

"It was as you suspected. Just the flu, God be praised."

"Kids are always sick. They play, and they pass whatever they have on to each other. I'll bet she's tired of
being in the house?"

"Yes, very much. She wants to go outside and play."

"That's great. And the boys?"

Roshan Malik talked about his children for the next
fifteen minutes. Then Beth passed him an envelope
with his stipend and sent him on his way. She waited a
few minutes for him to clear the area, and to settle the
tab. She'd given a lot of thought as to the best place in
L.A. not to accidentally bump into an al-Qaeda operative. And the bar at a four-star Beverly Hills hotel was
definitely it. The Bureau would stand for it as long as

they weren't on the line for anything more than a club soda with lime.

But as soon as she got back to the Federal Building she intended to take a look at some video.

"If they never talked around Roshan, how can there be something wrong?" Supervisory Special Agent Benjamin Timmins demanded.

"They never talked in front of him," said Beth. "But they talked when he wasn't in the room. They go to his house and it's all small talk and smiles. Before, when he left the room they used to huddle and plot. That's how we got the Russian guns. Now they just sit there, not even saying a word to each other. It's like they know they're under surveillance."

"That's crap," said Timmins. "You've been harping on this ever since the seizure at the port, like you wanted it to be a self-fulfilling prophesy."

"I do *not* want it to be a self-fulfilling prophesy." Calm down, Beth, she ordered herself. "Okay, Ben, then how do you explain all the clamming up everywhere we have a camera and a microphone?"

"Nothing's going on," said Timmins. "They're being cautious. It could be anything. What do you think, Sondra?"

"I don't see anything out of the ordinary," said Dewberry.

Typical, Beth thought. If Timmins thought he saw angels fluttering outside the window, she'd be taking down a description of the wings. "Roshan feels it. He thinks something's going on, too."

"All CI's get that way, you know that. He may even be picking that up off you."

Beth had to count down from ten to keep from saying what she really wanted to. "I thought he was just being paranoid, too. At first. Then I watched the tapes. And now I think he's right."

"Watched the tapes? You don't speak Arabic. How can you tell what's going on?"

"I don't have to speak Arabic to notice how people act. Have you seen the tapes?"

"I don't have to. I read the transcripts when Washington sends them back from translation."

"Do you want to see some highlights?"

"It doesn't matter," said Timmins. "We're turning this case, including running Roshan, over to the L.A. office."

"And why are we doing that?" Beth asked.

"Because that's what a Fly-Away Team does," said Timmins. "We come in, we assist the local field office on a counterterrorism investigation, and then we move on. We can't tie up a Fly Squad on case development. That's a field office job."

Suddenly it dawned on Beth why she'd been wracking her brain trying, unsuccessfully, to figure out the logic behind Timmins's moves. Because she'd been thinking about making cases and running what looked like a valuable long-term informant. And Timmins wasn't thinking about that at all.

As long as their Fly Squad was tied up on what seemed like a long, drawn-out case in L.A., it wasn't available to respond to anything sexy like Chechens coming across the Mexican border.

So that was why she was going to have to turn Roshan over to the L.A. office. Probably the same reason the Russian arms shipment had been seized instead of played along. Timmins got his credit for the bust, and the L.A. office was getting her informant. Immediate results—everyone looked good. And as an added benefit, if she was right and the surveillance had been compromised somehow, the L.A. office would be holding the bag for it.

Timmins really was good. Beth decided not to let him know she was on to him. No matter how much she'd love to rub his face in it. This had to be saved for the exact right moment.

So she saw that Timmins was ready for a fight, and instead replied, as meekly as she was capable of, "All right, Ben."

Timmins had suspicion written all over his face, but really, what could he say to that?

Chapter Nineteen

The hunter's moon made the night landscape glow bright in Abdallah Karim Nimri's night vision goggles. Too bright, but one of the penalties for having to move so quickly was not being able to choose the conditions he desired.

The four Ford Expeditions—two armored, two not—were spread out widely as they slowly climbed through the arroyo. No dirt bikes leading the way tonight. Rafael claimed they were required elsewhere. Nimri was furious at being cheated. But what could he do when they dismissed his arguments? He was totally dependent on Los Zetas, and they knew it. It was ever the same; the more money paid, the less value received.

He was not one of those brothers who did no training and no preparation, counting on the righteousness of their cause to obtain God's protection. The Saudis were particularly like that, regarding themselves as God's chosen people. Such arrogance tempted God's wrath. But Nimri knew there were times, and this was one, when everything that could be done had been, and the rest was in God's hands.

His eyes kept shifting from the landscape outside to the GPS receiver mounted on the dashboard. In this desolate land driving maps would not do. He had downloaded topographic information into the GPS. And even that only gave an approximation of the terrain.

Their entire route was also programmed into the GPS. This he had insisted on. Los Zetas could pick the route, but he was going to know where he was at every moment. Especially in relation to his destination.

Even without the dirt bikes, Rafael had been as skillful as before, picking their way over goat paths and dry creek beds. It made the going slow but secure. The Los Zetas bulletproof Expedition was in the lead, the other one last in the column. The middle two vehicles held Nimri and the Chechens, with only a Los Zetas driver.

They had all slowed, waiting for the lead Expedition to reach the top of the arroyo.

Nimri glanced again at the GPS, and as he lifted his head back to the windshield a beam of bright white light flashed across their front, washing out the image in his goggles as if he were staring at the sun.

As Nimri tore the goggles from his head, a booming amplified voice was issuing commands in Spanish.

"La Migra!" the Los Zetas driver shouted.

The spotlight was issuing from a white SUV a little higher up on the ridge. It had the lead Expedition in its grasp.

Nimri heard safety catches coming off behind him. "Wait!" he ordered. He reached up and pressed the button to open the powered sunroof.

A figure popped up from the sunroof of the lead Expedition. Nimri knew what was going to happen next.

Agent Mike Rodriquez of the United States Border Patrol was standing beside the open door of his white and green Chevy Tahoe, microphone in hand. He was working solo, as was usual along the border. There weren't enough agents to even consider putting two in each patrol vehicle. He'd already called for backup, but he wanted to stop that SUV before it reached the top of the arroyo. They'd been hearing rumors of black SUVs crossing for months, and now he'd finally got one.

Like pencils of light, the line of red tracer bullets skipped down the path of the spotlight and seemed to be absorbed by the white SUV. An instant later the hammering sound of machine gun fire made its way down the arroyo.

Nimri watched as another machine gun opened up from the trail Expedition behind them. That line of tracers wavered a bit from side to side, then settled down to intersect with the other directly onto the SUV.

The tracers leaped out and died down as the two machine guns traded off their fire. The spotlight either went out or was shot out. There was a pause in the firing, Nimri guessing that both gunners had stopped to put their goggles back on. The tracers started up again.

Agent Rodriquez was hugging the dirt. Jesus Christ, *machine guns*! He'd lost the microphone and was yelling into his belt radio but getting no response. Not unusual in the west Texas hills. Unable to reach anyone on any of the frequencies, he crawled back to the Chevy on his belly. Machine gun bullets snapped through the steel as he pulled himself into the open door, staying near the floorboard. He stretched his arm out but he couldn't reach it. So he pulled himself in a little more, pieces of glass and metal falling down on him like snowflakes.

Each time Rodriquez tried to rise up the fire made him flinch back, like trying to touch a hot stove burner. It wasn't showing any signs of subsiding, and he knew they might be moving on him even now. Finally he said fuck it and lunged up, stabbing his finger onto the red button on the computer console, sending off the automatic emergency signal with his GPS location.

Now there was Kalashnikov fire from the Expedition behind Nimri. A more methodical *bap-bap-bap* rather than the rapid hammering of the MAG machine guns.

He would have been surprised if Temiraev had been able to resist. He shouted into the walkie-talkie for them not to waste their ammunition.

Unable to turn around in the narrow confines of the arroyo, the lead Expedition was backing down the slope, fast, the machine gunner in the sunroof still firing.

As it neared Nimri's vehicle there was shouted Spanish over the radio. The Los Zetas driver threw open his door and leaped out into the night.

Nimri had been expecting that sometime, but he would have liked a little warning. He lifted himself over the center console, slid into the driver's seat, and pulled the door shut. "Machine gun, up in the roof," he ordered. "Wait for my command."

The Los Zetas Expeditions were retreating by bounds, firing as they went. Nimri knew his choice was to either follow them back across the border, or go on. Other Americans would be arriving soon.

"Follow me," he said into the walkie-talkie before jamming it between his legs so he could shift into drive. "Short bursts," he commanded the machine gunner. "Do not waste ammunition—just keep their heads down."

He headed up the arroyo. This driving wearing the night goggles was not as easy as it seemed. He did not go up the slope as slowly as the first Los Zetas did—he could not afford to—and the SUV bounced wildly.

"Are they following?" he shouted. He could not use the rear mirror with the goggles on, or hear the radio over the noise of the machine gun.

"They follow, they follow," one of the Chechens called out from the backseat.

Nimri almost had them to the top of the arroyo. He worried about puncturing the gas tank or oil pan, but it was no time to tarry.

Mike Rodriquez crawled down the line of the ridge on his stomach. The mesquite turned into blackbrush that held him up and ripped his uniform to shreds. He thought he heard approaching engines over the machine gun fire, and thought about shooting back. But everything was still being aimed at the Tahoe and he knew his muzzle flash would bring it all down on him. As he crawled he kept testing his radio. Finally a voice replied.

As Nimri and the Chechens crested the ridge, they saw that the Border Patrol vehicle was on fire. A tracer must have found gasoline. Nimri didn't like that at all—it would be a beacon in the night for the Americans.He could hear Temiraev's vehicle still hammering away. It made him furious, even though he knew it had to stop soon. And as they went over the ridge and lost sight of the burning SUV the fire did stop. What kind of fools painted their vehicles white? Nimri asked himself. Then the answer occurred to him: ones that expected their quarry to run back across the border when the white vehicle was seen. Not this time.

The GPS directed them down a finger that led off the opposite side of the ridge. And through brush that was as high as the hood. Could this be right? Was the machine faulty, and leading them the wrong way?

The slope steepened, the Expedition suddenly began sliding sideways. Nimri cut the wheel to straighten them out, applying the brakes carefully. But by the time they reached the bottom he could smell burning brake pads.

They halted before a wall of brush. Nimri felt helpless. "Do you see anything that looks like a trail?" he called up to the machine gunner.

"Yes, twenty meters to the left," the Chechen replied.

"Next time tell me!" Nimri shouted.

"You did not say to watch for this," was the Chechen's insolent retort.

"Watch for the Americans and watch the ground!" Nimri shouted back. A perfect view from the highest vantage point in the vehicle, and the fool keeps silent.

While the conversation was taking place, and before Nimri could get moving again, Temiraev's Expedition came roaring down the hill and almost slammed into them, the driver swerving away at the last moment.

Nimri knew Temiraev had to be driving. He turned left and punched through the brush.

It was little more than a path, a pair of tire ruts cut deep into the earth by the rain washing off the hills. They became so deep that Nimri had to climb the Expedition out of them, afraid the oil pan would definitely be punctured. It reminded him of Afghan roads.

This route was fine for a slow, unhurried infiltration, but not when already discovered and speed was essential. Nimri found it maddening. At least he was driving. Otherwise he would truly have gone mad.

Finally they broke onto a better track, almost a dirt road. Nimri sped down it, glad to be making up time. But it stopped abruptly at the base of another hill, requiring another slow climb through rocks and brush.

Cresting that hill, the GPS pointed him downward. Nimri still distrusted it, but the dashboard compass showed them continuing roughly north, and that was the direction they needed to go.

He hated not being able to see the ground properly. The goggles, combined with the concentration required, were making him feel sick again.

The Chechen machine gunner suddenly shouted, "Ai! Left, left by God! Turn left!"

Nimri swung the wheel over, and the vegetation fell away before them. Erosion had cut a deep gully into the side of the hill, and they had almost driven into it.

"Well done," he called out to the machine gunner. "Now guide us to the bottom of the hill."

"More left," the gunner shouted down. "Go slowly."

As he began moving again, Nimri picked up the

walkie-talkie to warn Temiraev when the gunner screamed, "Stop! Stop!"

Nimri jammed on the brakes, though it was not until he heard the noise that he realized the warning had not been for him.

Temiraev had been coming down the hill too fast again. Seeing Nimri stopped he had also applied his brakes. But with his downhill speed he skidded. The front tires went into the gully.

Nimri watched with dismay as the Expedition dropped into the gully and disappeared from view. "What has happened?" he shouted.

"They flipped over on one side and are sliding down the hill," the gunner shouted back.

"Get us down," Nimri yelled. "Quickly."

It was again infuriatingly slow as they had to skirt the edge of the gully and then cut back across the base of the hill.

Nimri almost screamed his frustration when they were halted by large rocks. "How far away?" he shouted up to the gunner.

"Twenty-five, thirty meters."

The gunner was pointing. "Keep pointing," Nimri ordered. He snatched up his AK and said to the others in back, "Wait here."

The fear Nimri felt was not that all in the other vehicle might be lost, but that Temiraev might be lost. He had always counted on Temiraev commanding the Chechens, and he commanding Temiraev. If Temiraev were dead controlling the rest might be difficult.

The air seemed alive with the sound of a million insects. Walking with the goggles turned out to be even harder than driving with them. Nimri could not see his feet and the ground both, and could not judge the distance to the ground. He kept stepping as if it was flat and having the sickening feeling of his foot continuing to drop. He almost fell twice, feeling as awkward as a baby. And, disoriented, kept having to look back for the gunner's outstretched hand.

Finally he came through the brush and found Temiraev and his men, and the Expedition still on its side.

"Any hurt?" Nimri gasped, from both exertion and relief.

"No," Temiraev told him curtly, deeply humiliated. "Again!" he ordered his men.

They were trying to rock the Expedition back onto its tires. Nimri knew they would never budge it. The light Toyota pickups they were used to in Afghanistan perhaps, but not this American behemoth.

"Leave it, my brother," Nimri urged. "We have no time. Move your equipment to my vehicle. We will fit everyone in."

"Once more," Temiraev shouted, unwilling for the sake of his pride to admit defeat.

His mean heaved, but to no avail.

"With the others we can move it," he said to Nimri. "I know this, by God."

Nimri realized he could not shout at the Chechen, no matter how much he wanted to. "There is no time! My brother, move them to my vehicle."

Temiraev whirled about, as if seeking further inspiration. Then he slapped his hands to his sides and, to Nimri's amazement, actually howled in frustration. Just as quickly, he began snapping out orders. And his men began dragging the equipment bags from the back.

"Let me rig it to explode, brother."

"No time," Nimri repeated firmly.

Temiraev gave up then.

Nimri paced in frustration as everything was gathered up. Too long, it was taking far too long. He led them through the brush, begging God not to let him become disoriented. For a moment he thought it had happened, then, thanks be to God, the Merciful and Compassionate, he saw his gunner waving from the roof of the Expedition.

They threw the equipment bags into the back, and had to fit in three men lying atop them. The rest were wedged in, grumbling in Chechen, with Temiraev and another joining Nimri in the front. Both machine gunners were standing half up onto the roof.

Nimri turned in his seat and made a last-second count of heads. Temiraev was sullen and silent. Nimri said nothing to him, afraid that anything might be taken as a rebuke and provoke violence.

They emerged onto a narrow dirt road that actually became wider as it wound through the hills. Less brush and more trees now, thick enough that they were a barrier to Nimri's goggles.

He was feeling more confident, especially as the GPS arrow faithfully followed the path of the road. They had been sternly tested, but had prevailed.

Then from up in the sunroof came the shout, "Helicopter!"

Nimri's heart sank. He begged God to forgive his presumption.

"Pull over, brother," said Temiraev. "They may pass us by."

Nimri backed into the first suitable space he could find between the trees.

"The engine," said Temiraev. He ordered the two machine gunners back into the vehicle and shut the sunroof.

Nimri knew that thermal cameras saw heat, but he did not know how sensitive they really were. He knew from Afghanistan that you could cover yourself with a thick blanket and be safe, but what to do inside a vehicle was a mystery. He cursed himself for not researching this when he had the time. But at least Temiraev had been hunted by the Russian helicopters with the heat cameras.

"Everyone," said Temiraev. "Keep your eyes on the

sky." He twisted around in his seat so he could look up through the sunroof.

Nimri did the same through the driver's window.

No one said a word, as if afraid the American helicopter also had microphones to hear them. With the windows shut and the engine off it soon became stiflingly hot.

Nimri could hear the helicopter but he couldn't see it.

Temiraev was looking up through the sunroof. *"Yob tvoyu mat!"* he spat in Russian. He did not repeat the popular Russian curse "fuck your mother" in Arabic, instead merely stating, "They have us."

The copilot of the French AS350B3 A Star used the joystick to lock the forward-looking infrared onto the SUV in the trees below. He was radioing the position as the SUV began to move.

Nimri opened the windows and sunroof.

"The hailstorm?" said Temiraev.

"When we are clear of the trees," Nimri replied. "You give the command. Everyone stay inside until then."

Safety catches began clicking again as Temiraev issued orders. He watched both the road ahead and the sky through the sunroof. The white helicopter was keeping pace with them. The color and the blinking lights made it easy to see. "You know what to do," he told them. "Be ready."

The Chechens were all shifting in their seats.

The trees thinned out up ahead. Temiraev weighed their speed. "Ready . . . Now!"

The two machine gunners popped up through the sunroof, firing from the shoulder.

Every Chechen who could access a window leaned out and emptied his Kalashnikov. In a span of ten seconds 500 rounds went up into the air, aimed for the helicopter to fly into. The technique had been pioneered decades before by the Viet Cong. Not all the rounds found their mark, but enough did.

The light helicopter shuddered from the hits. The copilot screamed that he was shot. Unlike military helicopters neither the aircraft nor crew carried any protective armor. Red warning lights were flashing as the pilot whipped it into a hard turn away from the red tracers that continued to float up toward him. He called out a mayday and, noticing the transmission warning lights, began looking for a place to set down.

The Chechens cheered as the helicopter ran away. "Be ready in case it comes back," Temiraev shouted over them.

Even partially deafened by concentrated gunfire, Nimri heard the machine noise of magazines being changed and bolts pulled back and released. He was driving as fast as he could and still stay on the road. The helicopter would certainly have used its radio. Every American policeman within range would be racing toward them.

The GPS told him they were approaching an intersection. As the dirt road emerged from the trees he crept forward slowly, looking for other cars. It was Texas State Road 1472, and a turn to the south would lead directly into Laredo, Texas. But not for Abdallah Karim Nimri. All the police and Border Patrol would be using this road.

But there was nothing in sight. Nimri turned left, heading north. Still driving without lights. After little more than a kilometer, the GPS arrow signaled another turn. Nimri found the dirt road on his right and turned onto it. He had to slow down to negotiate some deep ruts.

Nimri first saw the halo of light on the trees. An oncoming car on the road they had just left. His first impulse was to speed up, but he knew that would leave a cloud of dust that would hang in the air for quite some time. "No one move," he ordered. Black with no lights—they should blend into the darkness.

All heads were turned around, watching the road. The diffuse light narrowed into the beams of headlights. The car flashed by at high speed. Nimri saw the lights on the roof. So even before the Chechens in the back were able to say, "Police," he had the Expedition moving.

Happy voices chattering in Chechen celebrated their escape. But Nimri was not so confident. And soon there were headlights cutting through the dust behind them.

Temiraev smashed his fist onto the dashboard and let loose with another Russian oath. *"Huyesos!"* Once again he did not bother to translate "cocksucker" into Arabic.

"I will stop and let you out," Nimri said calmly. "Not everyone. Finish it quickly and I will come back."

Temiraev responded with an enthusiastic blow to his arm that almost sent them off the road. He barked out a few quick orders.

"After we go around the next curve," said Nimri.

It was just ahead. As soon as they made it Nimri stopped hard, skidding to a halt as the tires refused to bite into the dirt road.

Temiraev and five other Chechens, including one of the machine gunners, poured out. Nimri was off again before the doors shut.

The American police might be fools, but he knew that if he stopped in the middle of the road they would never approach him.

Then he heard it. The same hailstorm of surprise fire that had greeted the helicopter. Nimri braked and turned around, driving carefully through the dust kicked up by his passage.

"Prepare to give support fire," he said to those in back. "But only when I order, and be sure of your targets."

As they drove up Nimri had to take off his goggles because the headlights of the police car were still on. It was black with a white hood and roof, and a map of Texas on the door. The windshield was so shattered he could not see inside.

Temiraev was strutting back and forth in the road.

"The lights, brother," Nimri called out the window. "The headlights."

Temiraev waved happily and smashed them with the butt of his AK. Nimri realized that he should have said to turn the headlights off. "Make sure the computer is destroyed. And push it into the trees. Quickly." A radio call must have been made.

Another shot was fired as Temiraev made sure to disable the radio and computer in the noisiest way possible. The Chechens pushed the car off the road. Now Nimri could see inside as it rolled by. The policeman was still behind the wheel, staring up at the roof, his khaki uniform washed dark with blood.

"Quickly, brothers. Quickly," he urged.

Temiraev herded his men back into the Expedition. He was happier than Nimri had seen him since that terrible basement in Antwerp. "A fine night's work, brother Abdallah. More of the blood of our clan avenged."

"Keep watch for helicopters," Nimri ordered the machine gunners, who were doing much boasting but little watching. "The rest of you, reload your magazines."

The talk subsided into grumbling, which Temiraev stopped with one sharp word of Chechen. "God is with us, brother," he said to Nimri. It came out like a reproach.

"All praise to God," Nimri replied automatically. "But our mission, my brother, is not to drive about America shooting policemen. However satisfying that may be."

"It is all pleasing to God," said Temiraev.

Nimri said nothing. It was why the lands of America had not been struck in three years. The Faithful awaited God, rather than realizing that it was God who was awaiting the Faithful.

He was amazed when they did not encounter any more police or helicopters.

What Nimri didn't know was that the original Border Patrol call for help had drawn every law enforcement agency in the region past them to the north. That Texas Highway Patrol cruiser had been racing along at the tail end of the surge. The trooper hadn't been sure that he really had caught a glimpse of a black SUV on that dirt road, so he was waiting to get a positive identification and license number before calling it in. And had been killed instantly by the initial ambush volley.

They eventually emerged from that dirt road onto Highway 83, where the goggles came off and the headlights on. And the machine gunners ducked back out of sight. They followed the highway south until it merged with Interstate 35. Nimri's head ached and his eyes hurt. His neck felt like a piece of steel. The tension followed by this uneventful drive through the empty Texas night had drained him.

They passed a highway rest area that Nimri examined for a suitable vehicle or two that they might exchange for the Expedition. Nothing.

At the same time the horizon began to brighten ever so faintly, the highway rose slightly and the blinking lights of a city could be seen amid the surrounding darkness. After everything, they had come back almost full circle. To Laredo, Texas.

"Keep your weapons away from the windows," Nimri instructed them. "But be prepared for a roadblock." They would certainly not pass any kind of close inspection. It would have to be another fight, with only the first moments of surprise and superior automatic firepower on their side.

The signs on the highway said Del Mar, and then Laredo. The were many trucks, even at that hour, but no police. Nimri waited for the trap. Temiraev kept holding his goggles up to his eyes and scanning the sky for more helicopters. There was no sound in the vehicle except breathing. And the Chechens were definitely not asleep.

The GPS directed him to exit the highway on the

northern outskirts of the city. They drove west, toward where the Rio Grande wrapped itself around one side of Laredo like an anaconda. It was an industrial area.

Nimri had learned his lesson about American neighborhoods. Too many eyes. Here there were businesses. And warehouses. Many warehouses.

At a traffic light a police car crossed slowly in front of them, looking them over. Nimri could hear the Chechens shifting in their seats again, preparing themselves. But the patrol car continued on.

They crossed train tracks. All the warehouses looked the same. In his tiredness Nimri strained to recall the directions. The correct cross street. There it was. An old wooden warehouse surrounded by a chain-link fence, topped with coils of razor wire. The fence gate was open. Nimri went through and waited, hoping he would not have to use the cell phone.

A train whistle blew, as if right beside them. It made them all jump in their seats.

Then, as if in a heroic tale, the sliding door of the warehouse opened to receive them. Nimri drove inside. God was truly with them. God was great.

Chapter Twenty

In Paraguay, Ed Storey knew it felt dangerous. The why was like a multiple choice exam. The undercurrent of illegality, the sensation of being too loud and too crowded, like everyone and everything was coming at him in waves. Now in Nuevo Laredo he knew exactly why border towns felt so dangerous. Because everyone, from the panhandlers and street vendors to the guy who sold him a newspaper, looked at him like they were trying to decide how much trouble it would be to take him off.

Everything about the situation felt wrong, and he didn't think it was the cumulative stress making him a little crispy around the edges. It wasn't right, and more important it wasn't *professional.*

And lack of professionalism could get you killed. How many times had he seen someone fall back on that old military attitude and say: fuck it, let's just get this over with?

Why did Lund rent an office as soon as he got into town? It wasn't like Paraguay—people didn't just roll into Nuevo Laredo and go into business. You had to approach each country differently.

Border towns tended to display all the clichés of both cultures. Nuevo Laredo was cinder-block architecture, run-down little kiosks in the open plazas, bullfight posters everywhere. And 7-Elevens and Pizza Huts.

The rental car they'd picked up at the Monterrey airport was parked a quarter mile away. Storey and Troy were walking down the Avenue Obregon toward the office address Lund had messaged to them. Not walking side by side, shooting the shit, oblivious to everything around them, but on opposite sides of the street, Troy a ways back covering Storey like they were fighter pilots and he was the wingman.

Storey had noticed the dark blue Lincoln Navigator when they'd passed it. There were plenty of SUVs around. But then there was the silver one at the other end of the street. Two Navigators with tinted windows wasn't a coincidence. It was a major problem.

Both SUVs were parked facing each other, with the office Lund had rented almost exactly in the middle.

Storey's feeling about ambushes was that the best way to survive them was not let yourself get into the kill zone to begin with. And if you did find yourself there, to move your ass out of it as fast as you could. Because if the ambush had been done right, you weren't going to be fighting your way out once it got sprung. He'd watched enough people try and fail in his own ambushes.

If he was wrong, no harm done. They'd circle back and link up with Lund.

Storey passed two subtle hand signals to Troy. "Danger" and "follow me." Troy was already passing the danger signal back. He'd made the SUVs too. As Storey waited for his partner to cross the street, he was checking out immediate threats on foot. A couple of possibilities, but nothing definite. So he figured that if anything was going to happen, it would come from the SUVs.

Storey walked into the closest shop, a *tienda*, or little mom-and-pop grocery store, running two fingers along the front of his shirt to open up the Velcro. He'd melted the Velcro with a lighter so it would open without that ripping sound.

The owner seemed a little nervous that Storey still had his sunglasses on. "How may I help you?"

Scanning with his peripheral vision, Storey saw that Troy was almost inside. "Where is your back door?" he asked politely in Spanish.

"You cannot use the back door."

Now the Glock was in Storey's hand. Troy saw it and his appeared also.

"Take the money!" the proprietor yelped.

Storey was already around the counter. He grabbed the Mexican by the collar and aimed him through the open doorway. "The back door, if you please."

In the storeroom the owner had to fumble around with his keys to get the door open. In Mexico thieves were the main problem—you paid off the fire inspector. He got it unlocked, and was about to push it open when Storey yanked back on his collar and slung him over to Troy.

Storey carefully and quietly opened the door a crack and peeked out. There was a red Chevy Suburban, also with tinted windows, parked about twenty feet down the alley. But not loading or unloading, not with that pile of cigarette butts under the driver's window.

A major part of the training was to blot out the usual torrent of irrelevant questions: who are they; how did it happen; what had happened to Lund and his team? Questions were always a mechanism to avoid focusing on the difficult matters at hand.

They were boxed in, and the box was going to be closing even tighter pretty soon. Troy told the proprietor, "Sit down on the floor and be quiet." Then he took a look through the door, seeing exactly what Storey had. Going back out to the street didn't strike him as a good idea. Whoever was in the two SUVs, they weren't going to care about how many civilians got caught in the cross fire. He and Storey weren't going to be running up or down that alley—it was a shooting gallery. The only way was to go over the cinder-block wall on the opposite side. But no matter how fast their climbing, their asses were still going to be hanging out while they did it.

He held a whispered discussion about this with Storey. Which illustrated the ambiguity of their situation, and Storey's own indecision. Usually Storey would have made his move and expected him to follow.

"Check out the front window," Storey said. He'd rather cross the street and go out the back of another store—*that* alley might not be covered—than get in a shootout he didn't have to. Because no matter how good you might be, nobody was ever guaranteed a win.

Troy returned a moment later. "You ever see more than one twenty-something guy hanging around on the street carrying a shopping bag?"

"Not unless they got weapons in it. Arabs?"

"Mexicans."

"Shit." That was why there was so many of them. And they probably wouldn't be worried about making a lot of noise. The cops wouldn't be showing up in the middle of this one.

"The longer we wait, the worse the odds are going to get," said Troy.

"The alley it is," said Storey. "Only one vehicle out here." They had a quick exchange of views. Storey snatched up an empty cardboard box to conceal his pistol in. And just before he went out the door said, "There's probably someone up on the roof."

He walked out into the alley, the cardboard box tucked under his arm, briefly turning full-face toward the Suburban just to see what would happen.

The engine immediately came on. So they were made, and the opposition had radios.

The Suburban lunged forward. A figure popped up from the sunroof, firing. He would have done better to wait until his sights were on target before hosing off that first burst, because Storey was familiar with the sound of AK rounds cracking by and he was already looking through *his* front sight. He fired the mini Glock almost as fast as the AK on full auto. After the fourth round the Mexican in the sunroof slumped forward, and the AK went clattering down the side of the Suburban.

Storey immediately dropped his sight picture to where the driver would be behind the windshield tint, and tapped out two more fast rounds. No stars and holes in the glass as he'd expected—the bullets just splattered on it. Bulletproof polycarbonate. Shit.

The driver tried to run him down, but despite the movies it isn't easy to hit someone who knows you're coming. The turning radius of an SUV is much greater than that of a human. Even though the driver swerved at him, Storey stepped away like a matador dodging a bull. As the Suburban passed he fired a round into each of the side tires. They were probably the run-flat type, but it would make the SUV harder to handle.

As Storey was ducking away, another Mexican with a rifle appeared through the sunroof. As he leaned over the side to fire down at Storey Lee Troy shot him in the back from the doorway.

After that Storey expected the driver to hightail it down the alley, but instead he threw it into reverse and came at him again. Storey kept his eye on the sunroof. All the windows were still closed, which meant the polycarbonate was too thick to roll down.

The driver hadn't seen Troy and hadn't heard the shot that killed the second rifleman. He was looking over his seat and concentrating on Storey.

As the Suburban backed toward him, Storey didn't wait to dodge as before but ran toward it faster than the driver could cut the wheel, sprinting past and putting himself in front of it again.

The driver braked to a halt, the rubber of the two

shot-out tires flapping on the pavement. As he paused to shift into drive again, Troy ran out of the doorway, leaped up on the running board, stuck his arm in through the sunroof, and blew the driver's brains onto the bulletproof glass.

Two rifles opened fire from the roof of the building. Troy launched himself through the sunroof, landing on both the driver and the other dead Mexican shooter. Shit, Storey had said to watch the goddamned roof.

Storey dashed for the cover of the side of the building, to cut down on their angle. An AK and an M-16. Their sounds were as distinct as the calls of two different species of birds.

Troy thrashed around in the front seat, trying to yank the driver out of the way so he could get behind the wheel. The driver's foot came off the brake and the Suburban shot back. It hit the wall on the other side of the alley, almost knocking him into the backseat. Goddammit!

Storey wondered what Troy was doing. Could there be another live Mexican in the SUV, that he was going hand to hand with? He stuck his head out a bit, almost risking a run across the alley. But the two automatic rifles on the roof opened up again.

Troy didn't worry about shifting; he went back to the dead Mexican. But whoever said that about dead weight wasn't kidding. There was blood all over the inside of the car, and brains splattered across the windshield. A couple of rounds came through the open sunroof, hitting the dash and ricocheting off the windshield. Shit! He twisted around and hit the button to close the sunroof.

Storey was pressed up against the wall, waiting for Troy to do something with the SUV. He didn't have a shot at the roof without exposing himself, and wasn't all that anxious to do that anyway with his pistol against two rifles. Troy needed to get a move on. They couldn't sit in that alley all day, and reinforcements—not theirs— would be arriving very soon.

Troy finally pulled the driver out of the way, and as he sat down behind the wheel the sunroof exploded over his head. The one part of the fucking car that wasn't bulletproof had to be right over his fucking head as they were shooting down at him.

Plastering himself against the driver's door, he shifted into drive and aimed the Suburban across the alley at Storey. Fewer rounds came in through the sunroof while he was moving, but they still kept coming in. Until he reached the dead space on the side of the building.

The driver's door opened up and Storey dove across Troy's lap. He crawled across and found himself atop two dead Mexicans.

"Watch your fucking feet!" Troy yelled as Storey spun around to get himself upright.

Troy stepped on the gas, heading for the cross street at the end of the alley.

Rounds thudded into the back of the Suburban. Storey looked over his shoulder. Three or four Mexicans coming out of doorways, shooting down the alley at them. Probably the ones who'd been waiting inside the office.

With the gas pedal on the floor and driving on two good tires and two hard run-flat inserts, Troy was fighting to keep the Suburban from wobbling all over the alley. "Left or right when we get to the end?"

"I'd go right. Left is the street we came from." Storey had climbed over into the backseat and was gathering up the one AK and all the magazines he could find. The other AK was out in the alley somewhere.

Troy was recalling the map he'd studied, trying to orient a route to one of the border crossings and back into the USA. Shit, they just needed to head north.

Then the dark blue Navigator pulled to a stop right in front of the alley exit.

"Brace yourself!" Troy bellowed. Fighting the wheel one-handed, he grabbed the seat belt with his left hand, dragging it across his body and snapping it in.

Heavy engine up front. Center the center of gravity. Troy aimed for the back wheel of the Navigator—less weight there.

It was like two tanks colliding. The Navigator spun around 180 degrees.

Troy's neck snapped back and the airbags deployed. Every time that happened he thought he'd gone blind.

The Suburban was spun around too, and as soon as he figured that out Troy cut the wheel over. He'd kept his foot on the gas the whole time and they continued lurching forward with a metallic shrieking sound.

When Troy got his eyeballs focused again he saw that the right front of the Suburban was all caved in. Probably a ton of metal pressing against the wheel. They weren't going far, and he didn't feel like bailing out in the middle of the open street. He had to find some cover.

Unable to do a lot of steering, he took the path of least resistance. Right across the street. Even floored and with the engine screaming and smoking, they ground forward at about ten miles an hour.

"You with me, Ed?" Troy yelled.

Storey had managed to look up and see what was going to happen just before the impact. He didn't manage to get a seat belt on, but the rear airbags kept him out of the front seat. He yelled back, "With you!" Though that was not entirely true. He knew they were still moving, slowly, but had no idea where. Until he got his head clear and saw they were about to ram into the front of a restaurant.

"Get ready to bail out!" Troy shouted.

They hit the restaurant, and at that speed if it hadn't been glass and thin wood they wouldn't have gone through. As it was, they only went in a few feet.

Troy tried his door. No go. He rolled onto his back and kicked away the few jagged shards remaining from the sunroof. Then he went out that way, slithering down the windshield on his stomach and sliding over the hood because there were timbers hanging from the ceiling.

He bounced up onto his feet, the Glock out in front. A few people were on the floor, a few were standing there looking at him in shock. Someone off to the side started screaming at him, and as he turned around to confront it, revealing the pistol, the sound shut off like pushing stop on a CD player. He checked everyone out—there'd be no trouble here.

Storey emerged from the sunroof right behind him. "Lead us out!" he shouted.

As Troy took off toward the back of the restaurant, Storey leaned around the side of the Suburban, trying to get a view of the street. Someone was staggering out of the Navigator, a pistol in his hand. Storey brought the AK up to his shoulder and squeezed off two rounds. He watched their impact—low and to the left. Where the sights were and where a rifle was shooting weren't necessarily the same thing. Making an instant correction by aiming high and to the right, he fired another double tap and the Mexican with the pistol fell to the street.

With ten more rounds Storey drove two more gunmen back around the corner. He shifted targets instantly, lining them up and squeezing off. Into the silver Navigator that was dropping off more gunmen into the cover of the parked cars across the street. Storey knew it was probably bulletproof, but it would keep their heads down. Someone was firing from the sunroof of the wrecked blue Navigator. Storey gave him the rest of the magazine until he disappeared from view.

A piercing whistle from Troy.

It had only taken a few seconds, and Storey knew they wouldn't be so damn quick to come across the street now. He dropped the empty magazine, letting it fall to the floor, rocking in a new one. He only had three left—ninety rounds.

Another urgent whistle from Troy.

Storey followed him through the back of the restaurant. The other side had more men. But they had to get organized, get on the radio, figure out what they were doing, then get moving without shooting each other. Where two men could just move damn fast.

They cracked the back door and made sure they weren't going to be walking into another situation. All clear. For now.

They both grabbed empty cardboard boxes from the jumble next to the door. Just as he'd done with his pistol Storey slid the AK inside his. With that prominent banana magazine, wrapping his jacket around it would only look like a Kalashnikov wrapped in a jacket.

Troy ripped open the bottom of his box and flattened it out, throwing it over the coil of razor wire atop the chain-link fence on the other side of the alley.

They climbed the fence, rolling over the cardboard to the other side. Troy yanked it off and threw it on the ground with the rest of the trash.

This time he took point and Storey hung back a bit to cover him. They walked fast but didn't run, knowing they had to gain some separation before the opposition realized they weren't inside the restaurant and began sweeping the area.

As they cut over onto the next street Troy turned and made a subtle steering motion with one hand. Storey nodded. They definitely needed a new car right away.

Storey turned toward the nearest storefront as a Nuevo Laredo police car sped down the avenue, siren wailing. Damn, it popped a U-turn at the next intersection and was heading back.

Storey had no idea how disheveled the two of them

were, how spattered with blood from their time in the
SUV with the men they'd killed.

The police car was a real problem. With Mexicans
gunning for them they'd last about five minutes in a
Mexican jail. If they even made it that far. He stepped
back into the storefront.

Troy was playing it cool. The police car skidded to a
stop in front of him, and two cops in blue uniforms
jumped out, brandishing their pistols and shouting,
"Hands up!"

Troy put his hands up. Storey stuck his hand into the cardboard box until he felt the wooden pistol grip of the AK.

The cops were waving their pistols around, not aiming
them, like everyone they'd ever run into had just given up.

Storey let the box drop to the ground and stepped out
onto the sidewalk. Getting a firm grip on the grooves cut
into the front handguard and pulling down to reduce
the muzzle jump, giving a hard tug with his forefinger to
make that long, creepy AK trigger break.

The first burst caught the nearest cop and threw him
back onto the road. Troy dropped to the sidewalk to get
out of the line of fire. The second cop just stared in
amazement as Storey's muzzle swung over toward him.
Another *bap-bap-bap-bap* and he was down behind the
side of his car.

Troy was back up on his feet and his pistol was out
again. He ran round the car and made sure the second
cop was dead. If you were going to shoot the public officials of an allegedly friendly country it was best not to
leave them alive.

Another shot from Storey as he did the same for the first
cop. The sound of that AK was going to attract attention.

Storey was already behind the wheel of the police car.
Troy didn't need an invitation. Storey changed magazines and passed the AK and last magazine over to him.

Only sixty rounds left. The keys were still in the ignition, the engine on. Storey pulled out fast.

Troy turned the radio volume up to see if they could figure out what was going on. About ten stations were yelling at the same time, drowning each other out. But he caught, "Los Zetas are moving to the Avenida Guerra."

"The Zetas?" said Troy. "What the fuck?"

"You missed the mission prep when you were getting your knob polished and doing nude wall climbing," said Storey. "They're cartel enforcers, ex-Mexican special forces."

"Cartel? What are they mad at us for?"

"Maybe they figured Lund and his boys were DEA. Maybe some Arabs hired them. Right now, who the fuck cares?"

"Okay, okay, so it's not a case of mistaken identity. Mexican special forces? That doesn't shrivel my nuts. I put Mexican special forces up there with Iraqi special forces. By the way, the border is in the other direction."

"You take a hit to the head?" Storey demanded.

"What are you talking about?"

"You think we'll make it through any of the crossings? Let alone to the U.S. Consulate?"

"I guess not," said Troy, a little embarrassed. "If they got the cops, we won't even make it on any of the roads out of town."

"Cops," Storey muttered. "That's a fucking mess right there."

"I know what you'd tell me," said Troy.

"What?"

"That's *way* down on our list of worries right now."

"You're right about that."

"Besides," said Troy. "I hear there aren't that many honest cops in Mexico. What's the odds you shot both of them?"

One of the hallmarks of both Delta Force and SEAL

Team Six was to carefully select and just as carefully train men of extraordinary self-control to explode into ferocious violence and then just as quickly revert to a calm, outwardly relaxed state.

They were far enough away from the scene now, and Storey turned off the flashing lights and siren that had helped them through the traffic. "We need to find a more inconspicuous car. You still got your tools?"

"Always." They both carried three simple tools, camouflaged as everyday objects, that could get them into and start any car in the world. That was also part of their training. Cars, locks, handcuffs. Originally Delta and Team Six had gone to prisons and consulted professional burglars and car thieves. Now the skills were passed along in-house.

In south Nuevo Laredo they found a Toyota Camry with a nice tint job on the glass that fit their needs perfectly. Troy got inside, deactivated the alarm, and had it running in less than forty seconds.

No one bothered them. Not with a police car there. Any bystander would have assumed that the police were either protecting the car thieves or stealing cars themselves. And not been surprised by either.

Storey followed him for about a mile. They dumped the police car near a junkyard, hoping the scavengers would arrive and in a few hours not even the skeleton would be left.

"I assume you've got some ideas?" said Troy.

"Nope, I'm stumped, I'm dry. It's all on you. What you got?"

Troy knew he was being fucked with, but it was time to show that there was more than one planning mastermind in the family. "Okay, they're going to be watching the border crossings. They're going to be watching the roads out of town. And the airport and train station. You feel like a little hike in the desert, maybe a swim in the Rio Grande?"

"You've got that SEAL ninja thing going again," said Storey. "Sure, load up a backpack with water, slip through the brush, swim across the border. If everything works out all right. If you run into someone, you're on foot in the desert with two pistols, one AK, and sixty rounds."

"Okay," Troy replied. "You don't like that. Even if they weren't before, they're probably all set up and in place by now. So I figure we should let them think they found us, draw them in, fuck them up a little, then slip out the back door in all the confusion."

"Now I like the way you're thinking," said Storey. "With one AK and sixty rounds, I assume you're thinking about an MA?"

"You got that right. And with those armored rides they're rolling in, we're going to need to make a few EFPs."

"I'm with you all the way," said Storey.

"The only thing that's hanging me up is the location. I don't want to fuck up any innocent bystanders or lay waste to any neighborhoods. I mean, I know we did that today, but it was them or us. I don't want to do it by choice."

"We're in total agreement," said Storey. He reached in his jacket and took out a Nuevo Laredo street map and a few pieces of laminated plastic. The drivers' licenses and ID cards of the Mexicans in the Chevy Suburban.

"When did you find the time to frisk those motherfuckers?" Troy demanded.

"I had a little time to kill while you were crashing into things," said Storey. "Let's see if one of these guys lived in a house we can use."

They cruised the streets, inconspicuous behind the tinted glass. Frequently passing heavy black SUVs, also with tinted windows. Also cruising slowly.

One apartment. One house in a crowded neighborhood. Then one dusty, run-down rancho at the end of a dirt road on the southeastern outskirts of town. The nearest neighbor was 400 yards away.

"We're not going to get any better than this," said Storey. "Let's grab a Yellow Pages and go shopping."

"There better be some car racers in this town," said Troy. "I don't feel like mixing up a batch of The Mother of Satan today."

This was the name given by the Palestinians to triacetone triperoxide, or TATP. Easily made from acetone, hydrogen peroxide, and other ingredients available at any hardware store or pharmacy, TATP was extremely powerful and easy to set off. But it was also extremely senssitive to impact, friction, and temperature change. Palestinian bomb makers regularly blew themselves up with their own chemistry sets.

As it turned out, they did race cars in Nuevo Laredo. And nitromethane racing fuel was available.

"We going to be grinding up fertilizer?" said Troy, hoping the answer was no.

"Too much time," said Storey. "Let's use regular household ammonia as a sensitizer."

The local crime rate meant that home security stores were very well stocked with a comprehensive product range for all income levels. Electric wire, soldering guns, and batteries were easy. Plastic kitchen storage containers in all sizes. A couple of propane tanks for the old gas grill. A cookware shop had some beautiful handmade copper serving plates. And a plumbing supply was happy to cut and cap steel pipe to their specifications. A cordless drill and bits, some camping equipment, a few boxes of energy bars, a case of bottled water, and a case of nails rounded out the list.

They also stole another car. A Jeep Cherokee.

The rancho was still unoccupied when they returned. As soon as they let themselves in and saw the mess they knew there was no wife. Though it would also have suited them if there had been.

It only took four hours of steady work to get everything

ready. The inside stuff was easy. The outside would have to wait until dark. The fact that the manufacturers of home security equipment were making their stuff wireless these days saved them a load of time.

"You want to make an anonymous call to the cops?" said Troy, after they finished cleaning up their materials and stashing them in the attic.

They'd been listening to the TV and radio all afternoon, and there hadn't been any mention of two wanted Yankees. "That might just get them suspicious," said Storey.

"How do we get the word out then?"

"Kill two birds. Send a message to Washington. Tell them about Lund, tell them we're holed up in a house and need them to get the Mexican authorities to get us out ASAP. Los Zetas will be here before dawn, thinking we're ripe for the picking."

"Suppose someone at the Pentagon command center actually has some street smarts and sends another team or the CIA to get us out instead of calling the Mexicans?"

"You're kidding, right?" said Storey.

"Okay, so I must have taken a hit to the head," Troy replied. "But what if some real Mexican good guys turn up here looking for us?"

"If that ever happens, which I doubt, it'll be two days from now. Los Zetas will be here tonight." Storey began composing the message on his PDA.

"Lund was a good guy," said Troy. "I hope they didn't take them alive."

"You don't get too many mistakes in the business," Storey said while he was writing. "Sometimes you don't get any at all."

They left the house after dark and set up their outside equipment. Their observation post had been chosen with great care. It couldn't be near any trees or cover in the vicinity of the house, because the opposition might very well choose those as avenues of approach. It couldn't be more than 100 feet away, the maximum range of most of their wireless gadgets. So they were in a shallow depression scraped from the sand, pretty much out in the open, in the middle of some tufts of wild desert grass. Covered with a big sheet of burlap.

This was when Storey always loved watching the transformation in his partner. Troy only acted impatient because he wanted to get on to the next thing. But if the next thing was to hide in the middle of the desert, he'd lie out there for a week, pissing and shitting into plastic bags, moving nothing except his eyeballs and his beating heart.

It wasn't like the usual observation post because there was no night vision equipment. But that didn't matter. Everything was set up for the enemy to hit the house. And they could do that at the time and method of their own choosing.

Only a little while after they slid into the hide, just a few minutes after 9:00 P.M., Troy heard something padding around. He hoped it was a wild animal, because a wild animal would soon be moving on. It was a dog. Troy could hear the sniffing as it came over to investigate. The worst thing that could happen, because even if the dog didn't hang around it would return. Attracting the attention of anyone who might be watching. Troy listened for an owner that might be walking it, that might come over to see what their dog was interested in. He couldn't hear anything. The dog probably got let out to roam, if it wasn't feral to begin with. Storey nudged him hard. Troy knew that if their hide was compromised they were dead. He lifted up the edge of the burlap. The dog gave a little growl, approaching cautiously.

It was a mongrel, like a terrier. Troy shot it with the suppressed pistol, reached an arm out of the hide, and dragged the carcass into the hole with them. He felt terrible about it. Just terrible. The karma was so bad they were probably going to be in there with the dead dog for a couple of days. And it was going to get hot in the daytime.

Storey felt bad about the dog, too. Even more so when his leg began to itch as the fleas began to migrate off the cooling corpse.

At one in the morning Storey felt someone out there. He didn't believe in a sixth sense. He believed that if you trained the other senses and actually paid attention to the input they were receiving, however subtle, your brain would process it correctly and give you the word. That was what five million years of being both predator and prey was all about. That was what getting a powerful feeling about something was all about.

He nudged Troy, so there would not even be the slightest noise of movement, like taking a drink of water. Now he felt more than one person around them. Troy nudged back. He felt it too.

Whoever it was, they were very quiet. Storey pressed two buttons on the remote control in his hand, and inside the house a light went off in one room and came on in another. An indoor/outdoor wireless AC control. Plug the box into any standard outlet, then plug the appliance, in this case a lamp, into the box. The remote turned the power on and off, as long as you were within 100 feet. Twenty-five bucks.

At 2:30 Troy thought he saw a file of men moving through the trees toward the back of the house. They'd correctly waited for the time of night when the human brain was operating at its lowest level of efficiency, but the moon was a little too high for the best shadows to conceal movement. A common mistake.

Inside the house all the curtains were closed so no one could see inside. The Camry was parked out in front.

Storey thought they might be going for a quiet entry, but at 2:45 the houselights went off as the power was cut. Good, Storey thought.

Then a single rifle shot, and an instant later two machine guns and, from the sound of it, about twenty more rifles opened up on the house from the front, back, and one side. Well, they didn't care about waking up the neighbors. Storey supposed he ought to take it as a compliment. He'd walked the whole perimeter of the house and grounds, and the fire support groups were positioned right about where he would have put them. So someone out there had some experience.

Now a rolling series of bangs and roars and brilliant white flashes. Storey was a little chastened to see his own technique intended for him. They were firing rockets at the windows. Not RPGs, though. Something else.

Then, more muted over the sounds of the continuing gunfire, some lighter pops. Storey was surprised not to hear any explosions after a reasonable delay. Then the question was answered as smoke began billowing from the windows. They were using tear gas. Storey worried about that. Tear gas burned really hot, and tended to set things on fire.

They'd used the rockets to blow the security grates off the windows, and hopefully cause some casualties, to open holes to fire the tear gas in.

A few minutes later the supporting rifle fire tapered off, though the machine guns kept it up. A couple of stray beams of light across the front yard told Storey they were going in wearing gas masks. A couple of the flashlights attached to the rifles had been switched on too soon. There were always a couple of screwups in every unit.

The machine guns and supporting fire shut off. The front and back doors blew within moments of each other. A harder, sharper bang and a brief flash lit up the living room. They were using grenades to clear the rooms, Storey thought. He would have done the same thing.

The constant rapping of rifle fire was indistinct, but

it was easy to follow their progress through the house by the grenade explosions and the rifle flashlight beams.

There were twenty Los Zetas in the house. They'd cleared the rooms methodically, in teams of four. The last team had just tossed a grenade into the last bedroom, and raked the room with gunfire. They blasted the closet before opening the door, expecting a gringo to be cowering there from the gas. It was empty.

Now there was just the bathroom. Again they fired through the door, aiming low. The team leader made a hand signal, and his lead man kicked the door.

Screwed to the door and the frame were the two halves of a normally closed magnetic switch, about the size of pair of rubber erasers, designed to burglar alarm a door. When the door came open the magnetic field between the two halves was broken, and the circuit closed.

In case the switch failed or was disabled, there was also a battery-operated wireless motion detector taped to the toilet. When the door moved it went off. But instead of activating an alarm it also closed a circuit.

In the bathtub, safe from bullets and grenade fragments, was a full ten-kilogram propane canister with kitchen storage containers filled with liquid explosive taped around it, and four compound detonators made from AK rifle cartridges. This bomb had a twin hidden under the rug and floorboards of the living room. But the cast iron sides of the tub channeled the blast wave beautifully.

It was known in the trade as an MA. Mechanical ambush.

Storey and Troy watched a bright flash light up the windows in unison with the explosion. The charges weren't big enough to level the building and make a mess of the neighborhood. Instead the whole house seemed to hop into the air, then the roof fell down on top of everything. Just a rolling cloud of smoke and dust after that.

After the explosion everything happened incredibly

fast. Four SUVs raced down the road with their headlights on. Troy was watching the prominent tree he was using as a mark. He hit the buttons on his remote as the first SUV passed.

Resting in the sand next to the road, with more sand piled on top of it, was a piece of steel pipe about eight inches in diameter, and the same length. It was aimed at the road like a gun barrel. The rear was sealed off by a welded steel cap. The interior was filled with liquid explosive and another homemade detonator. And the front end was covered by a slightly concave copper serving dish that fitted the diameter of the pipe perfectly.

A few seconds after Troy pushed the button on his remote the explosive detonated and the whole force of the blast was directed out the end of the pipe, firing the copper plate like a cannonball. Except the force, which was incredible, pushed the center of the plate out and folded the outside edges in on itself, forming it into the shape of an aerodynamic slug. An EFP, or explosively formed projectile. Before it even reached the road that copper slug was moving at a speed of 2,000 meters per second and capable of penetrating a main battle tank.

It hit the black Expedition on the front passenger door and ripped right through, turning all the metal and plastic and bulletproof armor into additional missiles. The slug cut the SUV completely in half, though not by any means neatly, emerging from the other side and continuing off into the night. There were no survivors.

Ordinarily the delay involved in any wireless transmission would have made it impossible to time a detonation to hit a fast-moving vehicle, particularly at night. But Troy hadn't set off the EFP with his remote. He'd merely activated a green plastic box nailed to the nearest tree. A passive infrared sensor-transmitter. Another home security item, to let you know if anyone was coming down the driveway or fooling around with your backyard storage shed. The transmitter box sent an infrared beam to a receiver. Anything that broke the beam would activate an alarm. Or just as easily fire a detonator.

By pacing out a few simple measurements an EFP could be aimed to hit any part of a vehicle once the front bumper broke the infrared beam. And it was absolutely automatic—no fallible human being to press a firing button too early or too late.

The infrared triggering technique had been developed by the Soviet KGB and first used by the terrorists of the German Red Army Faction, who planted an EFP device in a bicycle saddlebag and killed the head of the Deutchebank inside his armored limousine in the midst of a squadron of bodyguards.

Troy had waited for the last second to activate it, not only because he didn't want to take out any civilian cars by mistake, but because the infrared beam could be seen by night vision devices.

They'd placed a whole line of EFPs along the road. When the first SUV exploded right in front of them the other three stopped and backed up fast. So the second vehicle didn't run into the infrared beam waiting for it. But it did back into the beam of the next device.

All that meant was that the slug entered just behind the rear seat.

The fourth SUV kept backing up. It hit another EFP and blew like a Roman candle when the gas tank went up.

The driver of the third SUV, after seeing those in front and behind explode, stopped. He leaped out and ran off into the night.

While Troy was activating the EFPs, Storey was punching buttons on his own remotes. As the house exploded and collapsed, all the Los Zetas outside understandably started running to get away from it. Except dozens of infrared beams popped on in two rough concentric circles around the house.

One of the machine gun teams, being farthest away from the house, was the first to decide to pick up and get the hell out. They were also the first to break an infrared beam.

Carefully positioned in a clump of grass to cover the distance between the infrared transmitter and its twin receiver was a plastic kitchen storage container filled with liquid explosive and detonator. The outside of the container had been covered with nails held on by duct tape.

Being homemade, the blast didn't achieve the perfectly uniform fan shape of an issue claymore mine, but it did the job. The machine-gun team disappeared in the smoke and were never seen again in their original form.

The SUVs were exploding. One was burning brightly. The homemade claymores were going off apparently randomly all over the place. Men were running in panic. Leaders shouting orders were ignored. It was chaos. A few Los Zetas started shooting at another group in the confusion, and now it became a full-bore firefight as others thought someone else had found a target and joined in. No one had the slightest idea what was going on.

Except Ed Storey, the master of the chaos. And his acolyte Lee Troy. Who watched the whole thing from the comfort and safety of their shallow hole in the sand. In the daylight Storey had paced out all the distances and marked the locations for the mines and the infrared boxes. Which made it easier to install the already constructed devices in the dark.

Because they'd had to stay so close to the house to make their wireless gadgets work there was a narrow gap in the mines right around them. In the firelight they could see someone running right toward them. Storey gave Troy a tap to be ready.

The Los Zeta had been running behind two others until they disappeared in an explosion that knocked him to the ground. Getting up, he didn't even realize that he'd dropped his rifle. He stepped on something soft that he looked down and saw was part of a body. He swerved to one side and began running again. Except this time it was a sprinting, panting, sobbing blind panic.

Something rose up from the ground in front of him. A terrible blow to the stomach, that he did not know had come from the butt of Storey's AK. All the air rushed out of his lungs, and he crumpled to the ground.

Troy stepped up and cracked him on the back of the head with his pistol. "Let's get the fuck out of here."

Storey took one step, then stopped. "Wait here a second. Keep him alive. I'll be right back."

"Are you fucking nuts?" But Storey had already slipped away into the darkness. God-damn. It was one thing to have balls as big as your brain. But forget about running into someone or catching a stray round in the middle of all this shit—even Storey the human compass might get turned around and not find his way back to the exact same spot in the middle of identical fucking hummocks of grass. Fuck. Troy dropped the Mexican into the hole and checked his pulse. Still alive. Silly shit didn't even have a weapon. Just a load-bearing vest with a bunch of magazine and grenade pouches that felt like it was made from cotton. Probably homemade.

The explosions had stopped, probably because all the ordnance had been expended. And the intramural Los Zetas firefight behind the house was dying down, probably because they'd run out of ammo. Son of a bitch! They should have been out of this and on the road five minutes ago. The survivors were going to start shaking themselves together pretty soon.

Storey's remote controls were lying in a neat row on the outer edge of the hide, each in a little groove in the sand that had been dug for them. Troy picked up the unit on the far left and aimed it at the road, deactivating the two remaining EFPs there. No sense in blowing up the ambulance crews or the mayor when he showed up in the morning to see what had happed. But any mines left around were the local bomb squad's problem.

Someone was coming up on the left. Troy raised his Glock. No more prisoners tonight. If it was Storey, well, he kind of felt like shooting him anyway.

It was Storey. Two rifles slung across his back and humping two wooden boxes. Troy thought it was a wonder the motherfucker's solid steel balls didn't throw up sparks when he dragged them over the ground.

A low whistle between the teeth confirmed that it was indeed Storey. "Can you carry him and one of these boxes?" he asked Troy.

"Only if we're getting the fuck out of here," Troy replied, lifting the unconscious Mexican up and throwing him across his shoulders.

"We're getting the fuck out of here," said Storey.

Moving slowly under their burdens, they set out west, away from the road, where the stolen Cherokee waited in a dry creek bed, camouflaged with the rest of the roll of burlap.

The moon was full up, making it bright enough to see by. It was still dark in the arid scrubland west of Nuevo Laredo, and the Mexican was regaining consciousness. He was naked, and his wrists and elbows were duct-taped behind his back.

Standing over him, Troy poured a bottle of water on his head.

The Mexican was somewhere between twenty and twenty-five, thin and wiry. Three gold neck chains. Expensive haircut, short and all gelled up.

He opened his eyes and discovered himself to be naked, with wrists taped and elbows pulled painfully together behind his back with wire. Two gringos were staring back at him. One white, one *negro*. The same two lethal gringos who had left eight Los Zetas dead on the street and then destroyed them this night with the exploding house.

"What is your name, my friend?" Storey asked in Spanish.

"L . . . L . . . Luis," came chattering out.

"Luis, let me tell you what is going to happen. I will ask you some questions. Answer them truthfully and you will live through this. Otherwise . . ."

Troy grabbed his ankles and forced him onto his back. Storey tied an overhand knot in a length of electrical wire and, applying one foot to Luis's throat to keep him immobile, placed the loop around his penis and testicles, cinching it tight. Letting the long length of electrical wire run through his hands, he tied the other end onto the bumper of the nearby Cherokee. Then he finished his sentence. "Otherwise we will go for a drive until your *chinga* and *huevos* come off. Then we will ask you the very same questions again. If you still refuse to answer, we will see what else you are prepared to lose. Do you understand?"

The key to any interrogation is whether the subject accepts the validity of the proffered threat. Luis believed. He had seen many similar sessions, many much worse, but always from the other side.

The *negro*, who had been jingling the car keys in front of his face, got into the Cherokee and started the engine. The white man raised his arm so it could be seen from the back window. The Cherokee crept forward until the wire was almost taut. The white man began to bend his fingers, and the Cherokee went forward an inch at a time. The loop cinched tighter. Luis knew they would do it. "The Arab will attack in Laredo soon! He knows everything the FBI does! Stop! Please!"

The white man made a fist and a slashing motion. The engine shut off and the *negro* rejoined them. The wire was as tight as a guitar string, and Luis's hips pushed forward to try and take off some of the pressure.

"I should have let him continue," the white man said. "You are lying terribly. You think you can convince me these Arabs told you so much? Why would they tell you so much?"

"They did not tell us," Luis gasped. "We found out."

"How? Do not make me impatient."

"They all spoke Arabic, and those Chechens their own language. The Arab did not speak Spanish, only English. They thought we did not understand Arabic, but we had a man whose father came from Iraq. He listened, but kept his understanding a secret. He learned many things from overhearing the Arab and the leader of the Chechens speaking. We also had microphones in the home they stayed in."

The white man seemed unconvinced. "What was this Arab's name?"

"Nimri. Abdallah Nimri."

This was the first time he had seen the gringos make any reaction, though it quickly passed away.

"And the leader of the Chechens?"

"Temir something."

Storey rested his hand on the wire.

Luis was crying. "I did not learn it."

"Let us start from the beginning," Storey said. "How many are there again?"

"One Arab and twelve Chechens."

Storey thought: only twelve? They must have disrupted things more than they thought. But first things first. "The four Americans in the office downtown. What became of them?"

They would now surely tear his privates off. "Dead."

"Where are the bodies?"

"Buried in the desert."

The gringos made no reaction at all. Luis would have

been comforted if they had screamed at him. They were truly men to be feared.

Storey unfolded his map, found a stick on the ground, and stuck it into Luis's mouth. "Show me."

Luis moved his head while Storey moved the map in front of his face. Then he bobbed it forward, tapping the paper with the end of the stick.

Storey pointed to the spot. "Here?"

"Right. Down. There."

"What is it?" Storey asked.

"An old pit. People throw trash there."

Storey marked the map. At least they'd be able to recover the bodies. "All of them there?"

"Yes?"

"How were they found?"

"They drove across the border and contacted a real estate agent. They rented the office but did not check in to a hotel or recross the border in the evening."

"How did you take them?" Storey asked.

Luis hesitated.

Storey snapped the taut wire with his finger.

Luis yelped, as much at the surprise of it. "Dressed as police," he answered immediately.

"Interrogated?"

"Yes."

Storey moved in to another line of questioning before it affected his temper. "From them you heard about the Arab and the twelve Chechens?"

"Yes," Luis said haltingly. "But not much."

"You already knew about them."

"Yes."

"Because they hired you?"

"Yes."

"Tell me about it."

It was a command, not an invitation. Luis told about taking the Arab across the border once. Then the Arab hiring them to take him and the twelve across the border. The story of running into the Border Patrol. Los Zetas returning and the Arab and his men moving on.

"Now, how did they know what the FBI was doing?"

"From the computer. The Arab would go to an Internet café and use the e-mail. He did not trust our computer. But Los Zetas also control the Internet café. The Arab was told of the FBI plans. I do not know who he e-mailed," Luis said quickly, seeing the look on Storey's face. "They knew their weapons had been seized in Los Angeles. They knew they had been betrayed by a man from Pakistan who they trusted. They knew the FBI was hearing everything with microphones and seeing everything with cameras. The Arab and the Chechen spoke of this. This is why they crossed the border before they planned."

It was not welcome news. Storey had intended to send a message off to Washington as soon as he'd heard enough. But if there was a leak he couldn't risk it. If Nimri was getting that kind of quality information he'd either move or hit an alternate target as soon as he heard about it. Once again al-Qaeda was moving faster than they were. "What did they do about losing their weapons?"

"Purchased replacements from us. For double their true value." Unbidden, Luis went down the list, and then looked at them as if for praise.

The *negro* spoke for the first time. "He's lying. He's lying about everything. How would he know?"

"I helped to unload everything from the truck," Luis protested.

Storey believed him. Luis was just the kind of weasel private nobody noticed in the background, who heard everything and knew everything that was going on in the unit. Soldiers gossiped about everything, and he didn't doubt criminals did the same. He despaired at hearing the list, though. With that kind of firepower they could take on any big-city SWAT team, straight up. Or even overmatch the president's Secret Service Counter-Assault Team.

"What will they attack in Laredo?"

"I do not know," said Luis, his fear rising as he saw their intensity.

"When will they attack?"

"I do not know."

Storey thought: What could be in Laredo? Was there some kind of last-minute campaign stop there? Was Bush going to be in Crawford, Texas, on Election Day? Maybe the Arab was going to launch from Laredo. Then Storey realized that, bottom line, nothing had to be in Laredo. Al-Qaeda just had to be in the United States and do something, anything, within range of reporters and TV cameras. Twenty-four-hour-a-day news would do everything else for them. "Where are they in Laredo?"

"An old warehouse on Carrillo Road. That is all I know."

"What is the address of the warehouse?"

"I do not know."

Storey gave the wire a yank. "You've come this far, Luis, why make it hard on yourself?"

Luis was sobbing again. "I've told you everything! Haven't I told you everything? I don't know."

Now the *negro* was hissing in his ear. "What shit. How would this lying little cockroach know about the warehouse but not know the address? He knows they will attack in Laredo but he doesn't know what or when. I'm going to take his tools for a ride, and when I come back I'll see if he wants to keep lying." He made a move to get behind the wheel.

"I only overheard!" Luis shouted. "Our men were saying that we also owned a warehouse on Carrillo Road, so they had to check and make sure the Arab's was not nearby, in case they were caught. This is all I heard! I did not hear the address! I did not hear the place of attack! I did not hear the time!"

"He's talking through his asshole," Troy said.

"They were to hide there," said Luis, trying to keep talking so they would not hurt him. "In the warehouse. I know nothing else after that. They may have left."

Storey had been thinking the exact same thing. He didn't think ripping Luis's nuts off would give them any additional answers. And now they'd gotten the mission-essential intelligence, it was time to start thinking about themselves. "Tell me the preparations your people have made to capture us."

Luis was desperate to appease them, and relieved to have something he could finally answer. It was like they'd figured. All the roads out of town had blocks on them. Even a few four-wheel drives cutting across the scrubland in case they tried to go off-road. The U.S. Consulate was covered. And the three international bridges had both Los Zetas and Nuevo Laredo police cars checking vehicles and foot traffic before they crossed to the U.S. side.

Troy stepped in close and murmured in Storey's ear, "Shit, they got more people than we thought. They wouldn't have to pull anyone off the checkpoints."

But Storey didn't reply. He didn't even give any indication that he'd even heard. He was just staring at Luis with that preternatural focus. Then something clicked and he dug the map out of his pocket. "You mentioned three bridges," he said to Luis. "Which three bridges?"

Luis was confused. "What do you mean?"

"*Which* three bridges?" Storey repeated, more harshly this time.

"Bridge 1, Bridge 2, and Bridge 3," Luis said, still puzzled. Then he added, to be helpful, "The three international bridges across the border."

"What about Bridge 4?" said Storey.

"That is only for trucks. Commercial. No tourists."

Storey turned to Troy with just the faintest hint of a satisfied smile. Then he began untying the wire from the bumper. He thought about having Luis make a call to his superiors, but being a weasel cut both ways.

"Are we done?" Troy asked in English.

Storey nodded.

Troy turned around with the pistol in his hand and shot a smiling Luis in the head. "I was almost starting to like the little shit," he told Storey. "So I had to remind myself he was out there trying to kill us."

"You know why?" said Storey. "You're used to interrogating al-Qaeda."

"Yeah, you got to stop yourself from killing those assholes."

Storey looked at his watch. "We're fast running out of time. We need put the headlights on and zero the sights on those two AKs."

That procedure only took a few rounds and a screwdriver.

"You drive," said Storey. "I've got a couple of things to do."

Troy started the engine. "I forgot to ask. What's in those two boxes?"

"One's full of loaded AK magazines. The other's full of grenades."

"Grenades? What kind?"

"Old M-26 frags. I'm guessing Mexican Army issue."

"Where the fuck did you find two boxes of mags and frags lying around?"

"That one SUV that missed the EFPs. Driver bailed out and ran. I guess they kept their reserve ammo in the back."

"You were running around in the road with two more live EFP shots out there?" Troy demanded. "What if you hit one of the beams."

"I placed them," Storey said, offended. "I sure as shit knew where they were."

Troy let it go. "How do we get the word out on this? If

we message the Pentagon command center they've *got* to notify the FBI. If we say the FBI's got a leak the FBI is going to say we're full of shit—you know the FBI. But the FBI's got a leak, and if they don't have people in Laredo they've got to move people into Laredo. That could take time, and al-Qaeda could be quicker than us."

Exactly what Storey had been thinking. "The FBI has people in Laredo. If Los Zetas was shooting machine guns at the Border Patrol, the FBI's in Laredo." He pulled out his PDA, extended the antenna, and began dialing. "We just have to go a bit outside the regular chain of command."

"Sounds like a court-martial to me," said Troy.

"You up for it?"

"Sure. Besides, I think we could beat it anyway. Are you calling who I think you're calling?"

"Yup."

"What do you think the odds of her being in Laredo are?"

"Never hurts to try," said Storey. "If not, we'll go to Plan B."

see the Pentagon command center they've got to

Chapter Twenty-one

Everyone had a hell of a time getting there. One van-load of FBI forensics people got lost on a dirt road and only found their way back by following the glow of all the flashing domes and portable spotlights.

Beth Royale had never been in the desert. It was amazing how cold the night was. She could see everyone's breath.

Beth didn't bother the poor Border Patrolman. He was sitting under one of the spotlights, wrapped in a blanket, surrounded by all the bosses from all the agencies, all barking questions at him at once. That, of course, was where her partner was.

The technicians were wandering around with metal detectors, looking for shell casings or anything that had been dropped. Camera flashes were popping. Others were taking impressions of tire marks.

The Border Patrol vehicle was charred and still smoking. That hydrocarbon torched car smell was all over the hill.

Starting at the bottom where the brush was flattened from all the vehicles running through it, Beth walked up the hill, following the cones that marked found shell casings like a trail of breadcrumbs. At the top was more pushed-down brush where they'd continued on. She walked past the limit of the spotlights into the darkness. Looking over those black hills as if she expected to see something. But she knew all the scattered headlights were law enforcement.

She walked back over the hill and returned to the ring of lights. One of the technicians was pacing back and forth beside some deep tire ruts, waiting for his casting medium to set. "What does it look like?" Beth asked him.

"Four SUVs," he replied. "All the same model, but I don't know for sure which one yet. Border Patrol says they were black, maybe Ford. One came up near the top of the hill here, opened fire, then backed down. Another one stayed at the bottom of the hill the whole time. Those two turned around, headed back to Mexico. Other two came up the hill, went over the top, and kept going. That's it for now. Is it true there's a state trooper missing?"

"That's right," said Beth.

"Poor bastard," the technician muttered. He knelt down and poked his cast to see if it was hard.

"Thanks," said Beth. She turned, and there was Karen the Spook. "Jesus, Karen, I wish you'd stop sneaking up on me like that."

But Karen was serious. "They wanted me to tell you before you heard it secondhand."

"My dad?" Beth said quickly.

"No, your family's fine." Karen paused, then said, "Your informant. Roshan. He's dead."

Beth just gave a little nod, as if the news wasn't unexpected. "His family?"

"No, just him."

"Go ahead, Karen."

"He got a call from the group, inviting him to a meeting in San Bernardino. Place they'd never had a meeting before. L.A. office put just one car on him. After an hour at the meeting four cars leave, going in different directions. Roshan's still there. They didn't have a wire on him because everyone had been getting frisked going into meetings.

They waited another hour, then went in. He was on the floor with his hands tied behind his back. Throat cut."

"And the whole group is gone," said Beth. No question there.

"They're looking for them now."

"Anything else?" Beth said crisply.

"No. We'll have to wait for the damage assessment, try and trace the leak."

"There won't be any damage assessment," said Beth. "The Bureau does damage assessments after it's been publicly embarrassed. The Bureau doesn't conduct damage assessments that are going to *cause* public embarrassment. Not serious ones, at least. Besides, there were so many grubby little fingers in this pie they'll never be able to narrow anything down."

"You don't have to be such a hard-ass, you know."

"I'll be goddamned if I'm going to cry, Karen. Let's get back to work."

Karen studied her face in the moonlight for a moment before saying, "Okay. Come on over to the car."

There was a map spread over the hood, anchored with stones.

"You mean you don't have it on your laptop?" said Beth. A map was so low-tech for Karen.

"Yeah, but it's easier to see on paper," Karen replied, clicking on her flashlight. "Here's where we are," she said, making a pencil circle around a ridge on the map. She slid the pencil over. "Here's where the Border Patrol helicopter got shot down." Another circle. "Missing state trooper made his last radio call from here. And he was heading north." A final circle and an arrow.

Beth leaned over the map, tracing the road networks with her finger. "So is it north to San Antonio, or south to Laredo?"

"What's in Laredo?" said Karen. "San Antonio. Or east

to Houston. North to Dallas. Or maybe just north to Crawford."

"Just what we needed, a president from Texas. I bet the Secret Service is shitting."

"Even if they don't make it there, they could make a lot of noise."

Beth measured the distances with her finger. "Anyway, they'd be in San Antonio or Laredo by now. We'll have to wait and see if two abandoned black SUVs turn up. Or more dead bodies."

"Or more dead bodies," said Karen. "They have AKs and at least one 7.62mm NATO machine gun, based on the shell casings. Which means either M-60, Belgian MAG, or German MG-3."

"That weapons mix sounds familiar," said Beth. "I guess they did find another source of supply."

A ring tone went off. Karen put her hand on her phone. "It's not me."

Beth flipped hers open and held the screen up to her face. "Who the hell could it be at this time of the morning? Weird number. Well, at least the Bureau's paying for the call . . . Beth Royale speaking. Ed! Where are y . . . yes, I'm in Texas. How did you know that? Just outside Laredo. Ed, how do you know about that? Yes, I suppose I can . . . all right, all right, I'll definitely be there. And if I'm not someone else will. Yes, I'll make sure I tell them. Ed, are you sure there isn't anything I need to know right now? Yes, I understand. You're damn right you'll tell me when you see me." She closed the phone.

"Ed *Storey*?" said Karen.

"If you can believe it," said Beth. "He's in Nuevo Laredo right now. He knows about the Border Patrol being shot up, and he knows there's a leak in the FBI. That's why he called me. He wants me to pick him up on the U.S. side of International Bridge 4 in Laredo at eight this morning. Unbelievable."

"Want to bet he isn't in Mexico on vacation?" said Karen.

"No."

"Mind a suggestion?"

"What?" said Beth.

"Remember the last time you two got together that wasn't a date? Bring something besides your sidearm."

"Okay."

"And be careful. Think of me surrounded by all these suits all by myself."

"Yes, Mom. I think I need to go check out with Timmins."

"If you can't find your partner, just make a half circle around him," Karen suggested. "She'll be the one with her nose up his ass."

Chapter Twenty-two

Abdallah Karim Nimri wanted to scream. But he could not scream at Chechens. Only Temiraev could. And he was as bad as the rest.

The past day had been nothing but unending grumbling. The warehouse, with no air-conditioning, was like an oven. It smelled of dust and mold and sour rotten wood. There was no way to cook food, so there was nothing to eat but fruit and candy bars and snacks. Nothing to drink but warm bottled water and juice. No place to wash except in buckets. By God, he had heard it all. All and enough.

He had insisted on preparing the explosives and weapons the night before, knowing it was more difficult to get men moving in the morning. Now they were washing and eating and dressing and wiping down their rifles. And every time he tried to hurry them along they gave him that expression.

He went to enlist Temiraev's aid, but Temiraev was praying. All Nimri could do was wait, boiling with frustration, until he finished.

Finally he was able to say, "The minutes tick away, my brother. If we are not careful it will be after nine, and we must have the morning."

After a daylong sulk, the prospect of imminent action

had brought Temiraev back to being himself. "God's will, my brother."

Nimri had heard *Inshallah* on the eve of every disaster. He was prepared to accept the will of God, once events had come to their conclusion. He was not prepared to hear it from the lips of men before a mission had even taken place, or as an excuse for their own failure. "Accept God's will but do not tempt His judgment, my brother. Our work awaits, and every second squandered could be the difference between success and failure."

Temiraev's face changed, causing Nimri to drop his hand in the vicinity of his pistol holster.

They stared at each other for a moment, then Temiraev clapped his hands together like a pistol shot. "Get to the car!" he shouted, grinning at Nimri. "Stop wasting time! Move!"

That finally roused them. Nimri heard the sound of boot steps on the wooden floors, and the metal clattering of weapons. He saw them heading for the vehicle, shoving candy bars into their mouths.

Nimri paused to embrace Osman, the Dallas operative who had arranged the warehouse and provisions. He had been silent as a mute in the presence of the Chechen fighters and the famous Arab commander.

"God grant you success," said Osman.

"A safe journey," Nimri replied. As soon as they left, Osman would cross the border and fly home to Yemen. Nimri would not leave any connections for the Americans to discover afterward. Those clumsy fools in California? They could fend for themselves. But Nimri wanted to preserve this operative for the future. "Take heed, brother, when I tell you that you have accomplished the tasks you were set perfectly. If you knew how rare this is, you would understand how highly I praise you."

Osman's face actually quivered with emotion. "Thank you brother. God protect you and watch over you."

Nimri broke the embrace. "Go to the door now and let us out."

No one was in the Expedition. All the Chechens were milling around outside it. At first Nimri thought they were afraid. Then he realized that no one wished to enter first only to be crushed by the others. They had wanted to steal another vehicle, but he would not allow it. "Brothers, get in the car." He gestured to Temiraev, as if to say: do something.

"Get in the car!" Temiraev shouted.

The Chechens wedged themselves in with more grumbling. Nimri got behind the wheel, Temiraev beside him. It was even tighter than before with the Chechens all wearing their full equipment harnesses.

The GPS was already programmed to guide them to their destination. Nimri started the engine and tapped the horn to signal Osman to open the warehouse door. He shifted into gear and proclaimed in a loud voice, "Victory or Paradise!"

"Victory or Paradise!" the Chechens answered him.

Chapter Twenty-three

At 8:00 A.M. Beth Royale was standing on the Customs island on the Laredo side of International Bridge 4, the World Trade Bridge. She was watching the Mexican side through binoculars. All six lanes of highway were empty. In front of her was the row of yellow Customs gates with their closed-circuit cameras and scanners. All closed. Weekdays the bridge closed at midnight and didn't open until eight.

The Customs supervisor beside her said, "You know which truck they'll be on?"

"No idea," said Beth. "But we won't have to go looking for them. They'll just show up."

"You know them by sight?"

"That I do."

"FBI or not," he said, "they're going to have to identify themselves."

"Don't worry about it," said Beth. He'd already made a copy of her ID, to cover his ass. She just hoped Ed and Lee still had passports. Or something.

"Here we go," said the supervisor.

A solid wall of tractor trailer trucks were coming across the bridge. Once across the Rio Grande, on both sides of that wide band of highway was chain-link fence topped with barbed wire. Then an expanse of empty grassland, mowed short to provide no concealment and burnt by the sun. More fence beyond. Designed to keep people from jumping out of trucks and disappearing into America before they reached the checkpoint.

The trucks rumbled up to the gates, brakes blasting air. Inside the control center they were watching the banks of TV monitors. Running licenses. Checking out drivers. They could only search a fraction of what passed through on any given day. The sight of all those trucks gave Beth cold chills. It was one thing to understand it intellectually. Another to stand there watching them push up to the border like a huge herd of migrating animals and wonder what or who might be inside waiting to make their way up the Interstate 35 into the heart of the United States.

She trained her binoculars from truck cab to truck cab, but all she saw were solo drivers.

"Do you see them?" Sondra Dewberry asked.

"Not yet," Beth replied.

"Does this happen on your Fly Squad all the time?"

"*This?*" said Beth. "Meeting Special Ops guys coming across the border? No. But things *like* this—outside the usual Bureau routine? They do tend to happen every now and again."

"But this in particular is out of the ordinary," Dewberry persisted, as if she really needed to have that confirmed.

"Yeah. But look at it this way. You'll finally get to meet my boyfriend." Beth smiled behind the binoculars, knowing Dewberry wouldn't quite know how to respond to that. And hopefully grant her a short interval of silence.

The trucks kept coming. Beth wondered how many of them had been parked and lined up on the Mexican side waiting for the bridge to open. She decided to quit looking down the road and only concentrate on those pulled up to the gates.

The trucks were pretty generic. Unmarked trailers

for the most part. Dull cabs with the names of freight companies. Probably no one wanted to get too wild with their paint job and attract the attention of Customs.

It was almost 8:30 and Beth could just feel Dewberry getting impatient. Then she caught a flurry of movement in a cab that had only held a driver a moment before.

"We're here," the driver announced.

The curtain opened, and Storey and Troy climbed down from the sleeping area in the back of the truck cab. Storey passed the driver a thick roll of cash. "Here you go, Bob. Just like I promised. We're getting out in front of Customs, and this is the easiest money you ever made."

Bob was flipping through the roll, checking denominations. "You're a man of your word. *Vaya con Dios.*"

"Amen, brother," said Troy.

They climbed down and shut the door.

"Let's get out of traffic and find Beth," said Story.

"I feel like kissing the ground," said Troy. "Like the Pope. There's Beth," said Troy. "Over there with the binoculars."

They each had a two-day beard. Both wearing suits and open-collared shirts that were looking pretty road-worn. As they got closer Beth could see stains that looked like rust on their clothes. She made a mental note not to ask about that when Dewberry was around.

Beth knew Ed would be too shy to kiss her in public, and way too proper to even think about it when she was on duty. He slipped an arm around her shoulders and gave her a quick squeeze. "Thanks for being here."

Lee, of course, was never one to pass up an opportunity to embarrass his partner. With a loud, "Beth!" he threw his arms around her and gave her a big hug and a kiss.

Beth gave him a friendly slap on the backside. "Good to

see you, too." She wrinkled her nose. "You're going to need a shower one of these days. What have you been up to?"

"If you only knew," said Troy.

"We really need to get moving here," said Storey.

The Customs supervisor took a step forward.

"Have you got your passports?" said Beth.

They dug in their pockets and handed over red diplomatic passports.

The supervisor looked the books over, compared the photos, and said, "Wait here."

As soon as he was out of earshot, Beth said, "He's going to make a copy to cover his ass."

Storey said, "He wants to look in our bags, everyone's got a problem."

"We'll see what we can do about that," said Beth. "Oh, Ed, Lee, I want you to meet my partner, Sondra Dewberry."

Storey gave her one quick appraising look and said formally, "Pleased to meet you."

Troy was giving her a different kind of appraising look. "Likewise."

"Beth's told me so much about you," Dewberry said to Troy.

Realizing what impression the hug and kiss had left, Troy burst out laughing. "I'm sure she has," he said finally. "But this is the happy couple." He was waving a finger between Beth and Storey.

Storey was wearing a faint crinkle of amusement across his face.

Beth's was red.

"Oh, I'm so sorry," said Dewberry.

"That's okay," Troy told her. "The best man doesn't always win."

"Any day, any day," Storey muttered as the Customs supervisor slowly ambled back up to them.

The supervisor handed back the two passports and

glanced down at the two duffel bags on the ground. "I don't suppose I want to look in there, do I?"

"Career-wise?" said Storey. "Big mistake."

That Master Sergeant authority combined with the country sincerity always worked, Troy thought.

"Okay, you can go," said the supervisor.

Hurrying them toward the car, Storey said, "Beth, we've got to move fast. We've got twelve al-Qaeda Chechens and Abdallah Karim Nimri in an old warehouse on Carrillo Road, according to last information."

"Nimri?" said Beth. "We heard twenty Chechens."

"Not all of them made it to the dance," Troy broke in.

"What happened to them?" said Dewberry.

Storey gave Troy the eye to dummy up.

Beth formulated her next question very carefully, like the lawyer she was. "How good is your source?" Not: exactly how did you come to know all this?

"Pretty good," said Storey. "The word is that there's a leak somewhere in the Bureau. Nimri's hearing what you're doing. I don't know how fast his information pipeline is working, or if he has real-time communications with it right now, but it's something we need to think about before calling the troops in."

"What's Nimri's objective?" said Beth.

"Don't know," said Storey. "Don't know where he's moving, don't know when. Don't even know if he's still at the warehouse. All we know is, his plan was to go to the warehouse. But he got in a firefight with the Border Patrol, and that wasn't part of his plan."

"That we know about," said Beth. "They shot down a helicopter, too."

"Really?" said Storey.

"And a State Trooper's missing," Beth added.

"Well, they got AKs, two MAG machine guns, a sniper rifle, LAAWs, grenades, and explosives," said Storey. "And night vision gear."

"What's the address on the warehouse?" said Beth.

"All we know is an old wooden warehouse on Carrillo Road," said Storey.

"Why do I think there's going to be more than one?" said Beth. "Let's run by and take a quick look, then we can decide what to do."

They finally reached the car.

"I'll drive," said Dewberry, sliding behind the wheel.

Beth stood there for an instant, flexing her fingers into a fist. Then without a word she walked around to the trunk, removing two heavy bulletproof vests, navy blue with gold FBI lettering. And an M-16 rifle. She donned one of the vests.

Storey and Troy were already in the backseat. Beth passed them the M-16. "Here, hang on to this for me."

Troy accepted the rifle and laid it on the floor. "Thanks, but we brought our own."

Sondra Dewberry looked into the rearview mirror and watched the two men donning the cotton ammunition vests they'd liberated from Los Zetas. "They've got hand grenades," she whispered to Beth.

"Don't worry," said Beth. "They won't go tossing them around. Will you, guys?"

"Not unless we clear it with you first, Beth," said Troy, rocking a magazine into his AK.

"They seem to have automatic rifles, too," Beth observed. "You guys pick those up in Mexico?"

"From the same people who sold them to Nimri," said Storey. "You think we can go a little faster?"

"They're not law enforcement," Dewberry whispered to Beth.

"It's okay to speak up," said Troy. "We can actually hear you back here."

"The president empowered them to act as such," said Beth. "The Posse Comitatus Act is suspended for members of Joint Special Operations Command. So until the Supreme Court says no . . . you going to put on your vest?"

"Not while I'm driving."

"Suit yourself," said Beth, slapping it down on the seat between them. "In that case you can drive faster."

"You want to stash the packs?" Troy said to Storey. The two daypacks held all the magazines and grenades that wouldn't fit in the vests.

"Keep 'em close," said Storey. "If we need 'em, we'll need 'em bad."

Dewberry kept glancing in the rearview mirror.

It was rush hour, but Beth didn't want to turn on the lights and siren. Clearing the loop road that fed the border bridge, they headed south on 1472. The traffic was heavy, everyone heading to all the nearby industrial parks. From San Bernardo they took a right onto Industrial Boulevard. Then across the train tracks onto Carrillo Road.

Storey was dismayed. They'd kept passing shiny new industrial parks on the drive down. And there wasn't just one old wooden warehouse, but rows of them. He'd hoped they'd be able to isolate the right one, then call in the FBI and the locals. But there was no way. And if they called in the troops right now, Nimri and the Chechens might very well notice all the activity and manage to slip out before the cordon closed.

"You can slow down now," Beth was telling Dewberry. "We really need to check these out."

They passed what looked like an old factory that butted up right to the edge of the road. A chain-link fence, and Dewberry braking suddenly. And less than twenty feet away, almost face to face, was a Chechen who looked like the brother of the ones Storey and Troy had killed in Rio, unlocking the padlock at the gate. And behind him a black Ford Expedition waiting to drive out.

"Shit," said Troy, giving voice to what everyone else was thinking.

Storey threw himself out the passenger door on the opposite side, Troy following right behind him.

With her side of the car exposed broadside to the gate, Beth popped her seat belt and dove into the backseat. As she landed she heard the loudspeaker pop on and Dewberry's voice, unbelievably, announcing, "FBI. Turn off the engine and show your hands out the windows."

Oh, my God, Beth thought.

Chapter Twenty-four

Abdallah Karim Nimri could hardly be faulted for that moment of frozen disbelief. Within his grasp. Within minutes of being within his grasp . . .

"Back up!" Temiraev bellowed into his ear.

Within the cramped confines of the vehicle, the Chechens fought for the buttons. And the windows rolled down so very slowly.

Chance contact was usually won by the side that fired first and put those rounds on target. Staying behind the front wheel, Storey rested his AK across the hood. The Chechen at the gate nearly had his pistol out. The post of Storey's front sight settled onto his chest, and the AK bounced twice against Storey's shoulder. His brain registered the Chechen falling, but he was already shifting targets. The fingers of his left hand draped over the receiver, pulling that awkward AK selector switch one notch up to full auto.

Troy was already there. He was aiming at the driver, but the Expedition was backing up fast and then spun around as the wheel was cut over. He squeezed the trigger, holding the AK down against the recoil, and didn't release it until the thirty-round magazine ran out. Contrary to all the rules of shooting, AKs didn't jam from overheating—AKs didn't jam from anything—and the only important thing was to get as many rounds into that vehicle in the shortest period of time. Fire superiority.

Nimri cut the wheel just as Troy fired. The first rounds impacted just behind his head and stitched their way through the backseat and cargo area. Screams and frantic thrashing as men were hit.

Storey fired full auto right after. Seeing Troy's aim, he went first for the engine and tires. When the Expedition stopped moving it was sideways to them.

"Get out!" Temiraev was screaming. "Get out and shoot back!"

The one-sided part of the fight was now officially over. Return fire thudded into the side of the FBI sedan. The driver's door came open. Annoyed at the interruption in his shooting, Troy leaned over, grabbed Dewberry by the back of her suit jacket, and dragged her clear.

A few Chechens were now out and shooting from behind the Expedition. One of them darted out into the open, hands in the air, running toward them. Shouting in English, "Surrender! Surrender!"

Storey was changing magazines. Beth hesitated—she couldn't shoot a suspect with his hands up. Dewberry stopped firing her pistol and shouted back. "Halt! Get down on your knees!"

The Chechen didn't stop.

Storey yelled, "Shoot him, goddammit!"

Jesus Christ, Troy thought. He swung his rifle over and shot the Chechen through the chest.

The Chechen blew up.

When the smoke cleared there were two shod feet standing on the ground. A scorched black circle, and two feet, jagged anklebones projecting up, in the exact center of the circle. Nothing else.

In the time it took them to regain their wits and get up from where the blast had knocked them over, there was a fast string of much louder, ripping cracks. Accompanied by the singing of metal under strain.

The sound told Storey they'd gotten a machine gun into action, and the holes told him the fire was coming right through the sedan. He threw himself back down onto the road. That was how quick the course of a gun-fight could change, once you lost fire superiority.

Also on the ground, though from a different perspective, Troy saw Chechens running for the warehouse under the protection of the covering fire. He pulled a hand grenade off his vest, yanked out the pin, and threw it from flat on his back.

Beth fired her M-16 dry, then realized that she only had one more magazine left. Slamming it into the rifle, she heard Troy shout, "Grenade!" She'd learned what that meant some time before, and threw herself down onto the ground.

The grenade hit the cinder parking lot, bounced once, and exploded near the side of the Expedition. Scoring the paint job and shaking the occupants.

Storey used the cover it provided to roll twice so he was now firing from a prone position, under the sedan engine.

After the first grenade blast Troy reared up and threw two more, taking the time for better aim.

Nimri had grabbed a rifle from somewhere—it was very confusing—and was firing out his driver's window.

Temiraev was shouting orders. "If you can move, run for the warehouse! Otherwise keep firing!"

He grabbed Nimri from behind and dragged him across the seat, over the center console like a speed bump, and out the other side of the car.

Troy's second grenade hit the side of the Expedition and bounced back before exploding, shattering glass and sending up new cries from inside.

The third grenade landed short but kept skipping

forward along the cinders until it came to a rest under the SUV.

Plastic explosives are not sensitive to heat or impact. Only a blasting cap, not fire or a bullet strike, will set them off. But when ignited they will burn. Very hot.

When the grenade blew there was an orange flash of gasoline within the black cloud. A few seconds later, still inside the smoke, a pillar of fire shot up. Pure white, and it rose and spread out until it had completely consumed the SUV. High-pitched wailing shrieks that barely sounded human, cut off by the bangs of grenades and LAAW rockets cooking off and scattering chunks of metal outside that burning shroud.

Storey dashed to his left to get enough of an angle to see the warehouse beyond the burning SUV. The last Chechen was going for the door, limping, carrying the machine gun. Storey took his time, not wanting that gun to get inside. He dropped the Chechen just short of the door. Changing to a fresh magazine, he ran back to the sedan, ducking every time another explosion rocked the Expedition. "Did you see how many made it back inside?" he shouted to Troy.

"I saw three, but I'm sure more made it!"

That was Troy the sniper, Storey thought. He was only going to report what he saw.

Troy checked behind him for the first time. Sondra Dewberry was sitting on the road, where she'd been ever since they were all knocked down when he hit the Chechen's explosive belt. She was shivering uncontrollably. Troy followed the path of her eyes. The Chechen's scorched head had landed in the road about fifteen feet away from her. Troy grabbed her upper arm, shook her hard, and shouted, "Get in the car! Get in the car!"

She didn't even look up at him.

Troy immediately dropped her arm and moved on,

writing her out of the fight. Not angry, just done with her. She hadn't been ready for it.

Now Beth ran over. "Sondra! Sondra!"

No reaction. Storey was yelling at her from inside the car. Beth jammed the M-16 into Dewberry's lap and ran for the sedan, jumping into the open back door next to Troy.

Amazed that the engine was still running, Storey threw it into reverse and backed up fast across the street.

Beth crawled over the seat and grabbed for the radio mike. She flipped the switch from loudspeaker and tried to get a call through. Just as amazed as Storey had been about the engine when the radio crackled out a reply.

Troy was passing Storey fresh magazines from the day-packs to replenish his vest.

Beth recounted the situation and demanded that every local, state, and federal unit respond immediately, particularly SWAT.

She'd thought that once they got across the street Storey would back them into cover. But he was shifting into drive. "Ed, what are you doing? We have to establish a perimeter and keep them inside that warehouse."

Storey said, "Beth, if they barricade themselves in there until the TV cameras show up, they'll have the incident they came for. They won't have to attack anything."

Beth digested that, realizing he was right.

Then Storey added, "If they get their sniper or a machine gunner up on that roof, or someone with a LAAW, we're pinned down. Nobody's getting near them."

"What the fuck?" Troy shouted from the backseat. "Are we waiting for them to get dug in?"

Sirens could already be heard in the distance. Of course, the substantial explosions might also have had something to do with it.

Beth keyed the mike. "Be advised, three plainclothes officers inside the warehouse. Two male, one female. Repeat, three officers, in plainclothes, inside the warehouse."

"Better buckle up," Storey advised as he stepped on the gas.

They shot across the street and hit the gate dead center. The chain snapped and it flew open.

The Expedition was still burning, and by now looked like a naked frame standing on wheel rims. Ammunition was still popping inside.

Storey made a wide turn and put the sedan between the Expedition and the door the Chechens had run into. Troy was firing deliberately into the door to keep anyone from sticking their head out.

Storey said, "Beth, would you lean out and grab that machine gun?"

For an instant Beth was taken aback by his calm good manners, considering the circumstances. She went out her door and grabbed the machine gun off the ground. Another weapon that wasn't taught at the FBI Academy. She passed it through the window into the backseat. Storey was speeding off before she even got her door closed.

"Didn't want them running back out to get it," he explained.

As they circled around the burning Expedition, Troy put down his AK and took up the machine gun. Only about twenty rounds left on the belt. He stuck the gun through the window and hammered those twenty rounds at knee height across the front of the warehouse. When he was done he pressed the butt catch, lifted the butt up, and pulled out the return spring and bolt. Dropping those parts on the floorboard, he tossed the now-disabled gun out the window.

Beth was retrieving the Remington 870 twelve-gauge pump shotgun from under her seat.

"Why the hell did you give her the M-16?" Troy demanded.

"There were only ten rounds left in the magazine,"

Beth replied, still under the seat trying to get ahold of the extra box of shotgun shells she'd crammed in there.

Storey went around the side of the warehouse at high speed. Then he saw it, three quarters of the way down. The warehouse was so old there were no back-in loading docks. Just the big barn-like doors in the front, and probably the back. But on the side here was a ramp leading up to a smaller loading door. A better idea than parking and standing around out in the open trying to breach a door.

He swung wide and turned to take the ramp, giving the sedan more gas after straightening it out.

Troy said evenly, "You crazy motherfucker. What if there's something heavy behind that door?"

Beth braced her feet on the floorboards.

The sedan shot up the ramp and hit the door squarely.

Chapter Twenty-five

Abdallah Karim Nimri threw himself on the floor as the bullets came through the walls. A medium machine gun, just like theirs. And grenades. American police were not armed with machine guns and hand grenades. He could not understand it. American special forces hunting them? But they carried the M-16. He had heard one, but the other fire against them was Kalashnikov. How could that be?

But that was a puzzle that had to be set aside for the moment. His heart sank as he took stock. There was himself, and Temiraev. Two more of the Chechens. And Osman the agent, who was armed only with a pistol. All that remained of his force. All but Osman with rifles, and one sniper rifle had been saved, God be praised. No machine guns. Only one of the LAAW rockets one of the Chechens had picked up. And only the ammunition and grenades they carried on their bodies. Nimri knew he should give thanks to God for what they did have, and prayed for forgiveness.

He could see that the other Chechens, and Osman, were totally dejected. Only Temiraev looked animated, as if the opportunity to fire a rifle, whatever the circumstances, had raised his spirits.

Nimri said, "Well, my brother. I am open to any suggestions."

"We hold this place against them, for all the world to see," Temiraev replied, making Nimri understand why men followed him. "Then die like heroes. What else can we do before the eyes of God?"

"And how do you propose we do this?" said Nimri, feeling his own spirits rise, however slightly.

Temiraev lifted his eyes up. "We must have the high ground, or else we can never keep them away."

Nimri's thinking it over was interrupted by a tremendous crash from the back of the warehouse. The whole building shook. "By God, what was that?" he heard himself say out loud.

"The Americans have blasted their way inside!" Temiraev exclaimed. "We do not have the strength to keep them out down here." He grabbed Nimri by the arm. "Up, my brother! We must go up! Quickly, we must reach the upper floor first or all is lost!"

When the FBI sedan hit the door, Storey was blinded by the immediate shift from sunlight to darkness. He thought it would be a good idea to use the brakes.

But even with the brakes applied the sedan skidded across the wooden warehouse floor until it slammed into a thick timber support post.

At least the airbags didn't deploy, Storey thought. He got out fast, rifle at the ready. Seeing no immediate threats, he said, "Everyone all right?"

"Crazy motherfucker," came Lee Troy's voice, quietly, from the darkness on the other side of the car. "Fucking door was probably unlocked."

"I'm okay," said Beth, pulling out the shotgun she'd secured in anticipation of the impact.

Troy handed Storey the daypack with his extra ammo.

Storey put it on, cinching the shoulder straps tight and hopping up and down once to make sure nothing inside would rattle.

His eyes slowly adjusted. There were no lights on, but there were sizable gaps in the planks of the outer wall. Probably for ventilation in the days before air-conditioning, Storey thought. They also admitted a good deal of sunlight. All the dust thrown up by their violent entry had turned it into beams projecting wild patterns all over the cavernous space. And just as deep shadows in the places they didn't reach.

Someone had been storing their junk. The warehouse was full of rusting old machinery and wooden crates of various sizes scattered around according to a plan, based on the amount of dust, that had long since been abandoned.

Storey felt his stomach tighten up. There were a million places to hide, to ambush from. It would be like fighting inside a haunted house.

He cupped a hand behind his ear. The sirens were right on top of them now, but there was something else. Fainter, near the front of the warehouse, he could hear feet pounding on wooden stairs.

Storey let his eyes follow the double rows of thick timber support posts upward. A dark board ceiling. A second floor. He thought about the height of the warehouse, and decided there could be only one other floor. Extra storage space for lighter items. Offices maybe.

In one corner of the back wall was a wood-frame stairway.

Beth was right beside him. A low whistle brought Troy over.

"You hear the feet on the stairs?" Troy whispered.

"We're going up," said Storey, pointing to the stairway. Just then he noticed that Beth had a SureFire light mounted on the pump handgrip of her shotgun. "No flashlights. No shooting unless there's no choice. If you see someone we don't, and you have time," he said to Beth, "let us know and we'll use grenades. Grenades first," he said to Troy.

Troy understood. When you fired a weapon you also let everyone know where you were. Making yourself a great target for the grenades Los Zetas had supposedly provided these assholes. Though maybe they'd all gone up in the SUV? He allowed himself to consider that.

But a grenade thrown without shooting might have come from anywhere. And could be thrown right over all these obstacles and into the cover behind them.

"Make your last radio call," Storey was saying to Beth. "Make sure the place is sealed off, but tell them not to enter. No shooting into here, even if they take fire. Tell them to stay under cover—there could be a sniper around. And watch out for suicide bombers trying to surrender. Make 'em strip nekked a safe way away."

Troy smiled in the darkness. You could always tell his partner was fired up when the country came out in his voice.

Storey finished up by saying, "Move slow and move quiet. No talking. These floors are going to creak, and the whole place is an echo chamber."

While Beth was whispering into her walkie-talkie, he said to Troy, "I'll take point. You tailgun. Keep Beth between us."

Troy approved. He knew Beth could handle herself, but didn't think she knew anything about grenades.

Beth got her transmission acknowledged and turned off her radio.

Storey started moving. Troy put his hand on Beth's shoulder to hold her back, then released her when the right interval had opened up between her and Storey.

Though Beth had graduated from the FBI SWAT course she thought, not for the first time, that a few hours' instruction in basic infantry tactics would have been helpful.

With his rifle aimed up at the hole in the ceiling,

Storey glided up the stairway one silent step at a time.
The whole thing was so flimsy it rocked back and forth
at every step.

Beth kept her shotgun at the high ready, away from
Storey's back. Troy was going up backward, his AK pointing down into the warehouse. Taking stairs, especially ones
as open as these, was a point of particular vulnerability.

Temiraev took charge, and Nimri was content to let
him do so. It saved him from having to think of both immediate and future moves at the same time.

Temiraev had spent the previous day nervously walking around the entire warehouse, so he knew the floor
plan well. "Murat and Nur-Pahi go to the rear, and take
the ladder to the roof," he ordered the sniper and his
spotter, passing the latter his binoculars. "Keep us informed of the situation outside, but be careful what you
say on the radio. Your first priority is to keep them away
from the building. Move frequently and do not expose
yourself—they will have snipers. You have but the one
rocket—use it well. In particular you must keep helicopters away, but do not waste your ammunition. Your next
priority is to kill as many as possible—you may expend
one third of your ammunition on this task. Seek out
those in authority, as you have been taught." To Osman
the agent he said, "Go with them and watch the stairs on
the far side. Keep the enemy off them. You know how to
use grenades?"

Osman nodded.

"Everyone give him one grenade," Temiraev ordered.
They were handed over. "Go now, and God be with you."

Storey stuck his head up through the stairwell. He'd
thought it might be a little brighter higher up, but he'd

been wrong. The lower ceiling made it even gloomier. And the smell of musty wood and mold was even stronger.

He was looking at a big storage space, stacked high with all kinds of old-fashioned wood office furniture. To the left was a ladder that seemed to go up to the roof.

Storey moved off the stairway and into cover behind the nearest stack of furniture, motioning with his left hand for the others to follow. Once Beth and Troy were up he stayed still to let their eyes adjust to the new light level. And listen, something experience had always taught him was crucial.

In the darkness, running feet coming toward them. Like a cat, Storey made a silent dash to find a place with a vantage point.

He moved so fast and so quiet that, even though she'd been watching him carefully, Beth almost lost him in the shadows. She had to hurry to keep him in sight.

Whoever stacked the furniture had left a narrow avenue down the middle of the space. Storey was on one knee, exposing only one eye around the corner. He felt Beth coming near, and without looking pointed to where he wanted her to be. Troy was facing the other way, still covering their rear.

Storey removed a grenade from his vest, peeling off the piece of electrical tape he and Troy had applied to keep the pins from rattling. He silently eased the pin out. As long as he continued to hold the metal spoon down with the palm of his hand the grenade was safe.

The footsteps were coming closer, and Storey instinctively made the time and distance calculations. He was going to use a technique that had been taught to him by one of the original Delta operators who, during Vietnam, had run recon into Laos with Command and Control North.

He held the grenade up to his right ear. Then he removed the spoon with his left hand, keeping hold of it.

This way there would be no metallic ping of the spoon flying off or hitting the floor. The grenade was up to his ear because when the spoon came off he had to hear the faint pop of the striker hitting the cap to start the fuse burning. Hang on too long after the spoon came off, and there would be a nasty accident.

He gave the grenade an arcing lob to clear the obstructions. The fuse only had a couple of seconds left from the original 4.5-second delay.

Wh-WHAP! The grenade blew just before it hit the ground, right in front of the first Chechen, who absorbed the brunt of the blast. He died instantly. Behind him the sniper was wounded by fragments. And Osman, who had been behind them both, was untouched.

The scream came right behind the blast, telling Storey he'd gotten someone. He wasn't about to move down or across that central passageway. Instead he backed up and headed for the side wall.

Deafened by the blast, Murat the sniper crawled over to the nearest cover. He wiped off the blood burning his eyes. His cousin Nur-Pahi was dead, lying facedown in a spreading lake of blood. The long G-3 sniper rifle would be a hindrance in such a confined space. Nur-Pahi's AK was on the floor out in the open. He drew the pistol from his belt. The Americans would try to flank him. And he could not hear a thing. He had to move.

Storey was stalking forward one careful step at a time. Beth had her shotgun aimed toward the opposite wall. Troy was still walking backward.

Murat thought he saw something near the wall. He kept his eyes fixed upon the spot. There it was again. A new shadow forming as something broke the path of a beam of light. They *were* trying to flank him. He could do the same.

Peeking from behind the boxes where he'd taken refuge, Osman saw Nur-Pahi's body on the floor. He'd lost touch with Murat after the explosion, and now felt more frightened about being left alone than he did about moving forward. But as he did, his foot hit a loose floorboard that creaked loudly.

Storey heard it. He stopped, crouched down, and began readying another grenade.

Murat saw the shadow stop and drop down. All he had to do was move one or two meters more, without making a sound, and as soon as the American moved again he would have him.

When Storey crouched down Beth remained upright. She squinted, trying to see through the gloom. Off to her right front were three desks, piled one on top of the other. Something moved between the legs.

As she swung the shotgun over, she pushed the light switch on the slide with her thumb. The SureFire popped on and Beth centered Murat's head in the beam, blinding him. She pulled the trigger and blew the left side of his face off.

Racking the slide to chamber another shell, Beth dashed around Storey—who was trying to manage one hand on a grenade and the other on an AK. Turning the corner, the SureFire beam caught Murat sprawled out on the floor. Remembering the one that had blown up, Beth fired two more rounds of 00 buckshot into him.

As soon as he heard the shotgun, Osman threw a grenade in the direction of the sound.

But he hadn't taken the same care with the spoon Storey had, and the *ping* could be clearly heard in the silence after Beth's third shotgun blast.

"Grenade!" Storey shouted, tackling Beth around the legs to bring her down.

Thrown too hard, Osman's grenade hit the wall above them and ricocheted off to explode somewhere behind them.

Storey bounced up and threw the one he'd already had in his hand.

It was also too long, exploding behind Osman.

Besides the deafening noise, the grenades had thrown up an enormous amount of smoke and dust in the confined space.

Storey grabbed the back of Beth's belt, hoisting her up onto her feet and into forward movement. They had to get out of the bull's-eye.

This put Beth out in front, even more so when Storey had to look back to make sure Troy was with them.

Osman saw the figure emerge from the smoke in front of him. Rushed and excited, he leaned around the support post he'd been hiding behind and fired his pistol one-handed.

Beth saw the muzzle flash and fired her shotgun on the run.

The buckshot pattern blew a volleyball-sized chunk from the timber above Osman's head. He threw himself on the floor and crawled to safety.

Racking the slide back, Beth lost sight of her target. Then there was just a leg disappearing behind the post. She fired at it.

Osman felt the terrible impact, as if a car had driven over his leg. But no pain, though he was sure that would come soon enough.

Hearing the explosions, Temiraev barked into his radio, "What is happening? Report! Murat? Nur-Pahi? Osman? Report!"

"I will go to them," said Nimri.

"No, I will go," Temiraev said flatly. He embraced Nimri and released him quickly.

"God be with you, my brother," said Nimri.

"Victory or Paradise," said Temiraev, disappearing into the darkness of the warehouse.

Looking down at the blood pumping from his torn calf, Osman knew he was finished. He thought about waiting for the Americans to come to him, but he might lose consciousness before they arrived. Or they might throw another grenade, robbing him of the chance for revenge.

He set his pistol down on the floor and took up a grenade in each hand, pulling the pins with the opposite fingers. The pain was beginning now as the nerves woke up from their shock. He would have to be quick. He pushed himself up onto his good leg.

Beth was kneeling, feeding fresh shells into her shotgun. As Storey moved out in front of her again, he mouthed the words: did you get him?

Beth shrugged her shoulders.

The pain was very bad now. With his back to the support post, Osman gritted his teeth against it. He could not wait any longer. He pushed himself around the post with a cry of, "*Allahu Akbar!*"

Swinging his rifle toward the sound, Storey brought the two luminous dots of the AK front and rear sights onto Osman's chest and fired two fast rounds.

Osman tried to throw the grenades, but his arms would no longer move for him. The grenades dropped from his hands as he fell forward, and he landed on top of them.

Storey was panting from the adrenaline. It wasn't the first time one of the stupid bastards had killed himself by yelling that God was great instead of keeping his mouth shut. Like God wouldn't know they were on the way.

Temiraev was close now. When he heard Osman's cry he dropped down behind some boxes.

These two explosions were more muffled than the others. Storey wasn't going to hang back and make the same mistake as before. He'd take advantage of the smoke and confusion of the explosions to get up on anyone else who still might be out there. Still moving in that fast low crouch, he advanced into the smoke.

And then in one step his foot didn't touch floor and everything dropped away and he was falling. Storey let go of his rifle and threw himself backward, twisting around and clawing away with his hands. They hit wood and slipped, and his jaw slammed together hard enough to chip teeth. He got ahold of something with his right hand, but then it broke off under his weight and he was dangling in midair, hanging on to the edge of the hole in the floor only by his left hand.

Osman's body atop the two grenades had tamped the explosions, focusing the force of the blasts straight down through the thin dry wood of the floor, blowing a hole the size of the man's body. Storey hadn't seen it in the swirling acrid smoke and had fallen right through. It was more than a forty-foot drop to the bottom floor of the warehouse.

Storey kicked his feet to swing his body so he could get a grip on the edge of the hole with his other hand. But the fall through the jagged wood had ripped his palms up, and the blood was loosening his grip.

Beth heard Storey's grunt and then something crashing. The smoke was clearing now, and as she got closer she saw the hole and the two big hands hanging on. Oh, my God. She knew she didn't have the strength to pull Ed up. "Lee, come quick!"

Temiraev heard the woman's voice, and made sure the safety was off his AK. He could not see her, but now he knew where to look. Bad conditions. Too dark to see properly, but too much light for the night goggles.

As Troy rushed up Beth knew she had to protect them. She didn't know that Storey had a pistol, and was afraid he'd be unarmed. So she set the shotgun down on the floor for him and drew her pistol, carefully stepping around the hole.

Temiraev was waiting behind the boxes for one of them to show themselves. He heard the sounds of grunting, and something scraping on wood, but was afraid it was a trick to make him open fire prematurely. He would wait for a sure kill.

Troy was starting to worry about falling into the hole himself. He couldn't get any traction on the wood floor in his street shoes. And he couldn't use both hands— he had to brace himself with one. Growing impatient with trying to brainstorm his way through the problem, he locked his right hand on the closest wrist and yanked up with all his might.

Looking for the best cover, Beth noticed some crates and moved toward them, putting herself out in the open.

Temiraev saw something moving.

Beth heard Troy's loud grunt of exertion, and thought it was a warning. She dropped to the floor.

A burst of fire went right over her head. She fired four fast shots in the direction of that huge white muzzle flash, then rolled toward the nearest support post. On her stomach behind it, she fired two more rounds, then saw something fly off her pistol. She twisted her wrist to look at it, but seemed all right. When she twisted it back to fire, the entire slide, including the barrel, flew right off the pistol and clattered into the floor.

Beth stared at the polymer receiver in her hand, exactly half of a pistol, as if it was all some kind of terrible practical joke.

The next *bap-bap-bap* of three AK rounds going by woke her up. She bent at the waist, tugged up her pants leg, and yanked the little Glock 27 backup pistol from her ankle holster.

Temiraev had lost track of his target when the muzzle

flashes stopped. He reloaded and fired a short burst in the same direction.

Thanks to Troy's brute strength, Storey was now at armpit level with the edge of the hole. The AK and pistol fire started up as he was swinging his legs to try and get them over the edge. It spurred them both to greater efforts—Storey whipped his body up as Troy grabbed for his belt.

Beth leveled the three green dots of the Glock night sights and fired. That big white muzzle flash thundered up in front of her again, and suddenly wood splinters were flying everywhere. Then she felt an incredibly hard blow to the chest, and after that felt herself landing on the floor with no memory of ever coming off it. Looking up and seeing the holes on her side of the post and thinking: was that supposed to happen?

When she was a little girl Beth had been bucked off the back of a horse, which then kicked her on the way down. This felt exactly like that, like she couldn't draw in a breath. Then, realizing that something bad had happened to her and getting really mad about it, she fired her pistol at that persistent white flash that just wouldn't go away. Then the pistol wouldn't fire anymore and she thought: what, again? Before realizing that the slide was locked back because the magazine was empty. She pressed the magazine release to drop the empty one, and reached for one of the long Glock 22 magazines in her belt pouch.

Temiraev was wincing from the .40 caliber hollow-point in his upper arm. The fire stopped and he thought he heard a magazine striking the floor and knew it was his best chance while it was just he and the one American. Howling like the mountain wolf to terrorize his enemy, he sprang up, firing as he came.

Beth slammed in the fresh magazine and yanked back on the slide to slingshot it closed and chamber the first round. She fired and the floor seemed to explode in front of her and more splinters were flying and it was like the trigger drill at the Academy when you had to pull it as many times as you could in a minute. Then something hit her in the head.

Storey was halfway out of the hole. "Go!" he yelled at Troy.

Through enormous pains, Temiraev had the grenade in his hand. But he could not seem to get his finger through the ring. It was incredibly frustrating, and he was not a man who dealt with frustration well. His neck felt wet, and that was equally annoying. Then there was the man with the black face, like Satan himself, lunging at him like the wolf he had been . . .

Troy fired two rounds into the Chechen's head. He took the grenade from the hand and moved it off to the side, afraid it was a booby trap with a zero-time fuse. He grabbed the radio off the Chechen's belt and clipped it onto his. Fucking Beth—she was really something. He wanted to check on her, but he stayed where he was, covering their front, waiting for the next ones to show up from the front of the warehouse. When he felt Storey's footsteps behind him, he pointed his arm over to where Beth was lying in the shadows.

Storey set down the shotgun and knelt beside her.

"I think I got shot, Ed. It hurts when I breathe, but I was too chicken to look."

"Just take it easy, honey," he whispered back. "I'll see what's what."

"You called me honey," she said. "That's so sweet."

There was the tearing sound of Velcro as Storey opened up the front of the flak jacket. He ran his hands over her chest, feeling for blood and holes. Then slid down her sides and around her back. Pelvis and legs. Then arms.

The hair on the side of her head was wet with blood. Risking it, Storey took the SureFire Combat flashlight from her belt and clicked it on. There was a crease right along the side of her head, an inch or so above the ear, where an AK round had skimmed by and broken the skin without entering the skull.

He moved the light down to her flak jacket. Two bullet holes in the front, and the ceramic insert, which was supposed to be one piece, was now several. The vest had stopped both rounds that did nothing but bruise up her ribs. He checked her pupils with the light. Equal and reactive. No blood in the nose or ears.

Holes in the post above her. For a stubby assault rifle round the AK really did penetrate. They'd gone right through the thick timber post to hit her. The post had probably slowed them enough to help the vest out.

"You've got some bruised ribs," he told her. "But they're not broken. And you got creased in the head. That's it."

"I'm not shot?" she demanded.

"Well, yeah. But just a little bit. What is it with you and these point-blank pistol shootouts?" Flicking out a pocket knife, Storey rolled up the arm of her jacket and cut the sleeve off her blouse.

"Do you know what that cost?" said Beth.

"I cut it—I'll buy you a new one."

"Oh. Okay."

"You just sit here," he said. "We're going to keep clearing down."

That provoked a radical change in mood. "Screw that," said Beth, rolling over and getting up on her knees. "I'm coming along."

"You sure about that?" said Storey, watching her wince from the pain in her ribs.

"Better believe it. My duty pistol broke on me. See if you can find it."

Storey was willing to go along with her plan to distract him while she took her time getting to her feet. He found the slide and receiver, putting the two back together.

She was on her feet now.

He slipped the pistol into her holster. "You sure you're okay?"

"Let's go, Ed."

"Okay, but you take over rear security. I'm going to hang on to your shotgun for now."

"That's why I left it for you," she said, passing over the extra shells from her flak jacket pocket.

Left him the shotgun and charged ahead with a pistol, Storey thought, shaking his head and then quickly hoping she hadn't seen him doing it.

The radio on Troy's belt crackled quietly. The voice was speaking Arabic. "Temiraev, what is happening?"

"Oh, I really want to tell him," Troy whispered to Storey.

Storey surprised him by saying, "Go ahead. It's probably Nimri, unless we already got him."

Troy grinned as he brought the walkie-talkie up to his mouth. "He's dead," he said in Arabic. "It's next time, Nimri. You remember Arlington, do you not?"

"Nice touch," Storey whispered.

Abdallah Karim Nimri stared at the radio in his hands. The same American agents as before? How could this be?

He dropped the radio, tears of frustration falling down his cheeks. Once again they were all dead, and he was left alive. And once again he had failed. No television images sent around the world for days on end to delight the Faithful and shake the Americans before their election. The explosives and rockets had all been lost. All he had was a rifle, a pistol, and a few grenades. They would shoot him down and, as before, deny that anything had ever happened. Why, God?

Nimri got control of himself. God was merciful and compassionate. God was great. If this was His will, then he was His servant.

* * *

"He can't have many guys left," said Troy.

"Let's go see," said Storey.

"You're not taking point with a pump shotgun."

"Don't get careless."

"I don't plan to," said Troy. "I plan on using up these grenades."

"Fine with me."

So they started off again with Troy tossing grenades into every bit of potential cover he saw.

Other than the noise making her head hurt worse than it already was, Beth felt all right. As long as she kept her arms tight to her chest her ribs didn't hurt. And she had to keep them there to shoot anyway.

They made steady progress, until the upper warehouse ended in two walls and a narrow hallway.

Troy snuck forward for a quick look. Offices along both sides of the hallway. That was a problem. If they stopped to kick each door, their shit was hanging out in the middle of the hallway. Passing them by could mean getting shot in the back.

He was still thinking out the best move when Storey signaled him to get a grenade ready.

When Troy was ready to throw, Storey walked up to the wall and fired the shotgun from about six feet away. At that range the buckshot didn't have time to open up into a wide pattern, instead blowing a softball-sized hole in the wall. Troy released the spoon, counted two to let the fuse burn down a bit, and whipped the grenade through the hole and into the office. Problem solved.

As they moved to do the same thing on the other side, a clattering of metal on wood came down the hallway.

"Grenade!" Troy shouted. And they all hit the floor.

But instead of an explosion there was a loud pop and a hissing sound. The hallway filled with white smoke.

Troy edged in to get a whiff of it, then jumped back as the pungent vapor hit his nostrils. "It's CS, not smoke."

Storey sent his fragmentation grenade down the hall in reply. It was probably a futile gesture. Running through CS without a gas mask wasn't a problem. Doing it and expecting to shoot effectively afterward was. That was why the Mexicans had tried to use it on them. "Let's wait a minute and see what happens."

"Even after it burns out they'll be crystals all over the hallway," said Troy. "We'll kick them up just walking through."

Beth saw the flash of orange through the smoke. Except this wasn't a muzzle flash. "We've got a fire."

CS grenades burned so hot they were always setting things on fire. Which was why the hostage rescue teams were always careful about using them. It didn't take much to ignite the bone-dry wood of the warehouse.

"Well?" said Troy, as the flames filled the hallway.

"It's time to get the hell out of here," said Storey. Nimri wouldn't be coming that way.

They ran back down the length of the warehouse, mindful of the hole in the floor. Reaching the stairway they'd come up, they found they had a problem. The top was all splintered wood, and the first section of stairs no longer there.

"Now we know where that grenade they threw at us went," Storey observed.

Troy grabbed one of the stairway supports and shook it. The whole structure swung back and forth with dramatic cracking sounds. "How do you like that? Asshole couldn't have hit it *intentionally* if you gave him a case of grenades and all day to throw them. Think we ought to go up to the roof, wave a fire truck over?"

"What if there aren't any out there?" said Beth. "You know how fast a building like this can burn down?"

"Follow me," said Storey.

He led them on another run back down to the middle

of the warehouse, this time stopping at the open-cage freight elevator. Except there was no power, and the elevator was down on the ground floor.

Storey pushed up the wood gate.

"Oh, man," Troy moaned. "Those rusted old cables are going to come loose from the roof as soon as we jump on."

His argument would have had more force if the fire hadn't spread across the entire width of the warehouse, and wasn't also racing along the ceiling. It was close enough to feel the heat, and the smoke was getting thick.

Beth holstered her backup pistol and took off her flak jacket. Holding it open in front of her, she said, "Ladies first." And leaped across the void onto the cable with the jacket wrapped around it as a brake. After a loud yelp from the pain in her ribs, she slid down out of sight.

Storey and Troy looked at each other, then shucked off their ammo vests to do the same thing.

Storey pointed to the cable. In this particular case the senior man went last.

Troy jumped. The cable was seriously frayed. He went down about twenty feet then stopped. This was not his idea. Beth's vest was covered in tough nylon, but the cotton of his hung up on the ragged steel. Shit. He felt Storey coming down and yelled, "Hold up!"

Storey dug in the soles of this shoes and squeezed the cable. He came to a stop right above Troy's head. "I don't want to rush you or anything, but I'm having a lot of trouble staying stopped here."

Really pissed now, Troy hung on to the cable with one arm and shrugged the AK off his back. He tore the webbing sling off and let the rifle drop. He was thinking about the ropes loggers used to climb up and down trees. He'd seen it on ESPN or something once. The opening up above them was full of smoke.

He whipped the sling around the cable, wrapped both

one end around each wrist, and let go, leaning back from the wire.

Holy shit, now he was going down like a rocket. Troy squeezed the cable between his feet. It wasn't helping much, even though it felt like his feet were burning off from the friction.

He piled into the top of the elevator and lay there with the wind knocked out of him.

Storey came sliding down as easy as you please, coming to a gentle stop. "Anything broken?" he asked.

"Fuck you," Troy gasped.

"You okay, Lee?" said Beth from down below.

Troy rolled off the top of the elevator, wincing as his feet touched the warehouse floor. His hands were killing him. Okay, two big second-degree burn blisters were starting to bubble up on his palms.

Storey hopped down, holding the nylon daypack across his chest.

Troy just stared at it.

"I reconsidered the cotton vest after you went down," Storey said apologetically.

"Guys?" said Beth. The upper floor at the front part of the warehouse was already starting to collapse.

"What about Nimri?" said Troy.

"Fuck him," said Storey. "He's either going to make it out into custody or his ass is going to burn."

"We better keep our eyes open in case he shows up before that," said Beth. When they reached the back door she tried her walkie-talkie. No longer working. She put the flack jacket with the gold FBI lettering back on. "Let me go out first by myself, see if I can keep you from getting shot by the good guys."

"Try to get everyone unfucked before the place burns down," Troy urged.

Beth went out the front door with her hands above

her head. Storey closed it behind her, turning back to watch the warehouse for signs of Nimri.

"Yeah, I know," said Troy. "You always get ambushed on the way back to the boat."

"Better get rid of your daypack."

The fire was raging now, with big pieces of the upper floor dropping down into the warehouse. They could no longer see the front through the flames. Troy kept sneaking glances at the ceiling over their heads.

Then Beth's amplified voice could be heard. "Everyone hold their fire. Okay, come on out, guys."

Storey slung his AK, muzzle down. "Better keep the hands up."

"Shit, just thinking about all the trigger-happy cops," Troy muttered. "My asshole's puckered up worse now than during the whole op."

They walked out the door, blinking into the bright sunlight. And they didn't get shot.

The FBI only let the Laredo fire department set up hoses to keep the fire from spreading. Otherwise they kept everyone away until the warehouse walls collapsed and the entire structure had burned to the ground.

Beth, Storey, and Troy didn't get to see it. They were immediately hustled into an ambulance and taken to Doctors Hospital.

Beth had the gurney, and Storey and Troy sat along the side with the EMT, who was the classically chatty type. A real people person.

"Boy, that was some fire," he said. "Who would have thought they'd have a meth lab that big right in the middle of town?"

The three of them just looked at each other. So that's what the story was going to be.

"Yeah," the EMT went on. "You all were really gutsy. Especially that SWAT guy."

Beth sat up halfway in the gurney. "What SWAT guy?"

"The one in the black fatigues, with the gas mask," said the EMT. "He came out the front, just as it was burning down. Waved the firemen in, gave them directions. Then he collapsed. He said the fire had melted the gas mask onto his face. We only had the one ambulance on site, so the cops told us to stand fast, they'd take him to the hospital in a police car."

All the Chechens had been wearing black fatigues. "What happened to him?" Troy said.

"I'm sure you'll see him at the hospital when you get there."

"We don't want to use an open radio net," Storey said to Beth.

Beth threw her legs over the side of the gurney and opened up her cell phone. "Ben? Beth. Yes, I'm still on the way to the hospital. Shut up and listen. Have you heard about the cops taking a SWAT guy in black fatigues and a gas mask to the hospital? Well, I suggest you ask around. Because everyone inside was wearing black fatigues, and there was no SWAT guy with us." She closed the phone. "He hung up. Must have been in a hurry."

"Son of a bitch!" Troy exploded. "Doesn't anyone ever get the word?"

"Uh-oh," said the EMT.

"Just between you and me," Storey advised the EMT. "You're going to be really tempted to tell this story. Career-wise, you don't want to do it. Take my word for it."

"Okay," the EMT said in a small voice. And then, "Thanks."

"Don't mention it," Storey said kindly.

They x-rayed Beth's ribs, CAT scanned her brain, and bandaged her head.

At Storey's urging, Troy also had some x-rays taken. While he was getting his hands treated they told him he had a hairline fracture of the tibia and put his leg into a cast.

Storey didn't have a scratch on him.

Beth and Troy ended up in adjoining stalls in the emergency room. Storey was sitting on the edge of Beth's bed. For something to do he'd broken down her pistol, and was examining the parts.

"Here we go," he said, peering into the receiver. "Your slide-stop spring broke when you were shooting. The part you saw fly out must have been the slide lock. No slide lock, nothing's holding the slide on but inertia."

"But it kept on shooting after I saw the part fly off."

"That's inertia for you. You're lucky it didn't fire out of battery."

"Great. How often does that happen?"

"Slide-stop spring breaking? Never heard of it happening. Of course, any part can break."

"Figures. It would have to happen to me. By the way, you were right about my backup piece. I definitely needed to reload. Your present saved my life."

Storey could feel himself blushing.

They didn't notice themselves talking louder than usual, since without earplugs their hearing had been affected by all the gunfire and grenades.

Troy's voice came from next door. "What present?"

Storey groaned, waiting for it.

"Ed gave me my backup gun," Beth said loudly.

"Now isn't that sweet?" said Troy.

"It saved my life," Beth said defensively.

Storey just shook his head.

"A gift that keeps on giving," Troy sang. "You always miss what's right in front of you. I can't believe I never thought to give a woman a handgun. Takes a redneck to come up with something like that."

"It saved my life, Lee," Beth said sternly.

"Am I interrupting anything?" said Supervisory Special Agent Benjamin Timmins, appearing from around the corner.

"Oh, Christ," Troy groaned at the sight of him. "Look, the last time you chewed our ass for saving your ass. I don't want to hear it this time. You want my ass chewed, go talk to my boss and have him do it. But I don't want to hear it right now."

"I'm not here to chew your ass," said Timmins.

"Imagine *that*," said Troy.

"No, on the contrary, I'm here to praise you," said Timmins. "You didn't follow procedure at all, for the most part, but everything you did forestalled an attack and then kept the opposition from getting the incident they came for."

Beth said, "Ben, how's Sondra?"

"She's in . . . another ward getting looked at," said Timmins.

"She was okay," said Troy. "She just wasn't ready for the kind of contact we rolled into."

Storey wondered where the hell that came from. Or maybe his partner was going to ask for her phone number after she finished her psych eval? "What about the guy in the black fatigues and gas mask?"

"The Laredo cruiser never made it here to the hospital," said Timmins. "We're looking for it. Did you happen to find out what their objective was?"

"No idea," said Storey. "I don't reckon there's much evidence left in either the Expedition or the warehouse."

"No, there isn't," said Timmins. "Don't worry, we'll get him."

"Sure you will," said Troy. "You might even find another snotty note from him in that police car."

Chapter Twenty-six

Normally, any sign on any bar advertising karaoke night was Ed Storey's personal signal to go elsewhere. But tonight he didn't have that option. This was a command performance. And he was late.

The place was crowded, but he'd been told to go right up in front. And sure enough, at the table right in front of the little stage was Beth, Karen the Spook, and Karen's husband Kevin.

A drunk fat guy was singing "Bizarre Love Triangle."

He pushed through the crowd, and heard Karen yell, "Ed!"

"I'm sorry I'm late," said Storey. "We got hung up at work."

"No, no, no," Karen said reassuringly, giving him a hug. "You called. You were good. We've been waiting for you."

In contrast to Karen's bubbly mood, Beth was scrunched up in her chair, arms across her chest, chin down, the very picture of defiant sullenness. She still had her coat on, and her usually rosy complexion was an even deeper red this evening. "Hi, Ed."

"Hi, Beth." Storey tried to fight off the smile he knew would put him in serious jeopardy. He shook hands with Kevin.

"We already ordered you a Coke," said Karen.

"Many thanks." Storey settled into the chair beside Beth.

"Oh, don't thank us," said Karen. "This is all Beth's treat. We're going out for dinner later."

Storey turned to thank her, but the vibe coming across was such that he chose to remain silent.

The fat drunk finished his song to unenthusiastic applause.

Karen raised her hand to the master of ceremonies. "C'mon Beth, it's showtime. After all, the Red Sox haven't won the World Series in what, a hundred years or something?"

Beth spoke her first complete sentence of the evening. "I want to thank you, Karen. You've taken an event that should be the ultimate cathartic moment in the life of every Red Sox fan, and turned it into something cheap and degrading."

"Stop or I'm going to cry," said Karen. "C'mon now, get your ass up on stage. I had to get the machine pro-grammed special just for you. It's amazing," she said to Storey. "People just don't seem to want to karaoke to Joe Cocker anymore."

"You are such a bitch," said Beth. "You are the evil bitch of all time."

"Yeah, yeah, yeah," said Karen. "Get on up there. And don't forget your coat."

Beth stood up. Storey also stood up, to take her coat.

"No, Ed," Karen said firmly. "I'll take care of this."

She peeled the coat off Beth's shoulders. Beth was wearing jeans, and the T-shirt tucked into them had been custom made. It was white, and embossed across the front with a full-face portrait of Karen. And the legend beneath it said: *My Idol.*

The sight made Storey real glad he hadn't helped her with her coat.

Beth trudged up the stairs as if it was execution block, looking like she wanted to open fire on the crowd.

Karen turned her chair around so it was facing the stage.

The MC, having been both well tipped and coached by Karen, gave her an elaborate windup, finishing with, "And let's have a big hand for Beth!"

The crowd responded, Karen turning around briefly to egg them on. Storey wasn't quite sure if he wanted to have Beth see him clapping.

The MC handed Beth the microphone, which she held like a billy club. The lights went down, and the music came up. Beth began to sing, to Karen, "You Are So Beautiful."

Karen was sitting with her face cupped in her hands, gazing dreamily at Beth. And it was affecting Beth's performance.

Storey and Kevin just looked at each other and shrugged.

It was coming across like a punk version, mainly because of Beth's attitude. And maybe because that made it totally unlike the usual karaoke performance, the crowd was responding with whistles and whoops after every stanza. Which only served to piss Beth off even more.

Storey heard the guy at the table behind them say, "What is this, some kind of lesbo thing?"

Storey turned around and told him, "Like most things in this life, it's probably what you least expect."